SACRAMENTO PUBLIC LIBRARY

828 "I" Street

D0350438

The
EMERALD
SEA

The
EMERALD
SEA

RICHELLE MEAD

RAZORBILL®

An Imprint of Penguin Random House LLC
Penguin.com

RAZORBILL & colophon is a registered trademark of Penguin Random House LLC.

First published in the United States of America by Razorbill,
an imprint of Penguin Random House LLC, 2018

Copyright © 2018 Richelle Mead LLC

Penguin Random House supports copyright. Copyright fuels creativity, encourages
diverse voices, promotes free speech, and creates a vibrant culture. Thank you for buying
an authorized edition of this book and for complying with copyright laws
by not reproducing, scanning, or distributing any part of it in any form without
permission. You are supporting writers and allowing Penguin Random House to
continue to publish books for every reader.

LIBRARY OF CONGRESS CATALOGING-IN-PUBLICATION DATA IS AVAILABLE
ISBN 9781595148452

Printed in the United States of America

1 3 5 7 9 10 8 6 4 2

Interior design by Lindsey Andrews

This is a work of fiction. Names, characters, places, and incidents either are
the product of the author's imagination or are used fictitiously, and any resemblance to
actual persons, living or dead, businesses, companies, events, or locales is
entirely coincidental.

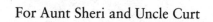

For Aunt Sheri and Uncle Curt

CHAPTER 1

BEING BETTER THAN EVERYONE ELSE WAS EXHAUSTING WORK.

That had been true for most of my life. I couldn't remember a time when I wasn't helping support my family, fighting for every copper we earned. If you slacked off in Osfro's bustling market district, even for an instant, then you were just opening the door for someone else to move in and snatch your triumph for themselves.

That hadn't changed when I moved into a household of girls all vying to marry wealthy men in a far-off land. Others here at Blue Spring Manor might think they could ease up, and that only worked to my advantage. Let them think they could coast now. Let them all hate me. I wouldn't lose my edge. I'd stay focused on my prize, never getting distracted by people or frivolity.

"Happy birthday, Tamsin!"

I stumbled to a halt in the doorway to my room, clamping a hand to my mouth to cover my shock at the sight that met me. Intricately cut garlands of paper hung along the walls. A little box wrapped smartly in silver tissue rested on my bed. A vase of rainbow-hued gladioli stood atop my dresser. And a plate of something lumpy and pink sat nearby.

As it turned out, not everyone hated me.

"What is this?" I swiftly shut the door. "Wait. How did you even know?"

My two roommates stood side by side, grinning broadly. "We have our ways," said Mira.

"Though we shouldn't have had to use them," chastised Adelaide. "Why didn't you tell us?"

"I didn't want to make a fuss. It's not a big deal." I walked over to one of the walls and touched the garland. "This is lovely."

"I made it," said Mira. At ease, a lilting accent crept into her voice, the result of having lived most of her life in Sirminica. Looking at her, so neat and proper in a pink poplin dress, one would never guess she'd had to fight her way out of a war-torn country. "Miss Shaw gave me the supplies the last time she visited."

"And I made the cake," piped up Adelaide. "It's strawberry."

I frowned. "What cake?" She pointed, and I turned to the plate with the oozing pink blob on it. "Did you now?" I asked. "All by yourself? Like, with a recipe and everything?"

"You're lucky it's your birthday, or I wouldn't tolerate that kind of sass," she returned.

I didn't believe that for an instant, seeing as she tolerated my "sass" on a pretty regular basis. Adelaide had one of the wittiest, most cheerful dispositions I knew, which worked as a good balance to my unending restlessness and Mira's quiet reflection. Everyone at Blue Spring was trying to rise from our roots and learn the ways of the upper classes, so you'd think Adelaide would be the one with an edge after working as a genteel lady's maid. And she *did* have occasional bits of brilliance about obscure aristocratic behaviors. But that was often overshadowed by her complete lack of practical life skills. Like sewing. And cleaning. And . . . cooking.

"Well, thank you . . . though you shouldn't have gone to the trouble. Um, especially the cake. It's kind, but you two shouldn't have wasted that time on me when you could have been studying."

Adelaide sat on the edge of her bed, swinging her legs. "Don't worry. I wouldn't have spent that time studying."

"Mira might have," I shot back.

Mira took a spot beside Adelaide and tossed her long black hair over one shoulder. "I don't think I would have either."

"Oh, come on, you two! If you really wanted to get me something for my birthday, it would be to get more serious about your studies. Time's running out."

"I *am* serious about them," Mira said indignantly. "Just not like you are. No one is."

"And we have loads of time," said Adelaide. "I'm not going to worry yet."

There was no point in chastising her. Adelaide would be Adelaide. I'd learned that six months ago when I'd joined the Glittering Court. Like me, she and the other girls in our house had committed to a year of learning etiquette, politics, music, and what felt like a hundred more subjects. These grueling days would pay off when we sailed to Adoria in the spring to find upper-class husbands who would elevate our standing in the new colonies. Some days I wished my two room-mates would remember that. Of course, I still had to be the best, but I would like to see them be, say, second and third best.

Mira did take her studies more seriously than Adelaide and, ever observant, had noted my late return. "Was there some sort of trouble downstairs? It looked like Clara and some others were trying to talk to you after class."

"As if that lot could give me any real trouble," I scoffed. "They were just sulking because I interviewed Florence about all the eligible bachelors in Cape Triumph."

Adelaide's eyebrows rose in astonishment. Florence was an alumna of the Glittering Court, and had returned from Adoria last week to tell us about her experiences. "You did what with Florence?"

"Remember how she wanted to rest after lunch? She's apparently gotten used to having a maid help her all the time—which is silly, since she started where we did—so I volunteered to help get her settled in the guest room. And then I used the chance to get as much information out of her as I could about all the men she knew over there."

Silence and stares met me. Then, Mira said: "Yes. Of course you did."

"I've been using what she told me to study up on some of their interests. For example, there's a prominent banker who's looking for a wife, and he's very into lawn tennis. Do you know what that is? I didn't, though I do now, of course. I've been reading about it on my breaks."

"Actually," said Adelaide, "I do know what it is. But how come you never told us about this?"

I shrugged. "Do you want to know? Do you want to start researching these men?"

"No," they both said.

"See, that's why I didn't say anything, though I'd gladly share . . . some . . . of it with you. But as for everyone else? Not a chance. And that's what I told Clara and her cronies just now."

"Tamsin, there is no one else like you," said Adelaide, her voice full of both admiration and disbelief.

Mira nodded, her earlier smile back. "And we wouldn't have it any other way."

"Tease all you want," I said, "but I'm telling you, something's going on around here. Each time Jasper visits—I don't know. I can just feel it. We have to be ready."

Adelaide was getting bored with the shop talk. "Can we be ready after you open your present and have cake? Please?"

I picked up the silver box. "Ah, well, I'm not so hungry just yet, but let's take a look at this." When I opened the gift, I found a polished wooden pen with a steel tip. It was nothing fancy, but it was clearly new and well made. "Where in the world did you get this? Neither of you have money to spare."

"Cedric picked it up in the city for us. After an absurdly rich husband, we knew this was the present you'd want most," Adelaide explained. "That other pen you were using was barely staying together."

"You're right. Thank you." An unexpected wave of emotion swept me. I didn't need friends to succeed in the Glittering Court, but it was certainly nice to have them. "And thank Cedric too."

"Hopefully you'll stop slacking on those letters to your family," said Mira, remarkably straight-faced. "I think I saw you write only three of them yesterday."

"Then you missed one. I did four." I looked down at the pen, feeling an ache in my heart at the thought of my family. Everything I did here was for them, but ironically, it came at the cost of being away from them. "The six blessed angels know how I miss them. First birthday I've ever been away."

"You're lucky," said Adelaide, growing uncharacteristically solemn. "To have a family like that—to be so close to them."

The wistful note in her voice reminded me that she and Mira had lost their families. Maybe mine was far away in Osfro, but at least I had them. At least I'd see them again.

"I am lucky," I agreed. I set the pen down and walked over to my friends, pulling them into a shared hug. "Because I have a family like *this* too."

We held each other for a few moments and then Adelaide said, "So. Is it time for cake?"

I'd meant it when I told them I felt like something was going to happen. It took almost two months before I was proven right. Before then, life marched along to its normal rhythm at Blue Spring Manor. Instructors came by each week to teach their subjects, rotating between us and three other Glittering Court manors. I studied. I relished Adelaide and Mira. I tolerated the others. And always, always, I wrote my letters home.

One winter afternoon, Jasper Thorn—one of the two brothers who'd founded the Glittering Court—summoned us to the ballroom. That change of routine immediately put me on alert. When we arrived and saw blankets spread out on the floor and caterers setting up around the room, I panicked even more.

"I knew it," I kept telling Mira and Adelaide. "Maybe this is a surprise test. One to get us thinking about the big exams at the end." Mistress Masterson, who ran the house, wouldn't tell us anything, and I watched anxiously for Jasper's arrival in the hopes of getting answers.

But the next person who walked through was a man I didn't know. I didn't recognize the couple who came in after him either. Or the woman and four little boys who soon followed.

I knew who the next people were, though. With a cry of surprise, I raced across the ballroom. "Merry! Ma! Pa!"

In an instant, I was engulfed by people whose hair was the same autumn red as mine. My thirteen-year-old brother, Jonathan, was trying to keep a stoic face but failing. His twin, Olivia, had no such reserve and cried openly as she hugged me. Little Merry, at three years old, had a much simpler reaction to a happy occasion. She squealed with delight and launched herself out of my father's arms, nearly knocking me over in the process.

"Careful there, love," I said with a laugh. "These shoes I'm in are meant for dancing, not acrobatics."

She squirmed and peered down at the shoes. "Ooh, look at the buckles! Look at your dress! Look at all of this!" Her green eyes stared around the room, growing wider with each new wonder she saw. "Everything is so beautiful. Is this where we're going to live? Can we see the rest of it? Can I see the dress from your letter? The one with green flowers?"

"Hush, child," said Ma, her eyes misty. "You aren't letting her get a word in."

I hugged Merry tighter and showered kisses on her. "That's fine with me. I hear myself plenty. I can't believe you're here! What's going on?"

Pa scratched at the red beard on his chin. "Not sure. We got the invitation a week ago, and they sent a carriage for us today."

"Well, I don't care what it's for, so long as you're here." I tucked Merry's curls behind her ears so I could better look at her beloved face. "I've missed you so much. I've missed all of you so much."

The room buzzed with happy reunions. Laughter and tears surrounded us as other girls reunited with longed-for families. I spun around, suddenly concerned about Mira and Adelaide, but then I saw them with their own guests. Mira was beaming at an older couple who looked to be Sirminican too, and Adelaide was giving a stiff hug to a boisterous woman in a tacky red dress. I urged my family over and made introductions. Mira explained that the husband and wife, named Pablo and Fernanda, were fellow refugees. The woman with Adelaide was Sally, a distant aunt.

Jasper finally arrived and called us to attention. Though old enough to be my father, he was handsome and always smartly dressed. He was also something of a showman and knew how to sell.

"First, let me welcome you here today to Blue Spring Manor." He held up his hands in a grand gesture. "You are our guests, and we are all at your service. Second, I want to thank you for the sacrifice I know you must have made in the last eight months by lending us your daughters. But it has been our privilege and our honor to have them, to help them develop the potential you surely knew they had all along. Today you'll get a glimpse into the world they've entered—a world that will be dwarfed by the riches and splendor they'll get when they marry in Adoria."

When we'd joined the Glittering Court, we'd done it with the understanding that we couldn't visit our families back in Osfro, and they couldn't visit us here. I'd had to accept the dreary prospect that I could very well be facing two years without seeing them. I'd long hoped for a reunion of this type but never dreamed it would happen. So, that vigilant, always planning part of me warned that something like this wasn't being done as a random act of generosity. I shelved those concerns—for now. Just this once, it felt good to relax my guard and be with these people I loved. Jasper urged us all to get food, and we brought it to the blankets, eating picnic-style.

Merry, never leaving my lap, found the setup delightful and

chattered on about it and any other thoughts that came to her mind. I listened contentedly, nearly bursting with joy. The others got a chance to share their stories too, the twins telling me about school, and Pa describing a building project he'd just been hired onto.

Ma, at one point, exclaimed, "Look at your hands! You'll never be able to do a load of clothes again."

I felt a flush of pleasure. I'd worked with her for years washing laundry for households throughout the city. It had taken a lot of care at Blue Spring to repair the damage of soap and lye, and while my hands weren't perfect yet, they'd improved by leaps and bounds.

"Not much longer and you'll be relaxing your hands too," I told Ma after we ate. "I'll make sure of it. I wish I could do something about it now. I hate the thought of you shouldering most of the workload."

She tsked. "Don't give it a second thought. You have better things to focus on today."

Merry, head leaning against my chest, said, "We all love and miss you so much. But I love and miss you the most." The poignancy of her words was underscored with a challenge as she glanced at the rest of our family, daring them to say otherwise.

I held her tighter. "I believe it, sweet one. I believe it."

And yet, as much as I reveled in every moment of being with her and the others, I was always conscious that it would have to end. At some point, they would be taken away from me again. I smiled, laughed, and gazed at their beloved faces while my dread grew and grew. Nausea stirred in the pit of my stomach; my hands sweated as I held on to Merry. When Jasper at last called an end to the gathering, I felt as though I was going to throw up.

Merry noted the signs of departure, like people gathering their things and exchanging hugs. She turned to me in a panic. "I don't want to go. I want to stay with you."

"I wish you could, love." My voice cracked. "You have no idea how much I wish you could."

"Then can you come back with us?"

"No. I have to stay here a little longer and finish my studies. But I'll keep writing every day. Twice a day, if I can. And before long, I'll see you all again in Adoria, and we'll live in a fine house—finer than this—with all the things you could ever want."

Merry's lip quivered a bit. "Why can't we just live in this one?"

"Livvy, Jon," said Ma loudly, "they haven't put all the food away yet. Why don't you take Merry over there and pick some sweets for the trip back? You'll have plenty of time for goodbyes."

Merry still looked troubled but allowed Olivia to take her from me. Pa glanced between them and Ma and, after a moment's deliberation, went over to the food too. "Six, child," said Ma. "You look ready to faint. Come sit down."

I shook my head frantically and clutched her arm. "I can't do it. I can't be away from her again."

"Yes you can." Ma's gaze was steady and clear as she patted my hand. "You've already come so far. You can't turn back after all you've done."

"I want to leave. I'm going home with you. Right now."

"Tamsy—"

"Ma, how can I do this?" I hissed, trying to hide my hysteria from others. "Eight months I've been away already. Eight months, almost nine! And it could very well be another year by the time you're able to sail over. It's practically half her life!"

"You're with us all the time. She talks about you constantly, and we read your letters every day. We reread them. Hush," she added, seeing me about to protest. Her voice lowered to almost a whisper. "And listen. I was going to write you, but you should know now. It won't be a year. It'll be six months."

"W-what??"

"You remember that the Wilsons were planning on coming to Adoria?"

I frowned, unsure how our neighbors fit into my breakdown. "Yes . . ."

"Well, Merry's coming with them. Her coughing spells were light this autumn, so we didn't need to buy as much medicine. It let us build up a nice bit of gold, enough to buy her a ticket! She'll be in Cape Triumph with the Wilsons in six months."

I stopped shaking. "Are you serious? That's when I'll arrive!"

"Yes. I know you won't have things settled yet, but I'm sure it won't take long—not for you. The Wilsons have a lead to work in the south but will stay in Cape Triumph a few weeks to look after her."

A fledgling hope started to rise in me, but too many other fears dragged it down. "But the money! If she needs the medicine—"

"She has plenty. We had a lucky streak. You know I wouldn't do anything rash, and you know the Wilsons are like our own blood. They'll take good care of her."

I stared off at the rest of my family by the food table. "It's still six months."

"Six months is less than a year. For the price of, what, not even a year and a half, you've ensured all the years of her life will be secure. And yours."

"And yours," I said in a small voice. "I'll send for you too."

Ma wiped at her glimmering eyes. "I know you will, Tamsy. Just get by a little longer. You've never backed down in your life, and I know you won't now, my girl. Did you find out what you needed to know?"

With great effort, I attempted to shift to business. "Yes. There was a girl here—Florence—who's pretty thick with Cape Triumph high society. She told me all about the men who'd been available when she was there, and it matched up with what Esme had said. I've memorized everything about them—and there are several who are pretty open-minded."

"Good. You'll have them all charmed in no time, I'm sure."

"I'm glad one of us is." Pa and the others were returning, and the sight of them made all the emotion swell up in me. "Some days, Ma, I'm just so worried . . ."

"Don't be," she said, her voice affectionate but firm. "Remember what you promised yourself: no defeat. Not ever again."

Only the others' return kept me from choking up again. Jonathan and Olivia hugged me, and Merry climbed back up into my arms. Spots of pink icing showed on her face.

"What's this?" I rubbed some of it away. "I thought you were just getting something for the ride back to the city."

Merry grinned, showing her one dimple. "There were so many, though."

"Oh, well, I suppose it's all right then." I pressed a kiss to her forehead. "Be a good girl. And the rest of you be good too. No skipping school, Livvy."

Olivia made a face. "I only do it on days Ma needs extra help."

"You won't need to do it much longer. A year from now, you'll go to the best school in Adoria. And you'll have a private drawing instructor." I ran a hand over Merry's hair as she licked her fingers. "And you, love, I'll be seeing even sooner than that. You've been so patient. Can you do it just a little longer?"

Time was a tricky concept at her age. Six minutes, six months, and six years all ran together. Her little face started to darken again, but then she gave a brave nod. "As long as you send more letters. And promise not to leave anymore."

I started trembling once more. "No. We'll never be apart again, I swear it."

Seeing my resolve falter, Ma touched my cheek. "I had my doubts about this Glittering Court, but I know now that you did the right thing. Seeing you like this, such a proper young lady . . ." She cleared her throat. "Well. It's clear this is what you were meant for. This and more."

"We're all meant for more. And we'll all have it," I told her fiercely. Another call sounded, urging the guests to finish goodbyes. "I should go get you the latest letters. I have a whole bundle I haven't mailed. But spread them out so you have something new to read each day."

I handed Merry to Pa and then fetched the letters from my room.

I peered at myself in the mirror as I left and was pleased to see how calm I looked. No trace of my distress, no sign that I was crumbling inside.

But as soon as they were gone—after many, many more hugs and kisses—I couldn't maintain the façade. My family walked out the front door, and I hurried back upstairs, not caring that I had to push my way through some of the other lingering guests. I burst into my room and went to my bed, burying my face in my hands. A couple of minutes later, Adelaide slipped in. Quickly, I rubbed my face on my sleeve.

"I'm fine," I told her when she sat beside me.

"It's okay to be homesick. You don't have to be ashamed about missing them."

"I'm not ashamed . . . but I can't let them—the others—see me like this. I can't show weakness."

Her blue eyes brimmed with compassion. "Loving your family isn't weakness."

I thought again about how she didn't have any family—well, except for that unexpected aunt. I was beyond lucky. And now I had to wait only six months for Merry! I tried to tell myself that, as Adelaide continued her attempts to console me, but the pain was too fresh to let go just yet.

At one point, I blurted out, "If you only knew what I had on the line—"

"Then tell me," Adelaide said urgently. "Tell me, and maybe I can help you."

Her words elicited a whole new ache within me. "No. If you knew, you'd never look at me the same."

"You're my friend. Nothing's going to change how I feel about you."

The temptation was overwhelming. I wanted to tell her and Mira both, to let out all the pent-up emotion that had tormented me these long months. And I wanted to clear the space between us. I wasn't lying to my friends, but I wasn't telling them the entire truth either. But I couldn't. The secret I carried was too powerful, too dangerous. One hint of my secret getting out, even accidentally, could ruin everything in Adoria.

"I can't," I told Adelaide. "I can't risk it."

She nodded, her smile gentle. "Okay. You don't have to tell me anything you don't want to. But I'm always here. You know I am."

"I know."

The door was suddenly flung open, and Mira rushed in. "Everyone's gone—the families. Jasper's calling for all of us to assemble back in the ballroom."

I jumped up. My earlier suspicions returned and—for now—I set aside my emotions. I had to be sharp. I had to be ready. "I knew it," I told them. "I knew something was happening."

And I was right. When the whole household was gathered downstairs, Jasper delivered an announcement that turned our worlds upside down.

"I hope you're all excited about Adoria, because we're going there—two months earlier than planned."

The news sent us reeling, and our composure dissolved into whispers and speculation. Two months early! That meant a departure in just over one month. Adoria, which had always been spoken of like some far-off fairytale land, was suddenly right at hand.

When we'd quieted, Jasper went on: "I know this change in plans is unexpected. But really, it's a reflection of your outstanding progress that we feel confident in bringing you to Adoria early. In just a couple of months, you'll be in a whole new world—adored and coveted like the jewels you are."

My heart pounded as he delved into details and explained how we'd be taking exams early too—within the next few weeks. The others gasped, but I knew I could pull it off. It'd mean some sleepless nights and frantic days, but that would have happened regardless of when we took exams.

A sudden and thrilling realization struck me. Going to Adoria early meant I'd arrive ahead of Merry. I could secure a husband in that time and have a household ready to go. Just like that, my earlier uncertainty vanished. My passion and focus were renewed. I was going to blaze through these exams and have my pick of prominent suitors in Adoria.

And everything was going to be perfect when my daughter arrived.

CHAPTER 2

THERE WERE SOME BACK IN MY OLD NEIGHBORHOOD who believed—and had told me—that Merry was a mistake. And I'd had a few choice words for those people. Merry wasn't the mistake. Falling for the lies and manipulation of her father had been the mistake.

My mother's laundry business had sent me into countless upper-class homes for deliveries and pickups, and I'd been continually awed at the excess and glamour—especially compared to our modest house in an overcrowded neighborhood. I wasn't ashamed of my family or what we had, but I became very conscious of the way our "betters" looked down upon us—assuming they even noticed people like us. We might as well have been fixtures or furniture to some of them. And that smarted.

But Harold Thomas Barnett III had noticed me. Harry spoke to me like an equal, wanting to know about my interests and dreams. He would share his too, and I'd linger with him after my deliveries, dazzled by the warm and sophisticated persona he put forth. He let me browse his family's extensive home library and borrow books on topics I'd heard of but never dreamed of learning: astronomy, philosophy, geography, and more. From there, he advanced into outright giving me gifts—mere trinkets to him, I realized later, but luxuries by my standards.

When Ma discovered those presents and learned what was happening, she no longer allowed me to deliver to him or anyone near his neighborhood. But her efforts came a little too late. I was too far gone, too in love with him and the idea of being in love. We met in secret, and when we were apart, he was all I thought about.

Beyond Harry's good looks and clever words, I think, was the sheer thrill of having something that was *mine*. In an existence where food and rent were always in doubt, nearly every decision I made had to take my family's future into consideration. And so, it was glorious to toss all of that aside and do something because *I* wanted it. I believed Harry when he started talking about marriage. We speculated about our wedding and our future home and how my family could finally have the comforts they deserved. We rarely talked about *when* marriage would happen, though. It was always *later, later* because he needed more time. Time to persuade his father, time to "figure things out."

I was barely sixteen the day I found out I was pregnant. And that was also the day he stopped talking about marriage. In fact, he stopped talking to me at all.

It had taken me a little while to understand what had happened—to accept that he was done with me, that I was thoroughly and definitively cut off. After months of trying to get through to him, I finally admitted defeat—but I swore then that it would be the last time I ever would.

And that was why, when Jasper Thorn had offered me a spot in the Glittering Court, I'd seized the chance and developed a plan. Insight from both Florence and a former laundry client, Esme Hartford, had given me advance knowledge of eligible Cape Triumph bachelors who weren't picky about a bride who had been married before. I'd created a backstory for Merry about how I'd eloped when I was younger and then lost my husband tragically. Once I was married, I'd tell my husband that tale. It would be a shock, but if I chose correctly, he'd be someone whose blinding love for me would accept it. So, I needed a husband who was rich, fine with a widow, and completely enamored with me. I was certain that man was out there, but to find him, I had to make sure all options were available to me. I had to meet and win over as many suitors as I could, which meant I couldn't be any less than perfect.

This conviction drove me as I went through the Glittering Court's exam week. I studied longer and harder than anyone else. I slept less and ate less than anyone else. The only breaks I allowed myself were to write letters. My family would need an extra-large batch before I sailed.

When our last exam came, many of the other girls were bleary-eyed. Not me. I walked into the test ready and eager. It was part of our etiquette curriculum and required us to create a proper place setting for a formal dinner—involving two dozen pieces. Around me, other girls stood at their tables, a bit taken aback by the array of glasses and silverware. But I set right to it.

One glass for water, another for champagne. One glass for red wine, another for white. Last and smallest of all, a glass for cordials. I set each piece of stemware down with care, slowly creating an artful arc around the plate's upper right side. My hand trembled, but it was from eagerness, not anxiety. After all, what did I have to be anxious about? I could do this with my eyes closed, and if the stakes weren't so high, I might have been tempted to try it.

Salad knife, meat knife, fish knife, butter knife, seafood knife. Why did there have to be separate knives for fish and seafood? I had no idea, but if our instructors said that was the way it had to be, then that was how I'd do it. The polished silver surface caught the chandelier's light, and I had a brief, surreal moment recalling the broken wooden cutlery we'd used back home. Our entire set contained fewer pieces than the glittering array before me. *But not for long,* I thought. *Chipped spoons will soon be a thing of the past for my family.*

Confident or not, I double-checked my work when finished. Then I triple-checked it. Perfection. In my best script, I wrote *Tamsin Wright* on the card beside the plate, and then I walked out of the exam without a backward glance.

I don't think I breathed until I reached my room on the manor's upper floor. I rested my hand on the doorknob and closed my eyes for a brief moment, reveling in my success. I'd done it. I stepped inside, my heady glory jolted into surprise when I saw Adelaide sprawled on her bed. "What are you doing here?" I asked as I shut the door. "Didn't you go to the dining exam?"

"Of course. Went there. Did it. Done." She spread her arms out over her head and shot me a grin. "Feels good, doesn't it?"

I'd been so fixated on my own performance, I hadn't really noticed who else was still there. Most of the others, I'd wager. Even with all the extra checking, I'd been one of the fastest. But apparently not *the* fastest. "How long did it take you?"

Adelaide sat up and shook out her mane of tawny curls. "I don't know. A few minutes. It wasn't that hard. I just hope you can get some sleep now. It's a wonder you haven't made yourself sick with the hours you've pulled."

At the mention of it, I yawned. "It just means I can sleep until the results come in. I don't know how I'm going to wait to find out how I did."

"We all know how you did. What I don't know is where you get that drive. I'm wiped out, and I did only half the work you did."

"Half? That's generous."

I took out a piece of paper from my bureau and settled back against my headboard. Where did I get my drive? Right here. *Dear Merry,* I began. So many thoughts and feelings were bursting in me just then that I had to pause to collect myself before continuing.

> *How are you, my love? I hope you're happy and well
> and being a good listener and helper while I'm away.
> I heard recently that you've nearly learned all your
> letters! You'll be reading in no time, which is good
> since I plan on getting us loads of books once we're*

set up in Adoria. Of course, I still hope you'll let me
read to you once in a while. Be sure and bring the
book of rhymes when you pack, and we'll read it at
bedtime, every night, just like we used to.

I've been doing a lot of studying too. I just
finished taking a dozen different tests in all sorts of
subjects and did wonderfully on all of them, even
though I'm too tired to remember a word of it right
now! Don't worry—it'll all come back before I see
you in Cape Triumph, and then I'll teach you all of it.

It's time for me to rest now, but I'll write again
tomorrow. And before long, I'll be able to tell you
all about the fancy clothes that are going to be made
just for me. I've heard all of the diamond's dresses
are white and silver. Can you imagine? I'll be sure to
describe each and every one of them. Until then, know
that I love you without end and think about you all
the time.

I had just signed my name when Mira returned. The knowing glint
in her dark eyes told me she was unsurprised that my mastery and
Adelaide's indifference had brought us both back early.

"Why," Mira asked, "are there two different forks for seafood and
fish?"

Adelaide looked startled. "Are there?"

"It's a mystery we shouldn't question." My tone was a match for
Mistress Masterson's. "That, and why the seafood one goes with the
spoons and not the other forks."

Now Mira did a double take. "It does? That doesn't make sense."

"Are you questioning Tamsin?" asked Adelaide.

Mira smiled through her weariness. "Never. I've done some dangerous things in my life, but even I'm not foolish enough to go there."

❧

The following three days felt like three years. The feast day of the glorious angel Vaiel gave us a brief respite, but as soon as the festivities were over, it was back to waiting and more waiting. I was practically climbing the walls when word finally came that Jasper had arrived with our results.

"It's about bloody time," I exclaimed, running to the stairs.

Mira, taller than me, easily matched my hurried stride. "Watch it. They might decide to take away an extra point for that."

I bit my lip. Her tone was light, but around here, there was no telling what a slip into the market district's slang might do.

We gathered in the library, standing with the grace and good posture drilled into us these long months. Jasper looked supremely self-satisfied, no doubt envisioning piles of gold where each of us stood. He liked us reasonably well, but it was no secret he ran a business and always had his eye on the next big payoff. I'd picked up on his ambitions very quickly, back when I delivered his laundry. And he'd picked up on mine.

As soon as Mistress Masterson posted the results, our orderliness devolved into a frenzied rush. The first thing I saw was that the list had forty names on it. It was a compilation of scores from all the girls in all the manors. My eyes immediately scanned the top . . . but my name wasn't in the first spot. Or the second. It was third, with a 99 written beside it. Frowning, I looked back up at the other two names. They were from other manors: Winnifred Cray and Vanessa Thatcher. They each had a 99 too.

I spun around in outrage. "How am I ranked third? The girls above me have the same score as me!"

A few of my chattering housemates fell silent. Mistress Masterson, clearly not grasping how disastrous this development was, regarded me with exceptional calm. "Yes. You all tied—it was very impressive. Really, what it came down to is aesthetics. Winnifred, the first girl, would look so lovely in the diamond coloring. Ruby's the next most precious stone, and that obviously wouldn't suit you with your hair. So third, as a sapphire, seemed like—"

"Sapphire? *Sapphire?* Everyone knows green is my best color. Isn't an emerald rarer than a sapphire?"

If I couldn't claim the honor of the Glittering Court's most exalted spot, then I at least needed to salvage something.

The dressmaker who'd accompanied Jasper, Miss Garrison, gave me a cheerful smile. "My green fabric hasn't arrived yet. Isn't likely to show until about a week before you sail."

"And the categories are approximated," added Mistress Masterson. I could tell she thought I was being petty, but she couldn't understand how much I wanted—*needed*—every advantage I could get to ensure my success in Adoria. "It's more of a gemstone *range* we're going for. We thought it best just to go forward with sapphire so that she could start on your wardrobe. Otherwise, she'd be working at the last minute."

"Well, maybe she could just sew a little damned faster." The words slipped out before I could stop them.

Mistress Masterson blanched. "Tamsin! You are out of line. You will take sapphire and be grateful that you're among the top three. *And* you will watch your language."

Her scolding snapped me back to what mattered. This wasn't a time to let my emotions run wild. Swallowing my anger, I took a deep breath and hoped I looked contrite.

"Yes, Mistress Masterson. I apologize. But I can retake the exams I did poorly on, right?"

It wasn't an option I'd ever expected to need. I'd been so confident that I would earn the top spot. And yes, technically, I had—as far as scores were concerned. But when we sailed to Adoria, when Jasper dressed us up and put us on display for Cape Triumph's well-to-do bachelors, I wanted *Tamsin Wright* to be the first name everyone saw on our roster. Not the third. I wanted people to wonder who I was, to go out of their way to meet the girl who led the pack. To find the girl who was the best. That had to happen, because I needed to find the man who was the best. Considering the struggling backgrounds we'd come from, most of my peers would be happy with any husband who could elevate them to a higher class. A class change wasn't good enough for me, though. I had to have my pick of suitors and seize a man who could and would do anything for me—and could accept anything from me.

Mistress Masterson's ire turned to surprise. "Yes, of course. Every girl can. Though, I'll be honest, with a ninety-nine percent rating, there isn't much else to achieve."

I lifted my chin. "Perfection."

She gave me her blessing, but until any scores or ranks changed, I was still a sapphire. One of Miss Garrison's assistants began taking my measurements and examining swatches of luxurious blue fabrics. They were all so beautiful, so far and beyond the plain cotton dresses I'd worn only a year ago. Half of my mother's laundry clients didn't have clothing this fine. I almost felt embarrassed for my outburst and could tell by the glances of many of my housemates that they thought I was behaving absurdly.

"Tamsin, you know that blue *is* striking, don't you?"

Jasper strolled over to me as the assistant draped sky-blue silk over my shoulder. He wore a neat gray suit paired with a navy jacquard waistcoat. The ensemble was smart and stylish, but it didn't flirt with flamboyancy the way his son's fashion choices sometimes did. Jasper's attention made me feel even more chagrined, but I hid it with a haughty tone.

"Yes, of course, Mister Thorn. And you know I'm grateful and willing to wear such dazzling gowns. But when you recruited me, you said I had a spark you almost never see around here. 'I need smart girls. Resilient girls. Girls who understand what needs to be done to secure their end goal and who will fight for the best deal.' Those were your exact words, sir."

Jasper laughed. "The fact that you can quote those words back confirms I was right. I'm not going to talk you out of retakes, but I want you to know that you shouldn't lose sleep over this. Women are still so scarce over there that truthfully, I could take girls off the street and ship them directly to the colonies with no polishing at all—I'd still make a hefty profit. So when a prospect like you comes over, suitors will line up. They won't care if you're third, and remember—the top three *all* get extra perks and exclusive invitations."

Something in my chest lightened. I felt back in control—more driven than ever. "Thank you, sir. You have no idea how much your words mean to me. I'm just fighting for the best deal, that's all."

"That makes two of us," he said.

Once I calmed down about my own results, I learned later that Mira had scored an astonishing seventh place. She'd faced the same disdain all Sirminican refugees regularly received when she'd come to Osfrid, so to place higher than most of our housemates—many of whom had looked down on her when she arrived—was quite a coup. I could hardly contain my pride.

Adelaide placed right in the middle of the list, which didn't surprise me at all. What did surprise me was her showing up for retakes the following week. She'd been subdued after the results came out but had never mentioned this.

Amusement sparkled in her blue eyes when she saw how shocked I was. "Hey, I can care about my future too."

"Since when?"

I retook only the exams I hadn't received a perfect score on, but Adelaide did every single one of them over again. It made for another stressful, sleepless time, and at the completion of my final test, I felt as though I'd used up every last bit of physical and mental energy I had. I staggered upstairs afterward and thought I might very well make good on my previous joke about sleeping through the days until the results came.

Mira, reading on her bed, greeted me with "There's a letter for you."

My heart nearly burst when I saw what it contained. Olivia had sketched a charcoal portrait of our family for me. Ma, Pa, Jonathan, Olivia, Merry. I drank in the familiar faces and felt tears prick my eyes.

Mira, passing by on her way to the door, did a double take and then backed up a few steps. "Sorry—I didn't mean to look. Wow. That's amazing. It looks just like them."

I swallowed back more tears. "My sister made it. She's very talented."

"The older one, right? Olivia?"

"Oh, yes, of course." Almost a slip. Almost. I tapped Olivia's likeness for emphasis. "She must have used a mirror to draw herself. She was practicing self-portraits when I left."

"Well, I think she's figured it out." Glancing at my face, Mira discreetly retreated, but not before adding, "Don't worry, Tamsin. You won't let them down. You're unstoppable."

"I hope so," I murmured, once alone. I gazed at each face, but it was Merry's that drew me back over and over. Olivia had perfectly captured the way Merry's curls lay this way and that against her little cheeks. She'd had those unruly curls since she was born, and for three years, I'd tried in vain to tame them. I traced their shape with my fingertips, smiling in spite of the gnawing in my chest. "Six, I hope so."

CHAPTER 3

THOSE WHO HADN'T RETAKEN THE EXAMS WERE ALMOST as excited as those who had to see the new results. We gathered with Jasper and Mistress Masterson just as we had before. Miss Garrison wasn't around, but Jasper's son, Cedric, had turned up unexpectedly, as he so often did. He was studying at the university in Osfro but would be taking a break to accompany us to Adoria and help with the family business. A few girls in the house had a crush on him, thanks to his dapper good looks and seemingly endless supply of charm.

He came off a little more serious than usual today. In fact, Jasper and Mistress Masterson looked solemn too, which was odd given their enthusiasm last time. A strange feeling twisted in my stomach, warring with the giddy overconfidence of my expected triumph.

Mistress Masterson cleared her throat. "I know some of you have been waiting for your retake results, so you'll be pleased they're in. Most of you showed improvement—for which I'm particularly proud. But there was nothing significant enough to warrant a change in rank or theme—with one exception."

My mouth went dry. My fists clenched at my sides. I'd done it. I'd really done it. I was going to be the Glittering Court's star in Adoria, the wife of Adoria's most prestigious man. No one would ever look down on Merry—or me—again.

Mistress Masterson's gaze shifted in my direction—but not *to* me. Rather, beside me. "Adelaide. The improvement you showed is . . . remarkable, to put it mildly. I've never, ever seen a girl make such a leap in scores. And . . . I've never seen a girl get a perfect overall score. We rarely have theme changes based on retakes, though of course it happens. And in this case, it's absolutely warranted."

Jasper beamed at Adelaide, though tension seemed to strain his smile a bit. "Adelaide, my dear, you've replaced Winnifred from Dunford Manor as our diamond.

"Everyone else who scored above your last result will move down a notch," Jasper continued. "All girls will still keep their gemstone themes, with a couple of exceptions."

They started talking about Winnifred, and the world spun around me. I feared I'd faint. After a few deep breaths, I regained my senses in time to hear Mistress Masterson say, ". . . we think she'll show best as a sapphire, and we've done a couple of other last-minute switches—which means, Tamsin, you can be an emerald after all. Miss Garrison expects the green fabric to arrive next week, and she and her assistants will work around the clock to make sure you're properly outfitted."

Her expression said she expected elation from me. I had to wet my lips a few times before my mouth could make words again. "But . . . if the ranks shifted, then that means . . . I'm fourth."

"Yes."

I didn't know what to say. I didn't know what to think. Everyone in the room was watching me, and I oscillated between humiliation and despair. I hadn't just lost my diamond rank; I'd also lost access to the elite three.

Jasper attempted to fill the silence with words that didn't make me feel any better: "You'll dazzle them as an emerald. Even if you aren't invited to *all* the elite parties, I know you'll be in high demand."

He went on and on with compliments for the rest of us and offered his congratulations to Cedric, who had recruited Adelaide for the Glittering Court and would earn a commission when she got married. For his part, Cedric seemed to be the only one in the room as stunned as I was.

They forgot about me after that. All anyone wanted to talk about now was Adelaide's amazing performance and how close we were to Adoria. Everything blurred into a haze, and I had no idea how I made it back to my room. I collapsed onto my bed, next to Olivia's folded picture. Seconds or maybe minutes later, Mira closed the door and walked over to me.

"Tamsin—"

"How?" I peered up into Mira's eyes, desperate for answers. "How is this even possible? I gave it everything, everything that was in me. I worked hard. I studied hard."

"Of course you did." She settled down next to me, her expressive face troubled. "It's just that Adelaide studied . . ."

The absurdity of what Mira couldn't bring herself to say almost made me laugh. ". . . studied harder than me? We both know that's not true. And my dreams are done."

"Of course they aren't!"

She squeezed my hand and started to offer reassurances that were cut short when Adelaide entered. At the sight of her face—that beautiful, blue-eyed face that had always appeared so cheerful and guileless—anger suddenly dashed aside my self-pity. I leapt up from the bed.

"What have you done?" I cried.

"I'm, uh, not sure what you mean."

The weak attempt at deflection only enraged me more. "The hell you don't! Has this all been some kind of joke? Coast along and then swoop in at the end to crush everyone else? How did you do that? How did you score perfectly on everything?"

Adelaide quickly grew somber. "I learned a lot of it when I worked in my lady's house. I was around nobility all the time, and I guess I picked up their ways. You know that."

"Oh yeah? Where were those ways in the last nine months? You've botched things continuously—but not always the same things! You run hot and cold, perfect at some things and then failing at the most basic ones. What kind of game are you playing?"

"It's no game," Adelaide said. "My nerves just got the best of me. Things finally came together during the retakes."

I didn't believe it. And I could tell Mira—who was very obviously trying to figure out how to calm the situation—didn't really believe it either.

"Impossible," I told Adelaide. "I don't understand how or why you've been doing this, but I know something's going on. And if you think you can just ruin my life and—"

"Oh, come on." She gave me a withering look. "Your life is far from ruined."

That hurt me almost more than everything else—more than the results, more than her lying. She really didn't know that she'd ruined my life. How could she? I sincerely believed these two would still love me if they knew about Merry, but I'd learned too well that secrets rarely stayed secrets when shared. Jasper wasn't going to peddle a bride with an illegitimate child, and there was no way I could endanger all I'd accomplished.

And as Adelaide and I continued shouting, the fury within me was directed at myself as well as her. If I'd told her and Mira about Merry, maybe Adelaide wouldn't have done . . . whatever it was she'd done. But there was no going back now. I had to salvage my future somehow, and I knew with a sickening dread that I wasn't going to be able to do it with Adelaide around. Every time I looked at her, I'd be reminded of what she had potentially cost me. I couldn't risk the effect that would have on me. More than ever, I needed to keep a cool and calculating head. That couldn't happen if I was constantly driven to rage or tears.

When Mira couldn't take any more of our arguing, she begged, "Tamsin, please stop and talk this out."

Blood pounded in my ears, and I bit off the next angry retort I'd had ready for Adelaide. Studying Mira, I felt a pang of sympathy. She hadn't asked for this, and now she would suffer too.

"No," I told her. Realizing then what I'd have to do, I shifted back to Adelaide. "I'm never speaking to you again."

I stormed out of our room soon thereafter and went straight downstairs to the wing that held Mistress Masterson's office. Jasper used it when he was here, and we generally stayed away. Finding the door ajar, I pushed it open without knocking. Jasper glanced up from his desk and didn't look entirely surprised to see me.

"Tamsin." He leaned back and rubbed his eyes. "There's nothing I can do to change the rankings."

"That's not why I'm here, sir. It's the ships I want to change."

"Ships?"

"We're still taking two to Adoria, right?"

"So long as none of them back out on me," he replied. Brides weren't the only things he sold, and part of the reason he'd accelerated our departure was so that he could get the jump on other merchants. But it also meant risking rougher sailing conditions, and he'd apparently paid dearly to hire the ships.

I wrung my hands in front of me. "Well, then, I'd like to switch off the Blue Spring ship and go on the other one."

He took this in for several moments. "I assume this is about Adelaide? Look, I understand you're disappointed, but getting caught up in petty drama with other girls is only going to distract you from success. Focus on your contract."

"I will, Mister Thorn—when I'm in Adoria. And it seems like I'll have better odds of that if I'm not miserable for the two months leading up to it."

That brought a wry smile to his face. "I see."

I waited, unable to read his thoughts. As the silence stretched, I had to repress the urge to beg further, to plead and wail about how I couldn't be trapped in a small space with Adelaide for that long. But Jasper Thorn wasn't indulgent or sentimental. He would make his decision with or without further persuasion.

"I normally wouldn't even consider it," he said at last. "You should be able to deal with this minor inconvenience. But honestly, I'm still reeling a bit too. Who'd have thought Cedric could bring in a girl capable of a score like that? When he showed up with her and the Sirminican, I thought for sure he was out of his mind. He still might be."

Jasper gazed off, seeming to forget I was there. I didn't fully understand the dynamics of the Thorn family, though I'd picked up a few things while delivering their laundry. They weren't openly affectionate, but I still got the sense that Jasper cared about his son and wanted him to succeed in the world. The thing was, I felt like Jasper wanted to make sure he succeeded *more* than Cedric did.

Snapping his attention back to me, Jasper abruptly asked, "Did she cheat?"

"I . . . I beg your pardon?"

"Do you have any reason to think Adelaide might have pulled this off dishonestly? Yes, I'd like to parade a 'perfect' girl around, but I don't want to discover some nefarious scheme later and unleash a scandal. Our reputation isn't just built on teaching young ladies to be genteel. It's also about *them* putting in the work and effort for it." The intensity of his gaze made me take a step back. "You live with her. Did you see anything?"

I hesitated as an unexpected power now hovered within my grasp. What would happen if I said that I suspected Adelaide had indeed done something underhanded? Would she be removed? Would they take me at my word? I could back up my claim with her moody behavior before the retakes. Others must have noticed. It was no indicator of guilt, but it could be damning enough to cost her her rank . . . and win me back mine.

Except I truly didn't think she'd cheated. She'd been dishonest—that I believed, though I still couldn't put all the pieces together. We'd retaken some of the same exams, and I hadn't seen any real way to cheat. No, Adelaide wasn't fooling us by pretending to know everything. She'd fooled us by pretending to know nothing. And no matter how angry she'd made me, I couldn't falsely accuse her.

"No, sir. I didn't notice anything."

He nodded and sighed. "Mistress Masterson thinks it's all honest too. I suppose it could just be luck . . ."

As he fell into thought once more, I asked nervously, "So . . . does that mean I can switch?"

"We'll see. I'm going to Swan Ridge tonight. If one of those girls will trade, you can do it. Our space is parceled out pretty tightly."

"Thank you, Mister Thorn. I appreciate it. And I won't let you down."

"I'm sure you won't. And despite this Adelaide situation, I have no doubt you'll fulfill your contract in no time."

I crossed my arms. "I'm not going to just fulfill it. You can set a high starting price, and I promise you it'll be met and exceeded. And my advance'll be paid right away."

"I don't doubt that either. I hope the money's been useful to your family."

"Very useful," I said, keeping my voice as level as possible. Like me, most girls here had worked a job or even two to help support their families. Losing that income for a year, even if it eventually resulted in a fortune, could seriously affect a family's short-term well-being. So, on occasion, Jasper advanced money to a girl that she would pay back—with interest—upon getting married. Usually, he lent silver, but I'd bargained for gold.

Jasper didn't know about Merry, of course. I'd told him we needed the gold for my sister's medical expenses, which was only half a lie. Merry frequently suffered from coughing fits that could almost entirely cut off her air. The doctor had told us it would pass as she grew older, but until then, his fees and her medicine had racked up a debt we'd struggled to keep up with. The Glittering Court's advance had lifted that burden and done so much more, now that Merry had her own ticket to Adoria.

"I'll let you know about the switch." Jasper's eyes returned to his paperwork, and I recognized the dismissal. After thanking him once again, I left the office, satisfied I'd done all that I could with that problem. Now I just had to figure out how to avoid my bedroom as much as possible for the next two weeks.

Evading Adelaide didn't turn out to be the problem. She made a few half-hearted attempts to talk to me but gave up when I kept refusing to even look at her. Mira was a different story, though.

In the time I'd spent here, Mira had always been unshakeable. And how could she be any other way? Her homeland had erupted into civil war, and she'd lived in horrific conditions while escaping to Osfrid, never knowing if she'd make it alive. And even after she arrived, survival had been a daily struggle.

But she'd endured, and her resiliency had allowed her to face the ups and downs of a household of ambitious girls with ease. I'd seen little faze her until this rift with Adelaide. Over and over, she begged us to forgive each other. It tore at my heart, realizing just how much she cared about us.

That just reaffirmed that I was doing the right thing. This had turned into a terrible, emotional mess that was drowning all of us.

I couldn't let the fallout with Mira and Adelaide be a distraction. I loved them both—yes, even Adelaide—but Merry was my greatest love. Everything I had within me had to go into improving my life for my daughter, and I wasn't going to be able to do that if I was also wrestling with the hurt of my rocky friendships.

Mira came to me that very last night with one final plea. "You two are ripping me in half! I've seen what happens when neither side backs down in a fight. No one wins, Tamsin, and I'm so tired of it. I'm tired of pain. I'm tired of loss. I can't do it anymore—and I can't lose you two."

"Mira, you will never lose me. No matter what else happens or where we go in this world, I will always be there for you." I took her hands and added reluctantly, "And whatever's happened between Adelaide and me . . . well, I know she'll always be there for you too."

I didn't say a word to her about trading ships, how a Swan Ridge girl named Martha had agreed to swap with me. I didn't mention it to anyone at Blue Spring, but they all found out the morning of our departure. We left from Osfrid's largest west coast port, Culver, and spent a blustery morning waiting by the docks as sailors readied our ships for boarding. I stared off at the churning gray waves as the other Blue Spring girls clustered nearby chatted about the adventures to come. Their chatter turned to gasps when my name was called with the Swan Ridge girls traveling aboard the *Gray Gull*. My manor—my former manor—was taking the *Good Hope*.

I couldn't bear to look at Adelaide and Mira. Instead, I kept my eyes fixed on the *Gray Gull*'s tallest mast as I walked forward. I tried to clear my mind of everything except the ship. I didn't want to think about how I was leaving my friends behind. I didn't want to think about how I was leaving my daughter behind and how—if I failed her— this agonizing separation would have been for nothing.

I knew how petty it must seem to everyone. It must have looked like I was having a temper tantrum, that I couldn't handle the blow to my pride. They were all welcome to think whatever they wanted, though. Their opinions didn't matter. What mattered was getting back on track.

Somehow, I made it on board without crumbling. And when the *Gray Gull*'s lines were let loose, I stood on the deck and clenched the rails, watching my homeland grow smaller and fainter until it disappeared entirely.

We were on our way.

After the excitement of departure, I climbed the narrow ladder below deck and sought refuge in my assigned cabin. It was tiny, almost the same size as the room I used to share with Olivia and Merry. I immediately began penning a letter but didn't get very far because my three new roommates burst in.

"You're the girl who got kicked out of the top three, aren't you?" one of them asked. "Because of that—what's her name? Adelaide? The one who came out of nowhere?"

Another girl regarded me with wide, intrigued eyes. "I heard you got in a fight with her! Did you punch her?"

"Bad luck, that whole affair," said the third girl. The contrast of her long black hair against alabaster skin gave her an otherworldly beauty. "You and I got the same score, you know. I'm Winnifred. You think you got it bad? Imagine how I feel, losing the diamond!"

They all looked pleasant enough, their expressions bright and eager. And they seemed ready to welcome me too, but I didn't want people who might like me and whom I might like in return. I didn't want to deal with the pain that would follow if another friendship fell apart.

I met Winnifred's expectant gaze unsmilingly. "Well, I have no idea how you feel, but I'm sure it's pretty good, since you'll still be at all the most exclusive events. Hopefully you'll find a way to cope with the agony of being pampered and adored." To the blonde girl who asked if I'd punched Adelaide, I said: "And of course I didn't hit her. Do you think I'd be here if I had? Six. They should add common sense to our curriculum."

"No need to be nasty about it," Winnifred shot back. "We're just trying to be friendly, that's all. It's a long trip."

"I came to the Glittering Court because I wanted a husband, not friends," I replied.

The first girl who'd entered leaned against the doorway and chuckled. "Quite the charmer, aren't you? I'm sure men will be falling all over themselves when they get a taste of that sunny attitude."

"Yes," I told her, "they will be falling all over themselves. Because when I set my mind to getting something done, I fight for it with every bit of energy I have. And I don't waste that energy on things that aren't worth my time." I glanced at each of them meaningfully.

"Well, it's a good thing you aren't looking for friends." Winnifred moved to the doorway, beckoning the others with a jerk of her head. "Because something tells me you won't be making many."

They left me alone, and I stared off at nothing for a long time, wondering how someone could exist and feel so empty. And then I continued writing.

CHAPTER 4

DESPITE MY ROCKY FIRST IMPRESSION, I DIDN'T SPEND the entire voyage as a complete pariah. The trip was too long, the space too small. The other girls and I had to interact with each other, though it never went beyond the bare-minimum conversation needed to coexist. And as time passed, I found myself growing less angry at the world. That blazing fury diminished, instead becoming a cold, leaden depression that sat in the pit of my stomach.

With no social life, I didn't have much to do during those long days. I had my letters, of course, and continued writing to Merry and my family at least once a day. I planned on giving Merry hers when she arrived in Cape Triumph, and I'd send the others back to Osfro when I found a ship carrying mail.

We had a meager library on board, but reading didn't really improve my mood. The books Jasper had sent along for our "entertainment" were all about Adoria. Some simply contained dry inventories of plant life and geographical features. But a number included accounts of the struggles colonists had faced. Plague. Icori attacks. Famine. I would have eaten up such terrifying tales of a far-off land in my youth, but they lost their luster now that said land was not so far off anymore.

I did, of course, have an unexpected opportunity before me. Sailing on the *Gray Gull* meant I was able to size up my competition ahead of our arrival in Adoria. Had I been on the *Good Hope*, I would have known nothing about these girls beforehand.

None of them were cutthroat—or if they were, they did an excellent job in hiding it. That didn't mean they weren't a threat, however. Some of the Glittering Court's highest-ranking girls were here, and they wouldn't need any sort of mastermind schemes to win over their suitors. But none of them were perfect, not even former-diamond Winnifred, so I just had to make sure that if I ever went head-to-head with anyone over a particular man, I was prepared.

"Have you noticed how Mistress Baxter fusses over Mister Baxter's clothes all the time?" remarked Polly one day. She was chatting with a group of girls in our common room while I worked on a letter in the corner. "She picks out everything he wears, lays it out each morning."

"It's cute," said Vanessa. The Baxters were an elderly merchant couple sailing with us. "Well, mostly. I heard he never gets to decide anything for himself about what he wears."

"It's smart," Polly stated. "You can't leave decisions like that to men. You've got to take things like that well in hand early on. It's what I intend to do."

I lifted out a piece of paper from underneath the letter I was writing to Merry. It was a list of cryptic notes, and I added: *P.A.: controlling, especially with appearance.* If Polly and I ever vied for a suitor who liked choosing his own clothes, I'd make sure that quirk of hers came up. And if we both happened to want a man who *liked* having everything dictated to him, then I'd know to play even more domineering than her.

Another time, during dinner, some girls were complaining about how tired they were of hardtack—the bland, biscuit-like staple of shipboard life. Winnifred said, "You know, if you marry a plantation owner, you'll have a stockpile of food like this. When you live outside of town, you've got to have backup in case some delay keeps you from getting supplies from the city."

"That's why I'm not going to live outside the city," declared Maria.

Winnifred's smile was skeptical. "Yeah? At least half of Adoria's richest men are landowners. You're going to pass on all of them?"

"Of course not. But lots of them also own homes in town. I'll marry one like that. If he doesn't have one, I'll insist that he rectify that immediately."

I made a note after dinner that potential suitors of Maria's had best be prepared for certain expenses.

And then, on still another day, I was enjoying the sun above deck and overheard Damaris engaging with one of the sailors. We weren't supposed to talk to them, but her father was a fisherman, and she constantly broke the rule.

"Why're you using a square knot?" she demanded of the man. "Shift that load, and it'll come right loose."

The sailor, under orders not to talk to us either, grimaced and ignored her as he worked.

"If it were me," she continued, "I'd use a sheet bend for that."

He jerked his head up. "You can't tie no sheet bend."

"The hell I can't."

This quickly escalated to a knot-making contest between the two, which drew the enthusiastic attention of half the ship. When it also drew Miss Quincy's attention, however, the competition came to an immediate halt. Damaris was banned from the deck for a week.

Back in my cabin, I wasn't really sure what to record, but I found myself smiling—and hurting. I was lonely. I missed my own friends terribly and wished I'd listened to Mira's pleas for peace. I'd raged because Adelaide had endangered something she hadn't even known about, but in those long, seafaring days, I began to wonder if perhaps she'd had reasons for besting everyone that *I* hadn't known about either. Had we both suffered unnecessarily because we'd been too afraid of confiding in the other? It was a sobering thought, and the fact that this question consumed me stood as proof of how distracting friendship was.

And, of course, I missed Merry the most. No amount of letter writing or reconnaissance ever chased away my longing for her. Merry and I had shared a bed for almost her entire life. In the days leading up to my departure for Blue Spring, we'd had her start sleeping with Olivia to make the transition less of a shock. I'd felt Merry's absence keenly at the manor, but I'd also been so busy with my work that I'd usually passed out pretty quickly at night. Here, in my narrow, rocking bed, I'd lie awake long into the night, aching for Merry's warmth beside me, wishing I could be sure her breathing stayed deep and steady.

We grew so used to the monotony on the *Gray Gull* that the storm took us completely by surprise.

It took the sailors by surprise too. I was above deck when a lookout spotted an ominous line of gray on the horizon. I'd been gazing moodily at the *Good Hope,* which always sailed nearby. Our crew came to life with an alacrity I'd never seen before, shouting and running as they scrambled to follow the captain's orders. Those of us by the rail squinted at the clouds and tried to understand what had spurred this urgency.

"Doesn't look like much to me," said Joan.

Her roommate, Maria, nodded in agreement. "Seems like a lot of fuss for nothing."

Even Miss Quincy expressed skepticism when one sailor curtly ordered her out of his way. She crossed her arms and glared at his back, muttering, "I shall have a word with the captain once this has all settled down. That sort of behavior is not appropriate, and he must do something to keep his men in line."

But beside her, Damaris stared at the horizon for a long time, her brow lined with thought. At last she turned around and said very quietly to us, "Go below deck."

"Damaris," chastised Miss Quincy, "there's no need for you to fret over—"

"Go!" yelled Damaris, making us all jump. "If you've got any damned sense, you'll all go now!"

We went, though Miss Quincy lectured Damaris the entire way—at least until the wind and waves hit. The ship's usual rhythmic rocking grew so severe so suddenly that many of us were thrown off our feet.

Miss Quincy stopped scolding or saying much of anything at all. She hunkered down into a corner of the common room, her face pale and pinched. Not knowing what to do, some girls sat beside her while others took shelter in their cabins. When someone tentatively suggested going outside, Damaris called her a name that would've resulted in solitary confinement for the rest of the trip if Miss Quincy had been paying attention.

"Stay sharp, because we might have to go back to the deck," Damaris informed us, her brown eyes grim. "If anyone in the crew tells you to go up, go. If you see any water in your room, go up. If the ship doesn't right itself, go up. Until then, stay out of their way."

"'If the ship doesn't right itself'?" I asked.

As though cued, the *Gray Gull* lurched wildly, tipping so far that the wall I slammed against gave the brief, disorienting sensation of being the floor. When the ship rocked back to its original position, Damaris shot me a pointed look.

Most girls stayed in the common room, so I went to my cabin, preferring the solitude to all the crying and wailing. I sat with clasped hands, murmuring a few prayers for our safety, but mostly offering pleas that Merry would be protected and taken care of if I didn't make it out of this alive. Winnifred entered at one point and sat on her own bunk. She'd given me the silent treatment for most of the trip, but after long minutes of listening to the wind and the thunder, she asked, "Do you pray to Uros? Or to one of the angels?"

"To Ariniel."

Her eyebrows rose. "Why her? Why not to Kyriel, to battle the storm? Ariniel only guards the ways."

"Then she'll know the way out of this. Seems like focusing on that is a lot smarter than running into a fight. No offense to the glorious Kyriel."

"I hope not." Winnifred almost smiled at me. "We can't risk any blasphemy right now."

A brief, taunting lull eventually marked the tempest's eye, and then the onslaught returned with new force. Winnifred and I didn't say a word after that until I spied water slowly seeping in between the planks of one of our cabin's corners. I jumped up with a startled cry, just as Damaris's voice rang out in the hall: "Get out! Go above deck! Above deck!"

Winnifred was out of the room before Damaris finished, but I hurried to my trunk, fumbling at the lock with frantic fingers. Damaris stuck her head in and shouted at me to move, but I didn't budge until the lid popped open. I grabbed the sheaf of papers that included all the letters I'd written on the voyage, as well as Olivia's drawing. With shaking hands, I wrapped the pages in a piece of canvas and shoved the bundle into my bodice. The whole time, water continued spreading across the floor.

By the time I reached the ladder leading up, the other girls had already gone above—except for Polly and Joan. They were forcibly dragging Miss Quincy along. Our chaperone looked like a sleepwalker, her blank eyes staring ahead without seeing.

I helped them get her out, and then we joined the rest of the passengers in a section of the deck that was more or less out of the crew's way. Around us, a nightmare raged. An eerie color, neither black nor green but some sickening mix of the two, had taken over the sky, obscuring all memory of the afternoon sun we'd stood in not so long ago. Lightning occasionally flashed above us, giving a brief view of the swelling, frothy waves. A blast of wind rolled the ship to its side again, sending people and equipment sliding.

We heard the first mate shout about pumping water out from below, and then another gust knocked down part of the rigging. It crashed near the helm, barely missing a few sailors. I shifted to my knees and peered over the railing as rain lashed my face. When the next bolt of lightning flared, I spied only darkness on the water.

"Where's the *Good Hope*?" I cried. "What's happened to it?"

"It was on the starboard side," yelled Damaris. "I don't know if it's there anymore."

I didn't dare go look, but I prayed again to Ariniel to guide both our ships out of this. And I prayed that no matter how this ended, Adelaide would forgive me.

Water sloshed over the deck a number of times, but amazingly, our ship always managed to right itself again. We were drenched by the time the winds began to slow, though my papers—tucked under my bodice—remained mostly dry. When it became clear we'd faced the worst of the storm, we then had to endure the agonizing process of waiting out the night to determine the extent of the damage. Even though the ship no longer heaved, we seemed to sit at an odd angle, and water continued leaking below deck.

As the sun rose, we dared to emerge from our huddle. That's when we learned the ship's rudder, and therefore its ability to steer, had been severely compromised when the rigging fell on the quarterdeck. A mainsail near the bow had also taken irreparable damage, and even the figurehead had been shattered to splinters. Damaris told us the crew had no real way to navigate the ship anymore, short of rowing.

"Which might be okay—except the captain's got most of the crew working on the leaks," she explained.

I studied the gray, gray world and wrapped my arms around myself, trying to bring warmth to my chilled body. "How are we moving then? We seem to be going at a good pace . . . faster than the wind is. But that doesn't make sense."

"We're in the northerly current," a gruff voice said behind us. We turned, and found a very haggard Captain Milford. "It runs up the coast of Adoria."

I searched frantically toward what I thought must be west. "Then are we there?"

"Not yet. But near." He glanced up at the crow's nest, where a sailor scanned the horizon with a spyglass. "The northerly's fast, and we can't really counter it now. It'll keep dragging us north for a while, but eventually it'll lean west. As soon as we see land, I'll have the men row hard."

"How far north are we?" I asked.

The captain ran a hand over his sodden gray hair. "I don't know. If the clouds clear tonight, I'll be able to tell, but right now I'm just going by the compass. We're well north of Cape Triumph, I can tell you that. The storm and the current have made sure of it."

He stalked off, and I tried to quell the unease in my stomach. *Well north of Cape Triumph.* What did that mean for us? Once we reached land, could we take another ship south? It'd be a delay, but I'd still be there ahead of Merry and have plenty of time to settle my situation.

No land came into sight that day or the next. The clouds didn't clear either. All we knew was that we were still going north, north, north. The sailors couldn't fix the leaks, and we were permanently sentenced to the upper deck. The crew brought up as much cargo as they could and then continued their tireless pumping to keep us afloat until we reached the shore.

I woke up on the third morning, hoping to see land, but only ocean greeted me. A flooded cargo hold had ruined most of our food supply, and the captain put everyone on strict rations, the passengers strictest of all. "The crew's doing the work," he stated.

I paced around restlessly, hating the not knowing. Where were we? Had the *Good Hope* survived? Were they too drifting aimlessly? Those questions consumed me as we continued drifting, until shouting from the sailors finally snapped me to attention. I jumped up with several other girls and heard repeated cries of "Land, land!"

We ran to the railing. At first, the horizon looked the same as it had these long, long days. Then I saw it—a dark smudge atop the water to the west, separating it from the sky. The crew buzzed with a new urgency as part of their number was displaced from pumping to rowing. Slowly, awkwardly, the *Gray Gull* turned, fighting against the swift current that wanted to keep dragging us north. The line on the horizon grew darker and more substantial. Soon we could see trees. And all of a sudden, I felt the ship lurch forward as we broke free of the northerly's pull. Without that hindrance, the rowers made greater and greater strides. We entered into a race against time, trying to make haste to land before the leaks drew the sailors back to pumping.

At a certain point, the rowers slowed as they assessed our landing conditions. The shore before us consisted of wide, empty tracts of sand watched over by a wall of imposing evergreens in the distance. The *Gray Gull* came in as close as possible before the captain ordered the anchor dropped, fearful we'd strike the bottom or other unseen obstacles. The ship couldn't handle any more damage. As soon as we'd halted, a mad dash to get people and cargo off ensued.

The passengers were allotted only a few of the dinghies, requiring multiple trips to ferry us over. Although the distance wasn't too far, the minutes dragged by as I watched the boats edge through the waves. The wind had picked up over the last hour, and even if it couldn't match the storm's intensity, it still challenged the little boats. One almost capsized and was saved only by a sailor's skillful maneuvering.

I wasn't so lucky. I volunteered to go in one of the last passenger dinghies, and when we were about twelve yards from beaching, a rogue wave flipped us over. I hit the sea face-first, and everything went black for a moment as the cold shocked my system. Water filled my lungs; the taste of salt flooded my tongue. Struggling, I managed to turn myself around and touch the bottom with my feet. The water was shallow enough to stand in, but my dress felt as though it had gained a hundred pounds. It became a trap. An enemy that wanted to drown me. Twice, I fell back into the water before my shaking legs finally stayed upright. Coughing, I tried to move forward, but my steps fumbled, and I had to fight for every inch. I struggled against the heavy dress, against the waves, against the muck sucking at my feet.

"Hold on, you're almost there."

An arm linked through mine, lending me support. I glanced over and found Damaris walking with me, a tired smile on her face despite her equally soaked state. She and I staggered out of the sea, onto a rocky beach dotted with patches of snow. The bitter wind that had made us capsize whipped around us, and I wondered if it was cold enough to freeze my wet clothing. We collapsed onto a small patch of bare sand and huddled together. Gently, she patted my back as I continued coughing. The bitterness between us vanished.

"It'll come out. You just got a mouthful, that's all. Happened to me plenty of times when my brother used to push me over our pa's fishing boat. I always got him back, though." I spit out seawater by way of answer, and Damaris pointed farther down the beach. "That one went over too. Cargo, from the shouting. The captain wouldn't make that much of a fuss over us."

Most of the water seemed to be out of me now, but my teeth wouldn't stop chattering. I watched anxious sailors right their flipped dinghy and try to recover a few bobbing crates. Beyond it, the *Gray Gull* sat at anchor, listing at a sharp angle as more little boats streamed from it. Seeing its damage from this distance gave me a horrifying new sense of just how much peril we'd been in.

I closed my eyes a moment, trying to push down my fear, trying to ignore the cold seeping into my bones. How had this happened? How was I sitting here, freezing on an abandoned beach, when I was supposed to be getting ready for balls in the grandest city in Adoria? This had never been part of the plan. I was supposed to be living a luxurious life, reuniting with my friends, and providing for Merry.

Merry.

Just thinking of her steadied me. When I opened my eyes, I felt a little calmer, and the world became clearer. The world. The *new* world.

Another dinghy rocked precariously in its crossing, and Damaris started to rise to go help, but then it recovered for a safe landing. Four girls climbed over the side, faces frightened and legs rubbery. I made a quick assessment of the other groups scattered throughout the beach. "That's all of us, then," I managed to say. My throat felt raw. "I wonder how long they'll keep going back for cargo."

"Until it sinks, I imagine. The captain's lost his livelihood. He'll want to scrape every bit of profit he can out of this." She waved as the newcomers shakily made their way over to us. "The more he can sell, the more he can recover."

"But he can't sell all of it. Some of it's Jasper's and the other passengers'."

"Yes, but where is Jasper? Where are *we*, for that matter? The captain's going to be looking out for himself. And we are too, I suppose. I hope you've been saving that energy of yours to get us out of this mess."

The four girls sat beside us, and we all snuggled together. "Thank the Six," muttered one. "You can't pay me to get on a boat again."

Winnifred gazed at the *Gray Gull* with a scowl. "Well, we may need one to get to Cape Triumph."

"Maybe we're not that far," said Joan hopefully. I watched with envy as she hunkered into a cloak that had managed to stay dry.

"Or maybe we are," returned Maria. "Maybe it'll take months to get there. Years."

Her melodramatic words elicited silence and glum expressions from the others. Years? I didn't have that. I had just over three months. That spark within me blazed back to life, countering the cold, and I sprang to my feet. "It doesn't matter where we are or how far! We *are* getting to Cape Triumph. The rest of you can sit around and mope, but I'm going to find Miss Quincy and make a plan right now. *And* I'm going to make a blasted fire!"

I stomped off, not caring if they followed, but a few moments later, I heard the sounds of rustling skirts and footsteps on the hard sand. Miss Quincy sat with the rest of our girls farther along the beach, but her mind was clearly elsewhere. She'd said almost nothing in the days since the storm.

I peeled a few freezing strands of wet hair from my face and stood over her. "Miss Quincy."

No response.

"Miss Quincy."

Nothing.

"Miss Quincy!"

She flinched and turned her gaze upward. "We need to get everyone together," I told her. "We need to make a fire. And then as soon as they have all the cargo ashore, you need to talk to the captain and find out where we are. He said earlier we were drifting north, and maybe he's got a better idea now just how far we went."

She looked past me, slowly taking in the long, desolate beach. Inland, to the west, the terrain turned to patchy forest dusted with snow. No sun was visible in the gray sky. There were no buildings, no signs, no indications that any humans had ever been here before us.

Miss Quincy licked her lips and simply said, "Maybe."

"Maybe what?" I leaned down to her, forcing her to meet my eyes. "Maybe you'll talk to him? Maybe he knows where we are?"

She looked away. "There's a lot to think about, Tamsin."

"We need to think about making a fire before we all freeze to death!" I had to resist the urge to shake her and remind her she was supposedly our superior, that it was her job to look after our party. Instead, I turned to the others and asked, "What can we burn around here?"

"Driftwood," supplied Damaris promptly. "If it's not too damp."

I sized up the girls, determining who appeared the least exhausted or terrified. "Polly, Pamela, Joan. You go search. Gather anything you can and set it in that open spot there."

The three looked surprised and then jumped to obey. There was comfort in being given direction, I supposed. While they searched, Damaris and I discussed kindling, and I made a point of speaking loudly and keeping my body language open to Miss Quincy, as though she was part of the conversation. I expected her to join in at any moment. She didn't.

When we had enough material for a fire, a merchant who'd traveled on the ship gave us the flint he used for cigars. Before long, he, the other passengers, and the rest of the Glittering Court girls had gathered around the humble greenish flames, taking what heat we could.

I rubbed my hands together over and over, trying to keep my fingers from going numb.

Out at sea, the *Gray Gull* sat far lower in the water than it had when we came ashore. The sailors still fought their way back and forth, and a sizeable amount of goods rested on the beach now. I strolled over to the pile, dismissing the nailed crates, and found a traveler's trunk that opened easily. I had no idea who it belonged to, but the cloak inside fit me. I gathered the rest of the contents and those of another trunk before heading back toward the fire.

"Hey," called a sailor. "What do you think you're doing?"

"Keeping us from getting frostbite, not that it's any business of yours." He glanced uneasily at his captain, out of earshot, but didn't stop me.

I handed out dry clothes first to the girls who'd gone into the water and then to anyone else who needed another layer, which was pretty much everyone. The clothing we'd brought wasn't exactly designed for wilderness survival. Miss Quincy still sat in her stupor, but some of the others began discussing what to do next. The *Gray Gull* had primarily contained cargo, so there were only four other passengers besides the Glittering Court cohort. Two were the Baxters, whom Polly had admired. The third passenger was a merchant too, and the fourth was a short-spoken man whose only plan was to find adventure and fortune. He'd certainly already achieved one of those goals.

As twilight fell, Captain Milford finally called an end to gutting the *Gray Gull*. He summoned all the sailors back to the beach and stared sadly at his disappearing ship. I allowed him a few moments of mourning before I strode over.

"Captain, we need to talk about we're going to do."

He gave me a scathing glance, his face ashen. "There's no 'we.' You're not my responsibility."

"Of course we are. We're your passengers."

"Passengers of what?" He gestured to the *Gray Gull*. "I've got no ship now. I was a fool to sail this early. I should never have let Monroe talk me into it."

I had heard the name a few times in our voyage, and it took me a moment to place it. "The *Good Hope*'s captain? Do . . . do you think they went off course too? Or that they . . ."

"My guess is they're about to dock in Cape Triumph. The *Good Hope*'s bigger and heavier. She was getting knocked about, but last glimpse I got, she was still intact and holding her own." His eyes drifted back to the *Gray Gull*, and he gave a heavy sigh. "At least I got part of my pay up front."

"And you'll get the rest from Mister Thorn when you take us to Cape Triumph."

Noticing the fire's glow, he ambled toward it. I followed along, several sailors in our wake. "Girl, I'm not an escort service. I've got to get my men and my goods out of here and try to regroup."

"Ahem," said Mister Baxter. "Some of those are *our* goods."

"Yes. And some are Mister Thorn's," I added. "I'm sure he'll give you a handsome bonus when you return them—and us."

The captain held his palms by the fire. After a few moments, he peered up at the darkening sky. "I wish we could see the damned stars."

"Can you make any guess at all where we are now?" asked the younger merchant.

"Still just north. If we're lucky, the current only took us to Archerwood. But we could be as far as Grashond. In the morning, I'll send some men south in the boats to see what they can come across. Uros willing, we're just up the coast from a major port like Watchful or Sutton. And if nothing else, there should be some fishing village nearby."

"I'll go with them," I said immediately. I needed civilization. I needed to be actively working toward Cape Triumph.

The captain snorted. "You will not. I'm not wasting the boat space. The bulk of us will make camp here with the cargo. You can stay or wander off as you like, but I'm not pampering the lot of you."

A few of the sailors eyed us speculatively, and I became aware of a new danger to add to our growing list. On the ship, the crew had had brutal orders to not even think about laying a hand on us. But out here? In the wilderness? Their captain had written us off. They didn't have Jasper to answer to anymore. The younger merchant might come to our aid, but the elderly Baxters wouldn't be fighting anyone off.

That would leave us on our own. The sailors outnumbered us and had an advantage of size and strength. Near me, Maria shifted, and I saw her eyeing the fire—in particular, pieces of driftwood near the edges. Not a bad weapon in a pinch, I supposed. Maria's gloom was irritating, but I had the impression she'd been a scrapper back in Osfro.

I put my hands on my hips as I faced down the captain. "You don't have to 'pamper' us, but you do have to help us survive out here until we can find some help! You don't think you'll ever cross paths with Jasper Thorn again? When he finds out you abandoned us, he'll ruin the reputation of any new venture you try to start up."

This gave the captain pause, but one of the other sailors snorted. "That's *if* he finds out what happened. We'll just tell him that you all were lost and—"

"Shut up," his captain told him. "Listen, girl, even if we're able to—"

"What's that?"

I started at the unexpected sound of Miss Quincy's voice. In fact, I was so astonished to finally hear her that it took me a moment to process her words and look where she pointed. There, out of the hazy western forest, riders emerged from among the trees. Nearly two dozen riders.

At first, they were only shadowy figures. As they came closer, I noticed finer details. Intricate metalwork on the horses' bridles like none I'd ever seen. Fur-trimmed coats of unusual patterns. The women had on pants. Some of the men wore their black hair far longer than Osfridian fashion allowed right now. All carried a weapon of some kind, be it blade, bow, or gun.

The captain muttered something explicit and then said more loudly to us, "Of course. Of *course* this would happen. We're not in Grashond. We landed on the far side of the damned Quistimac."

I pulled up a mental map of Adoria and tried to picture the Quistimac River. I couldn't quite recall its exact placement. It was in the northern part of Adoria, I knew that, but most of our study at the manor had focused on the richer, commercial colonies to the south—the ones we were likely to marry into. Winnifred asked the question that was on my lips.

"What's on the far side of the Quistimac?"

The strange riders reached the beach, and the captain grimaced. "Balanquan territory."

CHAPTER 5

BALANQUANS.

My chest tightened. Our Glittering Court education had covered all aspects of Adoria, but the Balanquans had warranted only a brief summary. That was because it was unlikely we'd ever do much more than pass one or two of them in the safety of a colonial town. There'd been no lesson covering what to do if we faced a small army in the middle of nowhere.

Almost two centuries ago, when armies had sailed from the Evarian continent to Osfrid, they'd found people already living on the island: Icori. The two groups had fought for years until the Icori, defeated, had yielded their land and sailed away. Most thought the Icori had perished on the Sunset Sea, so it had been a shock when Osfridian explorers "discovered" Adoria and found our ancient foes had made a new home for themselves.

But someone else had been in Adoria long before the Icori, someone we'd had no experience with. The Balanquans. An empire shrouded in mystery. People who didn't act like us, dress like us, or speak like us. They remained neutral toward the Osfridian colonization of Adoria—as well as the renewed fighting with the Icori—and traded with Icori, Osfridians, and Evarians alike. The Balanquans were more advanced than the rest of us in certain technologies, and their goods were highly prized. They kept their techniques secret, and rumors abounded about northern cities filled with wonders. Few outsiders had ever seen those cities, however, as the Balanquans were fiercely protective of their territory. And since it wasn't really known if those fabled advancements extended to weapons, everyone gave the Balanquan borders a wide berth.

"Easy, boys," murmured the captain. The sailors had tensed up, and the few with weapons—mostly knives—had reached for them. "They could easily kill us all. Let me do the talking."

Several of the Glittering Court girls cowered closer to one another, whimpering and pale in the fire's flickering light. Most of the riders slowed to a halt, but one horse trotted boldly forward, bearing a woman in an exquisitely draped coat made from layers of black wool edged in silvery fur. It reminded me of flower petals and would have been the envy of many of Osfro's fashion-conscious crowd. A cap of the same luxurious fur covered her dark hair, framing eyes that were both sharp and wary.

"You're trespassing," she said in accented Osfridian.

"Not by choice, friends, I assure you," replied the captain, wearing a smile that looked like it hurt his face. "As you can see by our ship there—what's left of it—we didn't have much say in coming here. We're lucky to be alive after the storm we went through."

Her expression remained hard. "We don't allow your people in our land. You aren't supposed to be here."

"Of course, of course. And in the morning, some of my men will be sailing south and—"

"No." This came from a Balanquan man who rode up beside her. His fur-trimmed jacket was simpler in cut, but the design on the wool was extraordinary, depicting fanciful patterns of teal and ivory birds. I didn't know which appealed to me more: the coat's beauty or its warmth. "You will not be traveling through our lands," he said. "You are *not* going to Askashi."

"Perhaps you'd like to escort us," said the captain. "My ship was filled with goods—you can see it all over there—and we'd be happy to trade in Askashi—"

"Most of that isn't yours," I interjected.

He shot me a furious look. "Quiet. This has nothing to do with you."

"Of course it does! Our future's at stake here too, and if anyone's going to be trading Jasper's haul, it'll be us. Otherwise, it's going south with us, and you'd do bloody well to keep your hands off it!"

The Balanquans' eyes fell on me, and I cringed. The woman scanned our group of girls. "Do you let women work on your ships now?" She sounded surprised, pleasantly so.

"Ah, no, these are our passengers, and as you can imagine, they need assistance out here in these conditions, so your help would—"

"Oh, *now* we're your passengers?" Turning from the captain, I faced the Balanquan woman with as much courage as I could. "Begging your pardon, mistress, but this lowlife was ready to abandon us to the wolves minutes ago and steal our benefactor's property! I wouldn't trust him either, if I were you. But the rest of us? We're just on our way to Cape Triumph to get married. You tell us the quickest way out of here, whatever you want, and we'll do it. We'll even pay you for passage." I didn't want the sailors absconding with Jasper's goods, but I was pretty sure he wouldn't mind if I bartered away a few things to get us back. I nodded toward the merchants. "And, uh, they're with us too. Also happy to pay, I'm sure."

The two Balanquans studied me for what felt like an eternity. I don't think they even blinked. Then, without another word, they rode back to their companions and began speaking in a language unlike any I'd ever heard. Internally, I wilted, unable to believe the way I'd just spoken to them. But I couldn't leave our fate in the sailors' hands. If I wasn't in Cape Triumph when the Wilsons arrived, I knew they'd take good care of Merry, but they'd also take her with them if they had to leave to follow their job leads in the southern colonies before I arrived. I could easily lose track of her.

"I hope you're happy," growled the captain. "You've most likely gotten us all killed."

"It's not like you were doing so well!" I hissed back. "Besides, you're not my responsibility."

I studied the riders and noticed that they didn't all seem to be Balanquans. A handful had lighter hair and skin and wore far less elaborate clothing. They looked rough and seasoned, as though the harsh elements didn't faze them at all. But were they Osfridians? Or some other people from Evaria? Would they be sympathetic to us?

The Balanquan leader separated herself again and returned to us. When she spoke, she directed her words to me. "We've decided to help you. We'll escort you to our outpost southwest of here, down on the Quistimac. You'll be given food and shelter. We can also transport some of your cargo tonight. We'll come back for the rest of it in the morning, at which time we can negotiate a fair price for our assistance." Her dark-brown eyes shifted to the captain. "A price everyone will pay for themselves, with their own means."

The captain sagged with relief. "Certainly. And then from there—"

"From there, we'll take you up the Quistimac to a ford near Constancy. Your own people can deal with you then. The trip should take about three days."

"Constancy!" exclaimed Captain Milford. "That's a landlocked farm town! If you want us in Grashond, fine. But at least take us to the coast, so we can get a ship in Watchful. We don't want to go farther inland."

"This isn't negotiable," said the Balanquan man who'd spoken before. "Traveling to Watchful passes through too much of our territory and the Icori's. Neither of us want you there. Going to Constancy keeps you mostly on the river and gets you back to your own lands faster."

"For which we are very, very grateful," I announced. I knew little about Grashond and nothing about Constancy, but I'd gladly take any of the colonies over a leaking ship or freezing beach. "When can we go?"

The Balanquan woman was watching the captain. "As soon as everyone agrees."

He threw up his hands. "Of course we agree. What damned choice do we have?"

⁓

It was fully dark when we reached the Balanquans' trading post, and by then, I couldn't feel any of my extremities. Bone weary, I just kept putting one foot in front of the other, telling myself that each step I took was another step to Merry.

The trading post sat on the bank of the Quistimac River, which appeared only as a dark ribbon this time of night. The post's main hub was a simple, one-room rectangular building, though when I passed close to its walls, I noticed fanciful and highly detailed carvings in the wood, similar to the designs in the Balanquans' clothing and gear. I'd learned along the way that our ship had been spotted by a trading party en route to this post and that they had sought out one of the patrols that guarded the Balanquan side of the river. The merged group of sentries and traders had then intercepted us at the beach.

We packed into the post and silently devoured the hard bread and dried meat our hosts provided. The closeness of so many bodies, along with a cozy hearth, provided almost enough heat to make me feel human again. As we finished our meal, Alisi—the Balanquan woman who'd led the party—beckoned me to the side of the room. I rose from the dirt floor on stiff legs and scurried over to her.

"Tamsin Wright, correct?" she asked. "You're in charge of these young women?"

I hesitated and glanced back to where Miss Quincy sat hunched under a blanket. "Y-yes. I suppose so."

"Between them and the others on your ship, we have almost fifty extra people. We can't fit that many in here for the night, but we'll pack in who we can. We have tents everyone else can use, but those too will be crowded. Once my own people are settled, I can give you about fifteen spots on the floor, plus a tent. Can you divide your charges appropriately?"

"Yes, of course. Thank you. What about the others from our ship?"

"We've given them tents." A knowing look crossed her face. "But the sailors will not be near you."

"Thank you." I pointed toward the gray-haired Baxters, sitting near my friends. "Let that couple sleep in here. Two more from our group will go outside instead."

"It's cold out," a new voice remarked. "You sure your friends won't mind you giving away those spots?"

Alisi and I turned to find we'd been joined by a few of the mysterious riders I'd noted earlier, the ones who weren't Balanquans. The young woman who'd spoken had her hood thrown back, revealing long golden hair in need of a good washing. Most of her needed a good washing, actually. She had dirt smudged on her face and stains on her thick leather coat that my laundress's eye knew weren't ever going to come out.

"Honestly, my friends'll just be glad to sleep somewhere that isn't in danger of sinking," I told her. "And I'll take one of the outdoor spots, so they can hardly complain over what I'm willing to do myself."

The woman rolled her eyes. "Oh, they'll always find a way to complain. That's the downside of being a leader."

I glanced at the Glittering Court girls huddled together over their rations. "What's the upside?"

"Still trying to figure that out." The newcomer turned to Alisi. "Dermoc's burn is starting to bother him again. Can we buy some more nettle from you?"

Alisi looked genuinely dismayed. "I wish you could, Orla. We sent the last batch to Askashi."

"I see. Well, it doesn't look infected yet, so he'll just have to put up with it until we're home. The question now is if *we* can put up with his grumbling."

"Wait, Mistress—what was it?—Orla?" I called as the hardened group started to leave. The golden-haired woman regarded me with impatience. She struck me as someone who didn't handle delays well. "What kind of burn is it?"

"Sparks blew onto his gloves while he was building a fire," she said after some hesitation. "They took hold and blistered the side of his hand before he could rub the flames out."

"Okay, wait just a moment."

Leaving them puzzled, I hurried out of the post, gritting my teeth at the icy wind that met me. Our cargo was stacked nearby, guarded by a couple of Balanquans who watched me closely but didn't interfere as I searched the pile by torchlight. I wasn't even sure if what I wanted would be here; it could have been left on the beach until morning.

"There you are," I murmured, spying a long, flat leather case. I carried it back inside and was intercepted along the way by Polly.

"Tamsin, even in here, it's still cold. I mean, it's better, but . . . isn't there something you can do?" She pulled irritably at the edge of her cloak, which was made of a wool that was very lovely and very finely woven—but also very thin. "We didn't come prepared to camp out in the woods for three days."

"What is it you think I can do?" I asked, taken aback by her tone.

"I don't know. But you get things done."

"I'll see what I can do," I muttered, returning to Orla and Alisi. "Here."

Orla stopped their Balanquan conversation and took the small bottle I handed her. "What is it?"

"Arnica. Not as good as nettle for burns, but it'll take the edge off it."

"I know it," said Orla. She peered at the rest of the box's contents, consisting of various creams, rouges, and kohl. I had grabbed the whole thing in my haste. "Strange medical kit."

"Oh—these are cosmetics. We keep the arnica around for blemishes." I felt idiotic even saying the words. Skin beauty seemed so trite, given our life-and-death situation.

Orla's smirk suggested she was thinking the same thing. She made a comment to her companions in yet another language I didn't know, eliciting laughter. To me, she said, "Well, Dermoc would welcome it. And maybe he'll even come out looking a little prettier. What will you trade for it? Food? I have coin too."

"Nothing. It's a trifle."

Orla's mocking smile vanished first into disbelief, and then suspicion. "You have to take something for it."

"I'd hardly charge to ease someone's suffering, not when the remedy is so cheap."

"Even someone you know nothing about?"

"I know he's in pain, that's enough. It's a gift. Take it." I meant it. I was happy to help, and besides, Orla and her group didn't really look like they had a lot to spare. I thought they might be hunters or trappers, and I was already building a mental image of them living in some derelict shack in the woods. Or maybe they were hired muscle the Balanquans kept around.

Orla wavered, finally accepting when Alisi said something to her in Balanquan. Orla thanked me gravely and left with her followers. When they were gone, I asked Alisi, "I would like to trade with *you*, though, if you're able. And we'll still pay for the escort, of course. A lot of our clothing isn't warm enough for these conditions, and we could use some hardier things, especially for the journey to Constancy."

"We have a few items we brought back from our own expedition." Alisi scanned my cohort. "And even though your clothing is pretty impractical out here, it would be sought after in other places. You can borrow blankets for tonight, and then we'll see what permanent solutions we can negotiate in the morning."

"Thank you." Before leaving, I asked, "Who was she? Orla? She's not Balanquan."

"No. Orla Micnimara is one of our Icori trading partners."

"Icori?" I craned my neck, peering at where Orla and her band sat talking and laughing in a corner. The Balanquans had been a hazy enigma back in Osfrid, but the Icori were regularly described in frightening detail. We had textbooks filled with drawings of snarling, half-naked Icori wearing tartan capes in gaudy plaid designs. Fantastic stories of their brutal, uncouth, and untrustworthy ways ran rampant, and I tried to reconcile those images with the reality before me. "But they're . . . I mean, they're supposed to be . . . well, shouldn't they at least be wearing tartan? And painting their faces blue?"

Alisi's smile returned. "Too cold for tartan. And woad makes a terrible mess. It's only used for very particular occasions."

"Oh."

"You look upset."

"Not upset. Confused." Orla had been flippant, but her overall air was congenial and polite. Also, she hadn't tried to kill me on sight, as many of our books suggested Icori regularly did. "I just thought Icori hated our people."

"That's often true. But she doesn't hate *you*. Not yet. Try to make sure it stays that way, and you'll go far around here."

CHAPTER 6

MY TENT WAS SO SMALL THAT THOSE OF US WHO STAYED in it pretty much ended up sleeping in a pile that night—but at least that kept us warm. We'd also raided the ship's chests for more clothing, and Alisi had made good on lending us blankets. Since the storm three days ago, my body and mind had been taxed to their limit, and I slept heavily in those strange conditions, recalling no dreams.

But I awoke first, unable to sleep when I knew there was so much that needed to be done—and that I was the only one who could do it. With a wistful sigh at returning to the cold, I crawled out of my blanket and sat up, trying not to disturb the other girls. Near the tent's entrance, Pamela shifted and opened one eye. I nearly urged her back to sleep and then, after a moment's thought, beckoned for her to follow me.

Outside, the posts' other inhabitants were stirring. The Balanquans looked as though they'd been up for a while, and new piles of cargo showed they'd even made a trip back to the beach. Captain Milford stood arguing with a small cluster of Balanquans led by Hashon, the man who ran the trading post. A crate full of tin cans—not Jasper's—stood open between them.

"They're going to come to us next to negotiate our 'fee,'" I told Pamela. "I want you to be in charge of it."

"Me?" she squeaked.

"Your family had a stand in the west market. You know how to haggle."

She shuddered, watching the Balanquans moving around us. "Yes, but not with . . . them. They're so odd. Look at the pants on that woman! Can you imagine? And they sort of have the upper hand here. How good a deal can I really get?"

"I think they'll be fair in bargaining. More or less. Alisi and Hashon seem decent, but we *are* an inconvenience for them. That dinner didn't seem like much, but for fifty people? That's a lot of food they gave up, and we should pay for it. They're going to sell us some traveling clothes, so just see what you can do to get us out of here without giving away *all* of Jasper's stuff." I tried to recall anything about Balanquan and Osfridian trade. "Silk. Start with that—they don't make it here. But stay out of our personal things if you can. Jasper brought clothing specifically to sell. Use that."

Pamela pointed at the haphazard collection of boxes and crates. "How do we know what survived?"

"We don't." A few other sleepy girls emerged from the post, and I summoned them too. "You girls start sorting and organizing the cargo. Find our own belongings and Jasper's trade goods."

I set the makeshift committee to inventorying and was surprised they didn't question the order, just as they hadn't while making the beach fire. Everyone felt lost in this new situation, but as long as I kept sounding confident in my directions, they thought I knew what I was doing. It provided reassurance for them but little for me. I was as adrift here as I'd been on the damaged ship and hoped my decisions would deliver us to a safe haven.

By late morning, we had nearly everything in order. We'd decided which of our goods would stay behind and which would go with us to Grashond right away. The Balanquans had limited boats at the trading post, so a handful of sailors were remaining with the cargo that wouldn't fit. The rest of us, along with a dozen Balanquans and the Icori, would sail west on the Quistimac.

Pamela had bartered well but summoned me to endorse the final deal. "I know you said not to trade our own Glittering Court clothes, but the Balanquans saw them and are insisting on some."

I followed her to where Hashon stood near boxes and trunks. Several elaborate ball gowns were draped over a crate—including my favorite: an off-the-shoulder dress of deep-green silk, trimmed in silver beads. Jasper allowed us to keep one dress when we married, and this was the one I'd wanted. I sighed, running my chapped hands over the delicate, iridescent fabric.

Any argument I might make had already been attempted by Pamela. In fact, she'd already talked Hashon down quite a bit—but for these dresses, he remained obstinate. As I took stock of the other things the Balanquans wanted and what we were getting in exchange—transportation, food, and several cloaks of fur and thick wool—I knew it was a good deal in purely monetary terms. But the personal cost of that dress hurt.

"Go ahead," I said.

Although we'd all heard and agreed to the travel itinerary last night, the full reality of what it meant didn't hit us until we actually walked up to the Quistimac. All eight of the post's boats sat tied at the river's edge, already loaded with our supplies and even a few horses. The flat, rectangular barges had sides about three feet high. They looked sturdy and secure, but there was no denying the truth: We would have to sail again.

I saw several girls come to an abrupt halt when they realized it, and even my stomach lurched. The day had dawned clear and mild, and sunlight made the Quistimac glitter. Birds sang in the towering trees surrounding it, and a light breeze suggested the weather might even turn warmer. But the river was still a river, and this one, pretty or not, was wide and deep with a swiftly moving current that we'd have to fight against.

The Balanquans travel this river all the time, I told myself. *They trust those barges. And it's not like we're in the middle of the ocean with no land in sight. The banks are right there.*

I took a deep breath and continued forward. "Come on, girls. Let's be on our way."

My confidence wasn't quite as effective this time. A few of my companions stayed rooted and shook their heads, faces drawn. Even one of the merchants blanched. Conscious of the Balanquans' impatience, the braver girls and I fervently made pitches to our terrified friends. We reminded them how fast the trip would be, how close we were to normal Osfridian life again.

In the end, we had to forcibly drag only two, and even they stopped resisting once aboard. I clenched my teeth when the lines were loosed, and the rowers took us toward the river's center. The barges bobbed and wobbled, just like any water vessel, and I kept my eyes fixed on the bank. Close. It was close, hardly any distance at all. I was a decent swimmer and knew that Damaris, sitting beside me, was an exceptional one.

The rowers refused my offers of help, and we moved swiftly, despite the contrary current. I watched the beautiful, rugged terrain go by and wondered what it would be like for Merry to play in all that space, instead of in a cramped city. In the midst of all the uncertainty in my life right now, I'd had little chance to appreciate the wonder of Adoria. A new, wild, and unexplored world. Although, was it truly unexplored? To Osfridians, perhaps. Most of the land around the river looked untouched at first glance. But on our journey, we passed by another Balanquan trading post and then, later, a cluster of unusual buildings that I was told was a Balanquan town. On the other side of the river, smoke drifted up from farther inside the woods, and I heard someone speak about an Icori camp there.

Thinking of the Icori reminded me that Orla and her entourage had a spot in my barge. Unease over being on water again had kept me from talking to them or anyone else. Now, I studied them covertly, still finding it hard to believe they were Icori. They wore the same nondescript clothing from last night, the leather coats and pants that could have belonged to any rugged Osfridian explorer. They laughed and joked easily with both the Balanquans and *Gray Gull* sailors.

Orla noticed my scrutiny and flashed me a grin. Her face was cleaner than it was last night, but only a little. "Hello there, little leader. How'd you sleep?"

"Pretty well, actually. Considering what's happened this week, I think I could've slept anywhere."

"I hope you keep feeling that way, because it's just going to get colder as we move inland."

I squinted up at the sky, where a pale sun peeped out between layers of drifting white clouds. "Not so bad now."

"Sure, but we're still feeling the edge of the boiling current. Nothing like that ahead."

"'Boiling current'?"

Overhearing, a sailor sitting behind Orla explained, "It doesn't really boil. But it's not cold like the northerly. Comes from a different part of the ocean, brings warm water."

"And warm weather," concurred Orla. "Go farther north up the coast, and you'll think it's almost summer."

I had a hard time imagining that the weather could get warmer going north. "Have you been there?" I asked her.

"Often. I always try to schedule my trade trips there for this time of the year." Her smile turned wry. "But in Grashond—and where I live, farther west—there's no question winter's still got its hold."

I tried not to grimace. "That won't make traveling south easy."

The young sailor who'd commented before nodded. "The roads get rough, and Uros help you if there's a blizzard. Those things come out of nowhere. You won't be able to travel at all."

You won't be able to travel at all.

"I have to," I blurted out. "How long does it take to get to Cape Triumph if the roads do stay clear?"

Orla's eyebrows knit in thought, and she said something to the Icori beside her in their language. It struck me for the first time that Orla spoke Osfridian perfectly, no trace of an accent. A man answered her, and Orla translated, "For a group your size? Maybe six weeks."

"Six weeks," I repeated bleakly. A long time on the road. But not the longest time. Not an impossible time. I'd still have well over a month to secure a marriage before Merry arrived. That should be easy for someone with my exceptional qualifications. And even in the unlikely event I couldn't find a husband right away, I'd still at least be in the city to meet the ship. We'd figure out something.

Noting my reaction, Orla asked, "You're anxious to see your betrothed?"

"Don't have one yet."

"I thought you were all going to Cape Triumph to get married?"

"We are. But we've got to find husbands first. That's the reason we came over here—to meet and marry respectable men."

"Interesting." Orla had another murmured conversation with her seatmates. Seeing my puzzled look, she explained, "I'm trying to decide if I like your situation better than mine. I already have a 'respectable' husband lined up, but I didn't have much say in the choosing. I'm going to meet him in a few weeks."

"Congratulations."

She shrugged. "We'll see. If I don't like him, I don't have to be around him that much. He's in Kershid—that's across Denham's west border. Once we're married, I can just visit him now and then. There are plenty of reasons my people would need me to stay up here—and I can make up more."

"That's a lot of travel for 'now and then.' Seems like you'd spend half your life on the road."

Orla appeared momentarily confused and then laughed in understanding. "Oh, you're thinking of what I told you. About six weeks on the road."

Now I was lost. "What else would I think?"

"Sorry, I'm forgetting you haven't been here very long. We rarely travel overland to go south. There's a river—the East Sister—that runs through our eastern territories. It angles down close to Denham's border. It's fast—not as smooth as this. But you can be on the west side of Denham in, oh, a week and a half."

"A week and a half?" I tried to picture Denham's width on a map. "How long to Cape Triumph? Is there another river?"

"No, no. Well, there's the bay—sort of. But most travel through there is by land, and I think that takes a week. Maybe a little more."

"But . . . but . . ." How could no one else see what I could? "That's three weeks, not six! We should just go that way to Cape Triumph."

Orla's upbeat expression abruptly darkened. "Ah, well. There are a few problems with that—the main one being that that part of the East Sister is almost entirely in Icori territory. Your people can't travel on it."

"Why not?"

One of her companions must have known Osfridian, because he interjected something just then that sparked an Icori conversation between all of them. Orla nodded at its conclusion and turned her attention back to me. "We've never allowed Osfridians unrestricted access to the East Sister, and because of their recent aggression, we've cut them off from it entirely."

Her words came out almost as a growl, and I glanced questioningly at Damaris, who'd been listening quietly. She shook her head, as confused as me. "What aggression?" I asked Orla. "If you don't mind me asking? I'm sorry for my ignorance. I just don't know what's going on."

"There's no way you could." Orla stared off across the river, her eyes brilliantly blue in this light. "Over the winter, your people—that is, other Osfridian colonists—have attacked a few of our settlements."

"Why?"

"No provocation. We attempted a talk once. They denied the attacks and claim *we* raided some of their land."

"'Claim'?" I asked, noting the word choice.

"We haven't." She threw up her hands in disgust. "We have no reason to. We've upheld the treaties."

I knew the accusatory tone in her voice wasn't directed specifically at me, but I felt it nonetheless. "I'm sorry. But now I understand why you wouldn't be so open to outsiders on your river. I hope things are sorted out soon."

"Not soon enough for your trip, I'm afraid."

"Oh, yes, I meant . . . I hope they're sorted out in general, not just for me. For everyone—your people, my people." I studied the vast shore, noting how the pines this far upriver were weighted with snow, whereas the ones at the coast had only been dusted. The air, though cold, felt pure and refreshing. Even with the oars and light conversation, everything seemed so quiet compared to Osfro. So still and calm. "There's been too much strife. Everyone came to this land for something better. It seems like we're all a lot more likely to get what we want if we work together."

Orla's crooked smile was back. "Lovely words, little leader. But not so easy to make happen."

"I know." I gazed back at the river, aching with memory. "Anger and pride are hard to give up."

"Something tells me you weren't thinking of Adoria when you said that."

Now I smiled, but I felt no joy. "You're right. I was thinking of a friend. We had a huge fight before I sailed here, and now I don't know when or if I'll see her again."

"Who was in the wrong?"

"Both of us."

"Would she say that?"

I thought for a moment. "I think so. Even if she didn't, I'd still apologize. My conscience isn't contingent on someone else's."

"I see" was all Orla said, and she spoke little for the rest of the day. But I could feel her eyes on me often, and whenever I looked at her, she appeared to be struggling with some great problem.

The journey to Grashond took three days but felt like three weeks. After the monotony of the river, we traveled cross-country and at first seemed to be wandering in the wilderness. The Balanquans and Icori moved with surety, pleased that the clear weather held. My Glittering Court companions displayed mixed reactions. Some pushed steadfastly forward, accepting this challenge as an inevitable part of their journey to marriage. Others were less positive.

"Ugh, this ratty old thing smells like woodsmoke," I overheard Maria say to Joan one day. "I can't believe Tamsin just handed over my best velvet dress for it. Is she trying to sabotage me? I knew she was ruthless, but I never saw this coming."

I gritted my teeth. The "ratty old thing" Maria referred to was a heavy fur cloak we'd bought in the negotiations. I couldn't say if it really did smell like woodsmoke, but I would've taken it in an instant, especially when we set out in the chilly early mornings. I still wore the same cloak I'd had on the ship. We'd acquired maybe a dozen pieces of heavy outerwear from the Balanquans, and I'd tried to distribute them thoughtfully.

Orla, walking nearby, overheard too and gave me a look that seemed to repeat her earlier words: *Oh, they'll always find a way to complain. That's the downside of being a leader.*

Around midafternoon, one of the Balanquans announced that we'd crossed the border into Grashond. I glanced around but found no marker, manmade or natural, that revealed how she'd known. Grashond was a young colony and largely undeveloped. Whereas some places, like Denham Colony, had been started specifically with commerce in mind, Grashond's founders had come here so that they could have a safe place to practice their religion. They called themselves the Heirs of Uros, and though they weren't officially heretics, they also weren't on great terms with the orthodox church that formed the cornerstone of Osfridian faith.

Eventually, our party reached a packed dirt road that grew wider and showed signs of frequent travel. We began to cover ground more quickly and could see farms—Osfridian-style farms—off in the distance, sending a new energy surging through us all. Some of the girls had been flagging up until that point, needing constant coaxing to keep moving.

But the sight of familiar buildings and ways of life changed our outlook. It was a comfort after the upended world we'd lived in for the past week. Our steps quickened, and finally, near evening of the third day, the outskirts of a bona fide village came into view down the road.

Pamela and Vanessa hugged each other. "We're almost there!" Pamela exclaimed. "We'll finally be with our own people! They'll keep us safe and . . ."

Her words trailed off as a gunshot rang through the air, echoing among the trees and sending birds flying. Our party stumbled to a halt, and the Balanquans rapidly drew their weapons. I was near the back of the group and shouldered my way forward to see what had happened.

Out of seemingly nowhere, the road ahead had become blocked by a group of men in dark-colored clothing—all in shades of gray, brown, or blue. Most wore wide-brimmed hats or caps of knitted wool. *All* of them wielded guns, every single one of which was pointed straight ahead at us, save one. That gun was aimed in the air, held by the man who'd fired it to gain our attention.

"Get out of here," he ordered. "Get out of here before we blast you to the oblivion of Ozhiel's hell." Those flanking him nodded and muttered similar sentiments.

Orla leaned toward me and murmured, "It looks like we've found your people."

CHAPTER 7

"Do you understand us?" one of the other men blocking the road demanded. He swiveled around, seeming unsure where to point his gun among so many targets. He finally settled on Alisi. "You aren't just in Osfridian territory. You're in Grashond—a land sanctified by the Heirs of Uros. We want no part of your unholy ways, so you infidels can go back to wherever you came from."

"Gladly," she replied. She looked almost regal this morning, with her hair pulled up in a cluster of intricate braids and shoulder-length earrings made of some purple jewel that glittered brightly against her coppery skin. I marveled at her composure, but then, she had the backing of her heavily armed people. They looked to be an even match for the men blocking the road. I didn't know which side would win if it came to a fight, but I was pretty sure my cohort would lose either way. "But first, we need to return something to you."

Alisi glanced over her shoulder, and the ship's captain lumbered forward, several sailors at his side. He made a half bow to the man who'd spoken. "Captain Jonas Milford at your service. Our ship took damage in a storm, and we've come to ask your help."

The gray-clad man regarded the captain with only slightly less disdain than he'd given the Balanquans. "Ship? Are you from Osfrid? We're a long ways from the coast."

"Not so long on the Quistimac," said Alisi. "We took them in, and now they're yours."

Some of the Grashond men had lowered their guns, but none

looked ready to welcome us with open arms. I dashed to the captain's side and faced the Heirs. "Please, sirs," I said, using my prettiest Glittering Court manners. "We'd be ever so grateful if you could let us stay with you while we regroup. We won't trouble you for long. We're going to Cape Triumph and will be on our way in no time."

Another of their number stepped forward, stern-faced. Actually, they all had stern faces. Between those and their drab clothes, they kind of blurred together. "You're just a girl. Why are you traveling alone with these men?"

"I'm traveling with a group of refined young ladies." I stood on my tiptoes and beckoned the rest of the Glittering Court to me. "We're on our way to be married."

The man who'd fired the first shot scanned my friends, then the sailors. He shook his head and scowled. "How can we bring in so many people?"

He and his somber companions huddled together, their conversation hushed but still audible. "We can't abandon those girls out here," one noted. "Their delicate natures wouldn't survive against this wilderness—or other threats."

He eyed the sailors and Balanquans askance as he spoke. I found "delicate" a little ludicrous after surviving a shipwreck and the hurried journey to get here, but I held my tongue. They could think whatever they wanted if it would get us to Cape Triumph.

"We can't abandon any of them out here," one finally declared, his voice grave. "Even the sailors. Uros commands us to show compassion to those who need it."

His companions considered this, and at last, they came to a reluctant consensus. The one advocating compassion faced Alisi gravely. "Very well. We'll take them all back. No doubt it will require much reflection and prayer, but to do less would show ingratitude to the angels who grant us mercy every day."

Alisi, restless and maybe bored, picked up her horse's reins. "You can do whatever you want, but we're leaving. Captain, I'll send some of our traders to escort the rest of your men and cargo in a few days. Farewell."

Even I was surprised with the alacrity in which she directed her party to unload our goods and leave them in the road. In Osfrid, I'd been taught that we were superior to everyone else in Adoria, but the Balanquans seemed to regard us as little more than children badly in need of a babysitter. The Icori, on foot, followed the Balanquans, but Orla stopped beside me and rested her hand on my shoulder.

"Good luck, Tamsin. I think your friends will be all right with you as their leader."

I studied the Heirs of Uros, with their guns and suspicion-filled faces. "I feel like we've gone from one storm to another, but thank you. Your regard means a lot."

Orla didn't move. After a few moments, she said in a low voice, "When I told you we'd barred your people from the East Sister, I left out some details. Officially, yes, it is off-limits so long as this conflict remains unresolved. But there are a few Osfridians we've had longtime relations with who have no part in policy. They've been our trusted partners and even friends since long before these recent attacks."

"Hey," shouted one of the Heirs, noticing Orla. "We told you to get out of here, Icori."

She ignored him and remained fixed on me. "The party I'm going south with soon is a large one—lots of barges and boats. It's not just about meeting my betrothed. It's the first real trade expedition of the season, and that has value for a lot of people doing business in Adoria. We've agreed to let some outsiders accompany us—for a price, of course. Most are Balanquan, but a handful of those rare Osfridian friends have also bought passage. One of them is in Constancy—his name is Jago Robinson. He's purchased a large number of spots on the barges. Enough for your group. If you can find him and convince him to give those up, I'll see to it he's refunded and you're allowed to purchase them instead. The rest of the space is spoken for, and there's no guarantee of a future trip you'd be allowed on."

"Icori! I'm talking to you!"

Rattled by the colonist's shouting and her startling offer, I stammered out, "Orla . . . I . . . I don't know what to say . . ."

Though her overall expression stayed earnest, a smile lit her eyes. "You don't have to say anything. Except that you'll remember the name: Jago Robinson."

"Jago Robinson," I repeated, a bit floored. "Thank you. Thank you so much."

She shrugged. "Well. Don't get too excited. He hasn't agreed yet."

Before leaving me, she paused to give the man who'd yelled at her a long, icy look. He opened his mouth to speak again and then reconsidered, contenting himself with repositioning his gun. Satisfied, Orla bid me farewell and then jogged off to join the Balanquans, leaving the rest of us alone with our ominous new hosts.

They directed us and the rest of the *Gray Gull* refugees to follow them back to town. The Heirs spoke in urgent, hushed tones as we walked. When we reached the heart of Constancy, my tension eased slightly. Although small, it was a real town, a town that evoked comfort and familiarity, despite its plainness. The streets had no cobblestone, and the buildings that lined the square had little embellishment or even distinction from one another. A few had shutters and glass windows, and those that had been painted were white. Signs marked ordinary businesses: a blacksmith, a tailor, a cooper. The town's residents stared at us from doorways and windows. They wore dark colors and drab fabrics like the men on the road had, but at least it was clothing of a familiar style: wool cloaks and dresses, cotton shirts and trousers.

The Heirs split us apart, taking the sailors one way, the merchants another, and then directing my party into the square's largest building: a church. "You may rest in here while the council convenes and decides what to do with you," one of the men said.

"Thank you," I said. "And I'm happy to talk to this council and answer any questions that might help."

"You'll provide the most help by praying," came the curt reply.

As soon as he and his companions left, I slumped against the wall. "Looks like it's time for our next strange adventure."

"Well, we're safe now. That's all that matters," Pamela said. When I didn't answer, she tilted her head to better meet my eyes. "We *are* safe now, aren't we?"

"Yes, of course," I said, wondering if I lied. The Balanquans and Icori had given us a better welcome in some ways, at least keeping us informed of their plans for us. But Constancy hadn't turned us away, and despite their unusual religious practices, the Heirs were still technically our own countrymen.

Restless, I paced the building, which resembled no church I'd ever been in. I'd heard the Heirs maintained a strict and simple lifestyle but hadn't expected this. Even our humble district church back in Osfro—which had always seemed so dull compared to the city's grander cathedrals—had more adornment. Here, the pine-planked walls wore only varnish and contained no art of any kind. The small, high windows that lined the room's sides contained clear glass, not stained, and were solely utilitarian. There was no altar, no incense, no gold or even brass candleholders. A simple wooden podium appeared to be where the priest would stand, and the congregation sat on narrow wooden benches that lacked even the threadbare pads of our pews back home.

An alcove in the back, far behind the benches, contained several shelves filled with books, papers, and other scholarly materials. I knelt on the hard floor to read the books' spines, all religious in nature. Most were copies of the usual holy texts. A few looked to be specific to the Heirs' faith.

Winnifred joined me. "Kind of a gloomy place to glorify Uros and the angels."

"I guess that's their way, though." I thought back to some of our history lessons. "They left Osfro because they were always getting into disputes with the priests over excess."

"Left? Or were they kicked out?" she asked pointedly.

"I suppose it depends on who you ask. I remember Master Bricker saying the king authorized this colony more to get them out of his hair than to approve of their beliefs."

"Listen to us," she said with a laugh. "Me from the bridge district, you from the market: talking politics and history like fine folks. But then, I suppose this is what it's all been for."

Not quite, I thought. We were supposed to have improved upon our education in order to rise from our backgrounds and find better lives. Analyzing the practices of a group that barely escaped being called heretics—one we now depended on for survival—had never come up.

After about an hour, three women entered with large bundles in their arms. *Finally.* We gathered around the newcomers, eager for an update. These women of Constancy were clad in simple, high-necked cotton dresses in shades of navy or gray, with heavy woolen cloaks. The oldest of them wore a bonnet, while the others, a little older than me, wore kerchiefs.

"You will change out of your clothes and put these on," the older woman informed us. "We are glad to care for you—it's our duty by Uros—but you'll have to abide by our customs while you're here."

"Yes, of course," I said. "And we're ever so grateful. We're happy to do whatever it takes to make this easier for you so we can be on our way."

The woman didn't return my smile and simply began handing out the garments, which were the same type as theirs. They had a wide range of sizes, and it took some doing to sort out what would fit whom the best. The dress I ended up with was navy blue and seemed to be exactly my size, which was a stroke of luck. Some of the other girls' were baggy or too long.

"It'll have to be let down," one of the younger Grashond women told me, kneeling to examine my hem. "Luckily, there's about an inch there."

The length looked perfect to me, but it didn't graze the tops of my shoes the way hers did. "Certainly, if you say so . . . but if you'll help me understand . . . is this length . . . er, indecent?"

"No," she said, with a small chuckle. "But it shows too much of the shoe and stocking. Someone poor may have worn-out shoes. Or perhaps they can't afford stockings at all. Long skirts and pants make it less obvious. Then those people needn't feel insecure or jealous of others. And those who have more can't easily lord it over the less fortunate."

"Ah. I see. Well, if you can lend me a needle and thread, I'll take care of it."

"Can you?" She looked pleasantly surprised. "You all look like ladies who are used to being waited on."

I took in my party's bedraggled state as I tied a kerchief over my hair. "Well, thank you, I think. But believe me, we've done plenty of waiting on others in our time."

I fastened the gray cloak she gave me with a plain pin. The wool was coarse and lacked the embroidery of my previous cloak, but it was so much warmer that I made the exchange without hesitation. Inner pockets held matching mittens. The young woman shook out my old overdress before folding it and exclaimed in delight, "Oh, look at that." She ran her fingers over the fabric, a pale green cotton scattered with white lilies. Mud from our overland trek had stained the hem, and seawater had splattered parts of the skirt white with salt. "What a shame it's ruined."

"There's a trick I know that'll get that mud out," I said. "Takes some soaking and a bit of time, but I can do it. If you could get me lye and—"

"You have much bigger things to worry about than a gaudy garment." The older woman stomped up and snatched the dress away, adding it to a pile in her arms. "Uros has spared your lives. The sacrifice of this frivolity doesn't even begin to repay that debt. You should be on your knees in gratitude. If you'd arrived earlier, you'd have been in time for our holy day services."

"Ah, how unfortunate. But I'll, uh, be sure and get to that kneeling soon. First, I was wondering if you could tell me what's going to happen to us? You see, we're very anxious to get to Cape Triumph, and—"

"The council will decide what's to be done with you, and that decision will come when it comes. If you have trouble accepting that, I'd advise adding a plea for patience to your prayer list."

She swept away, and the woman who'd helped me scurried after her. They made their way to the third woman, who was kneeling by Polly's ankle and wrapping it. Polly had tripped over a branch earlier that day and been in some pain. As I watched, Vanessa leaned toward me.

"Did you know? She's a doctor, that woman. A real, honest-to-goodness doctor."

"What? Are you sure?" Female doctors were unheard of in Osfrid. I found it hard to believe there'd be one here, when the Heirs were rumored to treat women very strictly.

"That's what she told me when I was over there," said Vanessa. "She said all the doctors here are women! Something about healing being a woman's domain."

Desperately curious, I headed toward the doctor, but she finished her work just then and departed with her two companions. That left us alone once more, and another hour passed before a middle-aged man with hair cut bluntly to his chin entered wordlessly and set down a basket of rye bread. He returned again briefly to deliver a barrel of water and a dipper. Our attempts to question him were ignored.

The sky had darkened to deep purple when another man entered. He paused to stomp snow from his boots and then took off a wide-brimmed black hat as he surveyed us. Vanessa, still near me, straightened up and murmured, "My goodness. Maybe there's hope for this place after all. Wish I wasn't wearing this frumpy old rag."

Compared to the other townsfolks' grim air, this young man was like the sun bursting into our room. Dark-gold hair framed a clean-cut face that had wide-set bluish gray eyes and the warmest, most sincere smile I'd seen since entering Constancy. That smile looked almost surreal after all the scowls we'd received so far. He wasn't much older than us either and took a minute to study each face with genuine concern. We studied him too, some more blatantly than others.

He seemed a little self-conscious at our attention, and Vanessa whispered to me: "Is he blushing? He *is*. Six, it's adorable." I would've elbowed her, except she was right.

Clasping his hands in front of him, he cleared his throat and, despite being flustered, spoke with the clear, loud voice of someone used to addressing large crowds. "Hello. And welcome. I'm so glad you're here. In Constancy, that is. Not just the church. But I'm glad you're here too. I'm Gideon Stewart, one of the junior ministers. From what I've heard about the dangers you've faced, the Six must love you—to save you from those dangers, I mean. Not put you through them. Anyway, I know you must all be tired and worried, but please be patient with us just a little bit longer. We're going to do our very best to take care of you."

He spoke those last words with such heartfelt feeling that it was impossible not to believe them. Smiles bloomed throughout the church. Maybe things really were going to be okay.

"Could I speak to whoever's in charge of you?" he asked. "Your chaperone?"

We all turned to Miss Quincy, who returned our gazes indifferently. When she shook her head and maintained her customary silence, I stepped forward. "I'll be happy to help you, Father."

He turned that smile on me full force, and its radiance nearly knocked me over. "Oh, no. Not 'Father.' Only Uros deserves that title. You can call me Mister Stewart when we're formal, Gideon when we're not."

He led me to the alcove in the back of the church, and a few of the other girls looked as though they now wished they'd volunteered to be the unofficial leader. Maybe there was an upside to this role after all. I'd have to tell Orla, if I ever saw her again. He dragged two benches over and beckoned me to one while he took the other.

"Now then," he said, resting paper and a small lap desk on his knees. "I was hoping to get the names of everyone in your party—their ages, families, that sort of thing. Can you do it?"

"Certainly." I could tell him that, along with probably a dozen or so of each girl's little idiosyncrasies.

"I suppose I should know your name first."

"Tamsin Wright, Mist— Er, begging your pardon. Is this formal or not?"

"Let's say not. Gideon is fine. How old are you, Miss Wright? Er, Tamsin?"

"Twenty."

"From?"

"Osfro. Market district."

Gideon's pen paused as he looked up. "The market district?"

"Yes. Is there a problem?"

"No, of course not." He copied down the information, his writing neat and precise. "And what's your family's occupation?"

"My father's a day laborer, and my mother's a laundress. I work—worked—for her."

He stopped again.

"Is there a problem *now*?" I asked.

"No, no. Go on, please."

"Let's see. There's Winnifred Cray. Eighteen. Also from Osfro, bridge district. Her father's a blacksmith."

He hesitated a moment and then created a new entry underneath mine. But he wore a frown as he did, and I was growing increasingly perplexed. Was he judging us and our backgrounds? Even without our Glittering Court glamour, I'd expected the New World to be more welcoming of varied origins. That was this land's great promise.

When I saw his reaction to Damaris's fishing family, I couldn't hold back. "Mist— Gideon, I really think there's a problem."

He leaned back, a chagrined look in his eyes. "Forgive me . . . I'm just confused."

"You and me both."

"It's just . . ." Gideon tapped his pen against the desk as he groped for an explanation. "You speak so eloquently. I saw the clothes that were carried away, and I heard you were all on your way to be married. So, my understanding was that you were, at the very least, upper-class gentlemen's daughters, if not minor nobility."

I laughed so loudly that others in the church turned and stared. "Minor nobility! Jasper and our teachers will be thrilled to hear that! It's quite a compliment you've just given us."

His complete bewilderment restored his appeal. "So . . . you *aren't* upper class? Or is it that . . . some of you are, and some of you work for them?"

Still delighted, I shook my head. "We've all come from humble places. The Glittering Court just polished us up so that we'll be more attractive to suitors in Cape Triumph."

"You don't have arranged marriages you're going off to? No betrothed? And what's the Glittering Court?"

I provided a brief summary of Jasper's operation and watched as all sorts of emotions played over Gideon's fine features. Astonishment, puzzlement, intrigue. Then, unexpectedly, concern.

"Ah, okay. We'll have to make it clear to the council that your organization is very structured and supervised, that marriages are certain. The idea of young and unattached women on their own . . . whose purpose is to attract men . . . it could be misunderstood by some . . ."

He blushed again, and that made me blush, realizing what he was getting at. "Oh! It's . . . no. It's not that."

"Of course it's not," he said quickly. "I can tell just by talking to you that you're obviously a principled woman. A woman of good character. And that's important to us. Which is why I'll make sure the others understand that you and your friends aren't . . . uh, of bad character."

"Thank you. Your help means a lot." I averted my eyes, still a little embarrassed at the potential conclusion. Taking in the strange and austere church, I couldn't help but add, "The whole town's help does.

But I feel so ignorant about your customs. I know we're only here for a short time, but I hope we're not making constant missteps."

This drew a new frown. "How long do you think you're staying?"

"Oh . . . well, I can't give you an exact number of days. We just need enough time to collect ourselves, make the arrangements, and be on our way." When he didn't comment, I asked, "We . . . we can leave, can't we?"

"Oh! Yes, of course. No one wants to hold you against your will, and I know the council's already decided it'll help get you to Cape Triumph. But . . . you know we're talking weeks, don't you?"

"I know. It takes six weeks to get to Denham." The pitying look on his face raised my alarms. "What? Isn't that right?"

"It is, except . . . well, Tamsin, you need to know: It's going to be six weeks before you can even *leave* Constancy."

CHAPTER 8

"MAYBE FOUR WEEKS," GIDEON AMENDED. "IF CONDITIONS look promising, but that can be dangerous."

I went very still. "I don't understand."

"You can't go until the worst of winter has passed. Blizzards stir up with no warning—even into early spring. You don't want a group your size caught in that."

I took a deep breath. "Okay. Six weeks of waiting. And another six to get there. So nearly three months until we get to Cape Triumph."

My heart sank. That sailor on the barge had mentioned the sudden snowstorms, but it had never occurred to me that those might delay when we could even *leave* for the south. I'd be cutting it so close to Merry's arrival. I wouldn't have a husband yet, but at least I'd be there to greet her and the Wilsons. Barely.

Then Gideon added: "Hopefully there'll be no delay in organizing the traveling party that'll go with you. We don't want you alone with those sailors, and I'm sure a number of traders here would benefit from the trip. So, there's a chance another week or two might get added on, depending on the planning."

More than three months. I had no words.

"Oh, Tamsin, don't look that way." Gideon took hold of my hand and gave it a small pat. "I know it's daunting to think of waiting that long. I know it's daunting to even be here at all! But look what you've survived. The angels brought you here safely—and maybe, just maybe, you're here for a reason. I promise to help you however I can. Now. Shall we work on the list?"

We went over the whole group, and he filled the sheet with neat lines and columns. We had just finished when the church door opened, and one of the men who'd met us on the road entered. "Do you have the information?" he asked Gideon. "The council's about to convene."

Gideon jumped up. "Apologies, Cyril. I'll be right there."

"Wait," I said. "Before you go—what is the council? Do they govern here?"

"Yes. It's made up of the town's ministers and a set of elected laymen. We can govern with both divine and human guidance."

"And you—they—are deciding what happens to us until we leave?"

"Yes." Gideon held up the list. "That's why this is so useful. Some—still believing you were ladies of pampered backgrounds—worried you'd have a hard time adjusting to our simple lifestyle in the coming weeks."

There was that awful word again. *Weeks.* A crazy notion of running away and heading south alone popped into my head, but what in the world was I going to do if I was stuck on the road during a blizzard?

On the road . . .

"Gideon—I'm sorry to hold you up, but I have just one more question. Do you know a man named Jago Robinson?"

Gideon placed the hat back on his head. "Jago? Do you mean Jacob Robinson?"

"Maybe. He's a merchant of some sort?"

A rueful smile played at Gideon's lips. "Well, I suppose some might think of him that way. Why do you ask?"

"I heard he might be able to get us to Cape Triumph faster."

"How?" His face turned inquisitive. "I hope no one's been telling you he's got some potion to control the weather."

"Control the . . . what? No, of course not. I just heard he could help."

"I wouldn't count on it, if I were you." Gideon's tone became carefully diplomatic. "He's not from here—just staying for the winter. We respect him as one of Uros's children, of course, but his ways are . . . well, let's just say, he's not so concerned about missteps as you are. Trust me, Jacob Robinson isn't going to get you to Cape Triumph. We will. Have faith."

Gideon told me we'd talk more later, once our arrangements were settled. When he reached the church door, he gave a polite wave of farewell to the others that was met very enthusiastically.

"Goodbye, Mister Stewart!"

"It was so lovely to meet you!"

"Do you do one-on-one prayer sessions?"

"If you need help with anything else, let me know!"

"No, let *me* know!"

As soon as he shut the door, Polly rushed to my side, the others right behind her. "Did I see him squeeze your hand?"

"He *patted* it," I said. "He was comforting me."

"I wouldn't mind if he comforted me," said Vanessa wistfully.

Damaris regarded me with awe. "Less than an hour, and you've already snagged the best-looking man in town. You really do get things done."

"That wasn't snagging," I protested, trying not to roll my eyes. "And you haven't seen any of the other men in town. Maybe some are even better looking."

Winnifred crossed her arms. "Doesn't matter how good-looking any of them are if they don't have enough gold."

"I don't even think it'd matter if any of them had the gold. What would they use it for?" Maria pointed at her gray dress. "To buy more of these atrocities?"

"That's unfair," said Joan. Most everyone had drifted over now. "For one thing, it's two sizes too big for you. And plain or not, the quality's good. It's nicer than what I used to have back home."

"When you were an innkeeper's daughter! Did you come all this way to sweep floors again? Because I didn't come all this way to peel potatoes, and I know Tamsin didn't come to wash clothes." Maria turned to me. "What did he say? Are they going to help us get to Cape Triumph?"

"Yes." I tried to smile under the weight of those expectant gazes. "They'll take us. But we'll have to stay here while they ready everything, so get used to that dress."

Faces lit up, and I had to walk away, lest someone ask for details on the timing. I couldn't dash that optimism . . . yet. Because even though none of them had to rendezvous with a child, a three-month wait wasn't going to go over well, and I had a feeling they'd look to me to fix things. That, or they'd blame me for them. The problem was that I was stuck right now. We all were. And I could hardly figure out a solution for our situation when I didn't even know what that situation was.

Trust me, Jacob Robinson isn't going to get you to Cape Triumph. We will. Have faith.

It was well into evening when our answers finally came. Five men of varying ages filed into the church, a few I recognized from earlier. Gideon came too, entering last. Even though he wore gray, it didn't seem to cast the same pall about him as it did the others. Maybe it was just the power of his good looks. Or maybe it was that cloud of optimism he seemed to walk in.

The oldest of the men, perhaps in his fifties, stepped to the forefront. He had iron-colored muttonchops and a heavy brow. "My name is Samuel Cole, one of the senior ministers here. We stand committed to do our duty under Uros to shelter you from both the elements and the uncouth sailors who traveled with you. We're offering them aid too, though they'll be living in a camp on the outside of town and assisting us with some of our harder building projects in exchange for their keep. And of course, they will have to obey our laws. As will you. Because of your age and gender, you will become dependents in our households and be expected to keep all customs and rules there too."

Damaris caught my eye at that, expressing a wariness I shared.

I gave a small shrug, uncertain of just what those ambiguous words might truly mean. By colonial law, they couldn't require us to convert to their beliefs, as we were all members—some more in name than practice—of the orthodox faith. So what else did "customs" entail? Just the wardrobe change?

"I'm eighteen," interjected Maria. "I don't need a guardian."

"In Grashond, unmarried women don't reach independence until twenty-one. That's in our charter and is nonnegotiable." Samuel scanned the room, searching for objection. None came. "Several of our households have generously agreed to take you in, and many more than that have donated your modest attire. You came here under the shadow of pride and ostentation, and that will not be indulged during your stay."

"Sir, if I may, what happened to the clothing you took?" asked Winnifred.

"It and the rest of your cargo have been secured for the time being," another man answered. "You'll have no need of it while you're here. Most will be returned when you depart, though some will remain behind as a donation to pay us back for our help."

"Donation indeed," muttered Damaris under her breath.

It would be a wonder if Jasper had anything left by the time we reached him. I stepped forward. "Not all of our possessions are, ah, ostentatious, sir. I have paper in my trunk I'd like to get, so that I can write letters home."

Samuel frowned. "It's best if you stay away from all of that entirely. You will have plenty of other tasks to occupy your time." He nodded to a wiry man in glasses. "Naturally, you'll assist your hosting family with chores, but you'll also have additional community tasks. Roger Sackett, one of our magistrates, has your assignments."

Roger unrolled a piece of paper, and for one surreal moment, I had a flashback to Mistress Masterson revealing the exam results. Girls gathered in anticipation, waiting to hear their fates. But, oh, what different fates these were.

"Polly Abernathy. You will board with Davis Lee's family. During the day, you will help to maintain his general store's cleanliness and keep accurate records."

"That's lucky," Vanessa murmured.

Polly's father had been a minor wool merchant, and she'd done much of his accounting. I'd heard that she'd scored perfectly on her arithmetic exams, and from her relieved look, she had no problem revisiting her old life.

"Winnifred Cray. You will board with Samuel Cole and help our blacksmith, Edward Fast, with tasks in his shop: cleaning the forges, bringing in fuel, and those sorts of things."

Winnifred appeared just as surprised as Polly—though not quite as pleasantly. She and her siblings had performed that type of labor for their father, and she'd complained about it a number of times on the voyage. It was hard, dirty work.

But as Roger went on, I realized with a growing horror that it was no coincidence that girls were getting work assignments matching their backgrounds. The council had divvied us up based on the list I'd given to Gideon.

"Maria Thompson. You'll board with my family and assist in food preparation for those households that have a particularly heavy burden when it comes to cooking—widowers, those with large numbers of children, the ill."

I started to feel queasy again, and Maria's earlier words rang in my head: *Did you come all this way to sweep floors again? Because I didn't come all this way to peel potatoes, and I know Tamsin didn't come to wash clothes.*

Just before he read my name, I stared down at my hands. Though they showed wear from the last week's strenuous conditions, they'd still held up and maintained my moisturizing efforts from Blue Spring.

"Tamsin Wright. You'll board with Samuel Cole and provide laundry assistance to those similarly strained households."

Ma had almost wept when she saw the change in my hands, and

now I nearly wept at what was to come for them. I was going to be spending the next six weeks working as a laundress once again.

Bleach and lye are nothing, I told myself. *Not after everything else that's happened. Moving on to Cape Triumph and Merry is what matters.*

I accepted my assignment with faux cheerfulness, and when the list was finished, we were divided up to go to our new hosts' homes. Considering all I'd had to do to keep everyone moving during this past week, it was more than a little unsettling to send them off to unknown places. But the Heirs assured us we'd all see each other around town, as well as at social gatherings.

Samuel Cole didn't impress me as a particularly warm or open man, but he had offered to take in four of us—more than any other household. During the carriage ride back to his home, which was about a mile from Constancy's heart, I learned that he had five daughters. All but one had married and moved out, and that one—Dinah—took care of the house for him. He had room to spare—so much so that they already had a boarder: Gideon.

"Well, that'll make this a little more bearable," Damaris remarked when we were preparing for bed later. She unbraided her wavy black hair and shook it out. "I won't mind seeing his face around."

She, Vanessa, and Winnifred were staying at Samuel's with me. We'd been given a large attic with two beds and a lot of drafts, but it beat sleeping outside.

"I don't think he'll be around very much," I told her. "I heard someone say he's studying with the other ministers in town. And it's not like you'll be hanging around here very much either."

She scowled. "True. I'll be too busy cooking with Maria."

"At least you'll have company." Winnifred held up the rough woolen nightgown we'd been given and winced. "You know, I'm really trying not to complain, but it's hard when I remember how we used to sleep in linen and silk at the manor."

I shared her wistfulness. My nightgown itched so much that I was tempted to just sleep in the navy dress I'd received at the church. The only reason I didn't was for fear of wearing it out. I had no idea if I'd get any others. Just before we came up here for the night, Samuel's daughter Dinah gave us a curt lecture on how appreciative we should be of our new clothes and to treat them with respect.

I tugged the nightgown on. "I wonder why Dinah's not married yet. She's what, mid-twenties? From what I gathered, they marry young around here."

"It is odd." Vanessa's words were smothered in a yawn. "She's not bad looking. Her face is a bit pinched, but the blue of her eyes is lovely. Maybe she didn't want to leave Samuel alone."

When Dinah woke us for breakfast the next morning, she informed us we had five minutes to be downstairs. It was a shock to get ready so quickly after the elaborate prep we'd had to do at Blue Spring. Here, I simply changed clothes, splashed water on my face, and tied the kerchief over my unbrushed hair. It was pretty much what I used to do before a day of working for Ma, which was fitting.

"Tamsin, why is your dress so short?" demanded Dinah.

I stopped in the kitchen doorway and looked down. Recalling my conversation in the church, I said, "Oh. I forgot to let it down last night. I'll do it when I'm back this evening."

"You'll do no such thing." Dinah placed a platter on the table and looked me up and down, her forehead creased with disapproval. "What would the town think of us if we let you out like this? Go upstairs now, and take care of it."

"But . . ." I stared wistfully at the table, set with bacon and steaming corn bread. A bounty after what I'd been subsisting on in my travels.

"You can eat when your work is done."

"What work is that?" asked Samuel, emerging from an adjacent hall. Gideon followed, wishing us good morning. We all responded loudly and cheerily.

Dinah gave him an unexpectedly warm greeting too, her hard expression softening briefly before turning back to her father. "Tamsin has some mending to do. It should've been done before—negligence on her part."

"Ah. Well, she can sit and say grace with us first."

"Of course, Father. And after the day's labors, I'll have her read a passage about the consequences of negligence. Gideon, could you help me select one?"

"I'd be happy to," said Gideon, who actually didn't look so happy at the prospect. "But we should keep in mind they haven't even been here a day. The angels counsel patience and mercy, and there's a lot our visitors don't know yet."

"Well, she knew last night she was supposed to do it. And I hope it really was just negligence and not a vain attempt to show off those shoes of hers."

"It wasn't!" I exclaimed. My shoes had been one of the few things I'd been allowed to keep. They were simple but refined, made of fawn-colored leather and lacing to my ankle. They'd been chosen as a sturdy, practical choice for the voyage, but they were showy by Grashond standards.

I sank into my chair, getting a quick smile of sympathy from Damaris beside me when I whispered, "Still hard to believe she's not married, huh?"

Sitting briefly for grace was worse than going straight to my room, because then I got an even closer look at the food I couldn't have. I grew heady on the aroma as Samuel prayed and offered thanks. When he finished, the others began filling their plates, and I slinked back to the attic. I took petty comfort in hearing Dinah say, "Winnifred, that is entirely too much butter. Put it back and go without for today so that you can better contemplate your gluttony."

By the time I'd adjusted my hem, my friends had already left for the day. The Grashond residents had made it clear to us that we'd have to start pulling our fair share immediately. We were here on their charity—well, that and whatever "donation" they extracted from Jasper's cargo. A small cloth-wrapped bundle sat on the table, so I presumed the breakfast within was mine. With no one else around, I wolfed the food down without remorse. It was delicious. Whatever her other faults, Dinah knew how to cook.

I'd been given directions to town last night. The way was pretty straightforward, and sun shining through the windows suggested a pleasant day. Surprisingly eager for a walk, I put on my cloak and was almost at the front door when Gideon rushed inside.

"I forgot to bring my— Oh." He sidestepped to avoid a collision. "I'm sorry. But this is lucky. I'd meant to catch you later, but now's just as good a time. Wait here a moment."

He darted down the hall, leaving me alone and puzzled. When he returned, he held a sheaf of blank paper. "Here. This is for you."

I took it with shaking hands. "But how? We're not supposed to have our belongings."

"This is mine," he said. "And now it's yours. Samuel keeps ink and pens in the common room that you're welcome to."

I caught myself clenching the paper and eased up so I wouldn't wrinkle it. The prospect of not being able to write to Merry and my family had felt so strange, making the distance between us seem bigger than usual. "Thank you. Thank you so much. You have no idea what it means to me."

His smile held a trace of wistfulness. "I know what it's like to be homesick. Writing letters isn't violating any sort of rule—just make sure you do it at night, after chores and prayers. And you'll have to hold on to your letters for a while. Not much mail goes out in the winter."

"Right." My brief happiness dimmed. "Because of the roads."

"Some mail gets out, of course. We're not completely isolated from the world, so you're welcome to send them if we hear of any courier headed south—but winter letters get lost a lot."

"I'll take the chance—at least for our benefactor in Cape Triumph. If he knows what's happened, maybe Jasper can help . . . somehow . . ." It was a far-fetched possibility, and Gideon and I both knew it.

"It's like I told you before," he said gently, "we'll help however we can. *And* you can have as much paper as you like. I have plenty, and perhaps it'll make the time go by faster."

It was hard not to smile at his hopeful look. "I'm sure it will."

"Tamsin? What are you still doing here? You're late."

I jumped at the sound of Dinah's voice. She stood at the bottom of the stairs, looking like a specter in her starched black dress. Gideon said quickly, "My fault. I held her up."

Dinah frowned. "Well, let's not waste any more time."

"I'm on my way to town too," Gideon said. "I'll walk with you."

Despite the sunshine, patches of snow still lingered in the shade. I was glad for the cloak and mittens and glad to be out and moving. And yes, I also liked having such nice company.

Gideon gestured around at the barren trees. "I know it looks bleak now, but it really is beautiful once the leaves come back and everything turns green. When I first saw spring here, after growing up in Osfro, I thought I must be seeing the world as it looked when it was new, right after Uros made it."

"You lived in Osfro?"

"Up until just over a year ago."

"Why would you come to a—" I shut my mouth, realizing what I'd been about to say.

"A place like this?" He laughed.

"Sorry. I didn't mean any insult."

"None taken. I came here for the same reason you did."

"To get married?"

"To find what I didn't have. I was disgusted by how self-absorbed Osfro was. Everywhere I looked, I only seemed to find selfishness, materialism, and depravity. People give themselves up to excess and impulse, with no thought for— I'm sorry. I sound like I'm preaching at you in a service."

"Trust me, this is unlike any service I've ever attended." Not the least of which was because our parish priest, Father Alphonse, had been a gray-haired, wraithlike man who always chastised me about Merry.

Gideon gave me a knowing look, and I turned my gaze downward. "Did you attend church services often?"

"Eh, not as often as I maybe should have."

"It's okay." I could hear his smile without seeing it. "I was the same, actually."

"Were you?" I glanced back, startled. "Then how are you a minister?"

"It's a long story. The short version is one day, I felt as though Uros was telling me to wake up and see the truth of the world. His great creation had become shallow. Showy on the outside, empty within."

"That's . . . a bit disheartening." It was the most tact I could manage.

"I know, but it opened my eyes to looking past the way society says who's important. What's a noble title or expensive clothes? That doesn't define a person's character. Just as stained glass windows and a golden altar don't make a church holy. I wanted to connect to Uros in a pure way, without the empty, repetitive services no one really listened to. I decided it was my calling to help others live more meaningful lives."

"And you decided to do it . . . here."

"Everyone thinks the Heirs' way of life is harsh and stark—and it can be—but that's because they strip away all the excess and know a person's worth is measured by their heart and good deeds." He stopped abruptly, blushing much as he had at our first meeting. "I *am* preaching at you."

"It was actually really eloquent. But don't think you'll be bringing me into the fold anytime soon," I added. "I rather like stained glass."

Yet his words stirred me. My family had always worked honestly and helped others, but that had mattered little to the upper classes. And when Merry had come along, even my own neighbors had judged me by the shadow of scandal, not the light of my heart and good deeds.

He laughed heartily at that, a warm, golden sound that wrapped around us. "I do too, to be honest. And they aren't evil. We just can't let outside glamour hide the truth. Look at you and how you helped your friends stay safe. Don't let fancy dresses and jewels obscure your bravery and compassion."

"I don't know that it was bravery. I just did what needed to be done."

He regarded me with unabashed admiration, and suddenly, I was the one flushing. "You're brave, Tamsin. And if no one's ever told you that, you're spending time with the wrong people."

I pretended to adjust my mittens as I groped for something to say. "That's clever, what you said about the stained glass. Those glittering colors are beautiful, but you actually can't see through them to what's on the other side."

Gideon came to a halt, his eyes wide. "That's an incredible interpretation."

"Wait . . . you weren't using the stained glass as a metaphor?"

"Not intentionally. I'm actually no good at coming up with elegant analogies like that."

"You just told me plenty of elegant things."

"Well, talking to you is easy. Preaching to a congregation is harder. My mind freezes up, and I start sounding choppy and dry. And then I get more flustered if I think I'm boring everyone."

"Try writing out your sermon ahead of time."

Amused, he began walking again. "I do, but I was a lazy student before my revelation. If I'd paid more attention in class, maybe I could compose my thoughts better. Oh, and I'm a terrible speller too."

Thinking of the way my companions swooned over him, I said, "Give yourself more credit. I'm sure at least half the congregation pays attention to you."

The town square was coming into view, and our steps slowed as we prepared to go separate ways. Gideon clasped his hands behind his back and kicked awkwardly at a clump of ice. "Thank you for a nice walk," he said haltingly. "I hope your day is pleasant."

As he turned, I blurted out, "Gideon? I . . . I'm an excellent speller. I always got good marks on my essays. If you'd like, I'll proofread your sermons for you." He gaped, and I suddenly felt stupid. "Sorry. I suppose it's presumptuous for someone like me to help write the word of Uros. I just wanted a way to thank you for the paper."

"No, no. It's not presumptuous at all. I'd love it. It's just . . ." His expression wavered between enthusiasm and doubt. "It's complicated. We'll figure it out, but for now, don't breathe even a hint of it to anyone."

"Okay . . ."

"I'll explain it later," he added, seeing my bewilderment. "It's just that the Heirs have their own ways of doing things. And doing things differently from those ways . . . isn't always met well."

"Yeah," I said. "I'm starting to figure that out."

CHAPTER 9

I BEGAN MY WORKDAY IN THE HOME OF CHESTER WOODS, a widower with a spacious house located right near a large, public well along the square. He was busy clearing land on his newly purchased farm outside of town and had offered up his home as my workplace. I had a list of families needing my services, and after learning their locations from a neighbor, I came up with a plan similar to what Ma had used. I went out and gathered loads from those households closest to each other, washed them, and let them dry while I retrieved the next batch.

I found a pen in the house and allowed myself a small break. With Gideon's paper, I settled down to compose my first letter in Grashond.

> *Dear Mister Thorn,*
>
> *I'm writing to let you know that the twenty Glittering Court girls aboard the* Gray Gull, *along with Miss Quincy, are all alive and well. The tempest we encountered near the end of the voyage damaged our ship severely and sent us significantly off course. The other girls and I are now residing in the town of Constancy, in Grashond Colony, where we have been kindly taken in by the Heirs of Uros. You'll find the specifics of our location on the next page, and I again*

want to reiterate that we are safe. Nonetheless, any
immediate assistance you can offer to bring us to Cape
Triumph quickly and comfortably will be very, very
appreciated.

Sincerely yours,

Tamsin Wright

My efficient methods more than made up for this morning's delay, and the clothes dried quickly in the clear weather. But oh, the toll it took. By the end of the afternoon, sweat poured off me, thanks to the steam. My hands were already starting to roughen, and I knew they'd get worse. Chester kept salve in his kitchen, and I used a little each day in hopes of slowing the damage. I consoled myself with thoughts of silk gloves in Cape Triumph.

Life fell into a stable, if dull, pattern over the next few days. The Coles maintained a rigid schedule for meals and labor, and what little chore-free time we had in the evenings was often spent in the sitting room. Samuel or Gideon would choose a passage from the sacred texts, ask one of us to read it aloud, and then encourage discussion. Although "discussion" mostly seemed to involve having us parrot back whatever the book had said.

Afterward, we had a small amount of supervised "socializing" time in the sitting room, but it was hard to speak freely with Samuel or Dinah around. Even if they weren't directly involved in a conversation, one of them always hovered watchfully nearby. Conversation grew easier when Gideon would join us. He brought that infectious good nature with him and liked talking to us about Osfro and what he'd missed in his time away. He also helped us adjust to Grashond. As an outsider, he had a good sense for which of the Heirs' customs we might accidentally overlook.

"What do you think they're doing right now?" Vanessa asked in a momentary lull one evening. "The girls in Cape Triumph?"

"Mourning us, most likely," suggested Damaris dryly.

"Jasper might mourn the loss of revenue, but none of the others know us," said Winnifred. "Except Martha. I know her from our district, and she knows the other Swan Ridge girls, of course. But you—Tamsin. They'll be crying buckets for you."

"Or will they?" Damaris's brown eyes sparkled, despite the morbid topic. "How ruthless were you back at Blue Spring? If you blazed through there like you did on the ship—too focused to make friends, using all that energy of yours to 'get things done'—then maybe they won't be too torn up about it."

I met her teasing look with exasperation. "Yes, yes, believe it or not, I did actually have friends back there."

Gideon glanced between us, those fine features of his turning quizzical. "Why wouldn't you? You seem like someone who makes friends everywhere."

My roommates laughed, all except Damaris. She scrutinized Gideon, glanced at Dinah's cold face, and then said, "Well, of course she does. We just give her a hard time, that's all. She's just got one of those natures, but then, so do you. It's why you get along so well."

"That's enough," Dinah said from across the room. "No wonder your heads are so empty, if this is the drivel you talk about. Up to bed, all of you."

My roommates and I scurried to the attic. Aside from walking into town for work, bedtime was the only spare moment we had to speak privately. It was also often my only chance to write letters, so I usually found myself multitasking—writing and talking at the same time.

Winnifred stifled a yawn as she watched me. "You'll have written a book by the time all those letters of yours get to your family."

"Did the letter you wrote to Jasper go out?" asked Vanessa, pulling one of the scratchy nightgowns on over her head.

"Yesterday," I replied. "There was a farmer heading east to Watchful. He took some of the town's mail with him, which was lucky. But it'll still take forever to cross Grashond, and then who knows how often ships carry mail down the coast? We'll probably beat the letter there."

"Oh." Vanessa sat on the bed with crossed legs. She sometimes had a blithe nature reminiscent of Adelaide's, but she was unusually subdued tonight. "I was hoping the letter would get there before anyone wrote to our families back home about us and the ship."

Silence. I set down my pen and met the others' gazes. In all my fixation on getting to Merry, I'd never considered that possibility. I knew Mira and Adelaide probably thought I was dead. They'd been near the *Gray Gull* when we took damage. Our loss would've hit them suddenly and acutely, and my heart ached whenever I imagined their reaction to my supposed death. The haunting memory of Mira's agonized face from the eve of our sailing was etched into my mind. How much worse was it now? And Adelaide . . . I couldn't imagine her pain either. Because no matter how things had ended between us, I knew she'd grieve for me and grieve hard. Her heart was big.

But my family? They seemed so far away and isolated in Osfrid, detached from any of this. As difficult as my setback with the *Gray Gull* had been, I thought of it as a problem that was bound to Adoria. The inconvenience affected me, and I would have this settled—eventually—hopefully before it would have any effect on Ma, Pa, and the others.

But of course Jasper would write to our families. The question was: How soon?

"The ships probably aren't running back east yet," I said at last. I had to lower my eyes toward the letter, lest my friends read my doubts. "He can't send anything."

The other girls relaxed, but only slightly. Vanessa asked, "Have you heard anything about when we'll go south?"

"They're waiting for the weather to clear."

Winnifred brightened. "Then it can't be much longer. It hasn't snowed since we've been here, and there's hardly any left on the ground."

I still couldn't look up, knowing what I did. "Then I'm sure we'll hear something soon. And they still have a lot of planning to do. We haven't even been here for a week."

A creak on the stairs was our only warning before Dinah stepped through the doorway. "Are you four still awake? You're wasting candles. And you." She turned toward me, hands on her hips. "You're wasting paper."

I finished writing my last word. "Gideon gave this to me."

"And Uros gave us the world. That doesn't mean you have the right to misuse either one. Gideon is a thoughtful, generous man and most likely believed he'd be helping you out with an occasional letter—not a nightly missive!" Dinah scooped up the blank stack of paper.

"Hey!" I jumped to my feet. "That's mine."

"Nothing in this household is yours. I will keep this and allow you one page on holy days. That way you won't squander it and run him out of resources—because he'd no doubt keep supplying you. Out of kindness and obligation, of course. I'm doing this for everyone's sake."

"'Be cautious of those who are too quick to act in your best interests and even quicker to tell you that they are. Too often, your best interests become indistinguishable from theirs.'"

That astonishing bit of scriptural recitation came from Damaris. Her solemn delivery was undermined by a saucy smile that broadened when she saw Dinah gape. "What?" asked Damaris innocently. "It was in one of the passages you assigned me to read this morning. I was trying to apply what I learned in my everyday life. Did I do it right?"

Dinah blanched, then reddened as fury set in. "You think that's funny? Quoting the holy books for your own insidious purposes? That's blasphemous and evil."

"Evil?" I took a few steps closer to Damaris. "I don't really think—"

"I don't care what you think!" Dinah's eyes blazed. "You're all wicked and selfish, and the angels wrecked you here to learn some humility. Damaris—follow me. Since you fancy yourself such a scriptural expert, you can sit down by the hearth and copy out the first three chapters of *A Testament of Angels* before you sleep."

When Damaris started to walk to the doorway, I put out a hand to block her. "That's huge! It'll take her half the night."

Dinah regarded me coolly. "Perhaps you'd like to keep her company and copy out the next three?"

I was about to snap back, "Only if I can use Gideon's paper," but then I caught Damaris's eye. She gave a tiny shake of her head, and after a moment of indecision, I dropped my arm and let her keep going.

I heard her return hours later, long after the rest of us had gone to bed. Lifting my head a little, I peeked over at the small window, which glowed gray in the predawn light. I snuggled back under the heavy quilt but couldn't fall asleep. Our morning wakeup came all too soon, and Damaris clambered out of bed doggedly, albeit bleary-eyed.

Every time Damaris yawned at breakfast, Dinah looked increasingly proud of herself. I wanted to shake that smirk right off her. Gideon, blissfully unaware of the drama that had taken place last night, kept chatting me up about a bridge that had been built in the market district after he'd left.

Finally, noticing my attention straying to Damaris, he said to her, "My goodness. You must not have slept very well."

She managed a wan smile. "I slept very well. I just didn't get much of it. I went to bed late. I got caught up reading."

"I see," he said. "Well, try to be a little more careful tonight—though I know how hard it is when you're in the middle of a good book."

"That's wonderful advice," she said sweetly. "Thank you."

Later, when my friends and I reached the town square and were about to head off to our jobs, I held Damaris back.

"When you finish prepping the food, come find me at Chester's. Half my deliveries overlap with yours. I'll take them, and you can go home early and sleep."

She blinked in surprise. "What? No. I can't. Er, you can't do that . . ."

"Of course I can. I told you, it's on the way. And you need some rest."

She yawned. "You think Dinah will let me?"

"I think you'll have to be sneaky enough to get in without her noticing."

"Oh, Tamsin," she said with a chuckle, "I'm glad you're with us."

The nice thing about having a job that sent me out so often was that I'd gotten a good opportunity to study the town and its inhabitants. Although a fraction of the size, Constancy wasn't so different from the market district in Osfrid. People and horses traveled the streets on various errands, craftsmen made their crafts, merchants sold their goods. The residents I passed didn't seem unkind so much as wary, but then, we were strangers who'd arrived with Icori and Balanquans. We didn't practice their ways and came from a place that had, in fact, persecuted them for those ways. I persisted in politeness and respect, hoping the townspeople would eventually accept us.

My attitude must have done something, because the old cobbler who lived next to Chester Woods greeted me as I left with my last delivery later that day. "Where to now?" he asked, tipping his hat.

Smiling back, I set down my baskets and reached for my mittens. "The Randalls, Johnsons, and Calvin Miller. Then I go home."

"You'll take the creek road?"

"No, I—" The mittens weren't in my pockets. Six. Had I left them at one of my stops today? I repressed a sigh and hoisted the baskets back up. "Sorry. What was I saying? Oh, I'm taking the north road. That's how someone directed me earlier."

"Nah. Save time on the creek road. After you go to the Randalls, head toward the school, and you'll come across a little track. Don't worry—it gets bigger. Stay on it, and it'll loop up as it winds out of town. Goes right past the pond Miller lives on and then crosses the north road just south of the Johnsons."

I had a pretty good sense of direction and tried to piece it all together. "If it's where you say, I must have crossed the creek road before."

He scratched at his forehead and nodded. "You surely did. You remember an orchard? That's Albert Thrace's land, right at the crossroads. North after that is Jacob Robinson's, then the Johnsons' farm a half mile later."

I nearly dropped the baskets. "J-Jacob Robinson's place?"

"Well, he's renting it. You would've passed it too—it has two red barns." The cobbler pulled a face at that. "Do you know him?"

"I just heard the name, that's all."

"He'll be gone soon enough, and good riddance. We don't need his kind of trouble." The cobbler squinted up at the sky. "If you wait another hour, I can drive you when I go home. The creek road runs right behind Samuel Cole's, and I'm not far after that."

"No, thank you." I was already running later than usual because of making Damaris's deliveries. I was also forming a plan. "I appreciate it, though. I'll just finish this up now—I don't want to keep these people waiting."

I hurried away, my heart pounding. Jacob Robinson! Or Jago Robinson. Whichever it was, I remembered the red barns. It was hard not to, since no other building in Constancy was painted a bright color. The cobbler's words echoed back to me: *We don't need his kind of trouble.* And Gideon, in his mild-mannered way, hadn't really spoken well of Jago either.

But I couldn't pass up the chance. Merry was on my mind, as always, but after Damaris's punishment, I was more motivated than ever to get us out of here. Everyone kept saying I got things done. It was time to prove I could.

CHAPTER 10

AFTER DROPPING THE LAST BASKET OFF TO A VERY GRATEFUL mother of eight children, I backtracked toward the house with two barns. Clouds were moving in from the north, chasing away our sunny day, and I quickened my pace to avoid both the chilly air and a scolding for being late to dinner.

Jago Robinson's home was more of a cabin than a house, built of logs that had turned gray in the elements. It was one story and had a small porch that looked like a recent addition, judging from its golden-hued timber. Farther back on the property, the red barns stood like sentries, and the land showed no signs of being farmed.

The new porch smelled of cedar and creaked when I stepped up on it. I set my empty baskets down and knocked, rubbing my hands together as I waited. When about a minute had passed, I knocked again and peered in one of the dark windows, hoping to get a sense if anyone was home.

"Do your parents know you're here?"

The voice came from outside, not within. I spun around. A man stood at the end of the porch, hands shoved in the pockets of a knee-length leather coat that had seen a lot of wear. A wrinkled brown hat sat crookedly on his head, and a scarlet scarf provided an unexpected flash of color in his otherwise drab attire.

"Are you Mister Robinson?" I asked.

He bowed. "At your service. Can't say I recognize you, and I know I'd remember if we'd met. What is it you're looking for? Got a cough?

Need something to make your hair grow faster? Want a baby? Don't want a baby? You know, I've got a ribbon that I think would be perfect for you. It's green—but not a dangerous green."

"A . . . dangerous green?"

"It's dark green. A gentle green. Nothing that'll get you in trouble, but it's got just enough flair to catch the eye. And yes, we all know the evils of vanity, but between you and me, I don't think there's anything wrong with a little indulgence like that. Seems like the true sin is not showing off that pretty hair Uros gave you, right? I'll give you a good price for it. Buy two, and I'll give you a *really* good price. Come in and take a look."

He sauntered in, and I followed him inside, mostly because I was too stupefied by this reception. The snug little cabin consisted of one room, divided into living and sleeping spaces by a stone hearth. It took me a moment to distinguish the two areas, though, because both the kitchen table and small bed were hidden by haphazardly stacked crates and bags.

My host immediately homed in on a pile and lifted a large burlap sack from it. After a bit of rummaging, he produced two green ribbons with a flourish. "See? What'd I tell you? Beautiful, eh? You can try them on, if you want. There's a mirror over in that box you can use. In fact, I'm selling it for a very reasonable price."

I pushed aside the ribbons he held up to my face. "Mister Robinson! Please, I'm not here for this."

"Oh. So, it is medicinal, huh? Sure, no problem. Let's go over to—"

"I'm not here to buy anything at all!"

He stopped midstep, and some of the enthusiasm in his face dimmed. "You aren't here to ask me to come to church, are you? I can't say I'm surprised they'd try again, and I appreciate the creative approach of sending a pretty girl, but I'm not—"

"Can you shut up for a few bloody seconds?"

I didn't mean to shout, but it was the only way to break through his prattle. After several weighted moments, he said quietly: "So. You aren't from Grashond, are you?"

"No! My name is Tamsin Wright, and I'm starting to understand why everyone gets so weird when I mention Jago Robinson."

He cocked his head. "Jago? No one in Constancy calls me that. And just how weird are we talking?"

I leaned back against one of the rough walls and crossed my arms. "Orla Micnimara calls you Jago."

"How do you know Orla?"

"If you'll stop trying to sell me stuff, I'll tell you."

"I won't say another word, I swear." In an unnecessary show of good intentions, he clamped a hand over his mouth.

Sparing him the intricacies of the Glittering Court, I explained how we'd been shipwrecked and then brought here by Balanquans and Icori. He listened in admirable silence, but when I got to the part about how the town had sheltered us in exchange for work, he lost it.

"Let me get this straight. There's twenty-one of you, and they've got you all doing forced labor?"

"It's not forced. I mean, it's nothing I would've chosen, sure, but they *are* putting us up. They gave us food and new clothing. I don't mind paying that back."

"New clothing, huh?" Jago eyed the skirt of my navy dress, peeping out from underneath the cloak. "Was your old stuff unsalvageable?"

"No. It just wasn't . . ."

"Yeah, I know." He tugged at his red scarf. "You have no idea how much grief I get for this. But back to you. So, here you are, washed ashore, deprived of fashion, living with . . . Who are you living with?"

"Samuel Cole."

"Wow, okay. So, they've put you to work, probably lecture you a few times a day, and now you're here because . . . ?"

"Because we need to get to Cape Triumph as soon as possible. The council says they'll help us but not until the weather's warmer, so we could have as much as a two-month wait before we can even leave!

But Orla told me how the Icori will be going south on the river soon and that you'd bought a bunch of spots. If you can just give up some of them, then we—"

"Whoa, whoa, hold on." He held up a hand. "That's what you're here for? To steal my passage south?"

"Not steal it, no. Orla will give you your money back so that we can buy the seats. You just have to relinquish them."

"'Just' do that, huh?" He circled the room, shaking his head. "Miss—what was it, Tamsin? You clearly don't understand business, otherwise you wouldn't suggest this with a straight face."

"I understand perfectly well. My mother runs a business in Osfro . . . ah, offering services to a whole roster of well-to-do clients. I helped her schedule them, keep track of accounts, and all sorts of things."

"Okay, great. And if she decided to take a few weeks off, with no one to cover for her, and those well-to-do clients took their business elsewhere, did anyone steal money from her? No. But she lost it all the same. And that's what giving up those seats means. Come spring, the roads'll be flooded with trade. If I get south ahead of the rush, all those people in Denham and Joyce that've been waiting the whole winter will come to me first. But if I'm behind, they'll find someone else."

"That's not a perfect analogy," I insisted. "I'm not asking you to give up the seats for no reason. It's an act of charity."

"Why should I show charity to someone I just met? I mean, I'm not a cruel man, but come on. Would your mother let income slip away like that? Or was your family so flush with gold, you could afford to throw it around to hard-luck cases?"

"Let's stop talking about my mother." I rubbed my forehead and walked over to one of the windows. Two gray horses grazed beside a barn. "What if we pay you? Give up the seats, get your money back from Orla. Then we'll give you a fee per seat to compensate for what you'll lose in trade."

Jago joined me by the window and leaned one shoulder against the wall. He took off his hat, revealing a burst of sun-bleached hair. "Your business sense might be wanting, but you're persistent, I'll give you that."

"So you'll accept?"

"Nope," he said cheerfully. "Well, that is, I probably can't accept whatever you're thinking of. You see all of this?" He gestured grandly at the stacks. "I've got more in the barns. To make up for not selling it early . . . I mean, I'm probably losing two gold in profit for each seat I give up. And I secured fifty seats. Do you have a hundred gold lying around?"

Not literally, no. But somewhere in Grashond, heaps of goods worth much more than that actually *were* lying around. Glittering Court brides usually cost over a hundred gold. Surely Jasper would see parting with additional property as a good deal to get us back in a timely manner.

"And I don't even know if we need fifty spots," I murmured, thinking aloud. "The sailors can fend for themselves. But we need space for our goods too . . ."

"Are you actually considering that?" Jago leaned forward, peering into my face with amazement. "You did hear me say a hundred gold, right?"

I met his eyes, which were an odd greenish color. No—actually, they were two different shades. One a pure green, the other green and hazel mixed.

"Yes," he said unexpectedly, "they don't match."

"Sorry. I didn't mean to stare."

"Oh, you can stare at me as much as you like. Besides, I'm used to it. The people around here think my eyes are some mark of the wayward angels."

"People are foolish. Your eyes are marvelous. Now. I don't have that much coin actually in hand, but I have plenty of goods to equal it."

"Marvelous, huh?" He tilted his head and studied me with a lopsided smile for a few seconds. Then getting back on topic, he said, "I need currency. Already got too much to trade and not enough space to hold it."

"What about jewelry? It's small. Easily converted to coin."

"True." He played with the brim of his hat as he thought. "It'd depend on the jewelry, I suppose. And we'd have to settle on a higher amount then. To offset exchange fees and inconvenience."

"How much higher?" I felt like the solution to my problems was right in front of me—except that solution was like water. Each time I tried to grasp it, it slipped through my fingers.

"And . . ." Jago walked away and resumed pacing. "Even if I get my money back from Orla, I still have to pay for transport south through some other means. That's another fee."

"Are you trying to gouge us? We need to get to Denham!"

"And you think I don't?"

"I think . . . I think you could show a little more heart," I said lamely. A headache was building, as was my frustration. I knew ultimately, if he was fixed on going, no deal of mine would matter.

Jago tapped his chest. "I've got plenty, believe me. It gave a little pitter-patter when I saw you at my door, even. But go ahead—give me your last, best shot. Move me to tears, and tell me why you're really so anxious to get to Cape Triumph. And don't say to get away from the Heirs, because we all want to do that."

Gripping the windowsill, I looked outside again as I collected my thoughts. I couldn't see the horses anymore. *Move me to tears.* He joked, but I might very well do it if I told him about Merry. And yet . . . how could I? I'd clung to my secret so fiercely that I hadn't even revealed it to my best friends, ruining a friendship as a result. Why would I give everything up to a stranger?

"To find husbands," I said at last. "We've been at a finishing school of sorts for the last year. It's called the Glittering Court. They bring girls from Osfrid and show us off at dinners and balls in the hopes of meeting wealthy suitors."

Silence. It dragged on and on. Mystified—as it was the longest he'd gone without talking—I turned around to see what had happened. Bewilderment filled those green-and-gold eyes.

"That," he said, "is incredible."

A glimmer of hope reared up in me. "Then you'll help us?"

"What? No, of course not. I just mean, it's incredible that that's the argument you're trying. Look, I feel sorry for you and your situation. Really. But come on. A month or so from now, you're on the road. Two more months, you're back with this Glittering Court, wearing bright colors again, and drinking champagne with some man who wants to keep you in luxury for the rest of your life. And you know what? The more I describe it, the more I don't think I actually do feel sorry for you. In fact, I feel less guilty for refusing you now than I did before. The crumbling of my financial future is much more tragic than you having to wait a little longer to practice what I'm sure are formidable flirting skills with rich men. You know, some might even say *you* are the one lacking in heart for even suggesting this to me."

"You don't know anything about me!" My pulse quickened with outrage, and I balled my fists at my side.

Jago threw his hands up. "I gave you a chance to tell me."

Frustrated tears pricked my eyes, and I stormed off to examine the closest stack of crates before he noticed. One box held a jumble of yarn skeins, suspenders, tin cups, and a few toys. I lifted out a wooden doll and ran my fingers over her face, painted with bright blue eyes and pink cheeks. I'd saved for a secondhand doll very like this one for Merry's last birthday, and I felt an unbearable tightness in my throat, thinking how she was going to turn four without me. I'd written her pages of birthday wishes before I left Osfro and scraped up a little money for gifts to leave in Ma's safekeeping. Over and over, I'd reminded myself the heartache would all be worth it when Merry and I were together in Cape Triumph.

Except I was here in Grashond. With no escape in sight.

The floor creaked with Jago's footsteps, and I sensed him stopping just behind me. When he spoke, his voice was soft. "Why did Orla even offer this to you? She doesn't usually go out of her way to help colonists."

"I . . . don't know." It hadn't fully struck me how strange this deal of hers might be. "We traveled together. I gave her some arnica, that's it."

"For a good price? I could probably have beat it."

Trust me, Jacob Robinson isn't going to get you to Cape Triumph.

"That's all you can say?" I set the doll down and stomped toward the door. "Goodbye, Mister Robinson. If you can't sell the seats, that's fine, but I'm not some traveling act that came by to give you a little entertainment this afternoon! This is my life, my world—not some joke!"

He scurried over, the crooked smile vanishing. "Now, wait, I never said this was a joke—"

"No, you just acted that way! I came here to make you a serious offer—a very fair one, I might add. And now, because you thought it was funny to toy with me, I'll probably be late for dinner. They'll have me writing scripture all night now."

"Aw, don't leave like this." He searched around and snatched up the ribbons. "Take these, at least. Two for one."

"Good *day*, Mister Robinson."

I jerked the door open and then paused in the doorway, glancing back over my shoulder. "And just so you know, I didn't charge her anything for the arnica. Can you beat that deal?"

I slammed the door and hurried to the road, afraid he'd come after me. The dark clouds had spread fully across the sky, which complemented my mood nicely. Scattered snowflakes drifted down, and I kicked at dead leaves and clumps of ice as I walked, trying not to scream my outrage to the world. Not that there was anyone to hear. Once I returned to the creek road and continued toward the Cole house, I saw no other homes or farms. *Maybe a good yell would make me feel better.* No, nothing was going to make me feel better.

Perhaps it had been too much to hope that a stranger would help me. And Jago was right that I wasn't exactly asking a small thing. The

Icori river route was even more valuable than I'd originally believed, now that I understood more about northern travel. Even those who braved the roads couldn't move the amount of cargo the river barges could. Jago had every right to want to hold on to his prize.

But he could have been nicer about the whole thing.

I brushed snow out of my eyes and secured my cloak. He hadn't actually been mean, I supposed. Not exactly. Mocking? That was closer. Had he ever at any point seriously considered helping me? He just thought I wanted a faster way to dresses and champagne. How could he know I was trying to get to the person I loved most—who needed me most—in the world?

I felt a pang, thinking again about Merry's upcoming birthday. I'd left Ma with reams of letters and what presents I could muster. Had it been enough? Did Merry even care about the letters I took such pains to write? Maybe she didn't even listen when they were read aloud. She was so, so young. Young enough to not understand a lot of things. Young enough to forget things more easily than adults did. Her safety and well-being were always foremost in my thoughts . . . but they were followed closely by a deep fear that maybe, after all I was going through, Merry was forgetting me.

The wind jerked my hood down, and I stopped to refasten it. As I did, I stepped out of the dark spiral in my head and got a good look at what was going on around me. It was snowing. *Really* snowing. Those whimsical little flakes that had first fallen when I left Jago's had given way to a steady, thick snowfall that was rapidly accumulating. The dirt road was already almost completely covered. I resumed my trek, suddenly very conscious of everyone saying how unpredictable the blizzards around here were.

I couldn't have much farther to go, though. I had a pretty clear sense of the way the roads were laid out, and even though I hadn't taken this one earlier, I knew by where it intersected the others that there wasn't much more than half a mile to the Cole house. I just had to stay on the road.

The wind played hide-and-seek, sometimes keeping still for a while, and then gusting with such fierceness that it nearly knocked me off my feet. I wished I'd thought to ask Jago for mittens. He probably could have given me an amazing deal. Thicker and thicker the snow grew. It coated my lashes, and the increasingly frigid air froze my nose and mouth. But what was most concerning was that I hadn't reached Samuel's house yet. I was certain I should've seen it by now, unless my calculations were radically off. That seemed unlikely. This was far simpler than the labyrinth of Osfro's streets, and I was sure the house would pop up any minute.

But would I know it? The highway I'd walked into town ran in front of the Cole property. This creek road ran behind it. Samuel's house was one of the bigger ones in Constancy and would be easy to spot from a distance—unless your visibility had been severely damaged.

I looked around at the swirling white world. What should I do? I couldn't be sure yet that I really had missed the house, so backtracking seemed premature. But if I had gone past it, then what was going to happen to me if I kept going? The cobbler had said he lived along it, so maybe I'd come across his home. Or any home. But what if I didn't? What if the creek road meandered out of town, and I ended up wandering lost in the woods? *You wouldn't wander long,* a helpful inner voice pointed out. *You'd freeze to death first.*

With no answers, I kept trudging forward. I could still see the shapes of trees along the roadside, and I checked closely for any sign of a larger building beyond them. The stinging snow made it difficult to focus, and each time I tried to brush my eyes clean, tears would freeze around them.

Twice, I almost walked off the road and didn't realize it until a tree materialized right in front of me. Between the wind and visibility, it was getting hard to even move in a straight line down the road. I *had* to have passed the Cole house. I needed to turn around. The cold began to numb my mind as well as my body. An overwhelming urge to

just sit down while I figured things out spread over me. I was so tired.
A small rest would help me make a decision . . .

No, Tamsin! If you give up now, you'll never make it to Cape Tri-
umph. Are you going to abandon Merry because of a little snow?
The thought slapped me to attention as my knees started to buckle. I
straightened up and gritted my teeth. I wasn't beaten. Not yet.

Resolved, I turned back the way I'd come. I'd only taken a few
steps when I just barely picked up on a strange noise beyond the wind.
Peering around, I tried to locate the source. Was I hallucinating now?
No, the sound was real. It was metallic and clipped, growing louder
and closer.

Bells.

CHAPTER 11

A DARK, BLURRY SHAPE BROKE UP THE WHITE HAZE, materializing into a sleigh pulled by two gray horses. It drew up beside me, and as the driver leaned down and held out his hand, I recognized the red scarf covering most of his face. Jago waited until I was settled in the seat beside him, and then gave me a heavy wool blanket, large enough to drape over a bed. I cocooned myself in it and slouched down.

He pulled the scarf away from his mouth just enough to shout, "Okay?" I nodded. He shook the reins and guided the horses to turn around, but we didn't go very far before he directed them to make a sharp, hairpin right. We crept our way down the road because of the conditions, and I had the sense Jago was searching for something. There wasn't much to see, though. I couldn't even be sure where the trees were anymore.

Twice, he stopped and walked around, holding on to a rope tied to the sleigh. I watched and waited, unable to speak in the wind and snow. When he returned from a third trip down, he redirected the horses to angle left. I felt the terrain below us change. The sleigh still glided easily over the thick layer of snow, but whatever was beneath it didn't lie as evenly as the road had. Minutes later, the shadowy outlines of buildings came into view. With some squinting, I recognized the Cole house and barn.

Jago brought us as close to the front of the house as he could and helped me down. He watched me stagger to the door, and then he drove the sleigh toward the barn, soon disappearing from sight.

The wind ripped the door away from me as I opened it, bringing a swirl of snow inside. Closing it back up required throwing all my weight against it. Once the storm was shut out again, I leaned back and covered my eyes, panting, scarcely able to believe I was here. With a barrier between me and the elements, the world suddenly seemed impossibly still and quiet—and warm, not that any of that heat was getting into me yet. My legs trembled, and ice crystals covered much of my face.

"Tamsin!"

I rubbed my eyes and saw Winnifred and Gideon rush into the foyer. They pulled me into the main sitting area, bringing a chair up to the hearth, while Dinah gave the others curt orders for hot water and more blankets. The whole household was here, thankfully. It took me a few tries before I could speak, and even then, my numb lips and tongue tripped me up.

"J-J-Jago is out-outside," I said.

Samuel leaned closer. "Jago?"

"Jacob Robinson?" asked Gideon.

I managed a shallow nod and sipped at the tea Vanessa handed me. "He found me on the road. I think he's in the b-barn. I hope he is."

"Surely even he's not fool enough to try and go back out in this," said Samuel, exchanging troubled glances with Gideon.

Pounding at the door provided the answer, and Gideon scurried to help Jago inside. A fleece-lined cap with earflaps had replaced the wide-brimmed hat I'd seen earlier, and a shaggy fur coat covered his leather one. A layer of snow had turned all of it white, except for that defiant red scarf. He pulled it from his face to accept a cup of tea. "Thank you. I put my team in your barn—hope that's okay."

"Of course," replied Samuel.

"We were so worried, Tamsin," Damaris said, wringing her hands. The other girls nodded anxiously.

"I was almost going to go out after you," Gideon added. "But the storm blew up too quickly. Samuel didn't think I could make it to town in time . . . and we didn't know where you were."

Dinah hovered at the room's edge, arms crossed over her chest. "You wouldn't have been caught in it if you'd been home sooner. Why were you late?"

"Come now, Dinah," said Gideon, a small frown on his brow. "I think we can forgo any chastisement, given the circumstances."

Dinah's lips pressed into a straight line at the gentle rebuke, but she said no more.

"How do you two know each other?" Samuel asked Jago and me.

How indeed? I could hardly tell them I'd gone off alone to bargain with their resident pariah. Luckily, Jago naturally had no shortage of words. "We don't, nothing more than a quick exchange of names. I was on my way back from town when I came across her. She told me she was coming here, and it was closer than my place." He bestowed a smile on the other girls. "I had no idea what company you were keeping here."

"They're guests of ours, and it's a good deed you've done tonight, Jacob. You are welcome to stay as long as the storm lasts." Samuel seemed to deliver both compliment and invitation with some reluctance. His eyes fell on me. "And as for you, I hope you appreciate how once again the angels have spared you from nature's wrath."

"I do." I glanced at one of the dark windows as it rattled from the wind. "I honestly don't know what I would have done if I'd been out there much longer."

Gideon's frown had deepened. "When this lifts, the council should reconsider the girls' work arrangements—at least for ones like Tamsin and Damaris, traipsing around all over the town. That's safe enough in the summer, but it's too easy to get caught by a storm this time of year. This one was especially sudden, even for those of us who know what to look for."

"What work arrangement is this, exactly?" Jago's voice was perfectly guileless, with no sign that he already knew something of our history. "And I hope someone will be so kind as to give me the names of your lovely visitors. I confess, I'm so dazzled by them that I'm starting to wonder if I'm actually still outside and just hallucinating."

Jago's words drew answering smiles from my friends. He was a little disheveled from the storm, but even I had to acknowledge a kind of charm in his cheeky air.

Samuel pointed to each of us in turn. "Winnifred, Vanessa, Damaris, and, as you know, Tamsin. Their ship ran aground on the eastern coast, and now they're staying with us until they can continue to Cape Triumph in the spring."

"Oh yeah?" Jago asked. "What's waiting for you there?"

"Husbands, hopefully," Winnifred explained, a note of intense longing in her voice. "We've worked and studied to become ladies of high culture so that we can meet distinguished suitors—if any are still available by the time we get there! Tamsin'll probably snatch up whoever's left. She never backs down."

For some reason, the praise made me self-conscious. "Come on, I'm alive and well. You don't have to say nice things about me."

A mischievous smile crept over her face. "Who said I was trying to be nice? I'm just commenting on your relentless nature . . . which, by the way, I'm glad to have around. It's no wonder we're able to keep getting through these storms and other disasters alive."

I smiled back, thinking what a long ways we'd come from that first shipboard meeting. The touching moment was shattered when Dinah announced: "What *I* wonder about is why you all keep getting into one disaster after another. Perhaps it's some kind of divine punishment."

Jago knocked back the rest of his tea and set the cup on its saucer with a clatter. "Seems more like divine *favor* if they keep coming through it just fine. You said yourself the angels are looking out for them, Mister Cole. Maybe your guests are carrying some divine message for the rest of us and we don't even realize it."

Silence fell. Samuel cleared his throat and said, "While it's wise for you to consider the way the angels influence everything in the world, interpretation is best left to those more versed in holy study."

"We'd be glad to have you at services someday if you'd like to learn more," added Gideon.

Jago shook his head with a grin. "Nah. Honestly, I feel more spiritual when I'm working outside in the fresh air. I mean, look around at the sun and the trees—even this storm. Uros made that. The church? *You* made that."

"Are you suggesting worshipping outside, like the Alanzans do?" demanded Dinah, horror twisting her features.

"Oh, goodness, I'm no heretic, Miss Cole. I just live and worship by my own beliefs."

"That's nearly the definition of heresy!" Samuel threw back his shoulders and looked on the verge of delivering a sermon.

Noticing, Gideon quickly said, "Now, uh, it's been quite a night. Perhaps we should focus on celebrating Uros, not debating Uros."

Samuel, still scrutinizing Jago, didn't even blink. "Especially since there's nothing to debate."

"Of course not. I'm just saying maybe we'd all feel better after some dinner." Gideon might claim he choked up at the podium, but he could deflect beautifully. "Can you eat, Tamsin? We held off when the storm started."

"That's a great idea." Jago fixed his grin on me. "And how lucky you didn't even miss it."

As we adjourned to the kitchen, Damaris took my arm and held me back. "Tamsin, I feel awful. I wish you wouldn't have delivered those groceries for me. You wouldn't have been running late if—"

"Hush," I whispered, giving her a quick hug. "It's my own fault that I was running late. You needed that rest. Everything worked out, and it was almost worth freezing to death to have Dinah be nice to me. Or, well, just not be awful."

It was hard to poke too much fun at Dinah when she served up another of her excellent dinners. Once I thawed out, I developed a raging appetite and devoured the bean soup and greens without pausing. The others recounted their experiences with the storm, and Vanessa told how she'd walked home with a student who lived far outside of town.

"The snow was just starting, and I'm so glad I decided to talk to his mother about getting a more advanced lesson book. Otherwise, I'd have been worried sick about him getting home! He's so clever. It's a shame they can't afford anything new, but I'm going to create a makeshift reader so he won't be bored."

Jago arched an eyebrow. "Sounds like *you're* the clever one. You must be quite a reader yourself."

Her eyes glowed. "Oh, yes. I love it. And I miss it. I used to finish a book every few days."

"No kidding? I didn't realize there was such a scholar behind that pretty smile. And—wait? What? Are those dimples too? Wow. You know, you should keep your mind sharp. If you need new material, I've got a whole load of books I picked up in Sutton. Histories, novels."

"She needs no such things," Dinah interjected. "The scriptures will keep her mind sharp."

"Of course, of course." Jago fell into eating again but couldn't stay silent for very long. "You know, I can't remember the last time I ate something so delicious. Miss Cole, you didn't do this all by yourself, did you? I can taste a dozen different spices. You must have had these girls chopping all day."

Dinah looked startled at the praise and then, astonishingly, flushed with pleasure. "Actually . . . I did it all, Mister Robinson. Cooking is something I take very seriously. And there are only a few spices in there, basic ones at that. You can do a lot if you know how to use them correctly."

Jago let out a low whistle. "My goodness. I'll have to come by with my spice and oil inventory one day. If you've got the talent to create a meal like this out of simple things, I can't even imagine what you'd do with ingredients from around the world."

Perhaps Jago's flattery put her in a good mood, because later in the meal, Dinah reduced the punishment Winnifred had received for teaching the blacksmith's daughter to plait her hair. "You're excused from writing an analysis of that passage. Just be sure you remember its message."

"Oh, I will," Winnifred assured her. "I already read it, actually. I adore that one section: 'Remember your heart. Remember that others love you for it—not for your power or accolades. The conventions of man may lie, but the heart will tell the truth.'"

Jago set his fork down with a clatter, and I wondered how many more shocked reactions he could contrive in one meal. "What a musical voice you have. Do you sing?"

"Not often. I prefer playing." Her musical voice became melancholy. "I miss the violin I used to practice on back at Dunford. Hopefully I'll have my own when I'm married."

"Well, I have a lute for sale. Hardly the same thing, but some of the principles are similar. With your astonishing skill, you could practice before going south and then dazzle your suitors. Not that you won't already. In fact, I'm sure you'll have so many, you won't even be able to keep track of them."

Samuel sighed loudly. "Mister Robinson, did you hear nothing in that quotation?"

"I heard a voice that made me think one of the six angels had come to recite for us," Jago replied gravely. Damaris put a hand over her mouth to hide a laugh.

"The passage was about guarding against vanity, and yet here you are, feeding into it by constantly doling out flattery to these girls while also encouraging materialism with your incessant attempts to hock your wares!"

"Can't help the selling. It's in my blood. And I can't really hold back the compliments either—not when there are so many worthy recipients." Jago made a sweeping gesture around the table. "Besides, I've got to win over people with whatever skills I've got. I'm not as fortunate as Mister Stewart there, able to enthrall with just a glance."

Gideon started at the unexpected acknowledgment. "I'm sorry, what?"

"I'm not criticizing," Jago said amiably. "Just stating the facts. One of us has to work a lot harder to win the attention of young ladies. Give you a sword and some wings, and you'd be Kyriel made flesh. Me? I get called 'cute,' but never 'dashing.'"

Samuel froze mid-bite, unable to believe what was transpiring at his table. Meanwhile, Gideon was blushing so strongly, even his ears were pink. Dinah sprang to his defense: "It's Gideon's fine character that earns him attention."

"I can believe that. He's one of the finest people I've ever met." Jago sounded sincere. "But you probably figured that out early on, Miss Cole."

"Oh, yes," she said, thinking she'd scored a victory. "I could tell how fine he was the moment I saw him."

"The moment you saw him, eh? Mmm-hmm, I figured as much," said Jago.

I looked down at my plate to hide a smile. Damaris, catching the joke also, kept her face serene, though laughter filled her eyes. "You sell yourself short, Mister Robinson," she said. "I think if you grew your hair out a bit, you'd be quite dashing."

Jago put a hand to his heart. "You think so? I never thought about that. Sounds like you've got quite the eye for style. I have a mirror that—"

"This meal is over." Samuel shoved his chair back with a screech and stood up. "Jacob, we'll make you a bed in the front room. The rest of you girls, help Dinah with the dishes."

"Can't Tamsin be excused from it?" asked Vanessa. "After everything she's been through tonight? Look how chapped those hands are."

"Most of that's actually from the laundry," I said, touched by her concern. "But if they recovered from over ten years of it in Osfro, I'm sure they'll bounce back from . . . um, however long we're here."

"There's no shame in showing the marks of honest labor." Dinah studied me, and either because she was still upbeat from Jago's compliments or simply thought the others might judge, she said, "You may rest by the fire, Tamsin."

Jago followed me to the hearth and looked out one of the windows while I settled in a chair. "Quite a storm."

"Are you talking about the one you just made over dinner?" I asked.

He laughed and settled in the chair opposite me, turning it around so he could rest his chin on its back. "I like to keep things interesting, that's all."

"Seems like you could go a little easier on your poor host in the process."

"Seems like you could go a little easier on your poor savior."

I think he used "savior" to bait me, but it wasn't far from the truth. "Thank you for that. I had no idea where I was."

"On the edge of wandering into the southern woods." His levity disappeared. "When I found you, you'd gone off on a small track that branches from the creek road. I just barely caught sight of you as I was coming. A bit of luck there. Or divine favor."

I shuddered. "And here I was worried I'd just passed the house! Six. Why did you come looking for me at all?"

"When I realized there was a storm coming, I didn't think you'd make it back here before the worst hit. So . . . I had to go." The teasing twinkle in his eyes returned. "I've got more heart than you think."

"I won't apologize for what I said earlier, even if you did save my life."

"Understood."

We lapsed into silence, and I stared into the crackling fire, watching the gold and orange flames with their hearts of blue. When I glanced up, I found Jago studying me.

"What?"

"I should have given you the ribbons," he responded unexpectedly. "Most of your hair was covered up earlier. If I'd seen it all like this, I would've handed them over for free."

"You're just saying that because you want to save face now that you know I gave Orla the arnica for free."

He leaned his cheek against his hand, his grin widening as he regarded me sideways. "I'm thinking you might have a little heart too. Your friends seem to think so."

"If you weren't so busy trying to make a sale, you'd have heard them call me relentless."

"I heard them fawning all over you. And I heard Damaris sounding pretty grateful on the way to dinner."

I groaned. "Were you eavesdropping?"

"Nope. Just in the right place at the right time to make me wonder if maybe there was more to you storming into my house than a selfish need for champagne and silk. Maybe you were there for your friends as much as yourself. And then that makes me wonder if I should be on my guard. I mean, I hear you don't back down. Are you going to come after me again?"

"You bloody wish I was coming after you, Mister Robinson." I held up my hand to cover a yawn. I was getting too tired to indulge his banter. "Don't trouble yourself anymore. I'll find a way, just like I always do."

He lifted his head and examined my hand. "What did you mean about ten years of laundry?"

"I worked for my ma. I told you she's a laundress."

"No . . . you just said she ran a business."

"She does. Unless you think that doesn't count as a business?"

The tone of my voice wasn't lost on him. "Of course it counts. I guess I imagined other sorts of businesses. A fine dress shop. An event planner. I wasn't thinking of anything so . . ."

". . . gritty?"

His customary smile flickered back to life. "'Gritty'? Not the word I'd use. But when you told me you were off to waltz and dine with Cape Triumph's finest, I figured you must have already had connections to get a ride like that."

"A ride?" I straightened up, suddenly awake. "I'm not here because of a ride! I'm here because I worked hard—because I scraped and clawed in Osfro and then poured all that was left of me into being the best at Blue Spring. You have no idea how much I've sacrificed for the pleasure of sitting across from you right now, Jago Robinson, and I'll be damned if you, the bloody Heirs, or even this weather is going to keep me from what I want."

It was a harsher response than he deserved; I knew he hadn't actually meant to offend. But it all just burst out of me before I could stop it. I was bone weary, and the weight of this last twenty-four hours— Damaris, Jago, and the storm—was finally getting to me.

Jago watched me, his face serious but otherwise unreadable, and I wondered if I'd shocked him to silence. That seemed pretty unlikely. And sure enough, a few moments later, he began, "Look, if you— Oh, hello." His green-and-hazel eyes focused on something behind me, and his expression became lighthearted once more. "Mister Cole. Miss Vanessa. Pull up a chair and join us."

Panicked, I jerked around, expecting to see Samuel condemning me to Ozhiel's hell for my language, but his stoic expression told me he hadn't overheard. Vanessa stood behind him, quilts in her arms. "We'll clear some of this furniture and make you a bed," Samuel said.

Jago stood up and stretched. "Thank you, sir, but if it's all the same, I'll sleep out in the barn tonight."

"It's freezing out there," I protested. Was this another joke of his?

Jago responded with a wink. "If the horses can survive it, so can I. I'll feel better keeping an eye on them, and Mister Cole will probably feel better having me out of the house."

Samuel stiffened. "I wouldn't have made the offer if I didn't mean it. Our duty under Uros compels us to show compassion to anyone who needs it."

Jago tilted his head and stroked his chin in a sign of exaggerated contemplation. "Is it compassion if it's duty? Shouldn't compassion, by its nature, be freely given? And if memory serves, isn't who needs compassion just a matter of opinion anyway?"

Gideon slipped in to hear that last bit and see Samuel's answering glower. Moving deftly between the other two men, Gideon asked pleasantly, "Jacob, will this be enough to keep you warm? I'm sure we can find extras."

Jago eyed Samuel a beat more before turning to Vanessa and her blankets. "That's more than enough, thank you."

"You're hardier than me," she said. "We slept outside a few nights on the way here, and I felt like an ice block each morning, even with that massive bear fur Tamsin got along the way."

"How so?" Jago layered on his coats. "Did she relentlessly hunt one down?"

"She traded with the Balanquans for extra things to keep the rest of us warm. She handed over her favorite gown, this lovely green silk that—"

"Enough," I scolded. "It's just a dress. And stop before you give him ideas. He'll try to sell me something."

"Who said I was thinking that?" He was all bundled up now, about to wrap the scarf over his face. "But if you *do* need more dresses, come to me first. Good night, ladies, reverends." He took the blankets and disappeared through the doorway to the foyer. Several seconds later, the wind burst in as he opened the door and was then shut out once again.

Samuel stared at the doorway, opened his mouth to comment, and then shook his head. He stomped off to the kitchen, Vanessa hurrying after him when Dinah called her.

"It's always interesting around here," I muttered to Gideon.

He cocked his head, listening to the wind. "I wouldn't have minded it being less interesting tonight."

"How long do these storms last?"

"Usually a couple of days. I've seen them go as long as a week."

"A week," I repeated, aghast. What would someone on foot do?

It was easy to feel mad about the travel delay when I thought it was done unnecessarily. To understand it, to see for myself that the reasons were sound . . . it just made everything that much more depressing.

We both grew quiet, but I could sense Gideon building up to something. His eyes looked everywhere but me. "Tamsin . . . did Jacob Robinson really find you on the road, or had you already gone to see him about getting to Cape Triumph early?"

Gideon might be mild-mannered, but he wasn't oblivious. I hesitated, wondering how severe the consequences were for visiting Jago. I didn't want to lie to Gideon, though, and something told me he knew already.

"A little of both. I went to see him and got caught in the storm on the way back home. He came after me when the snow started."

Surprise flitted across Gideon's features. "Interesting. Well, what did he say? Can he get you to Cape Triumph before spring?"

"No." I sat back down and felt the earlier disappointment flood me. "The Icori would actually have been the ones getting us there, but it would mean Jago would have to stay behind and lose some of his profit. I offered to compensate him, but he still said no."

"Ah." Gideon settled down in the chair Jago had been using, flipping it forward again. "That's more what I'd expect. I'm sorry."

"Why is there so much friction with Jago?" I asked. "Is it just because of his personality?"

"It's a lot of things, I suppose." Gideon leaned back and sighed. "One is that Jacob sells things . . . some of which aren't legal to sell in Grashond. He gets around that by having clients meet him over by this tributary of the Quistimac—about a mile or so out of town. When the colonial charter was set up, Grashond and Archerwood both wanted that water route and were granted joint ownership. So, if he's making a sale on its banks of something illegal here but legal in Archerwood . . . he can dodge any repercussions."

I laughed before I could stop myself. "I'm sorry," I said, seeing Gideon's surprise. "I shouldn't have . . . It's just very clever, that's all.

Er, maybe 'devious' is a better word? What kinds of things is he selling?"

"Rum and wine come up the most." Gideon managed to make disapproval still look radiantly handsome. "And then whoever he sells it to usually gets drunk and ends up getting punished by the council. But Jago gets off on technicalities."

"I can see why that'd be irritating, but is that really so bad? Drinking definitely can cause trouble, sure, but it's not like Jago's out there killing scores of people or anything."

"No, not yet." Gideon's expression took on an uncharacteristic grimness. "But he might be doing it any day now."

CHAPTER 12

"Gideon! Stop it. There are enough reasons for people to dislike him without spreading horror stories and accusations." But even as I spoke, a chill ran through me at the solemn look in Gideon's eyes. "It *is* a story, right? Like Dinah saying we're being divinely punished?"

Gideon took his time to answer. "It's a story in that no, it hasn't happened yet. And no, I can't predict the future to say that it most certainly, without a doubt, will happen. But he's set us up for it."

"You're going to have to back up. I know Samuel wouldn't have let Jago in here if he might just turn around and start killing us without warning."

"That's true," Gideon admitted, "and I should have been clearer with my choice of words. If people die because of him, it's not that he'll be doing it with his own hands so much as his actions. But he'll do it just the same."

"Gideon—"

"I'm getting there, I promise. When he first rented his place in Constancy last fall, he was always looking to make a sale—just like now. Once he'd found a place to rent, he paraded around a lot of goods we don't see much of, one of which is an herb—bitterroot—that grows on the southernmost coast of Adoria. It makes a pretty powerful medicine that can treat a lot of things—and for some illnesses, it's the only thing capable of working. It's vital to have on hand in the winter. There've been plagues in Adoria that can wipe out a whole town in the span of a week."

"What happened?" I asked, my voice coming out as a croak. I didn't like hearing about damage caused by a shortage of medicine. It hit too close to home, dredging up memories of how hard it had been getting the medicine Merry needed to treat her cough.

"Jacob had a supply of bitterroot in his inventory and made a deal to hold on to it for the winter in case we needed it. We would be the only ones allowed to buy it. But then . . ." Gideon stared into the shadows, his thoughts lost in the past. "But then, the Icori offered him a huge sum of gold if he'd sell it to them—and he did. He broke his agreement with us because a better deal came along. Now, we have no protection. We've been lucky so far this winter, but if any plague or fever strikes . . . well, we'll just have to pray."

"Can't you get more from someone else?"

"Not easily. We have to import it from the southern colonies, and even there, it only grows in late spring and early summer. It's scarcest this time of year, and if you even can find it, sellers mark it up dearly."

A sickening feeling twisted my stomach at the continuing similarities to my own life. My family had frequently felt the sting of selfish apothecaries inflating the price of Merry's medicine. The thought of that happening on a larger scale, to a whole town, was appalling.

Recalling some of the abominable practices I'd seen, I asked, "Did he try to coerce you into paying more than the Icori? Like, start a bidding war?"

"No. He just absconded with it one night."

"Seems like someone who's so proud of his negotiating skills—and hungry for gold—would have pushed his advantage."

"Maybe the Icori offer was just too generous to pass. He was still getting gold from them long after it happened."

Jago had told me himself he was a businessman, but I hadn't really grasped the full extent of his drive for profit. That joking exterior hid a nature far more calculating and ruthless than I could have imagined. "Did the council do anything?"

"It was still technically his, even though he'd 'promised' it to us. So, he was punished for deception, not theft, and had to pay a fine for the breach of sale. That's all that could be done, short of banishing him from town. But he sells enough other critical things that the council grudgingly agreed to let him stay on." Gideon scooted forward and rested one of his hands on mine as he peered anxiously into my face. "Are you okay? You look so upset."

"I'm not. I mean, yes, I am. Who wouldn't be? I've seen what happens when— Well, anyway. It's just an awful thing he did. My first impression of him wasn't so great, but after he helped me in the storm, I figured I should give him more credit."

"And maybe you should—a little. I mean, I don't think he's an evil man. I don't think he wants people to suffer—he's probably more inclined to help others, just like he did tonight. But I also don't think he can look beyond his own goals enough to consider the consequences of his actions to others." Gideon's eyes glittered in the firelight as he deliberated. At last, he proclaimed, "When it comes down to it, I believe Jacob Robinson sold our medicine out of greed for himself, not maliciousness for others."

"That's not going to matter to someone who dies of a plague," I snapped. "That's not going to matter to some mother whose child . . ."

When I choked on the words, Gideon squeezed my hand tighter. "You're right, of course. But it matters to Uros and the angels. At the end of days, a crime born of petty selfishness will be judged less harshly than one born of deliberate menace."

I slipped my hand away and stood up. "Then they're more forgiving than I am."

The snowstorm was gone by morning—and Jago with it.

"He left just before you came downstairs," Winnifred told us as she brought biscuits to the table. It was her morning to help with breakfast. "Shoveled the whole area between the barn and house. He must have been up since dawn to do it."

I had mixed feelings about having missed Jago, particularly since I now had mixed feelings about Jago, period.

"A nice gesture, but it's probably just as well he's gone." Samuel walked over to a frosty window and rubbed his fingers against it. "Can't imagine having him underfoot if the storm had lasted longer."

Gideon entered and caught that last bit. "It may be over, but we're still snowed in until the roads are cleared. I'll start shoveling after breakfast."

"Sounds like today will be an excellent time for a thorough house-cleaning," declared Dinah. "I've already made some lists of how we'll divide up the work."

The other Glittering Court girls and I exchanged dismayed glances as we sat at the table. After the prayer, Gideon said in an overly casual voice, "Dinah, if it's not too much trouble, would you mind adjusting Tamsin's workload to free her up for part of the afternoon? I have a number of sermon drafts that need recopying. I've marked them up with so many corrections that they're barely legible. Today would have been a good day for me to do it, but shoveling has to take priority now."

Dinah set down her fork. "Why, Gideon, if you needed this done, you should have just asked me. I would've been happy to do it for you."

"This household depends on you," he replied smoothly. "I wouldn't dream of taking you from your duties. You're too important. Besides, Tamsin's just come out of very rigorous schooling and can hopefully catch some of my spelling and grammar mistakes along the way."

"I should think so. She scored perfectly on all our composition and rhetoric exams," Damaris added unexpectedly. "She knows all about exposition and persuasion. There's probably no better assistant to help you write those sermons."

I looked at her in astonishment. Samuel swiftly said, "Copying a sermon is not the same as writing one. She most certainly wouldn't be doing the latter. But I see no harm in her cleaning up your drafts. Assuming Dinah can spare her."

Damaris piped in again, "I'll help with any extra jobs."

"Very well then." Dinah spoke with obvious reluctance, but the others' expectation was too great for her to go against. "But not until this afternoon."

Later, as Damaris and I scrubbed the larder floor, I demanded, "What was that all about? There being no better assistant than me?"

She flashed me a grin, much like the one she'd had when challenging the sailor to a knot contest. "Are you saying someone else *would* be better?"

"No, of course not. But I don't follow what you were doing."

"Just getting back at that bitch Dinah." Damaris spoke in a low voice. "She's mad for Gideon, you know."

"Is she?"

"Yes! If you weren't so busy doing other people's chores and surviving blizzards, you'd have noticed. I'm certain it's why she hasn't married yet. I found out that she'd been considering some proposals but stopped when Gideon moved in. My guess is she's holding out for him—for when he finishes his studies and becomes a senior minister. But from the way he looks at her—or doesn't look at her—she's going to keep waiting."

"Wow. You've taken a lot of time to think about this." I dipped my rag into our bucket of water and wrung it out. "And where do I fit in?"

Damaris sat back on her heels, eager for a reason to take a break. "Well, even you must have noticed how huffy she gets when he talks to us. I think she's jealous that we can all get caught up in stuff she doesn't know about, like life back in Osfro. And she gets extra put out because he talks to you the most."

"He does not."

"Oh, really? When's the last time he gave me paper or invited me to be his secretary?"

"He didn't specially seek me out for that! It was just something that came up when we were talking about his sermons the other day."

"Exactly—because you guys are always talking! Now, back to

last night. You should've seen the way he went on and on about you during the storm. I thought he was going to defy Samuel and head out after you! And oh, Dinah . . . she didn't like that at all. I'm pretty sure the only thing that made her more upset than him being worried about you was when you showed back up alive."

I rolled my eyes and returned to scrubbing. "Dinah may not like me, but even she doesn't want me dead."

"I don't think she does either . . . unless she starts worrying that all that bonding time of yours poses an actual threat to her plans."

"Then thanks for endangering my life by going out of your way to get me more bonding time with him."

She dunked her rag in the water with a flourish, splattering both of us. "Had to be done. I mean, I hope your life really isn't at risk, but if it is, then take comfort in knowing it's for the noble cause of getting her back for making me copy that damned book all night."

"Oh, well, if it's noble, then sure, that's fine. And here I was worried you were doing something petty, like trying to off me to reduce the competition in Cape Triumph."

"I never thought of that," she said wonderingly, lifting her eyes from the bucket. "You see, that's why you're on top, Tamsin. You come up with ideas the rest of us don't."

I almost choked on my laugh. "Well, if you like that, here's a few more gems for you. First . . ." I glanced behind us. "Don't get caught calling A Testament of Angels a 'damned book' around here. Second— and I seriously mean this—don't provoke her. Or any of them."

Damaris's expression sobered. "She deserved it for taking your paper."

I almost felt like crying, thinking of the loss of those letters. It was like another wall had been slammed between Merry and me. "It's just paper, Damaris. We need to stay on these people's good side."

She gave a snort of amusement and returned to scrubbing with a wry smile. "That's assuming we were ever on their good side to begin with."

✌

After a small lunch, I settled down by the fire with stacks of Gideon's papers, unsure what to expect from sermons written for the Heirs of Uros. They turned out to be more interesting than I'd imagined, and I quickly understood the problems Gideon had been trying to explain. His message in each one—be it honesty, faith, or hard work—eventually came through, but he meandered around before getting to it. Some lines shone with his passion for the topic; others were stilted and clumsy.

I cleaned it all up as I wrote out the new copies, making better word choices, cutting the mundane, and rephrasing what need clarifying or just a little more polishing. The work was engrossing, and I barely noticed the time going by until Gideon came inside for a break two hours later. His face was flushed from the cold, and melting snow sparkled in his hair. I urged him to a chair and then scurried to bring him hot tea from the kitchen.

He brought the cup to his lips, pausing just to savor the warmth. "Thank you."

"You're frozen through!" I exclaimed. "I wish I could grab a shovel and help you out."

"I couldn't allow that. Not after you were almost swept away in a blizzard last night. It'd be cruel to make you shovel what very nearly trapped you."

"Actually, I'd feel like I was getting back at it. Its attempts to block our roads are no match for me."

He laughed and set the tea down. "I doubt many things are. My goodness. Have you done all that already?"

I followed his gaze to the stack of corrected sermons. "I hope it's been helpful. You'll probably read them and regret ever getting me involved."

He took the top page and skimmed it, his misty blue eyes widening. "Wow."

"Eh, is that good or bad?"

"It's . . ." His silence left me uncertain until he looked up with a big smile. "It's amazing. Look—right here. I spent paragraphs trying to explain this, and you did it in just a few sentences. I could never do anything like this."

"You were the one who *did* do it. I just tightened it up and moved things around."

He picked up another page. "Okay, I did this one. 'Fear can bind you up and block off parts of your life. You need to recognize that and not let fear inhibit the way you want to live.' And you did this: 'Fear is a cage, and we are our own jailers.'"

"I might have gotten carried away with the metaphors," I admitted.

"No, it's great. It's like you understood what was in my head and translated it." Happiness lit him from within, making him look as angelic as Jago had hinted. But then, that glow dimmed. "I can't use this. It isn't right. Maybe most of it is my intent, but you've had enough of a hand in it that we've blurred domains. Has anyone explained those to you?"

"I've heard the term here but didn't realize it was something special."

Gideon glanced around, ascertaining we were alone. "Domains are how we divide our responsibilities—the work, duty, and crafts of everyday life. Some jobs anyone can do. Some are only for women. Some for men."

A memory of our first night here flashed through my mind. "Is that why the doctors here are women?"

"Yes," he said, delighted at my deduction. "Healing is a woman's domain. So are weaving and dyeing. But tanning and cobbling are men's."

"And let me guess. Writing is a man's domain?"

"No. In fact, the teaching of essential worldly education—writing and arithmetic, for example—is a female domain. Whereas spiritual education . . ." He gestured grandly toward himself. ". . . is a male domain. That's why I told you not to say anything about this plan. It could be misinterpreted."

I picked up one of my corrected pages. "Because I can help you improve your craft so long as I'm not actually doing it."

"Exactly."

"That's ridiculous—er, sorry," I added quickly. Gideon was so personable that I became too comfortable around him sometimes, forgetting his role as a minister in Constancy. "But if someone gets hurt, and you're the only one around, you can't help? Or if you do, are *you* going to have to stay up all night copying out scripture?"

The angelic smile took a rueful twist. "When you put it like that, it *does* sound ridiculous. Yes, I could help—there are always allowances for special circumstances. But in general? We follow the domains in everything we do." He glanced longingly at the pages.

"In a home like this, discipline and minor infractions fall to the lady of the house to manage—Samuel and I have no say. Something bigger—say, if one of you tried to recruit followers to a new god— would threaten the larger spiritual well-being of the town. That's a male domain and would fall to Samuel and me."

"You said teaching grammar and writing is okay for a woman, right? Then think of me as being your instructor. All my proofing and editing are just teaching aids, showing you ways to improve your craft. And you can read over what I did to make sure I really didn't change any of your meaning. If so, change it back."

"That's a bending of the rules worthy of Jacob Robinson," Gideon said with a chuckle. "But I suppose it's okay if you aren't actually inserting new or radical messages . . ." His eyes drifted again to the sermons, and I found his moral conflict oddly endearing. Most people wouldn't have thought twice about accepting work that would boost their image. "But we still can't tell anyone just how much you helped," he said after long moments. "And that's what I hate—the dishonesty. Holding back secrets. Though I truly don't think any domains have been broken here . . . I just worry others might misread it."

"I can certainly understand why you'd worry about that."

Catching my tone, he stood up and patted my shoulder. "Stay strong, Tamsin. You're doing wonderfully here. Although . . . I have to ask, was there any reason you mentioned staying up all night to copy scripture? Were you just using it as a random example of punishment?"

I didn't answer immediately, but something in my expression or body language must have given me away.

"Tell me," he said gently.

I sighed. "Well, it started with the paper you gave me . . ."

He listened to me recount Damaris's story, his face remaining neutral. "I see," he said when I finished. "Well, I'm sure Dinah thought she was doing what was best for you girls." He sounded doubtful, though.

"Do *you* think it was best?"

"It's not my place to say. You're dependents in her household. Decisions about your well-being are in her domain. Here." He handed me some blank paper from the stack I'd been using. "To replace the last batch."

I started to reach for it and then felt angry on his behalf. "Dinah should give back what she took!"

"I'm not going to undermine her authority."

I scrutinized his mild expression, trying to discern the truth. "But you *do* think she was out of line."

"Do you want it or not?" He moved his hand to take the paper, but I was faster and snatched it away.

"Oh, I'll take it. But I do hate that you're wasting yours on me. Especially when I've got plenty in my luggage. This would be so much simpler if I could just get into it."

"I don't think it's a waste, and it's better that the cargo remain undisturbed. Aside from the council's decision about it, constantly getting in there and rifling for this and that would be a hassle."

Hoping for casualness, I asked, "Are the goods that hard to get to? I know exactly where the paper is in my trunk."

"Finding your trunk might be the difficult part. It's all spread out in different places."

"Wait—I didn't realize our things weren't all being stored together. I hope none of it gets misplaced."

"No, no. It's quite secure, and the council has a list of how many boxes and trunks are being kept where. Some's in the meetinghouse, some in the school . . . I can't recall the rest. But they're all safe places." After collecting the rest of the pages, he walked over to the mantel and surveyed the books atop it. He plucked out a slim volume and handed it to me. "This is my own copy of *The Ruvan Followers*. It's where a lot of our ideas about the domains came from. Take a look at it in your free time."

"Free time?" I could barely say it with a straight face, and as if to emphasize how far-fetched that notion was, Dinah suddenly entered.

She put her hands on her hips. "Tamsin, I could really use your help washing some bedding. You've spent quite enough time lounging around out here—and worse, you're distracting poor Gideon. I knew this wouldn't end well. Gideon, if she hasn't finished copying, I'll do it for you."

Gideon gave her a beatific smile, and it almost knocked her over. Damaris was right. "No need, Dinah. Tamsin's done plenty. She's done more than I imagined." He stood up and looked me over, and the spark in his eyes seemed to come from more than just his new and improved sermons. "*She's* more than I imagined."

CHAPTER 13

BY THE END OF THAT SNOWBOUND DAY, I WAS MORE exhausted than if I'd done my usual laundry regimen. But oh, that house sparkled. Dinah had had us scrub and polish every corner of it. When I dragged myself up for bedtime, the other girls immediately noticed the new paper.

"How'd you get that?" asked Winnifred.

I set it and the book down. "Gideon gave it to me when he heard what Dinah did."

Damaris winked. "Nice work. Remember, it's for the greater good."

"He gave you a book too?" Vanessa perked up. "What kind?"

"What kind do you think, around here?" I held up *The Ruvan Followers*. "It's not a book of sonnets! And he lent it to me."

I didn't need my friends to warn me about protecting the paper. I slid it under my mattress, keeping one piece out for that night's letter. When I finished it, I held it a moment, wondering when it and the others I'd been accumulating would ever get out of this town. Who could say? I didn't even know when I'd get out.

I hid the letter with the paper and used my last bit of free time to read Gideon's book in bed. While it did lay out some of the domains, the sections he'd underlined tended to be about helping others and improving one's character. It was like peeking into his mind, which seemed to imagine a purer way of life that didn't require so much of the Heirs' strictness. *He's wasting his time here,* I thought. *We all are.*

❧

"We won't be going to church today."

Samuel's somber face was even more somber than usual as he delivered that greeting the next morning. Gideon, also subdued, explained, "We didn't quite finish clearing the road yesterday. And then we got a little more snow last night. Nothing like that storm—but enough to be a nuisance. The carriage might get stuck."

He looked so crestfallen, I couldn't stop myself from blurting out: "Could we walk? I don't mind." Vanessa gave me a horrified look.

"I considered it," said Samuel. "But some places still have more than a foot of snow. It'd make for hard travel—especially in your dresses. So. Uros's will is what it is. We'll have a devotional day at home."

Winnifred peered at the empty kitchen table. "When's breakfast?"

"No breakfast on holy days," said Dinah. "We don't eat until midday."

As that depressing thought settled over us, the faint jingle of bells suddenly sounded from outside. The other girls looked puzzled, but I knew immediately what it was. Samuel moved swiftly to the door, and we scurried in his wake. He flung the door open, just as Jago pulled his sleigh up in front of the house.

"Good morning, good sirs and misses." Jago bowed with a flourish before hopping to the ground. "I thought you might be stranded, so I came to help you get to church today."

Stunned silence fell. At last, I asked, "For how much?"

He grinned. "This one's on me."

Samuel's shocked expression slowly transformed to one of wonder. "Why, Jacob, you have no idea how thrilled I am to hear you'll finally be attending services. Though I don't think it's appropriate to wear that flamboyant scarf into church. We focus on the spiritual, not the material."

"Oh, yes, I'm aware of that, but I'm afraid I'm not actually going *into* the church. Just taking you since I know how important it is to you. I'll find other ways to amuse myself while you're busy."

Samuel's brow furrowed, but Gideon preempted any protest. "As you said, Samuel, Uros's will is what it is, and it looks like it has provided for us."

We quickly fetched our coats and cloaks. Samuel and Dinah sat in the front seat with Jago while the rest of us piled into the hold in the back, which could have held a few more people. Then we were off to town, the sleigh nimbly flying over the snow. The only thing that slowed us was a fallen limb across the road, but it was soon moved.

"You've done two good deeds, Jacob, one upon the other," Samuel remarked when we arrived. He paused to help Dinah down. "It's given me hope that something might be changing within you, that the truth might be speaking to you after all. Are you sure you won't join us?"

Jago politely declined again and held out his hand to the rest of us girls. Vanessa, Winnifred, and Damaris rewarded him with pretty thanks and well-honed Glittering Court smiles as they alighted. When it was my turn, I whispered, "What are you playing at?"

"What do you mean?"

I held back as the others shuffled into the building. "You know what. You don't do anything out of pure altruism."

"Except that time I saved you from wandering off in a blizzard. And if you must know, you're also the reason I came by today."

"Whatever for?" I stroked the mane of one of his horses, hoping it would look like they'd been the distraction. They were a lovely team— silvery gray with black manes and tails.

"I've been thinking about your sad, sad situation. And I decided to help."

I spun around. "You'll sell the seats?"

"No, of course not. But I might be able to get you someone else's space."

"Whose?"

"There's a trapper who lives near the Icori border. They like him, he's traded with them, and he's sending some furs down with the expedition. We're old friends—I could probably talk him into postponing his shipment. I'm pretty good at deal making, you know. But it'd cost you."

"Of course it would." Knowing what I knew about him now, I wasn't surprised. "How much do you want?"

"Not me. I'm doing this out of the kindness of my heart. But my guess is it'll run what you and I were discussing—about a hundred gold or so. Up front."

"That's a lot of money."

"Aren't you sitting on all sorts of wondrous objects?"

"Not literally. It's all locked away." No one stood near us, but I dropped my voice. "I don't suppose . . . you'd want to break into the meetinghouse for me, would you?"

He scoffed. "*With* you? Yes. For you? No. I'm barely tolerated as it is around here. If they caught me breaking in alone, there's no telling what they'd do."

"Are you saying it'd be better if you were caught with me?"

"Well, then I could claim ignorance and say you'd asked me to help and that I did it unwittingly. And if that doesn't work, I'll at least have company in the stocks." I couldn't acknowledge anything so ridiculous, so I turned toward the church. "Wait, Tamsin."

"What?" I asked warily.

Jago leaned close to me, like he was adjusting the horse's bridle. "If the weather's clear, they'll let you go outside and get some air during the luncheon. I'll wait behind the meetinghouse."

Before I could question that incredible statement, Dinah ordered me into the church. Jago climbed into the sleigh with a wink, and I hurried to Dinah, rattling off excuses about admiring the lovely horses.

The Coles, as a minister's family, had a designated pew near the front of the congregation, but my companions and I were sent to the back rows. I didn't mind this at all, as it gave us a reprieve from Dinah's watchful eye. Several other Glittering Court girls had made it through the snow and sat nearby, so we had a small reunion until we were shushed when the service began.

It opened with announcements and short prayers, and my mind wandered, wondering if Jago had been serious about helping me. I believed he was. What I didn't know was why. I set those musings aside when Gideon took the podium. His sermon lasted almost a full hour—and it was one of the ones I'd revised for him. As strange as I found the Heirs, it was a thrill to have my words delivered to such a large crowd. And he delivered them well. I'd seen him falter and stammer when he was unsure of himself, but when he was confident in his message, he was a commanding force. The warmth and genuineness that infused his everyday actions amplified his words and made others want to listen. And his face alone made some of them want to listen too—if my companions' dreamy expressions were any indication.

Seeing the uplifting effect his closing had on the congregation made me swell with pride—for him and, yes, me. The program that followed was far less inspiring: a mix of community business, small prayers, and lectures. It was a relief when recess was called for the luncheon, but it left me with the sudden decision of what to do about Jago. The congregation rose and stretched their legs, some going to help set up the food and others walking outside.

"Thank goodness," said Damaris, rubbing her back. "I thought I'd faint with hunger."

My eyes fell longingly on the food table, but from what I could gather about the process, we wouldn't be among the first served. Quickly, I refastened my cloak. "Cover for me. If anyone asks where I am, say I went out to walk to get some air until we could eat."

Three astonished faces stared at me. "Um, what else would you be doing?" asked Vanessa.

"Just help me," I hissed, squeezing between the benches. "I'll explain later. Maybe."

After the stuffiness of the packed church, the frigid cold hit me with a jolt, sharpening my thoughts and making me reconsider my choice. Staying in the church was warmer and wiser. As I wavered at the building's threshold, a group of small children scampered past, their laughter stirring the old ache in my heart.

Could I pass up any chance to get to Merry faster? I plunged forward, trying to look as casual as the others who mingled and walked about the square. No one paid me especial attention, and I easily slipped unnoticed from the open area to a more private section behind the church's neighboring buildings.

Constancy's meetinghouse, I'd learned, was a recent addition. Early settlers had used the church for all gatherings, and it wasn't until the town had flourished more that a proper hall had been commissioned. By then, the square was ringed with other businesses, and so the meetinghouse was being built two blocks away, some of its timber still only sealed and not painted.

A few snowflakes drifted by, and I squinted upward, panicked. But the clouds that stretched overhead were white, only lightly tinged with gray. There was no sign of the dark, billowing masses that had marched across the sky during the blizzard. Exhaling, I continued on and didn't see a soul until I rounded the back corner of the meetinghouse. There, Jago waited for me, his lanky form leaning near a window.

"I didn't think you'd come," he said.

"I didn't think you would either. I thought you might be tricking me."

"Not about breaking the law."

"I've heard you break the law quite a bit."

"Have you?" He straightened up and looked supremely pleased. "I don't break it so much as bend it."

I studied the imposing building. "Yes, I heard that too. Does that mean you can get us in without doing anything illegal?"

"Eh, not so much." He shoved his hands in his coat's pockets and followed my gaze. "For all their talk about focusing on character and morals, they're not a very trusting lot. These windows are locked from the inside, and breaking the glass out would be noisy."

"So how do we get in?"

With great drama, Jago pulled a key ring from his pocket. "Through the door."

"You have a key? Why didn't you just mention that earlier?"

"Well, I didn't have it then." After trying a few keys in the small back door, he finally found one that let us inside. "One of the councilmen was so moved by my generosity in getting you all to town today that he kindly lent me use of his stables and kitchen while I waited. And it just so happens he owns one of the town's master keys."

"And he kindly lent it to you?"

"I found it after a little exploration of the rest of his house."

"Did he kindly lend you use of the rest of the house?"

"He didn't prohibit it," Jago said slyly. "And of course I'm bringing this back. No harm done."

Considering I'd solicited his services to sneak in here, I supposed I couldn't judge.

Much of the meetinghouse's interior still remained unfinished. The walls hadn't been sanded, and rushes covered the floor. A long table sat on a dais at one end, and partially constructed shelves occupied a back wall. And near those shelves, I spotted a pile of goods from the *Gray Gull*.

I hurried forward, relieved to find such a big haul. I'd been half afraid that the cargo would be so thinly spread out around town that only a few things would be stored here. Better still, none of the crates and trunks before me appeared to belong to the crew or other passengers. They were all either Jasper's or one of the Glittering Court girls'. The few unlocked trunks contained personal possessions of no use to me. The crates of trade goods were nailed shut, but Jago and I managed to get a few open using tools from the shelving construction.

Jago lifted a pink silk dress up to the light. "Looks like you can replace the one you gave away."

"Six, Jago. Just when I was starting to give you the benefit of the doubt. I can't wear pink with my hair."

"You can wear anything." He held the dress beside my face. "And what's this about starting to give me the benefit of the doubt? I thought we had an understanding."

I pushed the dress away and said, "Want to take it to your trapper friend?"

Jago studied me a moment, well aware I'd dodged his question. "Tempting, but no." He folded the dress up with more care than I would have expected and set it back down. "Louis is like me—won't want to deal with large objects that might take time to sell. Jewelry's still best. It's small and easy to convert."

"We should have plenty of that." I searched through the next crate and found it filled with books. "Wow. I had no idea Jasper was selling these."

"It's smart. They're not rare in Adoria but not nearly as common as they are in Osfrid either. Lots of folks would love to build up their libraries."

I lifted up a leather-clad novel I'd heard of but never read. It was a popular romantic adventure, and the book just fit in one of my cloak's inner pockets.

"Are you stealing that?" asked Jago in mock horror.

"Borrowing it for Vanessa."

"I hope that lot appreciates what a good friend you are. What's that look for? Are you laughing?"

I was. After collecting myself, I explained, "I . . . it's just . . . it's funny, that's all. There was a time—not even that long ago—that I think they would have been shocked to hear me called their friend. And I'd have felt the same about them. But yes . . . yes. We've become friends."

"Did that happen before or after you started looking out for them?"

That one gave me pause too. "After, I suppose."

"And you helped them because . . . ?"

"Not everyone needs an ulterior motive," I said sharply.

"Of course not. I'm just trying to understand how you think, why you'd step up for people who—if I'm reading you right—used to not like you."

I pulled off the next lid. "I stepped up for them because someone had to."

This crate held more dresses, but underneath them was a trove of accessories—including a jewelry box. We broke the padlock and then knelt beside each other as we spread the box's contents over the floor. He regarded it all with a practiced eye and began separating pieces out.

"This is costume, so is this. This one's silver, but the gems are glass. That's genuine. This one's costume . . ."

I knew the jewelry we'd wear out in Cape Triumph was real, but I also knew most of it was already safely there, used from year to year. New additions to the collection that were especially valuable traveled in Jasper's own luggage. This cache must be what he was selling, and I hoped there were enough authentic items to make up Jago's price.

"This," he said, after much shuffling and mumbling. "This would do it."

The set he waved to contained five necklaces, two bracelets, and four rings—all gold with differing gems. "That's worth a hundred gold?"

"A little over. To cover differences in trade and exchange."

"Done," I said.

Jago regarded me with amusement. "No hesitation, huh?"

"It's a small price to get us all back quickly." I frowned. "Assuming the Icori honor Orla's offer. What if they don't?"

"I'll need to confirm it all with her, but if that's what she said she'd do, then she'll do it. She's a stickler for honesty and integrity." He spoke with an admiration that seemed contradictory, given his own dubious morals. "Which, I admit, is part of why I'm even doing this."

"What do you mean?"

"Orla doesn't much like Osfridians—can't say I blame her, given her experience." Carefully, he began placing the rejected jewelry back in its box. "And yet, she thought well enough of you to suggest this."

"She must think well of you too, to sell you passage in the first place."

"Believe it or not, most people outside of Constancy think well of me. Some even like me. I've done a lot of traveling, a lot of trading. You get more done by making friends, not enemies." He scooped up the remaining jewelry and held out a necklace adorned with emeralds. "What about this? Green would look good on you."

"Green looks *great* on me, but I think the Coles might have a few things to say about me wearing that around the house. Or anywhere in Constancy. I honestly can't believe no one's taken that scarf away from you yet."

"No law broken in wearing it—it's just frowned upon." He straightened the last crate and strolled to the back door with me. "They think I wear it because I'm vain."

"Are you?"

"I wear it because it's warm. And yeah . . . maybe I do like the flair a little. Everything I had growing up was a hand-me-down—so faded, you couldn't tell what their original color used to be."

"Same here," I said. "We got the neighbors' handoffs, mended them for me, and then patched them up again for my sister."

"Lucky you, being the oldest. I had three other brothers who got dibs on clothes before me. They were practically threads by the time I got them, but that's how it is when money's tight." He self-consciously touched the red fabric at his neck. "Money's still tight, but I couldn't pass this up. It proves something to the world. Plus, I got a good deal. Why, Tamsin . . . what's this? Are you smiling at me?"

"I just understand it, that's all."

He smiled too. It had a different quality than Gideon's. Gideon's was more polished and practiced. It made you feel good because of its beauty. Jago's made you feel good because you wanted to keep smiling back.

"But," he said, "you still don't trust me."

"Of course not. I barely know you."

With the goods repacked, we stood up and walked to the door. "Well, Orla recommended me, didn't she?"

"Yes, but I don't really know her either. Can I trust her? Can I trust the Icori? Sometimes I can't even believe this plan is contingent on traveling with Icori! I'm so anxious to get to Cape Triumph that it's the least of my worries. But if you'd suggested one month ago that I go on a river trip with Icori, I'd have thought you were crazy."

It all came out in a burst, but Jago pondered it very seriously. "Don't believe the propaganda. Most Icori are trying to do what's right and get along in the world, just like everyone else. Can you trust every Icori? No. No more than you can trust every Osfridian. But I'm telling you, though, if it's in Orla's power, she'll see it through. She's a good friend to have."

"I'm glad, but it sounds like you're saying I should trust her because you trust her. And I should trust you because she trusts you and . . . well. You see where the logic starts to break down."

"And yet here you are."

I shrugged and stepped aside so that he could open the door. "Here I am. Because you're pretty much the only help I've got right now."

Jago turned the knob and flashed me one of those smiles. "Trust me, I'm the only help you need."

CHAPTER 14

I MADE IT BACK TO THE CHURCH IN TIME FOR THE SECOND half of services, and no one aside from the Glittering Court girls had noticed my absence. The only punishment I faced was self-inflicted: I'd missed lunch. By the time we piled back into Jago's sleigh, I was dizzy with hunger.

He drove us home, declining Samuel's stiff invitation for supper. Again, Jago gallantly helped each of us down. Clasping my hand, he examined both sides of it. "If you're worried about your hands, you should wear your mittens more often."

"I lost them." I watched Dinah's back as she entered the house. "But I'll let my fingers freeze off before I let her know. She'll have me writing about negligence using my own blood."

"Well, let's hope it doesn't come to either one of those ends." He checked the horses' bridles and then hopped back up to his seat. "I'm going to head out early tomorrow to see Louis."

"How long will that all take?"

"Depends if I make any stops. But I'll be back within the week either way."

The thought of his absence from town made me feel oddly alone. We had too few allies, and despite Jago's quirks, it was comforting to have another outsider around.

"What a lovely service," Dinah told Gideon at supper that night. "I don't think I've ever heard Uros's truth put so eloquently. 'Fear is a cage, and we are our own jailers.' I can't get those words out of my head."

"Me either," I chimed in. Gideon wouldn't look at me, but a smile flickered over his face.

"It was an excellent message," Samuel agreed. "Ned and Lowell spoke to me about it afterward, remarking on your progress. Next time, you need to encourage people to succeed—but also make them understand the dire consequences of not succeeding."

When I retired for bed later, my friends immediately clustered around me and demanded to know where I'd disappeared to.

"I can't tell you," I said, eliciting groans. "It's not all settled, and even though I trust you, I can't risk it accidentally getting out yet."

Vanessa flounced on her bed with a pout. "Can't you tell us anything?"

I paused in unbuttoning my overdress. "Well, I brought you a present. It's in my cloak."

Vanessa dove for it and pulled the novel out. "I've been dying to read this! Where did you get it?"

"You're better off not knowing."

"I hope you'll share that," Damaris said, leaning over Vanessa's shoulder.

"Of course. After I finish it." Vanessa clutched the book to her chest. Beaming, she told me: "Tamsin, you have no idea how glad I am that you get things done."

Although no new snow fell overnight, the roads still weren't fully cleared the next morning. A neighbor drove us to town in his sleigh, and I found myself looking forward to the day, despite its labor. The last two days had been stifling, and I was glad to have the freedom of my own schedule again.

After the neighbor delivered us to the town's square, Gideon offered to walk with me to Chester's. "You really helped me out with that sermon."

"You did all the work. That delivery was incredible."

"Because I had the right words. You really know how to get through to people. A gift like that . . ." He straightened his hat and gazed at the morning activity in the square. "Well, it's something you should do on a regular basis."

"Somehow, I don't think I'll have many chances to do it in Cape Triumph."

"You could do it if you stayed here." His eyes turned downward as he kicked at the snow. "Is there any reason—any person—that might persuade you to accept this way of life?"

"What? No. Well, maybe if the angels themselves came down and—" The sight of his serious mien drew me up short.

"I'm sorry," he said quickly. "I shouldn't have—"

"No, I'm sorry, I—"

"It was out of line—"

"It was—"

We both stopped trying to talk over each other, falling silent at the same time. Then our eyes met, and we started laughing. "It must sound crazy to you," he said. "We've known each other for, what, just over a week? But I'm telling you, these moments with you have been some of the happiest in my life."

I watched admiringly as he ran a hand through his hair, the pale winter sunlight turning it to burnished gold. I couldn't help a pang of wistfulness. He *was* terribly good-looking. And kind.

"Gideon, I don't know what to say. I've loved spending time with you too. I think you're the only bright spot in this town."

He vehemently shook his head. "No, there's more to it than you realize. I swear. If you could just give it a try and really open yourself up to it . . . I think you'd see what I see. I know the dazzle of Cape Triumph and its wealth are alluring, but it's all a pretense. You have a radiant spirit, Tamsin. Do you really want to cover that up by being around others who don't?"

A radiant spirit. No man had ever said such a thing to me, not even Harry, back in the days when every word out of his mouth had been worthy of a love poem.

"It means so much that you think of me that way. Not many have," I added, a catch in my voice. "And I'll be honest—I don't think many people around here share that opinion."

"That's just because you've been living with the Coles. If you and I were—" He cleared his throat, red flooding his cheeks. "If you were my wife, running your own household, things would be a lot different. And you saw how powerful that sermon was! With your help, I could really get through to people. We could inspire them instead of scaring them."

"I'd love to see that," I said sincerely. "And if things were simple for me . . . well, who could say? But they're not. I'm committed to an expensive marriage contract and have a lot of complicated things in my life to look after. Do you understand what I'm saying?"

"I do." Though he was disappointed, his eyes glowed with an inner light. "But knowing you think well of me, even a little, makes me happy."

"I think well of you a lot."

We stood like that a few more moments, wrapped in a warm sort of contentment. "I suppose I shouldn't keep you," he said at last. "We'll talk more later?"

"Of course."

His unexpected proposal left me with a flood of conflicting emotions as I walked to Chester's. Who could have seen that coming? Damaris would probably claim she had, I thought wryly. I felt guilty for refusing him and even guiltier that I wasn't head over heels in love with him—not that I expected to be with anyone I married. I did care about him, though. Gideon was an amazing person, and I'd be lucky to find a man half as good and kind. If he'd spoken to me like that in a Cape Triumph ballroom, his pockets full of gold for Jasper, I'd have probably said yes in an instant.

I was so distracted that I didn't even notice the small cloth bundle on Chester's kitchen table until after I'd made my first round of laundry pickups. Sometimes, if he had leftovers, Chester would leave me a biscuit or piece of cheese. Touched by his thoughtfulness, I unwrapped the cloth and found . . .

. . . mittens.

I tried them on wonderingly, trying to identify their unbelievably soft, black material. Cashmere? Angora? How could it feel like silk and still be so warm? Along their cuffs, tiny silver beads had been stitched with exquisite care, like a sprinkle of stars across the night sky. But when I put my arms down, my dress's sleeves settled over the cuffs, concealing that taboo glamour.

"Oh, Jago," I murmured, "I suppose you think you're being clever." Maybe he was. Anyone glancing at me wouldn't think I wore anything but a respectable pair of Grashond-approved mittens. Unable to help a smile, I tucked them into a cloak pocket, unsure if I'd risk wearing them. Even if I didn't, it made my steps a little quicker and my heart a little lighter, knowing I was carrying a secret bit of sparkle with me.

A few days later, an overnight storm dropped enough snow on the roads to snarl travel again, reminding me again that winter still had us in its grasp. We were dreading an arduous walk to town that morning when, luckily, a sleigh-owning neighbor came by and offered a ride. As we gathered our things, Dinah suddenly came thundering down the kitchen stairs and roared, *"What is this?"*

Samuel, reading papers in the sitting room, leapt to his feet. "Dinah Cole! Control your volume."

Dinah rushed up to him, her eyes blazing with fervid outrage. "Look! Look what I found!" She threw something to the floor. It hit with a loud thump, and I clamped a hand over my mouth to hide a gasp. It was the pilfered novel.

Samuel picked it up, leafed through the pages, and then slowly raised his eyes. Whereas Dinah had reacted without restraint, he spoke with a chilling, more frightening control. "Where did this monstrosity come from?"

Dinah pointed up. "It was in the attic. I found it when I went up to retrieve Gideon's book."

I had no chance to feel affronted at Dinah borrowing my borrowed book, because the horror of what else had happened was too overwhelming. Vanessa was supposed to hide the novel before going to sleep, and she must have forgotten last night. And I'd forgotten to check. Now, standing beside me, her face was so ashen, I thought she might faint.

By then, the racket had brought Gideon out of his room. Samuel strode over to my friends and me, holding up the book. "Whose is this?" he asked in that impossibly emotionless way.

I wet my lips, ready to speak, but Vanessa had shaken off her shock. "Mine, sir."

Incredulous, I began, "No, it's—"

"It's mine," she said more loudly, shooting me a glare. "I wanted something to read."

Samuel gestured toward the mantel, with its multiple copies of scripture. "There are plenty of things to read."

"I just wanted something different to read."

"Vanessa—" I tried.

"Quiet, Tamsin." This time it was Samuel who cut me off. "Those books are the only things you need to read. Trash like *this* is prohibited."

Vanessa's collected countenance faltered. "Did I break the law?"

The dam on his anger burst. "You broke a moral prescript! You brought wickedness into this household!" Samuel spun around and hurled the book into the fireplace.

Aghast, I made it halfway across the room before Gideon caught hold of my arm. "Tamsin, let it go."

My chest ached as I watched the burning pages. I felt like crying. "What a waste."

"Yes," said Samuel. "A waste of paper and leather. A waste of time. A waste of your thoughts. Novels like that encourage recklessness and abandonment of principles. Now. Tell me where it came from."

Vanessa didn't know, of course, but she answered promptly: "I found it."

"Found it?" scoffed Dinah. "You don't find a book like that lying around here!"

Her father held up a hand to silence her. "I'll handle this. Spiritual discipline is my domain. But Dinah *is* right. You didn't find that book here."

Vanessa lowered her gaze. "No, sir. I found it while I was walking home one day. There's a half-built barn, over on the north road? I got curious and went to explore it. I found this in a bag there."

"I have trouble believing that," he said. "I pray to the angels you aren't adding lying to your list of transgressions."

Gideon shifted, his eyes growing troubled. "That's the Erskin barn, isn't it? He had those men from South Joyce working on it last fall. The ones that ran off? They weren't really known for their exemplary behavior."

"Yes, but they also weren't really known for reading either." Samuel stared hard at Vanessa for a long moment. "If this really happened a few days ago, why didn't you bring the book to us immediately?"

When Vanessa didn't answer, Dinah was all too happy to. "Because she knew it was wrong. She knew we'd take it away."

Jerking my arm from Gideon's, I took a few steps forward. "None of this is true! It's my fault. I found the book."

"Yes, you found it." Vanessa looked up at me, her expression woeful but serene. "And you tried to tell me to do the right thing."

Samuel glanced between us. "What are you talking about?"

"Tamsin found the book in the attic and wanted to take it to you. I begged her to wait and said that I'd do it myself. But . . . I didn't. Now she's trying to take the blame."

"Vanessa!" I exclaimed.

Samuel's eyes bugged out, his contempt filling the room. "You lied to her, were deceitful to us, and purposely concealed corrupt literature. This cannot be treated lightly." He waved the rest of us toward the door. "Get to your jobs. I will not allow someone so degenerate to mingle with this good town's citizens—especially its children. Tamsin, take over her duties at the school today. The laundry can be delayed."

"But—"

Damaris practically dragged me out the front door as I tried to protest. "Vanessa made her choice, Tamsin."

"She's being punished for what I did!" I hissed.

"*You* didn't leave the book out."

"It's still my—"

"You'll just get both of you in trouble," Winnifred interjected. "And we need you to get us out of here. She stepped up to take the fall—let her."

The anger and indignation burning in my chest distracted me all day as I tried to do Vanessa's job: assisting at the town's school. Normally, that duty would have been a pleasure, but my mind kept straying to Vanessa as I walked around the classroom, tutoring the children as needed and making sure they stayed on task.

I missed spelling errors while proofreading compositions, and once, I showed a girl how to use addition for a subtraction problem. The schoolmistress gave me a disgusted look and muttered, "I hope Vanessa's back soon. Or that we at least get a better scholar to fill in."

When I arrived home in the evening, Vanessa wasn't there. We learned she'd been taken to town and was completing "solitary penitence" at one of the magistrates' houses.

"She'll spend three days alone, in a room with modest amenities," Samuel told us gravely. "She will speak to no one. Her only companions will be the holy books, and she will prepare a statement of atonement to be read aloud at this week's service."

We'd heard a few "statements of atonements" in church. One had been from a woman accused of too much pride because she'd boasted about how her family's cow was the most beautiful in Constancy. Another atoner had been a man who'd gotten hold of some contraband wine—probably from Jago—and accidentally walked into his neighbor's house, thinking it was his. The man had apparently gone right to the kitchen table, sat down, and demanded dinner.

My friends and I had tried not to giggle at the drama surrounding such silly-sounding confessions, but now, the thought of Vanessa having to stand in front of all of those judgmental faces and humiliate herself left us stricken. I longed to talk to Gideon, certain that he could help. This was a moral matter, not a domestic one. It was his domain. But he was swamped with work one of the other ministers had just given him, and all I could do was vent to Winnifred and Damaris at bedtime.

When Vanessa returned on the third day, she looked as though she'd been away for three months. Her face was wan, and dark hollows shadowed her eyes. She hadn't bathed or changed clothes, and she was thinner than when we'd first arrived in Constancy after a week of strict rations.

She tried to put on a cheerful front, assuring the rest of us—especially me—that her confinement hadn't been so bad. "It was a break from Dinah's nagging! I might as well have been on holiday."

But Vanessa couldn't leave the Cole house until her atonement in church later that week. I found out that in addition to her confession, she would have to arrive early and sit outside the square wearing a sign that said DECEIT. It wouldn't be removed until after her humiliating confession.

The more I heard about it, the more I seethed. The town that had been merely irritating before had become something sinister. We needed to get out.

After nearly a week with no word from Jago, I decided one afternoon to find out if he'd even made it home yet. Working in the school restricted the freedom I'd once had to wander town, and I had to wait until late afternoon before I could hurry off down the winding creek road. No one answered when I made it to his door, but as I turned to leave, a huge mountain of a man came ambling out of one of the barns. For a terrified moment, I thought some criminal was raiding

Jago's property, but the man casually held a rake against his shoulder and gave me a friendly wave.

Hesitantly, I approached. After a few fumbled communication attempts, I learned that the man was Belsian and worked for Jago. He spoke little Osfridian, and the Lorandian I knew, though similar to Belsian, wasn't enough for anything extensive.

"Arnaud," he said, tapping his chest. He had to be around seven feet tall. A grin split his bearded face.

"I'm Tamsin. Is Mister Robinson here?"

He pointed west. "Mister Robinson left away."

"Away from Constancy?"

"Yes. To visit."

"When will he be back? How many days?"

Arnaud shrugged, but I couldn't tell if he didn't know the answer or just didn't know what I'd said.

"When you see him, can you tell him Tamsin came by? Tell him I'm desperate to talk to him?"

"Yes, yes. I will tell him. 'Tamsin is desperate for you, Mister Robinson.'"

"Eh . . . that's not quite what I had in mind, but if it gets him to me, it'll do. Thank you, Arnaud."

"Goodbye, Miss Tamsin." He returned to his chores, whistling.

A bitter wind blew around me on the walk home, and I slipped on the black mittens. Even without a blizzard, it was always cold around here. Really, I felt as if I'd never properly warmed up since setting foot on the *Gray Gull*. Cape Triumph, rumored to be hot and balmy in the summer, seemed to be on the other side of the world from this dreary place. It was like Grashond was intent on wearing down both my body and mind.

"I hope you're as great a deal maker as you say, Jago," I murmured to myself, "because I don't know how much more of this I can take."

CHAPTER 15

THE FOLLOWING DAY, A LEAK IN THE SCHOOL'S ROOF forced us to relocate to the meetinghouse. Laborers were still finishing its interior, but the great building had more than enough room for us to work on our lessons. The cargo I'd raided with Jago had been pushed farther to the back and covered in tarps but otherwise appeared undisturbed. I couldn't help but note the irony of having it right in front of me after the caper we'd had to pull off during church.

The townsmen were installing shelves today, and we frequently found ourselves shouting to hear one another over the hammering. So, it wasn't that shocking when the schoolmistress developed a headache so severe that she had to go home early. It was midafternoon by that point, and she instructed me to just read aloud from one of the holy books.

I chose a particularly exciting passage I'd discovered in *The Ruvan Followers* about a woman who, full of devotion to Uros and the angels, successfully organized Ruva's defense against invaders. I'd never heard it before, and judging by my students' rapt faces, most of them hadn't either. And as the hammering continued to interrupt me, it became unlikely they'd ever hear it. Finally, frustrated, I shut the book and was on the verge of dismissing them early when Gideon walked in the front door.

"I passed Mistress Darcy as I was leaving the church." His expression grew warmer as he looked over the children. "I thought maybe you'd all like to go sledding for the end of your school day."

Excitement rippled through them, and they quickly gathered their things. "Is that allowed?" I asked in a low voice.

"What, playing? Having fun?"

I gave him a pointed look. "Well, it's not like I've seen very much of that in my time here."

He sobered a little. "Which is part of why I'm here. I wanted to talk to you. I know you haven't been very happy recently."

"How can I be?" I asked as we walked outside. Gideon paused briefly to pick up some bark sleds leaning against the building. "One of my friends is being humiliated unjustly."

The children, freed of schoolroom formality, scampered around us, some running ahead to a location apparently known to all. Gideon watched them fondly as he contemplated his answer. "Is it unjust?"

"She didn't do anything wrong!"

"She lied. She read a book she wasn't supposed to—and hid it because she knew she wasn't supposed to read it."

It took all my self-control to keep quiet about my role. "It's just a book."

"A book that glamorizes many of the things we try to avoid. Gambling, drinking, stealing, vanity, infidelity, insubordination."

"But it's not advocating them. Not exactly." The book's hero was a displaced prince who became the champion of an oppressed city and helped launch a rebellion. His ladylove was the wife of the city's ruling tyrant—a cruel man eventually killed in a swordfight with the dashing prince.

"Perhaps not," said Gideon. "But some might not see it that way. It could give them ideas and tempt them into trying something wayward."

We'd passed outside of Constancy's heart and now walked through a copse of snow-covered pines. "So you just get rid of anything that *might* make them think of doing something wrong? People don't need an example to fall into bad ways. They can do it on their own."

"Oh, I know. But there are some who never would have had dangerous ideas on their own. Surrounding ourselves in only the finest behavior prevents straying and shows people that it's possible to live in a righteous way."

He sounded so nice and reasonable, which made it hard to take my anger out on him. Also, he was dressed in a shade of gray today that brought out the blue in his eyes. It would *almost* have been a distraction if I weren't so worked up over Vanessa.

"Everyone's overreacting," I insisted. "And it's really depressing that you can't read fiction here."

"We can. There's actually a small collection of acceptable books with stories that completely align with our beliefs."

"It must be a *very* small collection."

We stopped atop a high hill with a long, gentle slope leading down to a meadow scattered with more trees. The snow blanketing it all was smooth and unbroken, and the children excitedly prepped their sleds. Gideon studied them a moment and then turned to me, his face drawn. "Tamsin, I don't want to argue with you. Not that this isn't important, but . . ." He gestured to the kids. "Perhaps this isn't the place."

I sighed. "You're right. I don't want to ruin their fun."

The children raced down the hill, some on sleds and some just tumbling down on their own. They'd laugh and help each other up, then trek back up the hill. Despite my woes, I couldn't stop from smiling at the sight of those rosy cheeks and excited eyes.

"I wouldn't have thought those sleds could get such speed," I remarked.

"Too fast for you?" Gideon teased.

"Hardly."

His lips quirked into a smile. "Is that so? Agatha! Winston! Bring that sled back up for Miss Wright."

"Wait a minute—" I began.

My protests were lost in their whoops of joy, and I gathered it wasn't common for adults to join their sledding. There was no way I could turn them down now. I took up most of the space on the sled they handed over, but one small girl managed to squeeze her way in front of me. We zoomed down the hill with cries of glee, though my weight threw off our balance at the end, and the sled tipped over. The girl and I flew off, with me hitting the snow headfirst.

I brushed it out of my face, laughing, and helped her stand. "Are you okay?" I asked.

She regarded me with enormous eyes. "Are *you*? I've never seen a grown-up dive into the snow like that."

Although she was a few years older than Merry, the girl's blue eyes and round cheeks reminded me so much of my daughter that I suddenly felt a searing pain in my chest, like some unseen hand was trying to tear my heart out. And when she shook the snow out of her brown hair, the sun spiked it with glints of gold, very much like Adelaide's hair would do. The fist on my heart grew tighter and tighter. Where was Adelaide now? The star of every party? Already engaged? And what about Mira? Was she still going through the motions of the Glittering Court, always watchful for a way out? In my mind, my two friends had endless possibilities stretching out before them. And me? I was stuck.

I closed my eyes and took a deep breath. *I've got to get a grip, or I'm going to lose my mind. Focus, Tamsin. It's the only way to get what you want.*

"Are you okay?"

My eyes blinked open, and I forced a smile back on for my little companion. "Of course I am," I told her. "And I bet you've never seen a grown-up do this either."

I put on my mittens and made a snowball that I promptly hurled into Gideon's arm as he trudged down the side of the hill. He peered around, shocked, trying to figure out which student had done it. By the time he realized it was me, I was already launching a second snowball. He was ready, though, and deftly dodged my throw. He quickly made a snowball of his own, and before long, our whole party was engaged in battle.

"All right, all right," Gideon said, when everyone was breathless and covered in snow. "Time to wrap up the warfare. We need to get back to town soon."

The eldest boy in the group ran up to him. "But Mister Stewart, can we please go see if the pond is still frozen first?"

Gideon, kneeling to help a small girl shake snow out of her hood, glanced farther across the plain. I could see a large gray indentation in the snow, just before the forest really took hold. "I don't see why not. But listen, nobody can go on the ice until Miss Wright and I make sure it's safe. Do you understand?"

Murmurs of assent answered him. We broke our way through the snow and reached the pond, which shimmered in the late afternoon sun. The girl who had sledded with me clapped her hands. "It looks just like silver!"

"It sure does," said Gideon, walking the pond's circumference. He found a fallen branch and began tapping different portions of the ice. "No human artist can match the beauty Uros creates, especially with winter as a canvas."

"Did Uros use a paintbrush?" asked one small boy, eliciting giggles from others.

Gideon stopped his inspection of the ice and regarded the group before him. All of them had gone quiet and serious as their little faces looked up at him. "Uros used something even better. His will. He used it to create everything you see around you—every bird, every snowflake, every wisp of cloud. Each one was created with meticulous thought and care. And do you know what Uros's greatest, most perfect masterpiece is?" Gideon waited a beat. "All of you."

This brought astonishment to some of them, skepticism to others. "But not all people are great or perfect. Uros made a mistake," said one girl.

"Uros doesn't make mistakes, Dora. His plan is flawless—the mistakes happen because of us."

A boy standing beside me mustered his courage to say, "How?"

An impromptu discussion followed, and Gideon answered their

questions patiently and respectfully, making sure everyone felt valued. He had no difficulty expressing his thoughts and looked far more at ease in the snow than he had at the podium.

Eventually sensing his little congregation's restlessness returning, Gideon gave them his blessing to go to the pond. They all approached it differently, some crawling or sitting, while others boldly strode out as if they wore skates. Some kept their balance; others, not so much.

He and I walked together, keeping an eye on them but also separating ourselves enough to speak quietly. "You're good with them. You teach them about faith much better than you do adults."

"I can't tell if that's a compliment."

"You understand how to get through to them." A boy came up to me, begging help to retie his scarf. I knelt down, using the opportunity to reflect on Gideon's manner. When the boy left, I remarked, "Actually, I think you can get through to anyone. That would have made a fine lesson for adults too."

"It was incredibly simplified," Gideon countered, clearly taken aback.

"So? I'll wager those kids learned more just now than they ever have in any hours-long service. And I bet the same would be true for half the town if they'd heard what you just said. You're always saying you joined the Heirs because you were searching for a purer, more direct way to connect to Uros. That seemed pretty direct."

"Oh, Tamsin. I know you mean well. But I didn't give up my old life, come all the way to Grashond, and study the finer points of philosophy and theology just so I could deliver ten-minute lectures outside." We stopped near the forest's edge, giving us a good vantage on the playing children. As engaged as he was with me, he constantly kept an eye on them, and his genuine concern for them touched me. Satisfied they were okay, he continued: "Have I ever told you what really drove me here?"

"You said you were disillusioned in Osfro."

He leaned against a tree, his gaze fixed on the plains beyond the children—or maybe he was seeing the past. "Yes, but my change of heart didn't just happen out of the blue. I don't like to talk about it much because it's embarrassing. I go on and on about people who are self-absorbed and obsessed with their own pleasures, but the thing is, I was one of them. I spent my parents' money on gaudy clothes and other nonsense. I went out to a different party every night, drinking myself silly. There were women that I—" The familiar blush filled his cheeks. "That's not really something to be discussed in front of a proper young lady. Long story short, I woke up one morning in the backyard of some house I didn't know, sick and dirty, with no money and no memory of the previous night. I'm not sure how I dragged myself home, but I passed out again when I got there. I was in and out of consciousness for a week, and when I finally stayed lucid, I learned I'd nearly died from a fever I caught sleeping outside. And that's when I knew I had to change."

I reached for his hand, well aware there'd be all sorts of fallout if someone saw the gesture. But I couldn't help it, not when the anguish of his past burned so fervidly in his eyes. It always seemed appropriate that his dazzling good looks were paired with a serene and affable attitude, so it was surprising that this raw moment almost enhanced his handsomeness. It made him real.

"Thank you for telling me that, Gideon—for trusting me enough to tell me that. I know how hard it is to talk about the darker parts of our pasts."

Gideon lowered his eyes to our hands, studying them before he answered. "Then you can see why I've worked so hard to fight through worldly distractions and immerse myself in the study of Uros—and why I need to get others to understand it too."

"I do see that. But I don't see what's so wrong with sharing your message in a way that's easier to grasp—even if, yes, it's simplified. If you really want them to understand, do the means matter?"

His pensiveness shifted back to amusement, brightening the mood around us. "You see, this is why I need you, Tamsin. Not that I fully agree with that line of thinking yet. But I love that you do think about it. You know how to get through to people, and we could do amazing things to fulfill my dream."

"You're giving me too much credit. Again." Neither of us had spoken of his tacit proposal until now, largely because Vanessa had overshadowed it. "And anyway, it's impossible."

"What if it isn't?" He squeezed my hand and took a step closer. "What if—"

His words were swallowed by a roar from the woods. It was our only warning before four men wrapped in brightly colored plaid came charging out on horseback. Two held guns, and two carried blades. All had blue paint streaked over their faces. They were riding toward a cluster of children, weapons aimed straight ahead. I wrenched my hand from Gideon's and tore off, diving in front of the kids as the riders skidded to a halt in the snow. Stumbling, I regained my balance and motioned the children even further behind me. Some screamed or whimpered. A few exclaimed, "Icori! Icori!"

Icori? Yes, I supposed these men did look like the Icori in my textbooks, even down to the wild way their red and blond hair had been teased to stand up. But it took me a moment to make the connection, because for the last few weeks, my mental images of the Icori had been replaced by Orla and her friends in their plain, practical leather and wool traveling clothing.

The riders jumped off their horses and advanced on us, their weapons still poised and ready. I stayed where I was, making myself the first obstacle they'd meet. "What do you want?" I demanded.

"You—you don't move, Osfridian girl," one ordered, raising a dagger to my throat. His tartan shirt was ripped open at the front, exposing a chest also painted with blue woad. One of his companions began moving among the children scattered farther out, herding us together.

"Hold on now," said Gideon. In my periphery, I saw him hurrying over to me. "There's no need for hostilities. Our people are at peace—"

An Icori with red hair grabbed Gideon by the front of his coat and threw him down to the ground. "No!" I cried. I started to move toward him, but the blade stopped me.

More gasps and screams came from the children. Leering, the Icori man rested his booted foot on the side of Gideon's face, pushing it into the snow. Raw fear poured through me, not for myself but for him and the children. My eyes scanned frantically around as I searched for a way to help.

"You have gold?" barked one of the men. "Give us gold."

The man whose blade was on me added, "Give us gold, we no kill woman."

"I . . . don't . . . have any gold," Gideon said. "But if you'll let me stand, I'll give you what I do have."

His assailant backed off, and Gideon slowly rose. They watched warily as he reached in his pockets, but all he brought out was a handful of mixed silver and copper coins. The red-haired man snatched them. "More."

"That's all I've got," said Gideon. "I swear by Uros."

The Icori looked expectantly at me. "I don't have any money at all. And neither do they," I exclaimed, seeing one of the men eye the children.

"Is there something we can help you with?" asked Gideon. "Do you need food?"

The Icori exchanged glances. "Yes," said one. "Give us food. Give us other precious things."

Precious things? This lot apparently had no idea who they were robbing. The Heirs of Uros weren't exactly the type to be walking around bedecked in silk and jewels. But at the Icori's behest, we gathered up all of the children's schoolbags and then waited under the watchful eye of a gun-wielding man as the other three ransacked the pile. Gideon took a step nearer me, angling himself protectively between me and our assailants.

The only food we had consisted of a few modest snacks sent by parents, and it was all immediately confiscated, as was anything of even meager value. A steel canteen. A bag with a brass buckle. A hornbook made of beautifully carved cherry wood. When they finished with the bags, the Icori examined our persons more closely. Objects made of fur—mufflers and hats—were taken, along with anything metal that was bigger than a button. Belt buckles, cloak pins.

Gideon and I made no moves to stop the Icori and continually assured the children that this would be over soon, that they only needed to be still and quiet, that no harm would come to us. This was undermined a bit by the Icori, who took a perverse delight in sneering and growling at the children.

"Please," said Gideon, when the last child had been frisked. "You have everything now. Let us go. These are innocent children, and we just want peace."

The Icori who'd first accosted me snorted. "Only coward want peace."

But they did seem to be backing off. They readied their horses and bagged up the loot. A couple shivered and rubbed their arms. I dared to think this nightmare might be over, when one Icori noticed he'd missed a boy's fur-lined coat.

"Take off, take off," ordered the Icori. He towered over everyone and had a thick blond beard. The boy froze, his face turning as white as the snow at that booming voice. Snarling, the Icori grabbed the boy by the shoulders and shook him. A repeat of the demand only terrified the young victim more, and I thrust my way to them.

"Enough!" I shouted. "How can you expect the poor thing to do anything? You're scaring him to death. Let me do it."

The Icori glowered at me but waited as I bent down and swiftly unbuttoned the coat. "Nothing to be afraid of, Alan. Let's just get this off so these gentlemen can be on their way."

Rather than soothe, my words had an opposite effect. Alan started fighting me, tugging back on the coat. "No, no! My ma made this, and now she's with the angels! They can't have it!"

"Hush," I said, seeing the big Icori preparing to intervene. "Your ma is in paradise and won't mind. She'll be proud of what a brave and selfless boy you are."

"They can't have it!"

My heart breaking, I finally wrestled the coat off him and handed it to the Icori man. As he started to turn around, Alan cried out, "You'll burn in Ozhiel's hell with all the other infidels! Eliziel will pass his judgment upon you, and all of your descendants will suffer until the end of the time!"

The Icori backhanded Alan in one smooth motion, sending the boy flying. The big man's face was red with anger, his nostrils flaring. He stormed to where Alan had landed and reached forward. I inserted myself between them and pushed back on the Icori's chest.

"Tamsin!" exclaimed Gideon. An Icori grabbed his arm as he tried to get to me.

"Let him go, he's a boy!" I yelled. "You've got the coat and a pretty good haul. No need to drag this on." The Icori's eyes still burned with fury, and he didn't budge. I yanked off my mittens. "Here—you missed these. How's that for a prize? Now, take what you've got, and go home."

He seized the mittens, running his fingers over the beadwork and silky material with approval. When he shoved them into his pocket, I thought the ordeal was finally over. But a few moments later, his gaze fell on Alan again, and the anger rekindled. This time, when the Icori advanced, I didn't just block his way. I smacked him in the face as hard as I could, landing what was probably a weak blow, save that my nails had drawn blood on his cheek.

He dabbed at it disbelievingly, and a few of his comrades snickered. He wiped the blood on his pants and focused back on me. "*Putce*," he hissed.

I started at the unexpected insult and then foolishly blurted out, "I've been called worse."

His hand closed into a fist at the same time a series of shouts sounded in the distance. The Icori flinched and looked around.

At the top of the hill we'd sledded down, the dark shapes of several people appeared. I couldn't make out any faces, but one called clearly, "Everything okay?"

Without a word, the Icori immediately retreated, securing their prizes and mounting their horses. They rode away and were long gone by the time our unexpected saviors from the *Gray Gull*'s crew reached us.

CHAPTER 16

I NEVER EXPECTED TO BE SO GRATEFUL TO SEE CAPTAIN Milford again. His crew had been living in a makeshift camp on the outskirts of Constancy and tasked with felling trees for a building project, but our paths never crossed. Although not forbidden, the crew was discouraged from spending too much time in town (unless they wanted to attend church services), and Constancy really wasn't the sort of place sailors went to for recreation anyway.

But the townspeople were very interested in the sailors now. After we'd made it back to the square and recounted what had happened, the council called an emergency meeting that was open for all to attend. Word spread quickly, and the church soon filled with almost as many people as I'd seen at the service. All of my Glittering Court companions came, along with their hosting families, except for Vanessa, whom the Coles still ordered to stay home until her atonement.

"They were Icori all right," Captain Milford said. The council had called him to stand by the podium and give his version of what had happened. "We were on our way to the valley to scout tomorrow's job, and that's when we saw them. All wild-eyed and vicious, dressed up in that crazy plaid of theirs. They were waving their weapons around, and I honestly don't know what those poor children would have done if we hadn't swooped in to save them."

Sitting with Gideon on one of the congregation's benches, I tried not to grimace. It was true the sailors' arrival had spurred the Icori's departure, and I was extremely grateful for that hasty resolution.

But the captain and his crew hadn't exactly done much in the way of swooping or saving, certainly not to the heroic extremes they described when testifying.

That detail was irrelevant, though. The real issue was assessing if Constancy was in danger or not. "They could be on the verge of a full-scale attack," one councilman declared. He gestured for the captain to take a seat. "Every family must arm itself, and we need to get word to the fort to send soldiers."

Another councilman treaded more cautiously. "I don't trust them any more than you do, but one rogue group doesn't mean an attack is coming. They just sound like thieves."

But his counterpart insisted, "*All* Icori are thieves. This could've been a scouting party that saw the children and decided to take advantage of easy pickings."

I shifted, trying to get comfortable, as they argued. Hunger gnawed at my belly, and I wished the benches had backs. People were continually arriving, and each time the door opened, a blast of cold air would roll over me. Once I'd given my own account of the events, there was nothing left for me to do but wait quietly and listen. Town policy and defense were male domains, and while plenty of women had turned out tonight, they weren't expected to ask questions or offer suggestions.

I didn't have much in the way of suggestions, but I was certainly beginning to build a mental list of questions as time went on. The assault at the pond still seemed surreal. At times, the emotions I'd felt during that terrifying episode would slam into me with full force and clarity. I'd start to sweat, and my pulse would race. Other times, I remembered the events in a manner so detached, it was as though it had happened to someone else instead of me—like it was just a story I was hearing or reading. And in those cooler moments, something about the whole encounter felt . . . off. But I couldn't quite grasp how. After all, it had been straightforward, hadn't it? We'd been robbed by men who looked exactly like what our books said Icori looked like. But that was what bothered me—because they hadn't looked at all like the Icori I'd actually met.

Off to the church's far side, the children who'd gone sledding sat on the floor. They hadn't testified, but the council wanted them on hand in case any questions arose. They looked even more tired than I felt as they huddled against the wall, and anxiety still filled most of their faces. I wished they could be allowed to go home and be comforted by parents.

"They should at least get dinner," I muttered.

Gideon tilted his head toward me. "Hmm?"

I nodded toward the children and whispered back, "I'm sure they're starving."

He studied them for several seconds and then, with murmured apologies to those sitting near us, slipped out of the row of benches. He approached a matronly woman standing near the children and said something into her ear. She nodded and left the church, returning ten minutes later with a basket of bread that she distributed to the grateful little recipients.

When Gideon sat beside me again, I flashed him a smile that he answered in kind. With the afternoon's sudden and dramatic turn, memories of its nicer moments had been shoved aside. Now, my mind wandered back to how affectionate Gideon had been with the children. He'd been as considerate of their needs during their play as he was now with their dinner.

Growing up, I'd always known I was lucky to have a father like mine. Plenty of the men who'd lived near us loved their families dearly, but they'd left most child-rearing—especially the emotional aspects—to their wives. But my father, no matter what else might be happening in his world, stayed firmly involved with our lives and needs.

Gideon would be the same with his children, I realized. My focus for the last year had been on finding a husband wealthy enough to give Merry the life she deserved. So long as that was secure, I'd accepted that I might not marry for love. I didn't need it and could be content in a household where my husband liked and respected me. But what about Merry? Was it enough for her to have a stepfather who liked and respected her? Was I making a critical mistake in not making a loving and nurturing stepfather as high a priority as medicine and education?

I sighed and tuned back in to the deliberations. The door opened again, bringing in a flurry of frigid air, and a pop of red couldn't help but draw the eye in that room full of subdued colors. Jago Robinson shuffled inside and stomped snow off his boots before finding an unobtrusive spot to stand near some farmers. He looked like he hadn't shaved in a couple of days, and his hat had more wrinkles than ever. When had he gotten back? He'd traded his lighthearted countenance for a much grimmer one, and his attention on the debate was hawk-like.

"Until the fort can send backup, I propose we post sentries of our own around the area. It's not like those children were playing out in the middle of the wilderness. They were barely on the town's outskirts! We can't let the Icori sneak up so close again."

That declaration from the lead councilman drew clapping and shouts of assent, though one timid man suggested, "Perhaps we should send a delegation to talk to the Icori."

A magistrate in the crowd stood up and dismissed that notion with a snort. "We'd be sending that delegation to suicide, more likely. And what talking could they do? You heard the report—those brutes could barely string two Osfridian words together. You can't reason with that."

That nagging sense of something being off played at the back of my mind again. Our assailants' Osfridian *had* been terrible. I never would have given it a second thought, though, if I hadn't met Orla. She'd spoken our language perfectly. Some of her companions hadn't, but they'd still communicated better than the men I'd encountered today.

The magistrate was still going: "We should spread word of this to other towns and forbid any Icori from entering Grashond. No more using our roads, no more trade in our towns. Icori who do should be imprisoned or removed. We need to put an end to these raids, and if it requires more offensive measures, so be it. The Icori must be stopped!"

Over the scattered cheers, a voice suddenly called out, "Oh, *come on!* The Icori never started anything. You're all acting like fools."

The noise faded, and heads turned. The lead councilman pursed his lips in disapproval. "Those are provocative words, Jacob Robinson. Perhaps you'd like to rephrase them."

The men standing near Jago parted, leaving a space around him that was particularly conspicuous given how crowded the church was. "Only if you didn't understand them," Jago replied. "I'm telling you, the Icori didn't attack today."

"We have a couple dozen witnesses who say otherwise."

"But there's no reason for the Icori to cause trouble. They're content with the treaties, and they comply with them."

Captain Milford, emboldened by his new celebrity status, jumped to his feet. "Then who did I see in tartan and woad, accosting those children out there?"

Jago hesitated. "I'm not sure."

A cacophony erupted, equal parts mockery and outrage at Jago's assertions. The lead councilman banged on the podium with a gavel. "Order, order!" When quiet returned, he continued, "Mister Robinson, while I am pleased to see you finally step through the door of this church, I think it best you abstain from participating in town matters—especially considering your bias."

My legs seemed to move of their own accord, and I suddenly found myself standing up. "Mister Councilman . . . with all due respect, I think Mister Robinson may be right."

Two rows ahead of me, Samuel rose, his face dark. "Tamsin, sit down. Gentlemen, I apologize. The girl is addled and easily influenced.

As her guardian, I take full responsibility—"

"I am *not* addled," I interrupted. "I just don't think those men we saw were Icori."

Gideon gave my hand a gentle tug. "Tamsin," he said softly.

Another councilman took up a spot beside the lead one. "Miss . . . Wright, is it? You just testified—under oath to the angels—about what you saw. Everyone heard you describe the tartan, the woad, their crude manner . . ."

"Because I did see those things. But it wasn't right." The hostility in the room was growing, and its pressure made me falter. "Like, the way they spoke . . . it was so broken. Almost perfectly so. Every word punctuated too much—like it was being contrived to sound like they didn't know Osfridian."

Samuel, still glowering at me, said, "Because they don't speak Osfridian! Of course everything is going to be slow and loud. It was a wonder they could utter any words at all."

"Well, they certainly seemed to *understand* Osfridian. One flew into a rage when Alan put down Ozhiel's curse on him. There are a lot of big words in that—why would he have gotten so upset if he didn't understand them? And why would he even care, seeing as the Icori don't believe in Ozhiel?"

Another of the town's ministers, one who served on the council, beckoned Alan forward from the cluster of children. "Alan Morwell, did you issue Ozhiel's curse?"

Poor Alan crept forward. As he did, I could see the side of his face was still red from where the bearded man had struck him. No one, not even the Heirs, actually believed speaking Ozhiel's curse could cause it to come about, but it was considered extremely vile and insulting—especially when uttered by a child.

"I'm s-sorry, Pa," Alan stammered. "He was taking Ma's coat, and I just got so upset. I didn't think he'd get so mad—I didn't think at all! Oh, you should have seen what a beast he was. He would've ripped me in two if Miss Wright hadn't given him those fancy mittens. And then when she hit him, I thought he was going to rip *her* in two, but then the—"

"Enough, enough." Mister Morwell held up a hand to silence his son. "Sit down. We'll discuss your behavior when we get home tonight."

I watched Alan slink back to his spot and hoped I hadn't gotten him in trouble. Turning back to the council, I continued, "Sirs, their tartans weren't right either. They were all ripped up so that their chests were bare—in the middle of winter."

"It's what they do," the lead councilman said. "Everyone's heard of the berserker Icori running shirtless into battle, impervious to the elements."

"They weren't impervious," I said. "I saw them shiver. They were cold. And when I traveled here with the Balanquans, the Icori in that party didn't bare their chests or arms. They didn't wear tartan at all. They were bundled up sensibly in coats and furs."

"What color were the tartans?"

The question came from Jago. I met his eyes, again surprised at his serious demeanor. "Two were red, one was green, one was blue," I answered.

"What other colors? The stripes and hashes?"

"I . . . I can't be certain. It all happened so fast. The red one had yellow lines, and green squares . . . I think? The blue was crossed with white."

"And the green had black checks," supplied Gideon, standing up beside me. "Does that mean anything to you, Mister Robinson?"

Jago nodded. "Those are tartans from three different clans. They wouldn't work together for a petty robbery. I mean, yes, I suppose a handful of renegades cast out of their clans could join up, but in that case, they wouldn't be openly advertising those clan colors while committing crimes. It'd be an insult to the clans they came from, and they know they'd be punished even more severely if caught."

The magistrate who'd spoken earlier snickered. "I think you give the Icori too much credit, but that's no secret. If I'm following this ludicrous exercise, you—and Miss Wright—are suggesting these men were not Icori, that they were imposters dressing in Icori clothing and pretending to speak like them."

"That seems more likely to me than the original accusation," said Jago.

The lead councilman banged his gavel when the crowd started buzzing again. "Then we're back to Captain Milford's question. If they weren't Icori, then who do you think they were?"

They were all looking at Jago, but I was the one who supplied the answer. "When I slapped the one threatening Alan, he, uh . . . called me a name. In Lorandian." I'd been startled at the time to recognize the name, but it hadn't occurred to me then that I shouldn't have understood it at all, not from an Icori.

"That's your extraordinary fabrication now?" Mister Morwell's expression had gone from displaying outrage at my impertinence to derision at what he saw as my lack of intelligence. "That Lorandians, dressed up as Icori, robbed you? Young lady, I can't decide if you're just looking for attention or are truly fool enough to believe what you're saying. Gideon, did you hear any Lorandian?"

"No, but I also don't know the language. If Tamsin says she heard it, I believe her."

"You're too trusting," said Samuel.

"I know Lorandian!" I exclaimed. "Enough of it, at least. I grew up by a Lorandian baker and had lessons in the Glittering Court."

"Different languages often have words that sound alike." The lead councilman pushed his glasses up, reminding me of our old history master giving a lecture. "It's entirely probable that there are many Icori words that sound like Lorandian. Or like Osfridian. Or anything. That black stone the Balanquans are always trading is called *reed* in their language. Completely coincidental that it sounds like our verb or the name we give the river rushes."

"This was not a coincidence, sir. The word he used was—from his point of view—very applicable."

"And what was this revelatory word?" asked Mister Morwell, his voice exasperated.

I glanced around uneasily, taking especial note of the children. "It was not a, ah, flattering term, sir. I don't think it'd be appropriate to say in a church."

Mister Morwell stalked back to his chair. "We're wasting time."

"What was it, Tamsin?" Gideon gave me an encouraging nod. "Go ahead."

"*Putce*," I said, scanning the congregation for any sign of recognition. I was certain a number of townspeople knew Lorandian, but I doubted any had lived near a hot-tempered baker who was always yelling at his wife.

I heard a startled exclamation from behind me and wasn't surprised that Damaris knew the word.

"What's it mean?" prompted Gideon.

I cringed under the weight of those gazes. I'd said far worse things in my life, but never in front of an audience like this. After a deep breath and a silent prayer for forgiveness, I blurted out, "It means 'bitch' in Lorandian."

I couldn't have elicited more outrage than if I'd started knocking over benches and punching people around me. The lead councilman had to practically bang his gavel to splinters before the outcry finally faded. When Samuel ordered me to sit down again, I did. There really wasn't anything else I could add.

Incredibly, no one discussed what I'd said. The council started talking sentries again, with the lead councilman saying, "Now, if we can move past this nonsense, let's start taking action before it's too late. We'll need volunteers to ride out to the fort in the morning, as well as to Piety and Reserve. Men willing to stand watch around our perimeters should meet me when we adjourn, and anyone who needs a gun should—"

"Didn't you hear any of that?" Jago broke from the throng and strode up to the podium, an action that was received with as much shock as my interruptions. "Those were imposters! If you start harassing real Icori and encouraging military interference, you're just to going to escalate an already tense situation!"

"They're the ones who escalated things! Not just here—we all heard about the raids earlier this winter."

"That wasn't them either," Jago insisted. "The Lorandians are doing this."

Mister Morwell threw up his hands in disgust. "To what end? We've always had troubled relations with the Lorandians, but their numbers in Adoria are too small to be any threat, and they know it. And I really don't consider one girl's vile language to stand as proof that those men were Lorandian when all other evidence points to the contrary! Really, Mister Robinson, if you're so partial to the Icori, perhaps you'd be better off with them."

"I'll go to them right now and arrange talks, if you'd like," Jago returned evenly.

"We've already discussed the futility of that. Now. Are you quite done wasting our time? You've never shown any interest in being part of this town before, and I'm honestly a bit suspicious as to why you'd start now."

Jago's jaw was clenched, and I could see his internal struggle to restrain both words and actions. A stillness fell as everyone waited to see what he'd do, but after several tense moments, he swallowed his temper and marched out of the church without a word.

The council continued with its plans and adjourned shortly thereafter to form volunteer committees. Families began to leave, and I stood up and stretched, grateful to be moving. I walked over to the children to check on Alan's injury. He assured me he was fine, and then I stepped outside to get some air. Cold or not, I needed it after the suffocating church.

Gideon followed me, and we stood off to the side of the door, our breath making wispy clouds in the crisp evening air. "What do you think of all of this?" I asked.

"I don't know," he admitted. "If they really were Lorandian

brigands, it seems like they could rob people without all the theater. But I also believe you're right."

"Really? About which part?"

My surprise brought on a wan smile. "All of it. I trust you on the language, and I didn't even consider all those little inconsistencies until you mentioned them. How you managed to be so observant and so brave during all of that is beyond me."

"I think I was more impulsive than brave. I could've made things a lot worse." I rubbed my hands together, reflecting on those moments. "I didn't think. I was just worried about Alan."

"My heart nearly stopped when you went after that man, you know. Even now, it gives me chills just thinking how something could have gone horribly wrong for you or the children."

Serious or not, I couldn't resist: "Are you sure it's that giving you chills and not the weather?"

"All I could do out there was pray to the angels when you were facing that man down. Of course, you've got enough divine favor that you probably didn't even need my intervention." He clasped my freezing hands in his gloved ones. "What you do need, however, are mittens. But we should be able to manage that without prayer."

"I don't know. I'll be going on my third pair. The angels might cut me off."

We stood together in comfortable silence, enjoying a rare minute or so of peace. Then, a sharp voice said: "Tamsin Wright, I pray daily to be worthy of the challenges laid upon me, and it's clear I'm being tested today."

I sprang back from Gideon and saw Dinah silhouetted in the doorway. "H-hello," I said as she stepped out to join us. She looked between me and him with an appraising eye.

"You know," she continued, "if I hadn't witnessed that outburst and offensive language myself, I wouldn't have believed even someone like you was capable of it."

Gideon put a hand on my shoulder. "Dinah, I know a few, uh,

inappropriate things took place tonight, but considering the extraordinary circumstances, I would humbly counsel leniency."

Dinah stiffened as her eyes tracked his hand. She had to wet her lips a few times before continuing. "Gideon, you're always so kindhearted, but it's my job to shape her character. And now I've just heard the most confusing thing. Alan Morwell was telling me about those 'fancy mittens' of yours, Tamsin. He said they were jewel encrusted, and I told him that was nonsense. Was he lying?"

"No," I said swiftly. "Well, that is, he was a bit mistaken. They had silver beads on them, not jewels."

"Why weren't you wearing your other mittens? The gray ones?"

"I—I lost them on one of my errands."

"I see. And where did you get these fancy replacements?"

I swallowed, unwilling to sell out Jago. "From our luggage—our luggage from the ship, I mean. Some of it's being kept in the meeting-house, and I took the mittens while we were holding class there today."

"I see," Dinah repeated, though her hard eyes said much more.

"There you all are." Samuel walked out of the church, Damaris and Winnifred behind him. He waved for us to follow. "Time to go."

Our party rode home without conversation, and I stared off into the darkness, apprehensive about both my fate and the Icori's. It was horrifying to think one incident could trigger a war . . . except it wasn't just one incident. Other towns had had run-ins with Icori, and Orla had insisted her people had been attacked without provocation too.

Speaking of Orla . . . how would these new developments affect my own travel plans? Would she take back her offer? Would the Grashond settlers even allow us to go with the Icori, if they were deemed an official enemy? Of course, until I talked to Jago, I didn't know if I even had travel plans.

We ate a sparse dinner of cold leftovers, and then, after a brief prayer, my friends and I were sent off to the attic while Samuel, Gideon, and Dinah had a meeting by the fire. I climbed the stairs with a heavy heart, knowing my future was on the line.

∾

The next morning, when we assembled for breakfast, Dinah told me, "You're lucky. Gideon spoke up for you and convinced us to overlook your breach of etiquette in church last night, seeing as it was part of an investigation."

Gideon, already sitting at the table, didn't really look like someone who'd achieved a victory. As I moved to take my own seat, Dinah held up a hand to stop me.

"That does not, however, excuse you from the transgressions of theft, vanity, deceit, and negligence."

"Me?" It was the only thing I could think to say, seeing as she seemed to have mixed me up with someone else.

Dinah ticked off my charges with her fingers. "Negligence for losing your mittens. Deceit for not confessing it. Vanity for wearing such garish replacements. And theft for stealing them."

"How . . . how can it be theft when it was our own stuff?"

"That cargo was off-limits to you," said Samuel harshly. "It's currently in *our* possession."

"That makes it theft?" I looked between the two of them in disbelief. "That's absurd, and you know it."

Dinah pointed at my chair. "Take that over to the stove and wait until the rest of us finish. You won't be eating this morning."

I opened my mouth to protest and then thought better of it. Fine. If they were going to make me skip breakfast because of some trumped-up charges, I'd do it with dignity. I'd show them how a person with principles and strength really behaved.

But, oh, I *was* hungry.

The Coles carried on like it was an ordinary day, though everyone else at the table wore a glum look. "I read through your sermon on integrity," Samuel mentioned to Gideon. "It's some of your finest work."

"Thank you," mumbled Gideon, eyes on his food.

"I liked the way you explained how deception casts a shadow on families and communities. But for the most part, your sermon only focuses on how things like honesty and honor improve lives. Maybe consider adding in a passage from the punishment of King Linus to show where deceit leads."

Gideon's eyebrows rose. "King Linus died in a pit of scorpions."

"Exactly. It's important to motivate people."

I wanted badly to speak to Gideon about what had happened last night and also to see if he could contrive any last-minute intervention before Vanessa's punishment tomorrow. Dinah went to town with us, however, and I had no chance at privacy. Gideon parted from us in the square, after giving me a long, searching look. I responded with a pained smile and then turned toward the school.

"No, you're not going there today," said Dinah.

"Am I back to doing laundry?" Damaris and Winnifred had gone off to their usual assignments, but maybe someone else had been recruited for Vanessa's former spot.

"No. Come with me."

Dinah walked briskly across the square with a self-satisfaction I found unnerving. I followed her to a residential section and watched with growing dread as she knocked on the door of one of the larger houses. A woman I recognized in passing but hadn't met answered and urged us inside. No introductions were made, and I wondered if I'd been assigned to help her. But as we passed through the exceptionally well-kept home, it didn't look as though she needed much in the way of chores done.

At last, we reached the far side of the house, and I stepped into a room that appeared to be an addition to the original building. It had walls that were still rough and unfinished, and a dirt floor scattered with hay. A narrow rectangular window near the ceiling provided lighting in the same way the church's windows did. This window was covered in greased paper instead of glass, however, creating a more muted illumination.

I took the strange room in and asked, "What is—"

The door slammed behind me. I was alone.

CHAPTER 17

I DOVE FOR THE DOORKNOB, BUT IT WAS LOCKED. "What's going on? What is this?" I pounded on the door until splinters made me stop.

"This is your home for the next four days," Dinah called from the other side. "Your place of solace to contemplate your wicked acts and pray for forgiveness. You didn't really think forgoing breakfast was the only penance you'd pay for those mittens, did you?"

"Penance for mittens?" I kicked the door a few times. "Do you hear yourself? You can't leave me in an empty room for four days over a pair of mittens."

"Two pairs, technically. And the fact that you don't realize how grave the situation is simply confirms why you should be here."

"I want to talk to Gideon! He wouldn't allow this." He'd been subdued at breakfast, but I was positive he couldn't have known this was coming. He wouldn't have just sat there without protest.

"Gideon can't help you, and once you've served your time, we're moving you to another house so that you won't be able to corrupt him with your seductive wiles anymore."

"My seductive . . ." I couldn't even stand to repeat it.

"Everything you'll need is there. That's all the food and water you'll get, so ration wisely. You have books to inspire you and help contemplate the errors of your ways, so use them. If you've written a satisfactory confession and appeal for forgiveness, you'll be allowed to go home in four days. You'll then be confined to your new residence until the next holy day."

Just like Vanessa, except I'd earned an extra day. I closed my eyes and leaned against the wall, knowing what Dinah would say next.

Or, at least, I thought I knew.

"You'll sit outside the church before services with a sign proclaiming your guilt. Later, you'll read your confession to the congregation, after which point you'll remove your sign." There was a pause. "And then you'll have your hair shorn."

I bolted upright. "What? Vanessa didn't have to do that!"

"Vanessa wasn't guilty of vanity. And this way, it'll be a little more difficult for you to tempt innocent men."

"Is that what this is bloody about? You being jealous of how Gideon feels about me? That he's interested in me?"

"Don't make it sound like he has a choice! You've used some sort of . . . beguiling . . . or whatever it is you learn at that school of yours. He'd never give you a second look if you hadn't muddled his mind, and I'm going to free him from you."

"Well, I've got some bad news for you. Getting me out of your house and cutting my hair isn't going to make him fall in love with you! Nothing short of a miracle will, so maybe *you'd* better start copying some passages and see if you can shore up some goodwill with the angels."

There was a much, much longer pause.

Then: "See you in four days."

"Wait!" I beat on the door again, splinters be damned. "I didn't seduce anyone! You can't do this! Not over mittens!"

The silence that answered eventually convinced me that Dinah and the lady of the house had left. I raked a hand through my hair—which was apparently on borrowed time—and began pacing the small space. When Vanessa had been taken away, Samuel had said she had "modest accommodations." Well, here they were. My four days' worth of rations consisted of four slices of bread and a tub of water. A chamber pot sat in a corner of the room. In the opposite one, several holy texts were stacked neatly beside paper, pen, and ink. That was it. Nothing to sleep on. Nothing to warm me beyond the clothes I already wore. And with no candle or lantern, my light would depend on the sun shining through the window.

Famished from missing breakfast, I quickly ate a piece of bread and almost grabbed another without thinking. No. I dropped my hand. If they were really going to leave me here for four days, I'd have to be careful with it and the water. In fact, I should have eaten only half a piece and saved the rest for tonight. I took a few sips of water and vowed to ignore the bread until tomorrow.

But what to do now? I couldn't bring myself to write that damned confession. What would they do to me if it wasn't ready in time? Give me another four more days' worth of meager supplies? Leave me to starve? I kicked at the wall in frustration, lost over what I should do. I'd put up with so much in Constancy. I thought I'd been patient. I thought I'd been reasonable—more than reasonable, really. And where had that left me?

I spent most of the day oscillating between despair and rage. I'd slump to the ground and curl up into myself, wishing I'd never set foot in Adoria or heard of the Glittering Court. But with enough time, I'd get fired up again and walk the little room, shouting and banging. Based on the house's orientation on the square, it seemed unlikely anyone would hear me. This room was in the back, and the building was long. In fact, recalling the larder and hall I'd passed through to get here, I doubted even the house's residents would hear me.

At last, as the light began to fade, I finally made use of the paper— to write a letter to Merry. I tucked it into my pocket when I finished, allowed myself one bite of tomorrow's bread, and then watched the room sink into darkness.

The dirt floor bothered me less than the chill did. The room had no insulation, and gaps in the paper window's seal let the wind sneak in. I gathered what hay I could around me and slept huddled against the wall shared with the rest of the house. I woke frequently throughout the night, reaching for a blanket that wasn't there.

I arose cold and sore the next morning, watching as my breath made clouds in the air. Vanessa would likely be sitting outside the church by now. The brightness of the paper window suggested a clear day, so at least she wouldn't have to endure rain or snow. The bitter overnight wind had faded too, and I felt like I was keeping watch with her as I hunched in a corner and rubbed my hands together. When I finally heard the church bell ring, I breathed a small sigh of relief. At least that phase of her punishment was over. Now she just had to get through her confession. If there was any positive side to my confinement, it was that I wouldn't have to witness her admitting guilt for taking a book she hadn't actually taken. I didn't know if I could have sat there and endured it. I very likely might have rushed to her side and raged at the crowd.

Was that what I'd do when my time came? Would I stand there and rail at them for their hypocritical, close-minded ways? Or would I too submit, meekly doing as I was told in order to get another day closer to Cape Triumph? Another day closer to Merry? A moment of humiliation before people I'd never see again was a small price to reunite with my daughter. Even cutting my hair was.

Except I was certain that bit had been a personal addition of Dinah's. I'd heard accusations of vanity constantly since being here, but no one else was walking around with shorn hair.

Another long day dragged by. I raged a little less, lethargic now from lack of food and sleep. I wrote a letter to Merry again but made no attempt at penning a confession. I wouldn't have minded reading the books to pass the time, but I resisted out of spite.

The third day passed more quickly, largely because I kept spacing out. Deprivation and cold had sapped my strength, moving me from tired to exhausted. My thoughts were dull, and sometimes standing up too quickly would make me dizzy. I didn't have the energy to write to Merry, and I knew I should work on the confession while I still had some sense. But I never picked up the pen.

Why? What are you proving? I asked myself when twilight fell. I lay on the floor, hands behind my head, watching shadows play about the room. *Suck up your pride, confess, cut your hair, and keep moving. It's the only way to Merry.*

No, it wasn't. I might still have Jago and the Icori . . . but I wouldn't know for sure until I got out of here. And to do that, I'd have to play Dinah's game.

Or would I?

Slowly, I sat up and studied the window. It was too high for me to reach. There were no handholds on the wall. There was nothing I could stack to climb on. But I could fit through that window.

I thought about that as dusk gave way to night. Moonlight just barely kept the window aglow, which hadn't happened the last two nights. They must have been cloudy. The rest of the room was still hard to see, and I moved slowly around it, feeling and assessing my accoutrements. I had the beginnings of a plan forming in my head, one that would make things go from bad to worse if it failed.

"But it won't," I murmured, taking off my cloak. I gritted my teeth against the cold and gripped the fabric tightly, trying to tear it. It held fast, as I'd expected, so I used the pen to stab at the cloak, creating holes to give me traction. Slowly, painstakingly, I tore the wool into strips about two inches wide. After that, I began disassembling the skirt of my overdress. I ripped two thirds of it into more fabric strips before determining I had enough. I tied them all together, end to end, and felt pretty proud of the length of "rope" I'd created.

But the exertion had taken its toll. I gave in to a brief break to regain my strength and brazenly ate all of my remaining bread. Then it was back to work.

With apologies to the angels, I started hurling holy texts at the window. Some missed, a couple bounced off the greased paper, but one struck in exactly the right way. Its corners tore the paper, creating a small hole. From there, it turned out to be relatively easy to expand the hole and knock out most of the paper. When I was satisfied with the opening, I tossed all the remaining books outside.

That required another rest. When I could drag myself up from it, I took one last deep drink of the water—and then dumped the tub out. Water spilled over the hay and dirt, and I winced at the waste. Then, I tied an end of the fabric rope through one of the tub's handles. The tub was narrow and oval-shaped. If the long side was horizontally oriented to the window, the tub would fit through the opening. If perpendicular, it wouldn't.

My first dozen attempts to throw the tub out the window failed. Most didn't get high enough. When I did manage a toss that reached the right height, the tub had rotated and couldn't fit through. I stopped to rest at that point, crouching on the muddied floor. The room wavered, my muscles were fatigued. With great effort, I forced myself up and resumed my task. After a few more bad throws, I finally got everything right, and the tub sailed out. The victory didn't last, though, because when I began reeling the rope in, the tub came right back in with it.

This certainly wasn't how I'd imagined my makeshift grappling hook working. And each failure was noisy since it meant the metal tub had struck the wall. I fully expected detection from someone inside or outside the house. But finally, the tub landed outside a second time, and this time I pulled it up slowly, making sure it stayed angled in a way that didn't immediately make it slip back in. When the tub was secured crosswise against a corner of the window and didn't return when tugged, I cautiously climbed up the rope and tumbled ungracefully out the window.

I landed hard in the snow, which was a foot deeper than it had been when I'd come here. The tub crashed down beside me, and I flipped it over as I surveyed the scattered books. I really had no use for them, but it seemed a shame to leave them behind. I also didn't want any of my escape tools discovered. Using the tub as a basket, I piled the texts and rope into it and then tried to stand. Everything spun around me, and I had to quickly grab the house to keep from falling. I closed my eyes, drawing breath and centering myself.

Stay strong, Tamsin. You aren't beaten yet.

Clutching at whatever scraps of reserve energy I could, I lifted the tub and set out. It had to be the middle of the night by that point. I expected easy passage through Constancy and was surprised to spy a few men out and about. Sentries watching for Icori, I realized. Evading them took a little care but wasn't too difficult. And once I was well along the creek road, I never saw anyone else.

I had little sense of time or scenery on the trip. Everything within me was focused on continuing along the road. *One more step, one more step.* Over and over, I told myself that. My limbs grew heavy, and I had trouble walking in a straight line. I constantly corrected myself, and more than once, I tripped and sent books flying. So many times, I wanted to stop but feared I'd never get going again. So, on I went, driven by thoughts of Merry and a warm fire and spiting Dinah.

If clouds had hidden the gibbous moon, I might not have found Jago's property in my addled state. But the two barns stood out starkly in the pale light, and I pushed through the chill and fatigue to quicken my pace to the dark little house. I gave the door three sharp raps and then waited, my teeth chattering.

"Who's there?" came a muffled voice.

"Tamsin."

A long silence followed, and I closed my eyes, thinking I might very well fall asleep there. Jago finally opened the door with a lantern in hand, just as a voice behind me barked, "Freeze!"

"Everything's all right, Arnaud," said Jago. He studied me in the lantern's golden light. "And I'd say she's already freezing."

Jolted to alertness, I turned and found the big Belsian man behind me. He walked around the porch, a rifle in hand. When he recognized me, he immediately lowered the gun. "Miss Tamsin! I did not know you."

Jago steered me inside. "It's okay. You can go back to the barn—and thank you."

A banked fire glowed orange in Jago's hearth, and I headed straight for it, dropping the tub along the way. I felt numbed and stupid, and even when I sank to my knees, the world kept wobbling and spinning. If I could just get warm, I could think clearly. I leaned in closer to the fire, its heat slowly spreading over my skin. After my last few stark days of existence, the glowing flames seemed almost friendly, like longtime acquaintances welcoming me home. Closer and closer and—

"Whoa." Jago grasped my arm and pulled me back. "You awake there?"

I blinked a few times. "What?"

He folded a heavy blanket around my shoulders and peered into my face. "You almost fell into the fire. What are you doing out here with no cloak and . . . Good grief. What happened to your dress?"

I searched around for the tub and pointed. "In there."

Jago bent over it, raising an eyebrow at the contents. He made no comment and instead brought me water in a tin mug. I drank it all in one go and asked for a refill. "I would've had more earlier if I'd known I was just going to dump it. But I thought I had to save some for tomorrow."

"What are you talking about?"

Why was thinking so hard? "The room. The room Dinah sent me to. I was supposed to write the confession, but I— Hey!"

Jago had abruptly withdrawn the refilled mug. "Were you at Magistrate Latimer's?"

"I don't know. It was on the square. Will you give that back? I'm so thirsty. Hungry, too."

"I bet you are. I know what goes on there." I lost track of him in the darkness as he walked to the other side of the cabin. When he returned, he carried a small bottle and knelt beside me. "You'll make yourself sick filling up your stomach like that. Start slow."

He brought the bottle to my lips, and the sweetness of apple cider startled me after my recent deprivation. After allowing only one sip, he slid his arm under my shoulders and led me to the pallet on the cabin's far side. I settled onto it with wobbling legs and let him drape another blanket over me. I was allowed one more drink of cider—a longer one—before I lay down.

"Don't you want to know what happened?" I burrowed into the pillow, my eyelids heavy.

He tucked the covers around me more securely. "Tell me tomorrow."

"It was the mittens."

"The mittens?"

"The mittens . . ."

∾

I felt like I'd only closed my eyes for a moment when Jago gently shook my shoulder. "Tamsin. Tamsin, wake up."

"No." I rolled away, planting my face in the pillow. "Let me sleep a little longer."

"It's noon."

Disbelieving, I sat up and squinted at the bright light coming in through the windows. Dressed in his leather work coat and battered hat, Jago handed me a bowl of what looked like porridge doused generously with honey. Sitting back, knees drawn up to his chest, he waited until I was about halfway through the bowl before he asked, "How are you feeling?"

"Better. But it wouldn't have taken much."

That got half a smile from him. "You're welcome. Now you have to decide what you want to do. I poked around town this morning and found out you're supposed to be released near dinnertime. What are your plans for when they don't find you? Go back to the Coles? Live in the woods?"

I pondered this as I ate a few more spoonfuls. "I don't know. I don't think I can do any of those things. I didn't really have much of a plan last night. It was just that, suddenly, there was no way I could stay there. I couldn't write that statement or confess in church, not over a damned pair of mittens."

"I heard you mention mittens last night, and I figured you were hallucinating."

"I told them I took the mittens from the storage area, so they branded me a thief, a liar, and a woman of vanity."

"No kidding?" He looked . . . impressed. "And here I thought it was just because you spoke out at the meeting."

"That too, even though Gideon technically cleared me of that." I held out my empty bowl beseechingly. Jago shook his head but traded me for a mug of water. After drinking, I continued: "The mittens were an excuse. If it wasn't those, Dinah would've found some other reason to lock me up. It's a long story."

"I'm sure it is. How would you like to go on a trip and tell me about it?"

I lowered the mug. "A trip where?"

"Oh, here and there. Does your Lorandian extend beyond insults?"

"Yes . . . why?"

"Because I was thinking of visiting some of them. And the Icori."

"Orla?" I asked hopefully. "Is your friend going to sell his space?"

"He's not. I'm sorry. He's worried if he waits much longer, no one will want to buy fur when the weather's warm."

Another blow. I looked down and played with the mug's handle. "Well. It was a long shot. Thanks for trying."

"But . . . I'll take you south."

Peering up, I searched his face for a joke and didn't find one. "What?"

"I'll take you. Only you. I can't make room for the others."

"Are you really . . . no. I can't abandon them here . . ." The words died on my lips. Would I be abandoning them? If the Heirs held good to their word, my friends would still eventually reach Cape Triumph. My going early wouldn't affect that. And if something did go awry, and the Heirs didn't make the trip, then I could tell Jasper. He'd most certainly take action to recover everyone. But, oh, it felt so unfair leaving them in this place while I went free.

Jago, watching my mental deliberation, said, "The Icori aren't leaving for two weeks, but I'm sure Orla would let you stay with her until they did. You can't come back to Constancy. As it is, it's going to be

Ozhiel's hell here when they find you missing today. I'd kind of like
to see it—but if you want to go with me, we've got to leave now. I
don't know if they'll figure out we're together, but I'd prefer several
hours' lead."

It's going to be Ozhiel's hell here. What kind of punishment would
the Heirs inflict for escaping confinement? I didn't want to find out,
and the only way I'd avoid it was by breaking *back* into my cell—
which was out of the question. So I could either become a fugitive
living in the woods after all or run off with Jago. One sounded as
absurd as the other.

"Why do you want to go to the Lorandians?" I asked.

"They have a post I've traded with before, just over Grashond's
far border. Sort of in a no-man's-land that neither the Icori nor Balanquans claim."

"You're going to try to find out if those Icori I saw really were
Lorandians, aren't you?"

"Yes. I don't want war breaking out around here. It's bad for business. It's bad for humans." He laced his fingers together and rested his
chin on them. "Anything else you'd like to know?"

"Yes. Why do you want to bring me?"

"Because it'll be handy having someone who knows Lorandian.
Mine's not that great."

"No, why are you agreeing to bring me south?" I could tell he knew
perfectly well what I'd meant.

"Ah. Well. You don't belong here. I want to get you to where you
need to be." His serious mien wavered as one of his crooked smiles
began to grow. "That, and I like you."

"Why?"

He laughed, noting my skepticism. "Will my answer affect whether
you join me?"

"I'm just puzzled. I'm not really sure what I've done to make you
like me."

That amused him even more. "What haven't you done, Tamsin?

You had me on day one when you said my eyes were 'marvelous.' You defy town councils, escape imprisonment by turning your dress into a rope. Oh, and I also thought you were going to hit me that first day."

"And you . . . liked that?"

"I liked that you *didn't*. That's the kind of self-control I could use in a traveling companion. You might not believe it, but sometimes I grate on people. Until you came along, I didn't think that anyone else could stir up this town more than me. Then you get in more trouble in two weeks than I did in six months."

I'd been smiling along as he spoke, but his last remarks jolted me from the light mood. He lifted his head, noting the change immediately.

"What's wrong? Aside from the obvious things, I mean. What did I say that brought on that look?"

I turned from his searching gaze. "Nothing . . ."

"Okay, I shouldn't have joked about you clashing with the town. It clearly wasn't funny twenty-four hours ago."

"It's not any of that . . . it's just . . ."

I nearly let the matter go, but now, all I could think about were the times I'd had to beg and bargain for Merry's medicine in Osfro, often while she was in the midst of a coughing attack that left her fighting for every breath. Resolved, I looked back up and met Jago squarely in the eye.

"I have to understand something. Why did you double-cross Constancy and sell their bitterroot for a better offer?"

Surprise and curiosity flashed over his face, finally resolving into confusion. "That's what's eating you? With everything else that's happened? Why?"

"Because it matters!" I sat up straighter. "I want your help, Jago. I *need* your help. But if it comes down to it, I'll take my chances alone before throwing my lot in with someone who risks a whole town's survival just to make a little extra gold!"

Our gazes locked, tension building, and I wondered if I'd meant my threat. How far would I go for Merry? If teaming up with someone guilty of despicable crimes was the only way I had to reach her, would I really refuse him?

"I didn't do it," Jago said at last. His was voice calm, level. No mockery. No outrage. "That is, I sold the bitterroot—"

"Jago! You—"

"—*but* I didn't double-cross Constancy. Not exactly. Like most things, it's a long story, and we don't have the time right now. I'll gladly tell you the whole tale later, but until then, you've got to decide if you can believe me when I say I wouldn't sacrifice the lives of a whole town just to turn some extra profit."

I wished I could read him. He looked sincere. He sounded sincere. And he'd helped me on more than one occasion. But he also made deals for a living. It was his job to get people to buy—or buy into— what he was pushing.

"You're a good salesman, Jago. How do I know you aren't playing me?"

"You don't. But I've never pretended to be anything that I'm not with you. And that's more than can be said for most of the people around here." He leaned to the side, eyes narrowed as he scrutinized me. "You're smiling. Why?"

"Because it's true. Because a lot of people who walk around here flaunting their righteous natures are the same ones who left me to freeze and starve. Whereas you mostly just keep trying to pawn your stuff off on me."

"'Pawn' indeed," he scoffed. "I sell quality merchandise at quality prices."

"Yeah? Then prove it, because we need to get going." I clambered to my feet, happy to find my legs steady again. "I don't suppose you can get me a good deal on some new clothes?"

It was a wonder Jago's face didn't crack from the enormous grin it had to support. "Aw, Tamsin, I thought you'd never ask."

CHAPTER 18

"Well, well, Jacob Robinson. Where are you off to today?"

"Afternoon, Chadwick. I'm heading over to Piety to see if I can sell a few things. Got to thin out my inventory before I head south."

"Oh yeah? How do we know you aren't actually taking ammunition to your Icori friends?"

"I don't trade in weapons, you know that."

"You'll trade in anything that turns a profit. Mind if we check out your hold?"

"Be my guest."

I closed my eyes and held my breath. Above me, there was a thump as someone jumped into the sled. The boards that made up the cargo hold's floor were less than an inch from my face. They sagged ever so slightly under the weight of the sentry's boots, but I had nowhere to move. I was enclosed in this wooden trap as securely as I might have been in my own grave, except that a coffin probably had more room. Crates and bags were shifted around and opened, their contents rifled through. At last, the man cleared Jago. Once everything was repacked, the sled went on its way, slowly building speed. I'd always felt like I was flying when sitting up above. Here, in this secret hold below the hold, I was acutely aware of every single bump and jostle along the way.

After an agonizing stretch of time—which probably wasn't nearly as long as it seemed—the sleigh slowed and came to another stop.

Once more, cargo was rearranged, and then the board above me popped off. Jago's face and a sunny blue sky beamed down at me. "I've smuggled a lot of things in there," he said, helping me out, "but you might be the most valuable."

I put my hands at my waist and arched my stiff back before climbing into the front seat. "I hope it's an honor I don't get again."

"Should be easy from here on out." He settled down next to me and picked up the reins. "Easier, at least. But keep your hood on. They didn't put sentries this far out, but we might pass a random traveler. Your hair's memorable."

I checked the fur-trimmed hood, making sure it was tied securely in place. This new cloak Jago had given me was blue—sky blue, not the solemn navy of the dress I'd worn before. And that dress had been replaced with a riding habit much more suitable for these conditions. Its skirt and close-fitting jacket were made of ivory wool edged in pink floral embroidery. Comparing it to my old Grashond attire, I felt like I was in a ball gown. I had new mittens, too, colored a brilliant rose.

"How much trouble do you think we'll get in if we're caught?"

"'We'?" Jago crooked me a grin. "Well. You're the fugitive who eluded their justice. I think you'd get in a lot more trouble."

"Well, you took off with me, *and* you're already under suspicion. I don't think they're just going to nod and wave you along your way."

He fell into thought at this, and the only sounds were the horses trotting and the swishing of the sleigh's runners on the snow. Jago had abandoned the bells, as they didn't lend themselves well to stealth. "Honestly, I probably *would* get waved off, so long as we weren't found together. There'd be no proof that I did anything wrong—well, this time. But as for you? I don't know. You haven't exactly broken a law—except in breaking out of their deprivation room or whatever they call it. But were you even in there legally to begin with? Did breaking a custom warrant it? They'd have the right to impose any punishment they wanted on a dependent, I suppose, which you technically are under Grashond law. But that's pretty tenuous, considering

you aren't a minor in any other colony and wouldn't be one in Grashond if you were married or male."

I gestured impatiently. "Okay, well, that's a lot of talking without
much of an answer."

He pondered that while guiding the horses around a sharp curve
with an effortless skill. "Well, let's put it this way. If anyone outside of
Grashond with any sort of sway looked into your case, I don't think
you'd be even close to a legally punishable offense. But, as you've
seen, custom and opinion carry as much weight as law around there
sometimes. Just as they thought they were justified locking you up
the first time, they'd likely think they were doubly justified in doing it
again—or worse."

"How could it get worse? Less food?"

"Eh, yes, but I was thinking of things besides the room. The stocks.
Less subtle ways of torture."

"Well, Dinah was planning on cutting off my hair," I said.

Jago's face turned incredulous. "What? Why?"

"As punishment for vanity—for taking the mittens. That, and . . ."
I stopped, nervous about delving into personal things with this man I
still didn't really know well.

He shot me a sidelong glance. "And what? Don't tease me. Tell me
the rest—because I can tell there's more. And it must be good, since
you're blushing."

"Watch the road," I snapped. "And if you must know . . . well, aside
from just tormenting me, she also thought losing my hair would make
me . . . uh, less attractive to others."

"'Others' being the good Reverend Stewart?" he guessed right
away.

"Yes." I sighed. "You can joke about divine favor, but it just seems
like bad luck to me that after surviving sea and snow, my biggest threat
came from living with someone obsessed with the idea that the man
she loves is in love with me."

"The way you say 'idea,' it's like you're suggesting it's all imagined in her head." When I didn't answer, Jago pushed: "You do know that he's in love with you? Or at least very, very, very fond."

When I didn't answer, Jago smirked, knowing he'd gotten close to the truth. "I've been around him when he's around you enough. And I saw his face when I talked to him in town earlier today."

"When was that?"

"While you were still asleep. It's how I got caught up on everything. I struck up conversation in the square and casually mentioned I'd heard something about you being punished, and he filled me in. Poor guy. He was pretty torn up about it, and hadn't heard until it was too late. He said it was his fault."

"It wasn't!" Poor, compassionate Gideon. How would it hit him when I turned up missing? "Maybe when you get back, you can get an anonymous note to him or something. Otherwise, I'll just have to explain when I . . ."

"When you what?"

I gazed at the road ahead, surrounded in leafless maple trees. The icy fingers of their branches stretched up to the sky like they were trying to hold on to it. "I was going to say I'd explain everything to Gideon when I see him again. But I suppose I won't see him again, not if I'm off to Cape Triumph."

"Does that bother you? Because I'm pretty sure you're just regular fond of him."

I left that provocative lead alone, even though I was dying with curiosity to know how Jago had drawn that conclusion. "Gideon was nice to me—nicer than most people in Grashond were. He's got a good heart. Too good to be there. He'll probably take my disappearance hard—so will my other friends."

"If it'll make you feel better, I really will pass them an anonymous note when I get back."

It did make me feel better, though it gave me a new worry. "Do you really want to go back there yourself? What if they link you to my disappearance?" The current plan was to go to the Lorandian trading post, and then Jago would leave me with Orla while he retrieved the rest of his cargo to take down the river.

"They might, but unless they actually find you with me, there's no proof. Arnaud won't say anything. He actually pretends not to understand any Osfridian when he's around the Heirs."

"How long has he worked for you?"

"Just over a year. He's an excellent guard, cook, and companion."

"Cook?"

"Mmm-hmm. And his twin's even better."

"Did . . . did you say twin?"

"Yup. Twin brother. You wouldn't be able to tell them apart. Unless you tried their cooking. Unsurprisingly, Arnaud doesn't get much of a chance to display his excellent culinary skills around here. Now, Tamsin. I'm trying to pay attention to the road, but I do believe you're smiling at me again."

"I smile all the time."

"Not *at* me very often, not in a way that seems like you approve of me or like me. At best, I get a smile that's like 'Oh, Jago, why do I put up with you and your quirks?' Most of the time, really, I'd say I get this grim smile of solidarity along the lines of 'Once again, fate has ground us under her heel, but onward we go, bearing our chains of bondage as best we can.'"

I laughed outright at that. "I'm certain I have never smiled in that kind of way! I don't even think it's possible."

"You'd be surprised. Pay attention the next time you're by a mirror. I've got one in the back right now that I was going to try to sell to the Icori, but you know I'll give you a better price if you want it."

"I'm glad to hear that. It's a relief knowing you haven't stopped trying to push your wares on me," I teased.

"Ah-ha! I knew it. I knew you secretly liked being kept informed about amazing deals for amazing products. You've just been toying with me."

"Jago, if I was toying with you, you'd never know it."

He shook his head, barely holding back laughter. "Tamsin, Tamsin. I knew you'd be good company, but I didn't know you'd be *this* good."

The first day of three passed peacefully, which felt decadent after the last few weeks of my life. We met no one on the road, and although clouds rolled in, the weather stayed clear. Jago delighted in hearing about how I'd escaped from the magistrate's house and even told me a little about himself. He'd been born in the colonies, which I'd presumed from his dialect, and came from a big family in Archerwood. I told him a little of my past too, but most of our talk hovered on common subjects—Constancy, the Lorandian puzzle.

We stopped once for dinner and then again to camp at sunset. Jago spent a long time caring for the horses, rubbing them down and making sure they had enough to eat. Their names were Pebble and Dove, and he spoke to them as he worked. I couldn't make out the words and teased once, "Are you trying to sell those horses something? Leave them alone. The poor things don't deserve to be swindled."

"You obviously don't know horses if you think they can be swindled that easily. At least not my horses." He patted Pebble's neck. "And Felicia's even smarter."

"Felicia?"

"Another horse I'm boarding in the south. She's a Myrikosi ghost— probably the only one in Adoria." His voice burned with pride. "She's half the reason I'm in debt and out 'swindling,' as you call it."

"Really? You do what you do . . . for a horse? Don't get me wrong. Pebble and Dove are probably the prettiest ones I've ever seen, but to rack up that kind of debt . . . I don't know. It doesn't seem worth it."

"You know a lot of things, Tamsin," he said solemnly. "But you don't know horses."

He had pen and ink in his supplies, and I wrote to Merry on the back side of one of the letters I'd written in isolation. With only a little light from the lantern Jago used for his work, I kept things short: *Merry, this was a good day. I'm getting closer to you.*

When Jago was satisfied with the horses' comfort, he took care of ours. He transferred some containers to the secret hold below the sled and moved others around to create a sleeping space. He laid down bags of seed for mattresses and more of those incredible blankets for bedding. Lastly, he set a long and narrow crate across the area to give us each a semiprivate spot.

"There we are," he said, helping me climb in. "Everything proper. Virtue secure."

I tested the firmness of the seed bags and found them surprisingly comfortable. "Thanks."

"Hey, who said it was for you?" he asked, putting on a dignified face. "I'm looking out for *me*." He snuffed the lantern and covered the hold with an oiled tarp.

"I'll try to control myself."

From the darkness came a great, exaggerated sigh. "Come on, Tamsin. Couldn't you try to sound just a *little* less sarcastic? Just enough to boost my self-esteem."

I covered a yawn. "Do you need a boost? It seems pretty secure to me."

"You aren't pulling any punches tonight, are you?" He didn't sound upset, though. Quite the opposite, actually. "It's a good thing that great heart of mine can take it." When almost a minute passed without a response from me, he asked, with some surprise, "No comeback?"

"I was just thinking . . ." The comment about his heart put the mystery of the town's medicine into the forefront of my mind. I'd wondered about the story constantly on this trip, but the companionable mood we'd had was so nice, I didn't want to risk losing it. Now, at the end of the day, when all was still, I couldn't hold back any longer. "What happened with the bitterroot?"

"Ah. I figured that'd be coming."

"Trying to avoid it?" The old anxiety and distress reared up, and I braced myself for the worst.

"No. I mean, it's just not something fun to bring up in casual conversation. I don't have anything to hide." There was a rustling as he shifted position. "But first, back up and tell me what you know and where you heard it."

Briefly, I relayed Gideon's account of how Jago had sold off the medicine promised to Constancy when the Icori made a higher bid. "And now the town doesn't have anything if some sickness strikes," I finished.

"You're right." My heart stopped, and then he clarified, "You're right about them being out of medicine. The rest? Well, that's a little fuzzier."

"Are you saying Gideon was lying?"

"I'm saying he told the truth as he probably knew it. But let's go back even further. You know I sell things that are illegal in Grashond? Passing through with them is allowed; owning them is not. When I realized I'd have to stay for the winter, I had to bargain with the council to bend some rules on storing contraband. They actually liked the idea of having backup supplies for the winter and struck a deal where I could stay as long as I didn't sell bitterroot, kerosene, or flour outside of Constancy. Those run short in wintertime."

"Did the town pay for them?" I asked, trying to follow the complexities.

"No. It was just held in reserve in case they needed it. I was free to sell any leftovers in the spring. And so, everything seemed to be fine. I got grief over the red barns and not going to church, but that was the worst of it. At least, it was until a wave of black fever broke out in Kerniall. That's where Orla's people live. Do you get black fever in Osfrid?"

"I don't know it, but we get our share of sickness, especially in the city." I was wide-awake now, propped up on my side. "How bad is it?"

"Very. If you can hit it early with bitterroot, the odds of recovery are pretty good. Kerniall didn't have enough, though, and the Balanquans weren't close enough to trade with. But I was."

I was glad the darkness hid my gaping jaw. "Gideon never said they were actually sick."

"He might not have known. The meeting I had was private—just me and the council. I explained how I wanted to give the Icori the stash I'd been holding. I told them I'd replace it—that I'd go to Patience for more. I even pointed out it was better if the black fever got stamped out in Kerniall before it spread. But the council refused. They thought it was too risky and said something to the effect that it wasn't our responsibility to look after heathens, that the Icori's best shot to beat the fever was to renounce their gods."

"Six have mercy," I muttered, appalled. "And that's when you sold it anyway?"

"I did. Sneaked off just like I did with you, but no one was doing checks then. The Icori insisted on buying it for market price, though I would've taken a lot less. They aren't beggars and thieves, no matter what most Osfridians think. They were still sending payments after the black fever was gone, which is probably where the rumors about me turning a higher profit came from."

"Why didn't you replace it afterward?"

"I tried." Genuine regret sounded in his voice, a far cry from the happy-go-lucky Jago I knew. "But I couldn't get out to Patience right away because there was such an uproar to deal with in Constancy. When I finally made the trip, I found out most of Patience's supply had been shipped to an outbreak in Watchful only a few days earlier. So, I went to a Balanquan post and salvaged a little there. It's not much, but it's enough to help in an emergency. The council doesn't know about it—I was tired of dealing with them."

"You're nicer to them than they were to you," I pronounced.

"'If you're on the path of right, and someone crosses it with wrong, you don't need to turn. Build a bridge over their path and continue on your way.' That's an Icori proverb."

"It's very noble," I said. "Were you thinking of it at the time?"

"Nah. I was just thinking no one should have to suffer if there was a relatively easy way for me to help."

"It didn't sound easy."

"That's why I said 'relatively.'"

I smiled but couldn't shake my guilt. "I wish Gideon had told me everything. I'm sorry for doubting you."

"You didn't know. He probably didn't either."

The honesty and humility in his voice pierced my heart. He was the hero in this story, not the villain. I sat up and reached over the crate. I couldn't see, and in my fumbling, my hand accidentally jabbed Jago in the face. He made a muffled cry of either surprise or pain, and I quickly pulled back. "Sorry. I was trying for your hand, to hold it in a gesture of . . . I don't know, solidarity. Admiration."

"Well, that makes more sense," he said. "I was worried you were trying to move in on my virtue, but it wasn't the best approach. And then I was worried it'd get awkward because I didn't really want to say anything in case that was some advanced technique you'd spent hours honing at the Glittering Court. Or worse, it was some technique you'd failed on, and that would be awkward too."

"Good grief, Jago." I flounced back down on my side. "You came up with all that? The whole thing took five seconds."

"Well, I can think pretty fast." Unable to handle the ensuing silence, he asked, "So . . . still want to hold my hand?"

"Eh, my emotional moment of being overwhelmed by your kindness is past. I mean, you still did a great thing."

"Oh. Okay, but if you change your mind, you can just come over here. Or I'll come to you. Whatever's easiest."

"Good night, Jago."

When a few minutes passed, I thought he'd conceded. Then: "If you want to hold it another time, that's okay too."

I groaned. "If I agree to, will you let me sleep?"

"Good night, Tamsin."

Our second day passed without incident, which was good, of course, though it also made for a lot of monotony. Jago never had a shortage of topics to discuss, but sometimes even he had to take a break from talking. Still, I came to enjoy his company more than I expected. Without the specters of the bitterroot or river passage hanging over us, we got along easily and developed a real rapport, though often it strayed into one of us seeing just how much we could exasperate the other.

He was a welcome diversion because when we weren't talking, I spent most of my time ruminating. The land had become stark and barren, the forests giving way to endless snowy plains. With little to see in the outside world, I turned my thoughts inward on the many uncertainties clouding my future. Merry, the trip south, finding a husband, the Lorandians and Icori . . . it was a lot to wrestle with, especially because I had no solutions for any of it.

I used our lunch break to write a quick letter, and that was when a horrible, agonizing realization nearly knocked me over. "The picture!" I exclaimed, the pen slipping from my hands. It bounced off the sleigh's seat and hit the ground. Jago, who'd been tending the horses, retrieved it.

"What's wrong?"

I slumped forward, burying my face in my hands. How had it not occurred to me sooner? When the storm had hit on the *Gray Gull*, I'd rescued some letters and the picture Olivia had drawn. They'd all been kept safely under my mattress in the attic, and in lonely times, I'd take the drawing out and gaze at my family's faces. After being locked up in isolation, I'd never returned to the Cole house, and the drawing had slipped my mind in the wake of my escape with Jago.

He climbed up now and tried to look in my eyes. "What's wrong?" he repeated.

I lifted my head, my breath coming in gasps as I fought to not break down into total sobbing. "It's gone! I left it at the Coles'. It was the last thing I had of them—of anyone I loved—and now—and now—"

I hopped down, unable to go on. I stalked away, pacing around our camp with no real destination as I swallowed back more sobs. I had the frantic, irrational notion that if I could keep moving, I could somehow escape my problems. Jago let me be, but finally, crushed by the weight of everything working against me, I sank to my knees and hid my face again, this time surrendering to the tears.

Jago's arm slipped around me, helping me up. "Now, now, this is no place to cry. That wind'll freeze your cheeks. I'll cover up the hold, and you can rest back there."

"No, no." I wriggled away from him and wiped my eyes with my sleeve. "I don't want to slow us down. Let's go. I'm fine now." Neither of us believed that, not with my rapid breathing and constant sniffling.

He didn't stop me from returning to the sleigh's seat, where I sat in misery and gazed off at the bleak plains, their emptiness a match for what I felt inside. How had I forgotten about the drawing? Why had I ever even kept it in my room? I should have had it in a pocket at all times.

"Hey, can you help me?" Jago called a few minutes later.

I blinked a few more times and then made my way to him as he stood by Dove. "W-what?" I asked, not meeting his eyes.

"Can you brush them for me? Something's wrong with Pebble's trace, and it'll take forever if I have to sort it out and then do their grooming."

I dragged my gaze to the silvery duo. "I wouldn't have the first clue how."

"Here, watch." He retrieved a box from the hold and showed me the grooming tools inside. After demonstrating how they worked, he removed the horses' harnesses and crouched down to figure out the trace's problem. Tentatively, I ran the comb over Dove's coat, trying to imitate what he'd done. The gray mare lifted her head, and I jumped back, afraid I'd hurt her. But she seemed curious more than anything and soon turned away.

I felt slow and clumsy as I worked, constantly questioning myself and going back to make sure I hadn't missed any dirt or matting. Jago was still puzzling over the gear, so I wasn't totally dragging us down.

Dove was sleek and shiny when I finished, and I took a step back to admire the results. She shook her head with a small whicker, and I like to think she approved.

Afterward, I did Pebble's coat. When that was finished, I asked, "Can I do their manes?"

"Sure," he said, not looking up. "But you don't have to. It's the sweat and wear I mostly want taken care of. They won't mind getting pretty, though."

Since he was still busy, I figured I might as well tend to the manes. I approached it like brushing my own hair, and he occasionally gave me pointers. There was a strange sort of comfort in caring for them. The things I grappled with were usually intangible. Touching something real and solid and seeing actual results provided a satisfaction I never seemed to get these days. When I was done, I took turns petting each of the horses, and Jago finally rose in triumph. "Got it," he said. "This should make it easier on them."

He hitched them back up in no time while I cleared the rest of the camp. Before long, we were gliding across the snow again, never mentioning my breakdown.

Later, when we stopped for the night, he went to the horses right away as he always did while I readied the hold and set out our food. This time, I watched as he went through his nightly routine, feeding them and giving them another rubdown after the long day of travel.

"More dried-out biscuits," he declared as he joined me at the fire. "I tell you, Tamsin, we eat like kings around here. And queens."

"You groomed those horses in a fraction of the time I did." I gazed into the flames, turning the biscuit around in my hands. "It wouldn't have slowed us at all if you'd rubbed them down after fixing the trace."

"There wasn't much to do tonight," he said easily. "You did such a good job earlier, I breezed right through it."

"Was the trace even broken?"

He stalled by taking a bite of his food. "Horses are easy," he said after a while. "Easier than people. If you're good to them, they're good to you. It's nice, a creature that's so uncomplicated, you know? I like to think it heals the soul."

We finished the meal without saying anything else. When bedtime came, I paused beside the sleigh, resting my hand on its side. Jago had been about to climb in but stopped when he noticed me.

"Before I left, my sister sent me a picture—a drawing she did of our family. She's good. It looked just like them." I tipped my head back, watching as clouds moved across the night sky, occasionally opening up pockets of stars. "I kept it safe in the storm on the ship and hid it under my bed at Samuel's. I never had a chance to get it back, and now, it's like . . . I feel like they—everyone who's against me—managed to take one more thing from me. And sometimes I wonder how much is left for them to take. How much more do I have inside of me to keep on going?"

"As much as you need." He put his back against the sleigh and followed my gaze upward. "I'll get the drawing when I go back to Constancy."

I shook my head. "It's just a picture. It's not *them*, and they're the ones I'm working for."

"I'll get the picture," he repeated. He swung up into the sleigh and held out a hand to help me.

As he did, I heard one of the horses neigh. I turned in their direction, even though I couldn't see them. "Could I . . . could I drive them tomorrow?"

"Do you know how to?"

"No."

"Okay. I'll show you how. Do you know how to ride?"

"No."

"I'll show you that too when we get some downtime."

I accepted his hand and laughed for what felt like the first time in ages. "You really think we'll have a lot of that?"

"For this, I'll make it."

CHAPTER 19

"LEAVE US BLOODY ALONE, JAGO! WE'RE DOING JUST FINE!"

"They'll get away from you. The weight in a sleigh is distributed so that—"

"Hush!"

Seeing him reach for the reins, I elbowed him away and leaned forward. Dove and Pebble immediately responded with more speed, and I whooped with joy. We flew over the snow, the wind whipping loose pieces of my hair around as it rushed by. Eventually, satisfied I'd keep control, Jago settled back and stopped his insistence on caution. No obstacle stood in front of us, nothing to block our way. Just wide-open land, waiting and beckoning.

It wasn't until Jago yelled that we were going the wrong way that I pulled back, gradually bringing the horses to a stop.

I returned the reins to him and said, "We should just keep going and going. Why all the hassle with everyone else? We can just fly to Denham in this."

"Two problems." He urged the horses into a turn, putting us back on course. "One: We won't do much flying if we run into a blizzard. Two: Those red barns will never get emptied out if I take off in this."

"And here I thought you were the fun one. Why did you paint them red anyway? One walk through that town should've made you reconsider."

"I don't know." He crooked me a grin. "I guess just to see what would happen."

It was the end of our third day of travel, and when we stopped for dinner, Jago told me we'd be reaching the Lorandian trading post, Lo Canne, soon. "Not sure if we'll learn anything about the so-called Icori attack," he said. "But I'm still banking on some of that stolen stuff working its way into trade circulation by now. If we're lucky, we'll see some." He wrapped up our leftover bread and put it back in our bag of food. "And I forgot to mention this, but you've got to have a wardrobe change before we go."

"You 'forgot,' huh?" I asked suspiciously. "What did you have in mind?"

After shuffling around in the wagon's hold, he returned with a bundle of clothes and a pair of boots. I examined them, noting the green-and-black plaid.

"Icori clothes?"

"Yes, ma'am. It might be suspicious if I show up with a well-dressed, proper Osfridian lady. But Icori come through all the time. That, and if any of the men who robbed you are at the camp, they're less likely to recognize you. People see what they're expecting to see."

That got through to me, and I changed while Jago discreetly packed up the back of the sleigh. When I finished, I wasn't sure what to think. The ensemble consisted of a thigh-length plaid tunic worn over chestnut-colored leather pants. A matching fleece-lined jacket came down to my hip and was belted with a black sash. The heavy, sturdy boots were far more masculine than any I'd ever worn, but they were also more practical than my shoes in the snow. Jago crossed his arms and looked me over.

"What are you thinking, Tamsin? Because I can tell you're thinking something. Is it the pants?"

I ran my hands along the sides of my legs, trying to formulate a diplomatic response. "This leather's wonderfully soft. And warmer than a skirt. But . . . they show a lot."

"They cover everything up," he said, but he knew exactly what I meant. "Balanquan and Icori women wear them all the time."

"That's well and good for them, but I've worn skirts my whole life! I'm not used to strangers seeing the shape of my legs."

"It'll be dark there," he said helpfully.

"It's not dark now."

"Yes, but I'm not a stranger. And I'm a gentleman. I'm not going to brazenly stare at your legs, even if those pants do make them look extremely . . ."

I narrowed my eyes. "Yes, Jago?"

He cleared his throat and glanced away. "Fit."

"Is that *really* what you were thinking?"

"It's one of the things I was thinking." He pulled a plain, dark-brown cloak from the hold and tossed it to me. "Wear this if it'll make you feel better."

I fastened it on, pleased with the way the cloak's folds wrapped around me. "Do I look the part?"

"You do, especially if you braid your hair. We'll pass you off as a fair Icori maiden from an isolated shrine by Kerniall. They don't have much contact with outsiders, so no one will expect you to know Lorandian. Hopefully, someone'll let something slip in front of you."

"I hope I can catch enough. I'm not fluent." I shook my hair forward and began to braid. "And what do I do if one of them tries to talk to me in Icori?"

"Not a problem. Because there's, ah, something else I forgot to mention."

I looked up. "Yes, Jago?"

He was trying to act chagrined, but the smile in his eyes betrayed him as usual. "You're a fair Icori maiden from a holy shrine . . . who's under a vow of silence."

"Does that really happen?"

"Sure does. I know it won't be easy, but it's a great way to keep our cover. You think you can pull it off?"

I rolled my eyes and returned to my hair. "Six, Jago. Of course I can pull it off. I'm not you."

We reached Lo Canne in early evening, though the dark clouds made it feel later. The Lorandian trading post was a motley collection of tents and shanties not far from a tiny tributary of the massive Heart's Blood River. It had a thrown-together feel to it, despite being a few years old. I'd felt bright and alive after driving the sleigh, but now, as we walked into the home of Osfrid's longtime rival and possibly the men who'd accosted me, my old wariness had returned.

A couple of men in leather and fur walked out to greet us, their faces hard and lined from so much outdoor living. They immediately started speaking Lorandian, and we quickly made it clear that we didn't. Neither of them knew Osfridian, but after a few minutes, they found someone who did—and someone who knew Jago too.

"Jacob Robinson!"

"Hello, Marcel." Jago shook hands with a short, barrel-chested man in a beaver fur cap. Messy black hair grazed his shoulders, and his accent sounded exactly like my old neighbor's.

Marcel cast an eager look at the sleigh. "You've come just in time. Do you have any nails or bacon?"

"No, but I have twine and cornmeal."

The Lorandian snorted. "How is that the same? Especially the twine?"

"I'm trying to offload them both, so you can buy them at a really low price now and then sell them later when someone shows up with nails and bacon."

"Pfft. I'm not the usual fool you deal with, Robinson." Marcel turned contemplative. "But show me that twine later."

"Absolutely." Jago rested a hand on my back to bring me forward. "Marcel, this is Breia Ipaeron. She's one of the servers at the Well, under a vow of silence."

Marcel bowed and rattled off a greeting in Icori. I smiled and responded with a nod. "We're always happy to see our friends from the Well," Marcel said, though his demeanor shifted slightly. Jago had told me the Lorandians were extremely superstitious about the Well. "What brings you—"

Another Lorandian man sidled over, his heavy brow giving the impression he was squinting. He spoke to Marcel in rapid Lorandian, challenging my rusty skills. One word I did distinctly pick out was "Constancy," though Jago could have spotted that one on his own. Marcel nodded when the man finished and turned back to us.

"You're a long ways out, Robinson. Haven't you been based farther east this winter? Constancy?"

"Yup, though I haven't been there in a couple of weeks. Got my watchman keeping an eye on everything. I'm going south soon on the East Sister and have to sell off the surplus I don't want to bring. Visited a couple of other towns and a Balanquan post, plus the Well—which is where I crossed paths with Breia."

Marcel nodded along and smiled, then held up a hand for Jago to pause. Leaning over, Marcel said something to the other Lorandian. Most sounded like a direct translation of what Jago had said, though I also picked up a Lorandian expression that meant "no problem."

When Marcel was ready, Jago continued: "The Icori need *reed* for one of the Well's sanctuaries, so she wanted to see if you had any close by before trekking to the Balanquans."

"Some, I think." Marcel scratched at his chin as he pondered. "Philbert was west of the river and just got back. He's got a lot of Balanquan goods—come see."

We followed Marcel farther into the camp, receiving scrutiny from the various traders. I noted two women as we passed, one as weathered and roughly dressed as Marcel, and the other looking as though she might be a lady of questionable repute.

A few others knew Jago, and when word got around about how extensive a trader he was, business turned serious. Traders began displaying their wares, bartering with Jago in a mix of Osfridian, Lorandian, and gestures. He in turn brought out goods from the sleigh, and before long, I felt like I was back in the market district. The Lorandians smiled at me in passing but otherwise showed the same unease around me Marcel had.

Philbert, the man with Balanquan goods, showed off all sorts of curious treasures, and it drove me crazy not being able to ask about them. He had several pieces of *reed*, a silvery black rock, that Jago haggled for on my behalf. The Icori believed it was sacred and used it for divination by scattering pieces and interpreting where they landed. Once my alleged business was concluded, I mostly just stood and observed, trying to understand what I could in the scraps of Lorandian conversation around me.

One of the traders had a saw that Jago was keenly interested in, but he wouldn't budge on the monetary cost. Jago thought it was too high but couldn't interest the man in an exchange.

"What about this?" Jago held up a small blue glass bottle. "A Balanquan waking elixir. What do you usually drink in the morning? Coffee? Tea? Add a few drops of this into your cup, and wow. You'll have a real eye opener there."

"I know those," the Lorandian said with a scowl. "They wake you up—day *and* night! I already have problems falling asleep."

Jago brightened. "Why didn't you say so?" He opened a crate and found a nearly identical blue bottle. "Balanquan sleeping elixir. One drop of this . . ."

"Your glove, danna. You ripped it."

It took me a moment to realize the Icori title was being directed at me. I turned away from Jago's pitch and found a very young Lorandian trader, certainly no older than me, standing nearby. Having my full attention now, he pointed at my hand.

"You ripped your glove."

I nodded, having noticed it earlier. The only Icori ones Jago had were old and worn so thin that they'd torn after snagging on one of the rein buckles. It was a minor nuisance, and I couldn't very well replace them with the pink mittens.

"She's under a vow of silence, friend." Jago, still holding a blue bottle, stepped away from his negotiations and moved to my side. He smiled as he spoke, but his eyes were watchful. "No need to worry, though. We'll fix it up later. I've got needle and thread in my sleigh—extra, actually, if you need any."

The boy shook his head emphatically. "No, no. Why bother fixing those? They're falling apart everywhere. The danna should have something nice and new. Take a look at these."

Bursting with excitement, he presented his prize for our examination: a pair of soft black mittens, edged with silver beads.

I didn't have to fake a vow of silence just then, because the sight of those mittens rendered me speechless.

"Well, how about that," said Jago, leaning closer. "They look just your size, Breia."

"Feel them," urged the boy, eager for a potential win. "Like silk."

Jago picked one up. "Cashmere, I'd say. Are these Balanquan made?"

"Real Evarian import. You won't find anything like these in Adoria outside of Cape Triumph." The boy thrust a mitten toward me. "Beautiful mittens for a beautiful lady."

"But this beautiful lady's a humble servant of the Well," said Jago. He made a great show of examining the mitten's construction, turning it inside out, and finally handing it back. "Not much need for high Evarian fashion there—if these are even genuine. Come on, Breia. Let's settle those elixirs and get some sleep."

The boy cast me a nervous look but then steeled his courage to scurry along with us. "Wait! They're genuine! Did you see the beads? You can have them for one gold."

Jago eyed the mittens a few seconds, seemed to waver, and then shook his head. "Too much, and I've got to finish this deal. Now, you, sir—sorry I stepped away. Are you still interested in that elixir?"

He resumed his negotiations for the saw, and it looked as though the sleeping potion was almost enough to do it. Noticing me, the saw owner asked hesitantly, "She's from the Well, right? Does she tell fortunes? Is that why she wanted the black stones?"

"She doesn't talk," Jago said brusquely. "But I see that the sides of your toolbox there are loose. You need to bind those up before it falls apart."

The boy with the mittens shifted from foot to foot as Jago bartered. As soon as he finished the deal—getting the saw in exchange for the sleeping elixir and a spool of twine—the young trader was ready to try again.

"Fifteen silver," he said. "That's a steal."

Jago knelt down to pack up one of his boxes. "I'm not parting with any coin."

"Ten silver."

"I mean it. I need to downsize. I'm only trading."

"Look how much your lady friend loves these! She can't stop looking at them."

"Oh, that I can believe," said Jago drily. Hoisting a bag over his shoulder, he rose. "How do you feel about cornmeal?"

"Cornmeal?"

"One bag for the mittens."

The young trader's brow furrowed. "Why would I want cornmeal for them?"

"Well, you've got to eat, don't you? Cornmeal's more valuable than flour out here. Doesn't spoil as much, less messy . . . and you don't need a bunch of extra ingredients to make something decent like you do with flour. I'll have to give you my grandma's corn bread recipe before I go. Easy to make, tastes like fine Evarian cuisine."

I could tell the boy had never considered trading for cornmeal, but he was considering it now. Such was Jago's magic.

"Okay then. I'll give you the mittens for . . . five bags."

"Five? Didn't you just hear me say it's worth more than flour? I'd give you five bags of *that* if I had it, maybe. But for this . . . I'll do two bags, and that's just because Breia wants those mittens so badly." Jago set the bag down and added another on top of it.

Just as the young trader looked like he was about to crack, a sharp rebuke in Lorandian made him wince. The boy jumped, spinning around as an older man with a dark-blond beard came striding over. Tall and barrel chested, he wore the same rugged, practical clothing as the other traders, but his long wool coat was much better quality than his peers'.

Firelight caught the side of his face as he launched into a lecture in Lorandian, and I nearly gasped. Fear flooded me, and I took a few hasty steps back, bumping into Jago. He put a hand on my shoulder and murmured in my ear, "What's wrong? Do you recognize him?"

Yes, I'd seen him before, but the circumstances had been very different. It had been far from this place, and he hadn't worn a finely cut wool coat then. He'd been clad in woad and worn tartan, bearing down on me as I stood in defense of Alan Morwell.

CHAPTER 20

I QUICKLY LOWERED MY GAZE, PRETENDING TO BE interested in the Balanquan rocks. In hoping we'd find some evidence of the men who'd robbed us, I hadn't expected to actually find *one of them*! And certainly not the one I'd been up close and personal with.

Fortunately for me, the big Lorandian's attention was focused elsewhere. From what I could follow, the boy was frantically explaining how cornmeal was more valuable than flour. The man cuffed him and called him a fool. *Corn*, *flour*, and *fool* were words I'd heard regularly from my Lorandian baker neighbor.

The bearded man looked right over me, recognizing that Jago was the deal maker. "Forget the cornmeal," he said in accented Osfridian. "Do you have any lard?"

"I have tallow."

"Let's see it."

While the two negotiated, I hovered in the shadows as much as possible, still fearful of recognition. The man's Osfridian was as good as Marcel's and not the stunted speech of our previous encounter. As the negotiations proceeded, Jago made subtle inquiries about anything else the man might have for sale, and eventually, they settled on two jars of tallow and a silver coin in exchange for the beaded mittens. Jago handed them to me, and the Lorandians departed, the older still scolding the younger as they walked.

We watched them go inside a little shanty, in front of which the saw's former owner and another Lorandian sat around a campfire. Jago picked up his goods and beckoned me back to the sleigh. Away from Lorandian eyes and ears, we sat together in the dark hold and finally conversed freely. "Was he one of them?" Jago asked immediately.

"Yes—the one who hit Alan and faced me down."

"Didn't *you* face *him* down? Regardless, I think after seeing him just now, it's safe to say the Icori robbers were imposters. And we've got the mittens as proof too."

I'd put them on, happy to have their warmth back. "Except nobody in Constancy—besides Alan—really saw the mittens. So there's not much in the way of evidence, aside from our word. Actually, it'll just be your word, since I can't go back."

"Not sure how much my word will be worth there. The Icori would believe me—or at least seriously consider what I had to say—but that won't matter if Grashond escalates hostilities."

"We need to show the town's council some item that was unquestionably taken that day, something that can't be duplicated. If you can bring *that* back from the Lorandians, they'll see that the thieves weren't Icori. Do you think any of the other items are here?"

"I think it's likely some are. He said he had fur and wool clothes to trade, but half the guys around here will too. Could be hard to prove something like that came from the Constancy raid."

"Maybe the hornbook?" I mused. "I think Lev's name was on it."

Jago stretched back against the sleigh's side, folding his arms behind his head. "Well, maybe in the morning, we could find him and say we need fur. That might be an opening to check out anything else he has."

"It still won't tell us why the Lorandians would go to so much trouble for these stunts."

"No, but I'll settle for simply convincing the Icori and the colonists that the other didn't attack."

He checked the horses and made our seed-bag beds again. As he did, I sat wrapped under a blanket and observed that a handful of

Lorandians were still up and around, some in earnest conversation and others drinking and laughing.

"Are we safe out here?" I asked Jago. "Do we need to keep watch overnight?" No one had threatened us, but a few of the traders had given off a hard, mercenary vibe, and I certainly knew what the man with the blond beard was capable of.

"I don't think we have much to worry about. I'm sure there are a few transients who'd be all for robbing a colonial trader, but some—like Marcel—value me too much as a partner. That, and half of them think you're a witch."

"But that one asked me for a fortune."

"Yeah, the Lorandians see it as sorcery, but at the same time, they have a secret fascination with it." He held out another blanket. "Want it?"

"Yes. I don't think I'll ever truly be warm in Adoria."

"I like your optimism." He set a rifle into his half of the hold and reached for the oilcloth cover.

"Why the gun? You said we don't have much to worry about."

"Eh, I'm just making sure we don't have *anything* to worry about."

I couldn't fall asleep. Too many things played through my mind. Even though it had seemed less and less likely the men by the pond were Icori, having it confirmed absolutely drove up the peculiarity—and danger—of the situation. The Lorandians were purposely misleading my people and the Icori. To what end? Making life difficult for the colonists was one thing, but inciting a war was a whole other matter. I'd liked the Icori I met, and despite my harsh treatment in Constancy, I'd liked plenty of its residents too. Chester Woods, the cobbler, the children, Gideon . . .

I didn't want anyone on either side hurt, and it was maddening to have proof of the deception appear so obvious to me . . . but not necessarily to others. Hopefully, we could find an innocent way to see the big Lorandian's other goods. Jago's persuasive powers weren't foolproof, though. It was too bad I didn't actually have mystical ones to lend him . . .

I sat up, my heart pounding rapidly. On one side of me, I could hear Jago's steady breathing. On the other, scattered voices from the Lorandian post. Gingerly, I pushed up the oilcloth and leaned over the partition toward Jago's side. It was too dark to see, but he inhaled and exhaled with the deepness of sleep and didn't stir at the sound of the oilcloth rustling. Retreating to my side, I felt around for the bag of *reed*. Once I found it, I regretfully unwrapped my blankets and climbed out of the sleigh as quietly as I could.

Outside, I smoothed the oilskin cover back and stood very still, waiting to see if I'd disturbed Jago. I hadn't. Closing my eyes, I took a moment to steel myself and then strode boldly forward, back to the camp.

I walked through it with purpose, barely sparing a glance for the Lorandians still awake. They looked at me, though—most with simple curiosity, others with apprehension. Chin up and eyes fixed ahead of me, I made my way toward the shanty that the boy and bearded man had gone into earlier. They were still up, sitting around the fire with two others—including the man who'd traded Jago the saw.

The group's conversation stopped at my approach. I stood before them and kept my face expressionless as I let my gaze sweep each face. After a bit of suspense, I focused on the man who'd asked Jago if I told fortunes. Never taking my eyes from his, I reached into my burlap bag and produced one of the silvery black rocks. I held it up and pointed at him.

He flinched, nearly dropping a brown bottle he'd been drinking from. I stayed motionless and just waited. Swallowing, he asked in Lorandian why I was here. The young trader told him in a loud whisper that I didn't know Lorandian, so the man switched. "What—that is, will you read my fortune?"

I nodded and waited again. "What do you want?" he asked uneasily. The group's fourth man gave a Lorandian suggestion I understood perfectly: "Pay her."

My "client" stood up and fumbled with his money bag. When he set a copper coin in my palm, I gave it a scathing look and then locked gazes with him. One of the others snickered. With a sigh, the man exchanged the copper for a silver, and I slipped it into my coat pocket. It was kind of amazing how much you could say without speaking a word.

I pointed at the shanty. Ordinarily, I'd expect to fear going off alone with a rough stranger like this, but it was clear I was the one who made him nervous. Nonetheless, he opened the door and gestured me in. As he followed, I heard one of the others murmur an angelic benediction.

Loud snoring promptly told me we were not, in fact, alone. My companion lit a lantern, revealing a small room crammed with dirty pallets and piles of boxes, bags, and furs. It smelled like sweat and rotting food. He shook a blanket-wrapped form on one of the pallets, and another man jumped up, swearing in Lorandian. After a brief argument, the sleeper left, grumbling, his steps quickening when he caught sight of me.

Once alone with me, my companion haphazardly shoved items aside to clear a spot. We knelt down opposite one another, and I spread my hands out, making a gesture that was half shrug and half *Well? Go ahead.*

He licked his lips a few times. "Eh, what now?"

I repeated the motion.

"Do I . . . that is, can I ask you a question? Will your spirits answer it?"

I nodded.

"Okay." Looking away, he turned contemplative. His face appeared troubled, but by his own thoughts now, not me. After a long drink from the brown bottle he'd carried in, he lifted his eyes. "Will she ever love me?"

It was hard to keep my face straight. I hadn't expected that sort of question from a man like him, certainly not spoken with such intensity and emotion. Hastily, I motioned for him to continue. I was going to need more to work with to understand him and accomplish my original goal. Fortunately, he was more than happy to elaborate.

His scarred face crumpled. "I know I'm not good enough for her. I've seen the way her family looks at me. They see me come through on my trips and criticize how I won't stay put. I think it bothers them more than where I'm from. They want her to marry a farmer like her father, but she still hasn't. And she always seems glad to see me." He took another drink and looked at me beseechingly. "Can you ask your spirits? Is there a chance? Will she love me one day?"

I took the black stones and rolled them over the dirty floor. When they stopped moving, I leaned close and scrutinized them, acting as though I was receiving all sorts of information. After almost five tension-filled minutes, he exclaimed in Lorandian, "Angels' mercy!" Then in Osfridian: "What do they say, witch? Will Gwen love me?"

Slowly, cruelly, I lifted my face toward his. After a few more beats, I nodded.

He fell forward, burying his face in his hands and rattling off Lorandian prayers of thanks. When he'd recovered, he looked at me again and asked, "What do I have to do?"

I stood up and walked around, trying to make sense of the cluttered shanty. Although not obvious at first, the clutter did seem to be divided four ways. I pointed at one pile and looked at him. He shook his head, puzzled. "What? That's not mine." I repeated this act until he indicated his belongings, which seemed to be composed of hides, felt, and more brown bottles.

Ignoring it, I turned my attention to the other traders' heaps, unclear which might belong to the large man with the tawny hair and beard. I began rifling through the items, eliciting surprise from my Lorandian companion, though he was too afraid to stop me. I knew when I at last came across the bearded man's things because they contained Lev's hornbook, Gideon's belt buckle, and a few other notable trinkets. But I didn't stop or call attention to them. Instead, I finished my sweep of all the piles and then returned to the watching man.

"What is it?" he demanded. "Please, what do I have to do?"

I held up five fingers, and after a little deduction, he gathered that I had five orders. First, I pointed at his belongings and made a sweeping gesture, like I was gathering it all up. I hid my fist away and took out the silver coin.

"Sell it?" he asked uncertainly. "Trade?"

I nodded, letting him interpret that as he wished. Next, I picked up a plate from one of his shanty-mate's items, displaying a painted pastoral scene. I tapped the house, and after a few tries, he guessed that he was to get a house. For my third instruction, I picked up a potato from a bag of food, and he immediately guessed, "I should grow potatoes." It confirmed what I'd thought by the name Gwen. It was an Osfridian name, almost exclusively used by those from the Flatlands region. I knew many had settled in Archerwood and grew potatoes and other root vegetables. His beloved was the daughter of a Flatlander farmer.

The golden ring I pointed to in someone's trunk had an unmistakable meaning. After returning it, I left the jumble of objects alone and stood over him with my hands on my hips.

"That was four," he said. "What's the fifth thing I have to do to win her love?"

I picked up the brown bottle, getting a strong whiff of whiskey, and poured it into a chamber pot.

"Hey!" He sprang up in shock but didn't touch me. He watched the last of the whiskey drip away and sighed. When I put the pot's lid back on and stared at him, he gave a weak nod. "Yes. I understand." He took the empty bottle from me, and even though I'd put back the plate, potato, and ring, his eyes traveled to where they'd come from. "And when I do these things, when I have the money to buy a house and farm, then I can marry her, and she'll love me?"

I pointed at the whiskey bottle.

"I'll stop. I'll stop if it'll get me Gwen. Will it? Do your gods swear it?"

I didn't feel guilty when I nodded once more. Would it win her? Maybe. He'd claimed she liked him. I couldn't know the whole story, but I felt mostly confident that, one way or another, his life would improve for the better if he stopped drinking and moved out of this place. Sniffling, he covered his face with his great hands and tried to muffle his sobs. I gathered my rocks and retreated over to a corner to give him space. When he settled down a few minutes later, he wiped his face and stood up. He regarded me calmly, his cheeks red and blotchy but his eyes remarkably serene. *"G-gormat. Gormat."*

I smiled, recognizing the Icori word for "thank you." Job done, I headed for the door, pausing to give him back the silver coin. "It's your payment," he said. "Why are you returning it?"

"Gwen," I answered. I left him there gaping, and it was hard to say if he was more astonished that I'd broken my silence or contributed toward his house fund. There was no way I could have kept that coin, though.

I stepped outside, just in time to see Jago tearing through the camp with the rifle, his face ablaze. "Where is she?" he demanded. "Where is—" Both his words and his feet stopped abruptly when he saw me. Outrage turned to confusion. He looked me over, checking for distress, and then studied those nearby. "What's . . . going on?"

No one answered. I smiled and glided forward, linking my arm through his. He allowed me to lead him away, and we walked out of the silent camp, Lorandian gazes following us.

As soon as we were back in the privacy of the sleigh, the expected outburst came. What I didn't expect was to be wrapped up in a fierce embrace. "Tamsin! Are you okay? Do you have any idea how much you scared me?"

"I'm sorry, Jago." I rested my head against him a few more moments before gently pulling away. "But I couldn't stop thinking about how we need to give the council hard proof. And then I had an idea for what to do—how to check out that man's possessions."

Jago lit a lantern, and there was not even the slightest whisper of amusement in his typically carefree face as he helped me into the sleigh. "I'm not surprised you had some flash of inspiration. It's what you do. Just please make sure the next time you do it, you bring me along! Six. I thought one of them had carried you off."

"I mean it, I'm sorry." He didn't look mad as we settled across from one another, but he didn't look happy either. "Drained" was probably the best description. "I didn't want to wake you because I wasn't sure you'd let me go."

"Like I could let or not let you do anything. At most, I'd just strongly protest."

"Well, I didn't want that either. And I think it was better I was alone. They're more afraid of me than of you, you know."

Some of the tension had faded from his features, and although he was still wound up from the scare, I could detect a glimmer of amusement—grim amusement, perhaps—in him. "What did you do?"

"Strangely enough, I counseled someone on how to find love and happiness. Oh, and I also encouraged him to take up potato farming."

Jago's smile returned, but it had a rueful quality. "Tamsin, don't tease me. I've gone through enough tonight."

I reached for the bag of stones and, with a flourish worthy of him, pulled out a fur-lined child's coat. "Does this look like teasing?"

Jago took it and held it near the lantern, where we could just barely read *AJM* lovingly handstitched in the back of the collar.

"The coat Alan Morwell's mother made for him," Jago said in awe. "Tamsin, how do you do these things?"

I scooted over to him so that we could sit side by side against the hold's edge. "I haven't really done anything outlandish since I broke out of captivity. I didn't want you to get bored."

He lifted the coat up one more time, shook his head, and carefully placed the garment into another bag. "There was no danger of that, but thank you for thinking of me. Besides, you're forgetting that you nearly poked my eye out the other night."

"I did forget about that, didn't I? Oh, and I suppose that's not the only thing."

I reached out and took his hand, entwining my fingers with his.

Looking down in momentary surprise, he shifted so that our hands were linked a little tighter. With a half-smile playing at his lips, he leaned his head back against the hold in contentment.

"No commentary?" I asked, not entirely faking my astonishment.

The smile twitched. "I'm afraid I'll lose this if I say something. Safer to stay quiet."

"Have you ever said that before?"

"Hush, and let me enjoy this."

I leaned back with him, basking in the buzz of unexpected warmth inside me. Turning, I studied his profile in the lantern's glow, intrigued by how the light picked out so many different shades of gold, everything from a deep bronze to a few strands that had been bleached almost platinum by the sun. Gideon might never have been a legitimate romantic option, but like everyone else, I'd admired his classic good looks. Jago was a jumble of contradictions by comparison. Nothing matched or stayed consistent, be it his eyes or his hair or even the lopsided way he smiled when particularly amused. I liked the contradictions, though. The sum of his imperfections seemed to create a special type of perfection that I found myself increasingly taken in by.

Sensing my scrutiny, he turned his head so we looked each other in the eye. "Yes, Tamsin?"

"We're the same height," I mused. "Not sure I ever noticed that before."

"Most women notice it right away."

"I like it. It seems . . . convenient."

He rested his free hand on my cheek, lightly running his fingertips along it before he leaned in and brought his face toward mine. My heart beat so heavily, it was impossible he couldn't hear it. And the sleigh's snug hold suddenly seemed smaller than ever because the intensity of his presence filled up every space. I was starting to close my eyes when he stopped, our mouths a few inches apart.

He stroked the side of my face again, sighed, and let his hand drop.

"I've taken a lot of risks in my days of deal making, but there are some even I'm afraid of."

Though we hadn't kissed, my lips tingled with the tantalizing expectation of it. "And here I thought a master salesman wasn't afraid of getting into any deal."

"True." He brought my hand to his lips and kissed it, sending a jolt through me. With what seemed like great reluctance, he released me. "But it's not being able to get out of this one that scares me. Now. We should get some rest. Scoot over there, and I'll make up our beds."

CHAPTER 21

WE SET OUT EARLY THE NEXT DAY FOR THE ICORI CITY of Kerniall, Orla's home. It lay two days from Lo Canne, and I was more eager than ever to get there. Once I was safely settled, Jago could make his return run to Constancy and show them the coat I'd pilfered while my "client" had had his emotional breakdown in the shanty. Jago would also be able to reassure my friends about me, and despite my objections, he swore he'd get my picture back.

The round-trip would take Jago about a week, and while I was eager for the results, the prospect of our actual time apart left me melancholy.

The placid landscape changed as we headed south, with trees and shrubs returning. The plains gave way to the foothills that heralded the mountainous border running along the Osfridian colonies' western side. I'd seen those mountains countless times on maps, where they were usually drawn in as neat little triangles. As they loomed in the distance now, their snowy peaks mingling with the clouds, I felt like I was looking at living creatures—and that they were watching me in turn.

Shortly after setting out on the morning of the second day of our trip, we reached a small river. A wide, sturdy wooden bridge let us cross, though most of the snow had melted off it. Jago walked alongside the horses, leading them at a snail's pace. The sleigh's runners noisily scraped the wooden planks but otherwise made the crossing without too much difficulty.

Once we were on the move again, I waved around at the white landscape. "What happens to the sleigh if all of this melts?"

"I have wheels in the back that I can attach and replace the runners. It's not as efficient as a regular wagon, but it'll keep you moving in a pinch. Neat idea. I picked it up from some Balanquans last fall."

"Balanquans, Lorandians, Heirs. Is there anyone you don't trade with?"

"In Grashond? Probably not." His eyes scanned the way ahead. "I don't think we have to worry about this melting quite yet. If anything, it's getting colder."

It was, and the wind was picking up too. By late afternoon, dark clouds were spreading across the sky. Jago had been telling funny anecdotes about various reactions to painting the barns in Constancy, but he trailed off mid-story at one point, his face growing increasingly troubled. When the first snowflakes began to fall, he deviated from the straight course we'd been following, turning toward a more treed area to the east.

"What are you doing?" I asked.

"We're going to need to make camp, and I'm trying to find a spot that's not in the open—but also unlikely to get a tree knocked onto it."

Snow fell steadily by the time he found a place he liked. Acting quickly, he hopped into the sleigh's hold and took out a few long, narrow wrapped bundles. He set them next to the horses and then returned to start tying down the oilcloth we used as a roof at night. "Go ahead and get in," he told me. "I'll be there soon."

"What are you going to do?"

He didn't answer but instead unrolled the bundles, which contained long, flexible rods. He began positioning them around the horses, and

I realized he was building a shelter of sorts. I hurried to his side. "What can I do to help?"

"Nothing—go get warm."

The wind snatched away one of the ties he was using to bind two poles together. I managed to snag it and hand it back. After watching him work for a few moments, I took up two other poles and began tying them together in the same way. Once he had the poles set as he wanted, he secured them into the ground with stakes. I helped hold them as he worked, fighting as the wind grew more intense and snow thickened. A slight panic rose up in me at the familiarity of it all, bringing a sickening remembrance of the blizzard in Constancy.

Don't worry, I told myself. *It's not the same. You have shelter and food. Jago knows what to do.*

When the frame was in place, he covered it all with more oilcloth, and we fought to keep it steady. The last corner of the oilcloth proved tricky to tie; it had grown knotted. Jago knelt down in the snow to work on it, and I hovered over him, unsure what to do but also unwilling to leave. At last, the horses' tent was complete, and after a few more checks, he urged me toward the sleigh's hold. The snow came down in sheets now, and we walked hunched over to protect our faces. Once we'd crawled under a gap in the oilcloth's cover, Jago bound that loose flap too. It blocked out the wind and the light.

He shuffled in the darkness, and after a few moments, a small spark glowed inside the lantern he always kept on hand. With the cloth pulled so tightly over us, we couldn't fully sit up, and he took care in placing the lantern where it wouldn't accidentally set anything on fire.

"Will the horses be okay out there?" I asked.

"Yeah. They're hardy. The tent keeps the snow off them and helps trap heat. Would they be okay for a week in there? No, but let's hope this runs the usual course of a day or so." He stretched out on his side, trying to get comfortable. "Sorry I didn't have time to arrange it into our usual setup."

There was still room to lie down, but crates and bags were scattered about, as opposed to the flat, open area he usually prepared on the seed bags. I managed to curl up on my side as well. "I'll take it over being stuck outside. And actually, I'm impressed at how fast you put together our shelter and theirs. I always wondered what people did with their horses in these storms."

"Well, not everyone travels with a setup like that for their horses. They'll survive just fine in most conditions. We didn't see storms quite like this where I grew up in Archerwood, but I remember one winter when I was a kid, a horse got lost outside during a two-day blizzard. When the weather cleared, we found her out in the pasture, hungry but otherwise not worse for the wear." He paused to listen to the wind. "But I'm not taking any chances with mine, if I can help it."

The word choice and emphasis piqued my curiosity. "Weren't the horses you grew up with yours? Or, well, your family's?"

"Oh, no. My family didn't own horses. We didn't own much of anything. There were seven of us kids, and my dad worked all hours for a big plantation owner. We got pulled into various jobs there too, and mine was working in the stables. I slept a lot of nights in that barn. I didn't mind it, though. It's like I said—there was a sincerity to the horses that resonated with me. I didn't have to deal with any of the cruelty or manipulation you get with people."

"Did you get a lot of cruelty or manipulation from people?" I asked, startled.

"More than some, less than others. Kids will always find something to pick on. I was small for my age, and the different-colored eyes were a pretty good target. And being poor, of course, always puts you at a disadvantage."

"Oh, I know."

"I'm sure you do," he said with a wan smile. "I tended the horses—but I couldn't ride them unless it was related to their care. It was made clear to me that I was too lowly to even imagine riding them for sport or convenience. And I sort of came to believe that—you know how it is, when that's the world you're in. But one day, I couldn't resist.

Most everyone was gone to a local festival, even the workers. So, I went for it. I took the youngest, liveliest horse there—this bay stallion named Moonshine—and rode. I rode and rode—let him go as fast as he could. It was one of the greatest moments of my life."

"And after that, you decided to make a career out of raising them?"

"Eh, after that, I got caught and was beaten pretty badly, but it lit something in me. Not long after that, an old peddler came through town and was looking to hire an assistant. He asked me if I thought I might be good at selling things and said that if so, I could leave with him the next day. I didn't actually think I was good at it, though."

"And yet, here you are," I said, startled at that plot twist.

"Here I am. I wanted out badly enough to give it a try. I wanted to take hold of my future, no matter the cost—which turned out to be a high one, seeing as I've spent a fortune on exotic horses that my first employer would say a 'lowly' guy had no business with." The pride in Jago's voice was unmistakable.

"To what end?"

"Racing." Jago's face glowed. "You've seen how Pebble and Dove move. Felicia's faster. Horse racing's starting to gain interest in Adoria, and I plan on raising and training some of the best. Once I get everything settled."

I looked at the spark in his eyes as he spoke, the purity and passion of his conviction shining through. It was a rare, clear glimpse into him, an honest window free of all the pitches and flattery he doled out normally. Neither of us had spoken about holding hands the other night, though I often thought about it. Sometimes, I'd see him watching me, and I suspected he was doing the same.

He reached for the lantern and snuffed it, explaining, "I want to save fuel, and we should sleep anyway. If this storm breaks anywhere close to dawn, we'll head out early."

"I'm too keyed up," I said. "I'm worried about the storm, about getting to Orla on time . . ."

"We'll be fine. I'll make sure of it."

His breezy confidence comforted me, as much as anything could while sheltering in a tarp-covered sleigh during a blizzard. "Okay, but I still don't think I'm going to fall asleep anytime soon. Talk to me about something. Tell me about, I don't know, horse gear."

"Pfft. I didn't realize my life's ambition was boring you. Why don't *you* tell me something for a change."

"Like what?"

"Sailing off to a strange land is a pretty big deal. You said yourself that you sacrificed more than I could understand to get here. So, help me understand. What were you running away from?" When I didn't answer, he added, "Or I can tell you about horse gear."

I rolled over to my back as best I could, pondering if I should answer. As I did, my fingertips brushed his arm, feeling only the leather of his coat. "Where are your blankets?"

"I put them on the horses."

"Jago," I groaned. "They have fur. You don't."

"I've got clothes. And it's not so bad in here."

"If you consider not below freezing being not so bad, then yes, I suppose." I pulled off one of my blankets and handed it over to him. He promptly handed it back.

"You're always cold. You keep it."

"Fine, you leave me no choice." I scooted over to him, maneuvering around the odd bag or box. Still wrapped in one of my blankets, I curled up against him and draped the second blanket over both of us. "And don't come up with some excuse or complaint. I'll keep you warm whether you like it or not."

"Do you hear me complaining?"

We shifted and rearranged ourselves until we were both comfortable, pressed together and lying on our sides. He put an arm around me, and I leaned my head against his chest. A long time passed before I finally said, "I'm not trying to get away from something so much as I'm trying to get to something."

"What's that?"

What indeed? Merry, of course. Always Merry. But so much more than that. The burden of it swelled up in my chest. "I don't even know where to start. The short version is that I'm trying to get a better life for my family, and I'll do whatever it takes to protect them." My voice caught at that last bit because Merry suddenly seemed so far away. I was out in the wilderness, huddled in the dark. She was going to be confined to a fragile ship on a mighty sea, the same sea that had nearly killed me.

Jago ran his fingers through my hair, brushing it from my face. "You'll do it, Tamsin. You're unstoppable. But you should make sure you get a better life out of this too."

"We'll see."

"That's not an encouraging answer."

As weighty as the topic was, I was starting to lose my focus a little because I was so distracted by his closeness. The hand that had toyed with my hair now ran gently along the curve of my neck, and at some point, I'd wrapped my arms around him, curling my fingers into his back. I'd had no interest in being with a man for so long that it was startling to have my body suddenly wake up like this. My attraction to him had grown by leaps and bounds in recent days, and now, I could scarcely think about anything except how badly I wanted to touch him and feel him touch me.

Somehow, despite the quickening of my pulse and breathing, I managed to coherently say, "The last time I was selfish, things . . . well, let's just say things went in an unexpected way. A world-altering way."

"Getting a better life for yourself doesn't mean you're selfish." There was a breathiness to his voice too, and I could feel the tension crackling in him as he continued trailing his hands over me. "You deserve to get something you want."

I lifted my head, leaning in so that our foreheads touched. "Well, maybe I could if that 'something' would stop talking. Unless you're still afraid of—"

The words were lost as he brought his mouth down to mine in a crushing kiss that contained none of the timidity he'd had the other night. My lips parted as the kiss grew more demanding, but I was just as eager, maybe more so. I pressed my body as close to his as I could, and when that wasn't enough, I pushed him to his back and then climbed on top of him. His hands encircled my waist and then explored the length of my legs as I finally broke the kiss and moved my lips to his neck.

We spent half the night like that, kissing and touching and wrapping around each other in a thousand different ways. Our clothes, though occasionally challenged, stayed on, and even though I held a craving for more, I also took a great deal of pleasure in what we could do now. Everything was still so new that there was no need to rush ahead. It was enough just to be together and linger over what we had.

We finally stopped, more out of exhaustion than lack of interest. I drifted to sleep in his arms, and though the wind still howled outside, the storm of worry and restlessness that usually churned within me was calm for a change.

CHAPTER 22

THE BLIZZARD SUBSIDED BY MORNING, AND I AWOKE to Jago's arm around my waist and cold oilcloth against my face. Feeling me stir, Jago opened his eyes and yawned, first looking at me and then to the dipping tarp. He poked at it and said, "It's got snow weighting it down."

Sure enough, when we managed to emerge from our den, we found everything covered in about two feet of new snow. But the wind had stopped, and the sun came out. I helped Jago take down the horse shelter, and Pebble and Dove greeted us with small whickers as they pawed eagerly at the ground. Jago tended to them with his normal affection, but it meant more to me now that I knew his history.

As we checked to make sure nothing had been left behind in our hasty camp, Jago started to put his arm around me. After a few seconds of reconsideration, he removed it. Seeing my puzzled expression, he chuckled and climbed into the sleigh's seat.

"Don't look at me like that, Tamsin. You can't expect me to know what to do."

I took the hand he offered. "You knew plenty well what to do last night."

"Oh, that was pretty straightforward," he said cheerfully. "Now? I'm not sure what you want."

I averted my eyes. "Me either."

"Then I'll proceed accordingly." He picked up the reins, and the horses zipped away over the unbroken snow. "Off we go."

I wasn't entirely sure what "proceed accordingly" entailed, but mostly, he seemed to be regular Jago, easygoing and witty. And chatty. But he didn't talk about last night or try to figure out what it had meant. My own self-analysis was unproductive. I almost hoped I could view what had happened as a superficial, lust-driven act. But while it was to some degree, I found I was just as interested in being with Jago as I was in being physical with him. And that wasn't sustainable.

The fresh snow let us make good time, though the land wasn't so flat and empty anymore. There were more trees than there had been to the north, and as we drew nearer the foothills, the terrain sloped up and was dotted with buttes and other oddly shaped formations. That afternoon, we came upon another road, the first we'd been on in a few days. Not long after that, we began to pass scattered homes, lone rectangular or round houses with barns and grazing animals.

"Is this Kerniall?" I asked.

"These are just outlying farms. The town's farther ahead—you can't miss it."

I leaned forward, hands clasped, eager to finally see this Icori town. The sleigh followed the road as it curved through a copse of elms and oaks, and when the trees thinned out, Jago said, unnecessarily, "*That is Kerniall.*"

Yes. There was no way you could miss it. The land gently swelled up into a wide, rounded hill with a blocky stone fortress—more in keeping with something from ancient Osfro—perched on top. Around it and scattered on the hill's sides were clusters of much smaller buildings, most perfectly round. Their cylindrical bodies were built of stone, and cone-shaped thatched roofs covered them like hats. A stone wall about twice the height of a man surrounded the hill's base.

The road ran right into a gate in the wall, guarded by four armed Icori. They wore coats made of overlapping pieces of hard leather, reminding me of feathers or scales. Fur hats and cloaks provided extra warmth, and when we reached them, I saw that the cloaks were lined with blue tartan crisscrossed with black and yellow. They appeared neither hostile nor welcoming as they scrutinized us and the sleigh.

When one of them greeted me in her language, I realized she thought I was Icori because of my clothes, which I hadn't changed since we saw the Lorandians. Jago answered in Icori, and then the conversation shifted to Osfridian. They didn't seem unwilling to admit a trader, even an Osfridian one, but were more apprehensive when he said we wanted to see Orla.

"Is she expecting you?" asked the guard who'd first greeted me.

"At this exact moment? No," admitted Jago. "But she won't be surprised that I—that we—are here."

The Icori talked among themselves and sent for a trade manager, who kept track of merchants and peddlers, Jago told me. I wondered if this manager might in turn fetch Orla. Her group had been on a trade expedition with the Balanquans, so maybe there was some sort of guild or association. The man who came to us was dressed in the first Icori civilian attire I'd really seen, a heavy wool coat edged in that same blue tartan, with a belt of copper disks hanging over it.

His face filled with delight when he saw us. "Jago Robinson! Welcome. Do you have any cutlery to sell? Tin or silver, I'm not picky."

"Does *everyone* know you?" I murmured.

Jago winked at me and shook the man's hand. They traded small talk, and then the manager spoke with the guards in Icori. We were admitted, and one of the guards hurried off, down a narrow road. The manager climbed into the sleigh with us, chatting with Jago while I continued gawking at this hillside town. The roads had no cobblestone but were laid out as efficiently as any substantial village or city I'd seen, lined with those remarkable round buildings. Judging from the people coming and going, carting things around, at least some of the buildings were businesses, but I couldn't read the Icori runes etched on their doors. We passed wagons and lone horses, travelers on foot carrying baskets and lumber. A few stared as we went by, but I think it was due more to the Balanquan sled. Most of the Icori I saw were bundled up for winter, but I did get some sense of the clothing underneath the layers of leather, fur, and wool. No one would mistake their fashion for Osfridian, but it was hardly the rags insinuated by our textbooks. The Icori wore variations of what you'd see among any other people—trousers and skirts, tunics and dresses. The cut and construction were different, some of the fabrics less refined, but nothing really took me aback.

The manager's home wasn't far away. It was one of the round houses and sat between some stables and a larger rectangular building that I took to be his business. He let Jago store the sleigh in the barn and reiterated a desire to do some deals. "And you're welcome to come back for dinner and lodging," the man added. "Though I'm sure you won't want to."

"I'll come back for some of your ale for sure. And to make you a deal on that cornmeal."

We told him goodbye, and I asked Jago, "You're always making these deals, loaded up with things to sell . . . how are you not living in a pile of gold yet?"

"Because it's uncomfortable to sleep on. That, and I've got debts bigger than this hill to pay off." He squinted up. "We've gotta go up to get to Orla. Are you okay walking? I can get us a ride."

"No, let's walk."

It felt good to stretch my legs after so much sitting, and the slope wasn't very steep. We passed through various residential and commercial neighborhoods, and I kept waiting for Jago to turn in to one of them. Exactly how far up did Orla live? But we didn't stop until we'd reached the hill's summit and stood before the stone fortress. In front of it, a courtyard was busy with activity. People and animals moved back and forth on errands and jobs, just as they had below. Two Icori, less formally dressed than the guards at the wall, stood watch at the door, but their posture was more relaxed. One was telling the other a funny story, and they didn't even glance at us.

I started to ask Jago why we were here when a voice said, "Well, Tamsin Wright, you found your way to us after all. And you found Jago Robinson too."

I turned, my eyes widening as the speaker approached. A floor-length cloak of pure white fur covered most of her body, but when she shifted, I caught a glimpse of a night-blue dress, the sheen of its fabric reminding me of velvet. Part of her reddish gold hair had been coiled into braids pinned at the back of her head; the rest flowed freely down in shining waves. All of her jewelry was silver: rings, necklace, earrings, and a braided circlet atop her head.

"Hello, Orla," said Jago.

Her lips twitched with laughter when she saw I hadn't recognized her. Even after Jago named her, I questioned myself. This fine lady didn't look much like the leather-clad adventurer I'd met who so badly needed to wash her face and hair.

"If I didn't know any better, I'd swear we'd exchanged wardrobes," Orla added, looking me over. The sharpness in her eyes hadn't changed. "But a lot can happen in a few weeks. Come inside out of the wind."

The Icori at the door bowed their heads deferentially as she entered. We followed her through a long corridor constructed of stone blocks that had an ancient and venerable feel, further enhanced by torches in the walls. But the room we ended up in was more modern, like the sitting room of some noble's country lodge. A wood floor had been built over the stone, and that in turn was almost entirely covered with thick wool rugs. An expansive river rock fireplace took up almost an entire wall. It provided most of the room's light, but there was also an assortment of torches, candles, and a kerosene lamp. The furniture was similarly mixed. There were rustic, utilitarian chairs that looked decidedly uncomfortable but also flowered plush ones that wouldn't have looked out of place at Blue Spring. Two small sofas with feet carved like bird claws drew my attention, and I ran a hand over the geometric pattern of the cushions.

"That's Balanquan," Orla said, coming up beside me. She'd removed her fur cloak, revealing the blue velvet gown's full effect. Its high empire waist was stitched in silver, making the skirt look bigger and more dramatic—but not nearly as much as the voluminous bell sleeves, which extended past her hands. This was not a dress designed for function. "Bought it from Alisi last year. She got the better end of that deal, but there was nothing to be done. Faiva wanted it too much."

"Who's that?"

"One of my sisters. Excuse me a moment." She went to the room's doorway, where a young man in plain linen had just arrived and now waited patiently.

As they spoke in Icori, Jago told me, "They also have a third sister who co-rules with them."

"What do you mean, co-rules with them? Is she . . ." I glanced over my shoulder, still in awe of Orla's transformation. "Is she a queen?"

"Not exactly. Maybe sort of a princess? Eh, that seems too formal. The Micnimaras have been the ruling clan in Kerniall for decades. Technically, their mother's the clan leader, but she's been sick a number of years and turned the power over to them. You didn't know?"

"How would I? I thought she was a hunter when I first saw her. Later, I thought maybe a roving trader like you instead. Why didn't you ever tell me?"

"I thought it must have come up in traveling! You never asked about it."

"Of course, how silly. Next time I'll be sure to find out if a random person I meet is a bloody princess!"

"Are you guys arguing?" Orla asked. She returned to the fire and flounced onto the sofa in a very unprincesslike way, stretching her legs out on a low glass table that appeared to be Osfridian.

I sat down on the other sofa gingerly, hoping my traveling clothes weren't too dirty. "No. Jago keeps forgetting to tell me things, that's all."

"Really? And here I thought Jago never had a problem talking. You can take your coat off, if you want. Just toss it over there."

"No, thanks. I'm still warming up."

"Tamsin's never warm enough," Jago explained from the other side of the room. He'd wandered over to examine some of its eclectic art collection. The stony walls displayed everything from an enormous aquatic-themed tapestry to a sheet of copper etched with rudimentary flowers to a Sirminican-style oil painting of a white-haired man and his dog.

"Well, then come over here and help her turn that couch toward the fire—it's heavier than it looks. No, really. Move it wherever you like, I don't care. If anyone complains, I'll just tell them you're un-couth Osfridians who don't know any better."

This Orla was starting to feel a little more like the mocking one I'd traveled with on the Quistimac. When she was satisfied with my sofa's position, she urged us both to sit and tell her "everything that's led to this point." Between us, Jago and I managed to piece together a recap of what had befallen me since she'd left me in Constancy. Partway through our story, the servant returned and filled up the glass table with platters of what I learned the Icori called "conversation dinner": sage crepes, venison sausage, dried currants, hazelnuts, and four kinds of cheese.

Our story concluded with the reveal of Alan's coat, and Orla was quick to understand the implications—even if she wasn't sure she be-lieved them. "That was certainly no sanctioned group that robbed you, though there was talk of retaliation after the Ipaeron fields were burned."

I looked to Jago for an explanation, and he said, "Upriver a bit, the Ipaeron clan have oat and wheat farms—huge ones. It's a big revenue source. In the summer, lots of Icori live out there and work, but they abandon it in the winter. A few months ago, all the buildings—homes and storage—were burned to the ground."

"No one was hurt, but they'll lose a lot of their growing season rebuilding in the spring," Orla added. "That's lost money for them and lost food for us. They didn't catch the men who did it, but witnesses saw them leaving the fields. They were Osfridians—all dressed in dark, plain clothes."

I knew firsthand that the Heirs had no qualms about engaging the Icori, but I had a very hard time imagining them doing it in that sort of way. "Are you sure they were Osfridian? If Lorandians could dress up like Icori, couldn't they just have easily dressed up like Heirs?" I asked.

"I would think so," said Jago.

"I suppose so too, but why?" asked Orla. "Your people have trouble with the Lorandians, but we've always gotten along. We trade with Lo Canne all the time. And the Lorandians have even been in talks with the southern clans for land."

That was news to me, startling for a number of reasons. But my mind was on the nature of these Icori and Osfridian skirmishes. When we first met, Orla had hinted at others having taken place over the winter, and Jago had later told me how they all were like the robbery and burning. Nothing large, no serious injuries. No leader claiming responsibility or making demands. The attacks weren't insignificant, but they also weren't on a grand enough scale to trigger definitive retaliation. Constancy's desire to outlaw Icori from Grashond was the most serious reaction thus far.

"It's just such a bizarre and convoluted tactic if the Lorandians are behind it." Orla pushed back her billowing sleeves to top off her wine. "I'll have to talk to Faiva and Stana. I don't care what games Lorandy wants to play with Osfrid—sorry—but we aren't going to be a casualty of it. I just hope I can convince others—I can already imagine the responses of some of my advisors. You're lucky your leadership job was temporary, Tamsin. Who knows what they'd be badgering you about if you hadn't escaped them?"

She meant it as a joke, as she did so many things, and her gaze was already turned inward, mulling over how to handle the Lorandian mystery. But guilt gnawed at my insides as I thought about the other girls still in Constancy, still under Dinah's thumb and the town's judgment for two more months. Had they had been punished for more minor infractions? What if my escape had made things worse for them? Stricter rules or punishment by association?

As I agonized over that, Orla gave her blessing for Jago to bring me south. She also confirmed I could stay in this mini-castle until then. Just over a week, and I'd be on my way back to the Glittering Court.

"Well, feel free to relax now," she told us, standing up and smoothing the dress. "I need to see if Stana's back for the night. I'll have the servants make up . . ." She glanced between us uncertainly. "One room . . . two rooms . . . ?"

"Two," Jago and I said at the same time, each of us pointedly looking away from the other.

Orla shrugged. "Okay, suit yourselves. If you're always cold, it seems like it'd be warmer having someone else around."

Orla bid us good night and issued orders to her servants. One of them, a young woman with hair even lighter than Jago's, let us know the rooms were being made up and that she'd be waiting in the hall if we needed anything. She left us too, and then we were alone by the hearth, wrapped in an awkward silence that had fallen after Orla's well-meaning suggestion about sharing a bed.

"You know, I really thought you knew," he said at last. "About her. Or at least knew she was someone important."

I surveyed the remnants of our dinner and picked up another crepe. "I figured she had influence, to be able to make those decisions about the river trip. But Icori princess never crossed my mind. I guess that explains why her Osfridian is so flawless."

"Yup, tutors and such."

"How did you get so friendly with her? It was before the medicine, right?"

"Right. I helped her procure some Evarian horses that would be pretty much impossible for the Icori to get otherwise. In exchange, she gave me some pretty favorable trade terms."

I slumped back against the sofa, still dejected over Orla's comment about escaping my friends. Jago, in that way of his, guessed my thoughts.

"You didn't abandon the others. They'll be okay. You didn't do anything wrong."

"I know they're competent. I know they're smart. They wouldn't have made it through the Glittering Court if they weren't. But that's not always enough in Constancy. Look what happened to Vanessa. Look what happened to me! I'm so worried there'll be more of that or worse. But what I can do? I have to be in Cape Triumph in two months." I leaned forward, elbows on my knees, and rested my face in my hands. "That's nonnegotiable."

"Then that's what you'll do." He drew me back and wrapped his arms around me. "Everything's going to be okay."

"Careful." I started to pull away. "What will Orla think?"

"Orla already knows."

"How?"

"Because she's Orla. You don't survive in her position without being observant."

I leaned against him and sighed. Being next to him like this made me feel as though everything really would be okay. Not because he'd fix things for me, but because I was reminded of the good in my life and why I had to fight for it. *I won't admit defeat again.*

Footsteps at the doorway made me jerk away, and I looked up, expecting to hear our rooms were ready. But it was Orla who returned, a handful of servants trailing her. All wore astonished looks.

"Word apparently travels fast," Orla said drily. "You've been summoned by Shibail."

Jago jumped to his feet. "I'll go right away."

"Not you." Orla nodded at me. "Her. But you may go along."

This drew speculative stares from the other Icori, and I hated being the only one who didn't know what was going on. "Who's Shi-Shibail?"

"Come on, and you'll find out," Jago said. "I swear, there's never a dull moment with you." He glanced at Orla. "Are you coming too?"

She crooked us a smile. "I'm not special enough. I wasn't summoned. I'll have someone escort you to the Well, though I'm sure you remember the way, Jago. Good luck."

With those ominous words, she swept away, and the blonde Icori girl bowed deferentially to us. After donning our coats and cloaks again, we followed her out of the keep and began the trek down the hill of Kerniall. It was evening now, and the wind had grown even more bitter.

"The Well is where you told the Lorandians I'd come from, right?" I asked. "It's a holy place?"

"Yes. Have you ever heard of the Predecessors?"

"No."

"Then you probably don't know that the Balanquans weren't the first people in Adoria?"

"What? No."

"Yes." He grinned at my shock, which was caused almost more from not knowing something about Adorian history than about the fact itself. "No one—not even the Balanquans—knows that much about them or where they went. All that's left of them are relics and ruins, but even the fragments they left behind are pretty impressive. The Icori believe the Predecessors were gods who prepared this land for them, and they credit the artifacts with magical powers. The Balanquans will tell you—in a helpful but haughty way—that the Predecessors were simply more advanced and had techniques none of us had discovered."

The information made me reel. "How have I never heard of this?"

"It isn't widely known in the colonies, probably because most of the sites and relics are in Balanquan or Icori lands. And I think Osfridians who have seen them assume it was all made by the Balanquans since they confiscated nearly every known Predecessor object found. The Balanquans don't do much with the ruins, though, which the Icori see as sacred places. So, the Balanquans let them set up shrines and maintain them." He paused as we stepped aside for a passing wagon. "Anyway, the Well is one of those shrines. It's pretty remarkable."

When we reached the bottom, another Icori was waiting for us, with a much smaller sleigh than Jago's. We climbed on and rode northwest of the city. I couldn't make out much in the fading light, but the driver seemed sure and relaxed about the way. The land turned sharply upward, growing very steep very quickly. We continued on for about twenty more minutes and then reached a stony outcropping blocking our way. It stretched on, like a wall, as far as I could see to my left and right.

We got out of the sleigh just as a man and woman landed beside us, having dropped down from some hidden spot atop the ridge. Both were armed with weapons and fierce looks, though they relaxed when the driver gave them an explanation in Icori. Then, the man who'd leapt down did a double take.

"Jago, is that you?"

"None other." Jago stepped down and shook the man's hand. "Good to see you, Cai."

"And you. You are welcome to the Well of the Gods." The man sheathed his blade and shot me a smile. "As is your friend."

"Tamsin Wright, Cai Ipaeron," said Jago.

"Welcome, Tamsin," said Cai. "Jago, I don't suppose you've come to sell food?"

"Not specifically, but I've got a few things that might spice up your winter rations. I've got lamp oil too."

The Icori woman stayed with the sleigh and driver while Cai led Jago and me through a gap between the rocks. It became a winding passageway that made me feel like I was in some sort of labyrinth. Evening's shadows darkened our path, and I couldn't see over the stony walls. The only thing I knew for sure was that the ground was sloping downward now, and carved steps soon let us descend at an even steeper angle.

We emerged from the rock maze without warning, and the whole world suddenly opened up. I stumbled to a halt and clutched at Jago's arm. We stood high atop a cliff, looking over a vast and very deep canyon. At its bottom—way, way, *way* below us—a river wound through, a little narrower than the Quistimac. On the canyon's far side, the setting sun ignited the sky with red, gold, and purple, and I could make out the dark shapes of mountains to the southwest. It made for a breathtakingly gorgeous—yet also terrifying—vista.

"That's the East Sister down there. Want a better look?" Jago asked me. I shook my head. We were about ten feet from the cliff's edge, and even though a wooden railing stood there, I couldn't imagine getting closer to that drop. When I simply shook my head, he squeezed my hand and tugged me to the left. "Come over here then."

When I dragged my gaze from the river, I saw that the stones we'd walked through didn't form a straight wall beside the cliff. They curved this way and that, eventually angling back from the edge, which was a relief. One curve in particular created a wide, sheltered enclosure that contained a handful of rectangular buildings. They were constructed of river rock and timber, and bonfires blazed between them. Among it all, a dozen Icori dressed like our companions went about their business.

"Is this a village?" I asked Jago.

"More of a camp, I suppose. They guard the Well and serve the high priestess—Shibail."

I cast a quick glance back at the canyon, wondering if that was supposed to be the "well." As we approached the buildings, people paused to study us. We walked past them and soon left the cozy-looking buildings behind. Ahead was only darkness, which seemed like a bad idea when you were so close to a perilously high cliff's edge.

But Cai moved assuredly, and before long a faint glow appeared. It came from a lantern hanging on a pole beside a particularly jagged section of the ridge. Two Icori stood by it, armed. They wore woad on their faces, the blue paint carefully drawn into spirals and whorls.

"They're going to see Shibail," Cai told them, and they moved aside, revealing an arched opening in the rock. "And now I leave you. Good luck. Come find Glyn about sugar and bacon when you're done, Jago."

Cai returned the way we'd come, and the painted Icori stepped through the arch, beckoning Jago and me to follow. Inside, we found a hollowed-out space completely surrounded in stone. And in the center of that space was an enormous dark hole. A chain with three-foot links came up from the hole, went through a pulley of sorts embedded in the stone ceiling, and then disappeared back into the shadowed depths. One of the Icori who'd accompanied us took a horn from the wall and blew into it three times. A few minutes later, it was answered by a creaking sound as the chain slowly began to move.

A chill ran over me, but it wasn't because of the wintry air. Jago said, "*This* is the Well of the Gods."

I watched with wide eyes and didn't realize I was gradually backing up until I bumped the wall. On and on the chain went, moving and groaning. I stood on my tiptoes, wanting to see more of the pit without getting closer.

"How deep is this?" I asked. "How far does it go?"

"All the way down to the river," said Jago. A giant sphere made of metal mesh suddenly emerged at the chain's end. "And we're about to go down in it."

CHAPTER 23

"No."

"Tamsin, it's perfectly safe."

"It's a metal death trap hanging over a million-foot drop!"

"It's not a million feet."

I dragged my gaze from the pit to Jago. "But it *is* a death trap?"

"No! The Balanquans made it. They're excellent engineers."

When the chain had stopped, the Icori had tossed out lines to pull the sphere up against the hole's edge. They'd secured it in place and opened its door. They must have been under a vow of silence like the one I'd faked, but they didn't need any words to express their impatience as they watched us.

"People do this all the time," Jago said. "Icori pilgrims come from miles away to make this trip, and most of them aren't personally invited by Shibail."

"What if one of the links breaks?"

"It won't. They're checked constantly. And this actually used to operate with ropes. It's a lot better now." When I didn't budge, Jago put his arm around me. "I'll be right beside you."

I shook my head.

"You want Orla to help you get to Denham? Trust me, she's not going to think well of someone who turned down a summons to one of their holiest sites."

That reached me. "You think she'd change her mind?"

"I don't know. She may still want to honor what she offered . . .

but her clan might overrule her if they think you've insulted Shibail."

I examined the Well again. Even secured with rope, the metal sphere never stayed still. It could probably hold three people, four if they got cozy. I wondered if Jago was bluffing about Orla, but the Icori's increasing incredulity at my reluctance made me think he could be right. And I *had* to have her help.

"Okay," I said. At least, that's what I tried to say. It came out as a half whisper, but Jago understood and guided me to the edge.

The sphere's opening was flush with the stone floor. Jago climbed in first and then helped receive me when the Icori handed me over. I crouched on the sphere's bottom beside Jago and felt my heart leave me as the Icori sealed the door shut. They untied the ropes, and the sphere swooped out to the hole's center, rocking back and forth like a pendulum. I screamed and covered my face. Jago patted the back of my hair and kept saying, "It's okay, it's okay." It was pretty much the same way he soothed his horses.

The horn sounded four times, and the sphere lowered with a jerk. Refusing to scream again, I bit my lip. The chain creaked as it labored to take us down, and all the while, the sphere swayed.

"Tamsin, look."

I hunched further down. "Isn't it enough I'm here?"

"You'll be glad, I swear."

I cautiously turned my head and opened one eye.

"Six!"

Sitting up straight, I gaped at the stone sides circling us. Every part of them had been carved and decorated. Some designs were flat, etched into the surface like one might draw on a piece of paper. Others were three-dimensional, rendered with astonishing texture and shape. Trees and flowering vines. Animals of land, air, and sea. Faces, both human and fantastic. A few times we passed sections that had been hollowed out into balconies, and statues of robed men and women solemnly watched our descent.

I leaned over Jago to get a better look at one of the balconies.

The people seated on it appeared so realistic, I expected them to stand up and wave. "Is that them? The Predecessors? They look human enough."

"The Balanquans will tell you they are."

"But I can also see why the Icori think they're gods." I hoped I wasn't being blasphemous, but it was hard not to believe magic had played a role in creating such a feat. Just one section of this carved onto the side of a cathedral would have been regarded as a masterpiece. To see this sort of skill, in such magnitude, and in such a place, was dizzying. "How did they do this?"

Jago watched a flock of flying fish go by. "I don't know. The Balanquans have theories. I know the Icori replace the torches with long poles. They have to come through in this sphere a few times a day to do it, and it's tricky work. Maybe the Predecessors had an easier way."

I'd been so consumed by the artwork that I hadn't even considered how the torches scattered among the stonework were maintained. We gazed in awed silence the rest of the way down. When we neared the Well's bottom, I saw an enormous crank wound with chain. It took ten Icori to turn it. Like those above, they wore woad on their faces.

My legs felt like jelly when I stepped out of the sphere, and it took my brain a few minutes to accept that the world was still again. We followed one of the attendants through twisting halls that quickly left me disoriented. Small alcoves were scattered along the way, occasionally with pilgrims resting or praying inside. Once, we passed a wide corridor with noticeably cooler air flowing from it.

"That goes to the riverbank," Jago said, seeing me slow my steps. "But we're going in tonight, not out."

"What exactly are we going to do when we get to this Shibail?"

"Dunno. Everyone who comes to the Well sees her. Sometimes, she just greets them and sends them on their way. Other times, it's more extensive."

"You've seen her, then? What happened?"

"She asked me a lot of questions. Some about my life, some that didn't seem to have any obvious purpose. I assume she must have gotten something out of it, though."

Our guide brought us to a set of double stone doors carved as intricately as the Well. "Wait. You are next." She had the thickest accent of any Icori I'd met so far, but it still didn't resemble that of the thieves in Constancy.

Several minutes later, the doors swung open. An Icori man and woman stepped out, escorted by another woad-marked attendant. Ours ushered us inside to a cavernous, mostly empty room. Its walls were of a different type of stone than I'd seen in the rest of the structure. This was lighter in color, polished to such a high gloss that it came across as mirror-like. It bounced the light of the torches around in a disorienting effect that made it seem as though the room contained more torches than there actually were. The vaulted ceiling was made of the same grayish rock as the Well, but it had been carved into a perfectly smooth dome. I again marveled at the skill to craft something so high.

At the far end of the room, five steps led up to a dais. As we walked closer and my eyes adjusted to the dim lighting, an old woman became discernible. She sat cross-legged, her indigo robes spreading out around her. An assortment of objects sat within her reach: a pitcher and cups, a small dagger, a bundle of grass, different-colored rocks. At the base of the steps, a small pool of water had been built into the floor. Beside it was a large copper plate with coins and cloth-wrapped bundles stacked upon it. Here, we stopped.

The woman, Shibail, scrutinized us with dark eyes. Her white hair was pulled severely back, displaying a single woad spiral painted on her forehead. I thought she might be smiling. After a minute, she lifted her gaze and said something in Icori. I heard the attendant's footsteps retreating behind me, followed by the sound of the doors opening and shutting.

I clasped my hands in front of me, wondering if I should curtsey. From his coat pocket, Jago produced a small jar of what looked like honey and set it on the plate. Shibail made a sound that could have been a grunt or a chuckle. When she spoke, her Osfridian was clear, its sound amplified by some trick of the chamber.

"Jago Robinson, you never need to bring an offering here."

"Then let me give it on her behalf, Danna Shibail."

The dark eyes flicked to me, and I met them steadily. "We don't see many Osfridians in the Well. What's your name?"

"Tamsin Wright, mistress."

"Where's your home, Tamsin Wright?"

"Until very recently, Osfrid. Now . . . I guess you could say I'm between homes."

"Why did you come to Adoria?"

"To find a husband."

"Did you?"

I hesitated. "I'm not sure which way you mean that. Did I find a husband? Or did I really come here for one?"

Yes, now she was definitely smiling. "It doesn't matter. You already answered. Do you speak to your gods, Tamsin Wright?"

"I know only one god—Uros, creator of all, attended by the six glorious angels. And I . . . I speak to them through prayer, I suppose."

"Your church's creed is 'There is only one god—Uros, creator of all, attended by the six glorious angels.' Did you intentionally change the wording?"

"Y-yes," I said, a bit taken aback that she'd known. "I thought that saying Uros is the only god would sound like I was belittling yours and . . . it, uh, it seemed rude."

She didn't comment and instead drank from a stone chalice that had been beside her. As she did, I cast a quick glance at Jago, hoping for a silent indication of whether I was behaving correctly or terribly, but his face was unreadable.

"Do they speak back to you?" she asked. "Uros and the angels?"

"Not directly."

"Indirectly?"

"I don't know." I tried to think of the last times I'd prayed—truly prayed, not just following along with the Heirs. "My ship was in a storm sailing here, and I prayed we'd get out of it. We did. Was it because of my prayers? Someone else's? Or was it the crew's skill? I don't know. And other times I've prayed for help with a problem, it eventually resolves through something I think of. I don't know if those ideas are divine or just from me."

"Both. Most visions and dreams are simply images and ideas locked away in our own minds. And we are divine."

Silence. It had a weight to it, and I shifted from foot to foot, uncertain if I was supposed to speak. I honestly had no idea how someone who'd neglected church as much as I had was constantly discussing religion these days.

"If you could have any three things you wanted right now, what would they be?" she suddenly asked. "Not people. Not abstract ideas like love or wisdom. Not sweeping sentiments for mankind. I mean three real, physical objects. What would you wish for?"

"Silver rue. It's an herb." It was also the main ingredient in Merry's hard-to-get medicine.

"I know what it is. What else?"

"Pen and paper."

She pursed her lips a moment. "That might as well be a single object, since you can't very well use one without the other. So name one more thing."

My mind blanked. I was too overwhelmed by being here to reason out something clever or poignant. And lately, everything I wanted was an end goal, like making it to Cape Triumph or escaping the magistrate's house. Pressured by her unblinking gaze, I finally asked, "What's your favorite thing to eat?"

A very, very faint flicker of surprise showed in her eyes and was gone in a heartbeat. I didn't think much surprised her, and I also didn't think she would answer, but then she said, "Honey, as Jago Robinson well knows."

"Then I wish I had some of my own to give to you. I don't like being beholden to others."

"I actually believe that. Most people I'd accuse of trying to appear selfless. Of course, you've done that, intentionally or not. You want each thing you named, but you want it because of someone else who wants or needs it. Someone sick needs the silver rue. Someone far away wants a letter to know what's happened to you. And you think Jago is inconvenienced, though I assure you, he is not." She drank again, allowing those words to sink in. "Isn't there something you covet for yourself? Some small pleasure? Some comfort?"

It was so similar to what Jago had said just before we kissed. Could she know? It was impossible . . . and yet, that piercing gaze seemed to see so much. "I'm sure there are many, Mistress Shibail. I just can't come up with any right now."

She picked up a small cup and poured some of the chalice's contents into it. "Will you share a drink with me?"

I didn't move. What was I supposed to do? Was this a test? A kindness? She'd been drinking whatever that was throughout our conversation, so it couldn't be poisoned. Unless the little cup was poisoned? If she really wanted me dead, it seemed like it'd be an easy enough thing to order one of her many attendants to take care of that. Would refusing the drink displease Orla? That was what decided it. Careful of the pool, I ascended the steps and accepted the offered cup. The drink tasted like cloves, a mixture of sweet and bitter and spicy. When I'd finished it all, I returned the cup and made my way back down. Jago watched me with wide, panicked eyes.

"Go to the wall, and tell me what you see in it," Shibail ordered.

I walked to the nearest one and peered into the shiny surface. "I see the torches and their reflections. I see the steps. And I can just barely see you and Jago watching me."

"You don't see yourself?"

"Well, yes, of course. I thought you wanted to know what else I could see."

"What do you see when you look at yourself?"

I leaned closer and touched my cheek. The wall wasn't a perfect mirror; my reflection was a little fuzzy. But I could make out enough detail. "My skin is dry. My lips are chapped."

"Why are those the things you notice?"

My reflection suddenly grew blurry, and I had to blink a few times to see clearly again. "Because I have to fix them before I go to Cape Triumph. I have to look my best. I have to be beautiful."

Again, my reflection went out of focus, but when it sharpened this time, I wasn't looking at Tamsin in the stone chamber. Jago's gifted clothes were gone, and I now stood in the off-the-shoulder green dress I'd yielded to the Balanquans. My skin was smooth and soft again. An emerald the size of an egg hung around my neck, and smaller ones sparkled in my hair, which had been arranged into an artful cascade of curls. It was exactly the same way Adelaide's had been styled when we first met, and I'd been so jealous of it.

Something moved behind me, and I spun around. Couples in silk and jewels of their own danced across a ballroom, underneath the glow of crystal chandeliers. The air hummed with conversation and laughter. Waiters offered champagne flutes. A string quartet played a waltz, and a cluster of men in expensive suits gathered around me, though all of their faces were shadowed.

"Has anyone ever told you that green is your best color?"

"I was going to tell her that!"

"No, *I* was! And I was going to ask her to dance!"

"You were not—because I was going to!"

"Gentlemen, gentlemen," I said, laughing. "No need to argue. I can dance with you all."

I glided around the room, moving from one set of arms to another. Each of my partners raved about my beauty and intelligence and swore he'd never know happiness unless I was his. "What will you give me?" I asked them.

"A carriage made of gold."

"A hundred servants."

"A new gown for every day of the year."

"A castle on a hill."

As the offers grew increasingly extravagant, my eye was caught by the sight of two small feet sticking out from underneath a tablecloth. Ignoring my admirers' entreaties to return, I darted across the room and knelt down by the table. I lifted the cloth and found Merry sitting behind it in a white muslin dress, her red hair curled identically to my own.

My heart sang at the sight of her, and I pulled her against my chest. "Why, Merry, what are you doing under here?"

She squirmed in my embrace and looked up at me solemnly. "Why won't you take anything?"

"What?"

"Aren't there things you want?"

"Loads. And we shall have them." I pointed at the shadowy suitors. "Didn't you hear all the wonderful things I've gotten for us?"

"You've done wonderfully, Mama, but isn't there something you covet for yourself? Some small pleasure? Some comfort?"

The words came out of my daughter's mouth, but they were like an echo. Where had I heard them? I tweaked her nose. "Are you encouraging me to be selfish, my love? You've been taught better."

Her serious expression remained unchanged. "It's not the same thing, and you know it."

"Why are you so saucy tonight? Come out from there, and we'll see if we can find you a cookie. There must be one at this party. If not, I'm sure I can coax some gentleman to go and get one."

Merry scooted forward with me and stood up. But she wouldn't follow when I gently tugged her hand. "What happens when this is all done?" she asked.

I put my hands on my hips. "When what is all done?"

"When we're all safe and secure. You and me and Granny and Grandpa and Uncle Jon and Aunt Livvy. When you have everything you want for us, what will you do?"

"You just said yourself that I'd have everything I want. I won't need to do anything."

"Then you won't be anything."

"Meredith Wright!" I exclaimed. "I don't know what's gotten into your—"

The room darkened. The music stopped. Looking up, I saw the candles on the chandelier go out one by one as though snuffed by some invisible hand. People cried out in alarm and searched frantically for an exit. Scattered tabletop candelabras provided the only light now, and multiple guests scrambled to snatch one. Collisions occurred, fistfights broke out. Some people gave up on light and ran blindly to the room's bare sides, groping around for a door. I scooped Merry up and held her close.

"Let's get out of here." I took a few steps forward and then paused, trying to recall if I'd seen any doors tonight. There had to be at least one.

People kept bumping into us in their panic, and I struggled to keep my footing and protect Merry. At one point, I found myself off balance—but no one was next to me. A rumbling filled my ears, and I realized the floor was shaking. The screams grew louder; glasses crashed and shattered. Someone who'd won a candelabra suddenly lost it when he tripped and fell. It flew up into the air, the light bouncing wildly, and then there was another mad dash to seize it. In that brief moment of illumination, I saw a spiderweb of cracks spreading across one of the walls. It began to collapse, crumbling away to reveal a night sky full of stars. But the cracks didn't stop there. The floor was breaking up too, and as chunks of it fell away, so did guests and furniture. There was nothing underneath this ballroom except a wide, dark chasm, and I watched in horror as people were swept away into unending blackness.

The hole kept advancing, the floor kept disintegrating. I turned and ran, but someone bumped into me, knocking Merry out of my arms.

She tumbled over the edge, crying, "Mama! Mama!" I dropped to my knees, ready to throw myself into the depths after her. To my astonishment, she was still there, clutching at a broken plank that was only barely attached to the ballroom's crumbling floor. The shaking had stopped and with it, the floor's destruction.

"Hold on, love. I've got you." I reached toward Merry, but my arms weren't long enough. I scrambled to my feet and peered around. "Help! I need someone to . . ."

What remained of the room was empty. Everyone had either fallen or found a way to flee, including my devoted suitors. I got down on the floor again, lying on my stomach. Merry still clung to the splintered board, her face deathly pale. I squirmed out over the edge as far as I could manage. One inch more, and I'd go down too. A cold wind blew up from the chasm, pushing all those fine curls into my face. I shook my head and extended my arm.

"I can reach you this time. Take my hand."

"I can't," Merry called. "I can't."

"Of course you can! My hand's right there." The floor shifted, and her plank wobbled precariously. I could see cracks forming in it. "Hurry! Grab hold of me!"

She reached out, but her little hand passed right through mine. "I can't grab hold of someone who isn't anything," she said. "There's nothing there."

Crack! The board she held on to broke and plummeted off into the night, taking her with it. I screamed as the darkness closed around her, screamed as my heart and my soul and everything that made me were ripped out of my body. The agonizing pain of it tore through me, destroying me, but what did it matter? I could not exist and draw breath if she didn't. I stepped forward, giving myself over to the darkness as I fell . . .

And I kept screaming until Jago gripped my shoulders and gently shook me. "Tamsin, Tamsin! *Tamsin!* Wake up!"

I didn't recognize him for a few seconds, and even after I did, it didn't calm me down. What could, after losing my daughter? I fought his hold, even hitting out at him.

"Let go of me—let me go to my child! We have to find her! She could've survived!"

"Ow, stop it! Tamsin, you're dreaming. No one's in danger."

"I saw her! I saw Merry go over! We can still get to her if—"

Four Icori burst in through the door. A small pine door, in a plain room with a river rock fireplace and stone walls. There were no chandeliers or dancers. No mirrors. No Shibail. And certainly no Merry.

I took in the Icori; I took in the room. And the more I did, the more the remnants of the dream fell away. My heart still pounded, and grief still burned in me, but I accepted that it had been a dream. This was my reality, not the crumbling ballroom. Slowly, slowly, I dropped my hands. Jago nodded at the Icori and said something in their language. They left.

For a long time, the only sounds were shifting logs and my ragged breathing. Jago settled back, watching me closely. We sat on a bed that rested in an elaborately carved wooden frame. The pillow and blankets looked damp, and I put a hand to my cheek. Sweat dripped down it, and I felt like my skull had been ripped apart.

I rubbed my eyes. "What happened? After the mirror?"

"What mirror?"

"The wall in Shibail's chamber. She asked me to look at it. And then everything turned . . ." I looked around, still trying to grapple with my circumstances. "I don't know. But you were there. You must know."

He handed me a mug of water. "She didn't say anything about a mirror or a wall. You took the drink and then passed out while you were coming back down the stairs."

"No . . ."

"I didn't realize how fast it'd affect you, or else I would have been ready. I wasn't able to catch you before you bumped your head."

I ran my fingers along my left temple and winced at a large lump. "So that's why my head hurts so much."

"Well, I think that drink gives you a headache regardless."

I lay back on the pillow and stared up at the beams on the ceiling. After such blindingly intense panic, my emotions had burned out, and now I just felt numbed. "What was it?"

"Not sure. I never asked."

I looked back at him. "You've had it? What happened?"

"I made it down the steps before I passed out and fell face-first into the pool." A brief, chagrined smile flitted over his features before they took a more troubled turn. "While I was knocked out, I dreamed about risk. I had all these choices, and the safe ones led nowhere. It was right around the time I was deciding whether to spend all that money on Felicia."

"What did we see? Is it . . . something she does? Something from the angels or . . . Icori gods?"

"I think it's what she said—stuff pulled up from our own head."

The images of the dream—or vision?—flashed through my mind's eye, and with them, the searing emotions returned. I shuddered. "Did Shibail ask me about wanting something for myself? A small pleasure or comfort? Or did I dream that too? Six, I'm not even sure what to believe now."

"Yeah, she asked you something like that."

"Merry asked me that in the dream too." I rolled to my side, resting my cheek against my hand as I watched the fire. I felt drained and numbed. "I suppose you heard me mention her."

"Yeah."

Let go of me—let me go to my child!

I sighed. "And I suppose you figured out that—"

"Your business is your business." He ran a hand along my back. "You don't have to tell me anything you don't want to."

A log shifted, sending up sparks. I followed their flight and waited for more from Jago. If not judgment, I at least expected questions. But he stayed silent, and the longer he did, the more I felt the need to fill the space. "She's in Osfrid—or was. She's about to turn four and is on her way to Cape Triumph with some family friends. She'll be there in two months."

"You must miss her."

My fingers curled, clutching the blanket. "It hurts so much sometimes, I think I'm going to die. I wanted to, in that dream."

"Don't say that."

"I mean it. It's this terrible, clawed monster eating me from within, and one day, I'm sure it's going to consume me entirely."

"If it hasn't already, then it's not going to. And it's not divine favor, Tamsin. It's just *you*."

I didn't realize I had a tear running down my cheek until he handed me a handkerchief. Somehow, that small kindness triggered a few more tears, and I hastily wiped them away.

"I'm sorry," he said fretfully. "I'm sorry if I said the wrong thing, which is weird for me."

I managed a small laugh and dabbed at my cheek again. "Oh, stop, or I'll end up crying for real. What you're saying, it's . . ." His beautiful eyes were so earnest, so nervous as he waited to hear what I'd say. It overwhelmed me, and I had to look away. "Well. It's . . . it's not wrong. Believe me, I normally hear some pretty awful things when this comes up."

"You missing your daughter?"

"No, me just having a daughter. People usually . . . well, think differently of me afterward."

"People are foolish," he said. "I pretty much think the same of you today as I did yesterday. Except now I know for sure you aren't moving mountains to get to Cape Triumph just so you can have your silk and champagne."

"Well, I won't mind the silk, truth be told, but even the thought of champagne is making me sick right now, after that drink." I peered around the room. "Where am I, and how did I get here?"

"We're back at Orla's keep—this is the room she gave you. After you passed out, some of the Well's attendants helped me carry you out.

Just so you know, I did most of the work." He straightened up and swung his legs over to the edge. "I should let you rest. Do you need anything else?"

I caught hold of his hand. "Stay with me, Jago . . . I don't want to be alone . . ."

"Of course." He kicked off his boots and stretched out next to me, gathering me into his arms. "I'll stay as long as you want."

I rested my head on his chest and listened to the steady beating of his heart. As I drifted off to sleep, I tried to think of the last time I'd told someone about Merry without getting a shocked reaction. But I couldn't recall any such time.

CHAPTER 24

IT WAS STRANGE BEING THE GUEST OF AN ICORI PRINCESS—
which was what I kept thinking of Orla as, no matter the technicalities.
She'd given orders to her servants to tend to anything we needed, and
if it was in their power, they made it happen.

After Jago slinked back to his own room the next morning, I found
a servant and asked for water to wash with, explaining that I hadn't
bathed properly in days. Before I knew it, servants were in my room
with a bathtub, hauling in buckets of hot water. When we went down
to breakfast later, I was asked what I wanted, and a cook immediately
prepared it.

Of course, the fulfilling of my wishes had to fall within the Icori's
abilities, which certainly weren't boundless. They didn't have the man-
ufacturing capabilities of the Osfridians and Balanquans, or access to
a world's worth of different ingredients. Little household items and
techniques that I took for granted in daily life were missing. Between
the Balanquans, Osfridians, and other Evarians, the Icori theoretically
had access to almost anything—but limited means to acquire it. Their
surplus resources mostly came from hunting and farming, and there
wasn't enough money there for the Icori to import on a grand scale
from their neighbors. The eclectic mix of random imported goods
I'd seen in Orla's hearth room was pretty typical of well-to-do Icori.
Those with humbler homes would have few or no outsider luxuries.
And often, the Icori might not have things I was used to, simply because they had a different culture.

So, I received biscuits and eggs as requested for breakfast, but the biscuits were denser than I'd expected, mixed with flour and an unknown grain. And I learned that the gauzy nightgown they gave me came from bark fibers, which I never would have guessed. It might as well have been silk, compared to what I'd had in Constancy.

Although the servants were quick to accommodate me and even quicker with Orla, the fortress's household still had an unexpectedly laid-back feel to it. Servants always acknowledged Orla and her sisters with at least "Danna" or a polite nod in passing, but no one fell to their knees, no trumpets blared. One servant laughed when I asked if Orla had the equivalent of handmaidens to dress her and style her hair. That would only happen on rare and very special occasions, the young woman told me. Otherwise, "the danna can take care of herself."

After breakfast, Jago and I were brought into a meeting with Orla, her two sisters, their advisors, and leaders of subordinate clans. We retold what we knew of the Osfridian and Icori skirmishes, what the colonists believed, and the conclusions we'd drawn about the Lorandians. They grilled us on details and regarded us with a mix of attitudes. Some, very conscious of the long and complicated history of my people and theirs, were wary and almost hostile. Other Icori officials didn't seem to care and were far more concerned with how we could be utilized to help them.

They dismissed us to continue their conversation in private, and Orla pulled us aside at the door. "When are you going back to Constancy to get the rest of your cargo?" she asked Jago.

"Ideally, tomorrow. Within two days for sure. I'll probably have to do two round-trips, and it'd be a good idea to keep a buffer in there for weather delays."

She nodded. "I understand. If you could wait those two days, I'd appreciate it. The others will have questions, and it'd be useful to have you around. I can send an extra sleigh with you if that'd help, and if there is a delay, we certainly won't leave downriver without you."

Jago agreed, and that left the two of us in the incredibly odd position of having . . . free time. We had no responsibilities. There was no need to plot how to get to Cape Triumph, because that was settled. The council wanted our observations, not our advice. We were on our own.

"Do you want to learn to ride?" Jago asked me, once Orla returned to her meeting.

I leaned back against the hallway's stone walls and crossed my arms as I looked him over. He'd had a bath too, and the morning light streaming through the windows made his sun-streaked hair glow with endless shades of gold. A guilty impulse to suggest we stay in my room reared up in me, but instead I said, "Sure. Looks like you managed to find the time after all."

He gestured to the meeting room. "Time found us."

We made our way down to the trade manager's home at the base of Kerniall's hill. He wasn't around, but his teenage son was and helped us get Dove and Pebble from the stables. "Father said if you came by that I should tell you not to forget to meet with him before you go." The boy fastened Pebble's bridle and stepped back admiringly. "He also wanted to know if you've changed your mind about selling these two. Or that other beauty, the one with the incredible hair."

Jago took Pebble's reins. "She'll be flattered, but none of them are for sale, I'm afraid. And I won't forget."

"Has he tried to buy them before?" I asked as Jago and I walked to the gate.

"Yup. He and others have offered me a king's ransom. Can't blame them."

"A king's ransom, huh? For someone always fixated on making amazing deals, it seems like you're passing up a good one."

"Hush. You'll hurt their feelings, trying to get rid of them." He patted Dove's mane. "Don't listen to her, girl. You're not going anywhere. You're going to help me make a fortune one day."

I understood why he wouldn't sell them to pay his debts. After all, the horses *were* the reasons for his debts . . . or were they? I didn't know what horses like these cost, but from all the business he did, it seemed like he should be close to paying them off.

We followed a road behind Kerniall that led to the East Sister. Buildings that probably played a role in transport and fishing clustered near the bank, which was even and flat around here, and docks and barges sat on the river itself. Even in winter, river activity was still booming, and Icori moved about on various jobs. Jago led us down a smaller track, away from the docks, to a clearing near some pines.

"Okay," he said, bringing Dove up beside a stump. "Up you go."

I stepped on it hesitantly. "No saddle?"

"You'll learn faster and better if you start without one. The downside is that you'll probably hurt a lot more afterward. Lucky you have all this time to lounge around and recover."

He helped me swing up onto the horse, and I wobbled as I tried to settle and stay balanced. I clung to Dove's mane for a moment and then had the sense to pick up the reins instead. She danced around a little, and I swallowed back a yelp. The ground seemed alarmingly far away.

"Easy, girl," Jago crooned. "You're fine."

Nervously, I patted her neck. "She seems okay."

"She's not the one I'm talking to. You've got your seat now, your balance looks good. Now, relax and just sit there."

"Just sit?"

"Just sit. Every muscle in your body's working to keep you steady right now, and we're giving them time to get good at it."

Dreams of galloping nobly across the plains, with the wind rushing dramatically through my hair, were banished as the morning progressed. After endless sitting, we advanced to walking and communicating with Dove's signals. Just before breaking for lunch, he let me take her out for a brief, gentle trot. It was tougher than I expected, and I struggled constantly to keep myself centered and still pay enough attention to direct her.

When he helped me down, my legs nearly collapsed out from under me. He laughed and offered his arm for support. "Told you."

I winced as I forced my stiff, sore muscles to obey. I'd never before thought about how many of them were in my body, but I was pretty sure just then that each and every one of them hurt. "This is the worst, right?" I asked. "It'll be better tomorrow?"

"Eh, let's go get something to eat" was his evasive answer.

We ate our packed lunch on a wide, flat rock, saying little as we basked in the sun and each other's nearness. Birds sang everywhere, and it was almost possible to believe spring might be coming to this land. Some snowy patches in direct sunlight had started to melt, though those in the shade remained frozen. When we finished eating, and Jago announced more trotting practice, I groaned.

"Come on, Jago! Can't I ride? Really ride? You're the one going on about how glorious it is to run free on a horse, but I'm never going to get to do it."

"You're not ready." But after a few moments of scrutiny, he smiled and said, "But you can do it with me. Come on, Pebble's been getting bored anyway."

Jago untied the gray stallion and helped me up. Once I was steady, he mounted as well, taking up a seat behind me. As he reached around my waist to take the reins, I forgot all about the thrill of racing. He felt warm and steady at my back, and I wished he'd wrap his arms around me more tightly. Then, Jago urged Pebble to a cleared path, and I was very much reminded of what Jago had been planning to show me.

Once he gave the signal, Pebble flew. Freed of restraints, with nothing but open land ahead, Pebble ran with an almost joyful abandon. His strong legs thundered beneath us, and I imagined them stretching as far as they'd go. The whoosh of air rushing by made tears sting my eyes, and the speed jostled and bounced us, but I didn't mind. It was glorious and terrifying all at once.

After only a couple of minutes, Jago guided Pebble into a curve and sent us back the way we'd come. Before I knew it, we were slowing to a halt beside Dove in the clearing. Breathless and laughing, I leaned back and asked, "Why did you stop it so soon?"

His hands rested on my hips, and he slowly slid them forward, wrapping me up to him. "It's not good to ride double like this—especially so hard—for very long. But now you see why I do so much for these guys? What it's all for?"

"Yes! And now I need to learn to do it on my own."

But I stayed where I was, loath to leave when his body was pressed up to mine. I turned to the side, trying to see him over my shoulder. He leaned forward and met me in a long, languid kiss that carried just as much heat as the rougher ones from the other night. Pebble pranced restlessly, and Jago and I broke apart with some reluctance.

But as soon as we climbed down, we went for each other again. As I wrapped my arms around his neck and melted at the feel of his lips, I began to think suggesting we stay inside hadn't been such a crazy idea after all.

At one point, I opened my eyes and caught a glimpse of the East Sister through the trees. To the north, looming like a dark sentinel, sat the unmistakable shape of the Well's jagged cliffs. All at once, the dream tumbled back to me, and with its return, all my earlier joy was sucked away. I unfolded myself from Jago and stalked away, suddenly despondent.

"Tamsin?" He hurried to catch up with me. "What's the matter?"

I pressed my hands to my forehead and halted. "We shouldn't be doing this! *I* shouldn't be doing this. I have no right to it! I shouldn't be out having a holiday when there's so much to do. Everyone's depending on me. The other girls are still in Constancy, and Merry . . . oh, Uros. Merry's out on the ocean right now."

I didn't stop him when he took my hand again. "Don't worry. Storm season will be done by the time they get to the western sea. You guys will be together before you know it."

He led me back to the stone we'd sat on for lunch. "What's your plan for her?" he asked.

"Before the delays, my plan was to be married and have a home ready for her when she arrived. At this point, though, my goal is just to make it to the city by the time she's there. But surely there's someone left who's wildly rich enough to bring the rest of my family over and cover Merry's expenses. He doesn't even have to be *wildly* rich. I just need to make sure we don't have to worry anymore." Deprived of talking about her for so long, I found myself going on and on. "She's sick a lot, and doctors and medicine add up. We've lived in constant fear. Can we afford the next treatment? Will we be choosing between medicine or food or rent? And anything other than those things, well, they were never even up for consideration. We didn't have a copper extra, and I don't want it to be that way anymore. I want everything for her. A safe, stable home. Education. Shoes without holes. Respect. That's what this is all about—the better life I mentioned. One without fear." My chest suddenly grew tight, imagining Merry having a coughing attack during the voyage. "She's got medicine with her, but Six. It worries me."

"You shouldn't worry. Even if you hadn't told me the details, I know you wouldn't have let any detail be overlooked."

"Yes. Yes." I took a deep breath. It was as comforting to hear someone speak of her as it was for me to talk. "I've done all I can for her trip. Now I've just got to secure that rich husband and make sure he's crazy about me."

Jago stiffened a little but didn't remove his hand. "How could anyone not be?" he asked, voice light.

"Well, some aren't going to be so crazy about a stepdaughter."

"But you've already taken that into consideration."

"Of course. I've got a story ready about how I'm the widow of some tragically lost soldier and that I had to hide it in the Glittering Court. I figure if someone's in love with me enough, he won't mind."

"Yes, he certainly wouldn't."

"That was why I fought so hard to be the best at everything. I needed to get first pick, to have as many choices as I could to get the ideal match. I just pray my best choices haven't been snatched up."

"Are you ever going to tell this husband the truth?"

"Before we're married?"

"Before, after, anytime." The tone of Jago's voice surprised me. And I didn't like it.

"In the long run? Who can say. But no, not before. I can't take any chances."

"So you'd be going into marriage under a lie."

I turned to Jago, so incredulous that I couldn't even form words right away. Instead, I brushed his hand away and got to my feet. "Don't preach to me, Jago. You've got no right to morals, not with the way you wheel and deal the gullible and push off liquor on people you know are supposed to avoid it!"

"That's not the same thing at all. They know what they're going into."

"You haven't had to make the choices I have. If there was some perfect, easy solution to all of this, I never would have set foot on that damned ship! I wish I could be good and honest in everything I do—I try to—but I have no regrets over what I've done to take care of my daughter, no matter how ruthless it seems. I'd do it all again, and I'd do worse!"

"Tamsin—"

"I'm done with riding today." I walked over to Dove and guided her toward the road. "I'll walk her back. If you'll allow it."

"Tamsin—" This time, he cut himself off. With a sigh, he took Pebble's reins and caught up to me, though he didn't say a word the whole way back to Kerniall.

Orla invited us to eat with her and her sisters, and a green cotton dress materialized on my bed where the nightgown had been. It was a less extravagant version of Orla's, with the same high waist and scooped neckline—but no gratuitously long sleeves. It was worn over a simple linen chemise, without a belt or clips, and felt absurdly comfortable for formal wear. I almost laughed as I dressed, thinking of the complexities of petticoats, underdresses, overdresses, and corsets that would be required for a comparable Osfridian dinner.

Jago and I were seated side by side, but the dark cloud still hung over us. We talked readily enough with everyone else but barely looked at each other. Several of the diners had been at the earlier meeting, and we learned that they'd voted to give us the benefit of the doubt on our story. This was largely because of Jago's insistence on the truth of what we'd discovered. Many knew him, and the bitterroot incident had earned him a lot of favor. That didn't mean the Icori would be openly declaring war on the Lorandians anytime soon, but Orla's sister Stana was already working on messages to send to outlying clans, apprising of them of the situation and warning to be watchful for more alleged Osfridian attacks.

Faiva, the youngest, was obsessed with coming up with schemes to catch the Lorandians in the act of wrongdoing, though few of her ideas were plausible. Orla was tasked with dealing with the colonists, in the hope of ensuring they'd stand down from any retaliatory actions until the mystery was solved. From her expression, it was clearly not a job she was thrilled about.

A guest delayed Jago as we were leaving, and I went to my room alone. Later, when he came knocking, I didn't answer. He left me alone after a few tries, and I sank onto my bed, my heart breaking. It wasn't just the fight with Jago that had me hurting. It was Jago himself. My brilliant plan to launch my daughter and me into a better lifestyle seemed tarnished now. I still had no moral qualms about marrying someone for money; it was done all the time. But since Jago had no money, he couldn't be that someone, and it bothered me. It also bothered me to even be bothered by that! I'd only known him a short time, and he'd driven me crazy for most of it. Doing . . . what I'd done with him during those few passionate times had only made this worse. If I'd displayed any shred of self-control, maybe I wouldn't feel so conflicted right now. Instead, I'd left both of us confused and upset and taken my eyes from what mattered most: Merry. I couldn't let that happen again.

When I woke, I felt a little more clearheaded, but it was underscored with a grim resignation. I knew what I had to do, and the sooner it was taken care of, the better. As soon as I'd cleaned up for the day, I headed out. But when I opened my door, Jago was standing right outside, his hand raised to knock. "Oh!" he exclaimed. "How's that for timing?"

I swallowed and glanced down at the stone tiled floor. "I was just coming to see you."

"Well, I was coming to see *you*. And Tamsin, look . . . about yesterday . . . I . . ."

I looked up, and the tension and his anguished expression were too much for me. "Oh, Jago—"

"Nope, nope." He held up a hand. "Don't 'Oh, Jago' me. I deserved that scolding. You were too easy on me, actually. I have no business judging you—you're right that I haven't been through what you have. I can't even imagine."

"Come in and talk." I stepped aside and waited for him to pass before I closed the door. "Look, I know you weren't trying to be . . . that is . . . I know you meant well."

He shoved his hands in his pockets and walked over to the fireplace. "Mostly."

"Mostly?"

I joined him, and in his profile, an array of emotions flashed by, too tangled for me to read. "What I said, I believe. *Why* I was saying it . . . well, that was me being petty over your hypothetical husband. My own hurt feelings, which have no right to be hurt."

My heartbeat suddenly felt so heavy and so fast, it was a wonder he couldn't hear it. "Why . . . why are you hurt?"

"Tamsin, you know why. I understand why you're doing this, but it's hard to be chipper about it when I . . ." With a heavy sigh, he turned around and walked back toward the door. "Never mind. I shouldn't bother you with my rambling."

"I don't know. I daresay I've grown accustomed to it. In fact, I kind of like it."

He stopped, his back to me. "No joking, Tamsin. Not today. I'm crazy about you—I have been since you walked through my door. But I'm not going to hassle you when you've got your sights fixed on better men."

"The thing is . . ." I took a few steps toward him. "I don't think I'm going to find a better man than you."

Jago slowly turned around and met my eyes, his green-and-gold ones so filled with emotion that its power nearly knocked me over.

"Now, that doesn't mean I can . . . Well, I still have to go to Cape Triumph and find someone," I continued. "Merry's still first, my wants come second—or not at all. And that's what I was coming to tell you."

His eyebrows rose, and he moved a little closer too. "You were?"

"Yes. I was going to your room to tell you that what we did in the storm and outside, well, that it has to stop. I wanted to make sure you knew that I still wanted to work with you and be your traveling partner but that I came to Adoria for a reason and will see that plan through."

"I get it," he said, face falling. "I knew it, I was accepting it. But when it's spelled out like that, it's harsh."

"Well . . . it's what I *was* going to tell you. And it's all still true! I'm just . . . not . . . saying it right now."

He looked understandably confused—but also hopeful. "Then what are you saying now?"

I took a deep breath and reached for him. "That I'm a little crazy about you too."

I think I might have actually been just plain crazy, too, as we came together and kissed. It was ridiculous. I'd just explained that we couldn't have a future, and yet, I couldn't stop kissing him. I melted into him and ran my fingers through his unruly hair, bringing him nearer in the process. For someone who'd been ready to walk away moments ago, he showed no hesitancy in the kiss. Neither did I, for that matter. It went on and on, and maybe it wasn't one long kiss so much as a whole bunch of little ones strung together.

Whatever it was, I lost myself in it and let go of worry and responsibility for a time. I tugged him toward the bed, and he followed without hesitation. We fell onto it together, still kissing and tentatively reaching for each other's clothing.

That was also when a loud knock sounded at the door.

We both bolted upright and stared at it. A childlike panic hit me, that somehow, impossibly, we'd been found out. But that couldn't be, and a few moments later, a servant's voice rang through: "Danna?"

Jago and I released each other, and after a deep breath to calm my racing heart, I walked sedately to the door and opened it. Shirsha, a young Icori woman who'd helped me a number of times, stood there.

"Oh, I'm so glad you're here. Dan Jago wasn't in his— Oh, hello." She peered past me in pleasant surprise. "Anyway, Danna Orla sent me. There are Osfridians here."

Jago strode to my side. "Osfridians? What Osfridians? Where are they from?"

"Grashond Colony. From a town called Cons-Constancy." She tripped over the unfamiliar name as she glanced between us. "And they're insisting on seeing you."

CHAPTER 25

IMMEDIATELY, AN IMAGE OF GRAY-AND-BLACK-CLAD HEIRS raising pitchforks at the gates of Kerniall popped into my head. I clutched at Jago's sleeve. "We have to get out of here. There must be some way to escape, right? Passages, a back door—"

"Orla wouldn't be calling for us if there was a threat," Jago assured me, though he didn't look all that easy about this news. "How many are there?"

"Three. One is a soldier."

Neither Jago nor I knew of any soldiers in Constancy. "What about the other visitors?" I asked.

Shirsha frowned, eyes thoughtful. "One is older . . . maybe forty? He doesn't have much hair, and what's there is black. The other is our age. Golden hair." A small smile played at her lips. "Very handsome."

"Gideon," Jago and I said together.

"Gideon wouldn't harm us," I said. "And that doesn't sound like Samuel. But what about the soldier? There isn't an army lurking somewhere, is there? Surely we haven't warranted that?"

Jago shook his head. "Orla wouldn't allow a soldier in if she suspected there were others lying in wait. If we're being summoned, the area's been scouted."

He started to follow Shirsha, but I stayed rooted to the spot. "I'm not going back there," I said when he noticed I wasn't with him. "I'm not going back in that bloody room—"

"You won't. I promise. There's nothing they can do to you."

"But what about to you? You said you weren't worried about going back for your cargo because there was no proof we'd taken off together. Well, if they see us now, there kind of is."

"Did they ask for us by name?" Jago inquired of Shirsha. When she nodded, he turned back to me. "They probably already know."

I followed with trepidation, more uneasy now about what would happen to him than to me. Shirsha took us back to the grand sitting room with the giant hearth. Orla was already there, fully decked out in princess attire, chatting with two men in dark clothing. Gideon turned when we entered, his face lighting up like a sunburst.

"Tamsin," he exclaimed. He rushed over to me and clasped my hands. "Thank Uros! I've been so worried about you! I'm so glad you're okay. I've missed you—we all have. No one knew what to think when you disappeared."

The other visitor's back was to me, and when he finally turned, I was relieved to see Roger Sackett, one of Constancy's magistrates. I wasn't really chummy with him, but I also had no grudge against him. What he thought of me was a different matter.

"Running out on a punishment is a serious matter," Roger said sternly. His eyes flicked to Jago. "As is helping a person do so. Or did you take her against her will?"

I found my voice again and came to life. "Of course he didn't! And I don't regret 'running out' for an instant. Especially since I didn't break any law."

"You didn't," a new voice said. Jago and I peered around, spying the soldier in a dim corner of the room. He'd been studying a sculpture so quietly, we hadn't even seen him at first. The black-haired man stepped forward, wearing the green uniform of the Osfridian army. "And I really hope I don't have to send word back to Osfrid of abuse of the charter. Everyone turns a blind eye to Grashond, but there may come a— Jago? Is that you?"

"Lieutenant Harper." Jago met the soldier in the middle of the room, shaking hands. "What are you doing out here?"

"Oh, the usual. Following up on kidnapping, treason, and attack by an outside force."

Jago's bewilderment left him short on words: "Wait...me? All that?"

Harper gave a small shrug of his shoulder. "That's what they say. When that's dealt with, I need to talk to you about some provisions. The fort's almost out of tobacco and flour. But we'd take cornmeal in a pinch."

"Oh, well, I can help you out there. But first . . ." Jago glanced back at the two Constancy townsmen. "Why are they here? You don't need them to arrest me. Are they going to try and cart Tamsin back?"

Gideon and Roger gave each other uncertain looks. "She certainly can't stay here with a bunch of—" Roger shut his mouth, remembering Orla was nearby. I could tell from his body language that she made him doubly uncomfortable: an Icori *and* a woman in charge of governance. "Well, there's no need for Tamsin to be an inconvenience here anymore."

"She's not." Orla had been observing everything with that mild, amused expression of hers, but her eyes were as shrewd as ever. "She may stay as long as she likes."

"And I actually won't need to," I added. "I'm going south with the Icori—to Denham and then Cape Triumph."

Gideon blanched. "Wait . . . what?"

I explained my travel plans. Gideon fell silent while Roger grew increasingly angry. "Are you out of your mind, girl? Going off alone with these people?"

"*These* people didn't subject me to starvation or exposure. They don't lower themselves to that sort of torture."

Orla shrugged. "Eh, don't sanctify us too much, Tamsin. There are plenty of things we don't take lightly. But no—I wouldn't starve someone over mittens or punish them for selling medicine."

Roger made a dismissive gesture. "That's the past. The present is this girl—who is not an adult—being kidnapped by a traitor sympathetic to a hostile nation and taken to that hostile nation."

"Okay, let's work through this," said Harper. He crossed his arms and came to stand next to me. "First off, she's not in Grashond, and she's—what was it, twenty? She's an adult in every other colony, as well as Osfrid. If she wants to stay—which she clearly does—she can. As for you, Jago, I didn't buy much into the claims of kidnapping, but it's no secret you're friendly with the Icori. That doesn't mean you're betraying secrets to them or conspiring with them, but enough is going on right now that I need to treat everything seriously."

Orla regarded him with a cool smile. "Is this where you get to the part about attack by an outside force?"

Harper's answering expression managed to be both apologetic and stern. "Constancy's council wrote to the commander of my fort in north Grashond asking for protection from the Icori. They aren't the first town to do so. Now, Mistress Micnimara, if things progress, I'm sure someone will suggest a formal sit-down between my people and yours, with a lot of people and a lot of opinions, that'll probably quickly go to arguing and grandstanding. You seem very reasonable and levelheaded, and so if you and I could reach a quiet understanding about the nature of your attacks—before someone's actually killed—I think it'd be helpful to all of us."

"I couldn't agree more," she said, getting comfortable in one of the chairs. "But the first piece of this 'quiet understanding' has to be that they aren't *our* attacks. Shirsha? Will you send for my sisters? And get us some tea and coffee while you're out. This may take a while."

It did, which surprised me. In my mind, I'd imagined a dramatic reveal of Alan's jacket, immediately clearing up all suspicions toward the Icori. Instead, Roger's first assessment was "How do I know you got that from the Lorandians? Seems more likely you got it here when those Icori thieves delivered the loot to their masters."

But he did keep listening. And more important, so did Lieutenant Harper. I soon realized it was a lucky break that he was the one the fort had sent to address Constancy's grievances. There were probably many other officers at the fort who would have come in with their opinions already settled on the Icori. Harper hadn't made his mind up either way. He was neither a pushover nor a warmonger. He asked a lot of questions and took note of everyone's views—me, Jago, the Constancy men, and the Micnamara sisters.

"Mister Sackett," he said at last. "I don't take what happened to those children lightly. I don't take any of the recent attacks lightly. That being said, I would *strongly* urge you not to instigate any aggressive actions toward the Icori in Grashond. Keep your sentries, but that's it. No outlawing of Icori or preemptive strikes. I know I don't have any say in municipal actions, but I'll be making the same report to my commander. He doesn't have civil authority either, but he does have the ear of the governor."

Roger scowled. "The governor's in Watchful! That place has nearly lost its way. What do they know about what goes on here in the west?"

"He'll know what we tell him. And if things change, and the evidence shifts, the military will act accordingly. But as it stands, the evidence isn't strong enough to implicate the Icori or vindicate the Lorandians."

Despite Roger's grumbling, I could tell that the evidence had affected him too. He was a magistrate, after all. It was his job to weigh the facts in legal matters. But he was also human, and his pride smarted at having to back down and give the benefit of the doubt to those he was so deeply prejudiced against.

"I can't believe this all stands on you believing Jacob Robinson about where they found the coat," muttered Roger, needing to place his frustration somewhere.

Harper smiled. "I've known Jago—or is it Jacob?—for two years, and he's always dealt fairly with us. More or less. I trust him."

"We trusted him too. He promised to keep that bitterroot safe and then sold it out right from under us!"

Faiva jumped up from her chair, fists clenched. "He saved countless lives! Probably yours too, if the fever had spread out of Kerniall. Jago is a hero, far more selfless than you'll ever be!"

Roger's eyes went wide. "Young lady—"

Harper shushed him before he had a chance to say something to one of Kerniall's three rulers that couldn't be taken back. Likewise, Orla rattled off a sharp rebuke in Icori, and after a few moments, Faiva sat back down with a glower. An odd, troubled look had come over Gideon's face, but I didn't have time to parse it.

Reassured that Grashond and the Icori were not going to war—for now—Harper and the sisters wanted to discuss the political implications of some of the other goings-on between the Icori and colonists farther out in Adoria. That didn't require the rest of us, and Shirsha led Jago, Roger, Gideon, and me to a small room used for weaving so that we could work out our differences. Not that there was much to be worked out. I'd made up my mind that I was going with the Icori, but I did have questions for our guests.

"How are my friends?" I asked Gideon. "Are they okay?"

Gideon pulled up a small wooden chair and sat down. "They are. They miss you, though, and there's been some friction since you left. A few went into a complete panic because they don't believe they're going to Cape Triumph now."

Those words tore at my heart, and I looked down at my hands to hide how I felt. After seeing the way Orla and her sisters held their own among men, I refused to start crying in front of these three.

"I don't suppose there's been any response to my letter to Jasper Thorn?" I asked hopefully.

"No. I don't even know if it's possible." Gideon's eyes narrowed as he did some mental calculations. "Assuming it made it straight to Watchful on the coast with no delays overland, it would have had to immediately get on a ship to Cape Triumph and get a same-day response from him. Then that letter would have to make the return trip with no delays. Even then, I'd say the soonest you'd hear back is another week, and that'd be extraordinary in the best of times, let alone winter."

I nodded. I'd expected as much. "Well, then the other girls will get there when they get there. And I'll be able to alert Jasper to their situation in person. Assuming everything goes as it's supposed to on your end."

Roger caught my tone. "I understand why you don't want to return to Constancy, but rest assured, we *are* going to honor our word to help the rest of the girls get to Cape Triumph. And believe what you want, but I am trying to protect you. I wouldn't want my own child to go off with those godless barbarians, and I don't want you to either." Despite his brusqueness, there was a sense of good intentions in his words. He believed he was doing the right thing.

"Thank you," I said. "Truly. But my decision is made. I'll write letters to the others that you can take back with you, and if there's anything I can do to help ahead of their arrival in Cape Triumph, I will."

Roger gave a shrug. Gideon looked truly disheartened, and I had a vivid image of the girls in Constancy wearing similar expressions. *No guilt,* I firmly told myself. I'd help the other girls if I could, but I was Merry's mother, not theirs. They would have to be their own advocates.

"Well, that's that." Roger slid his stool back and rose. "I did my duty but failed with you, girl. Rest easy—we'll give a faithful report to the council of what happened. Let's see if Harper's ready, Gideon. If we leave now, we can get a good jump on the day. Gideon?"

Gideon hadn't moved. He wore that same troubled look I'd noticed earlier. Slowly, he lifted his eyes to Roger's. "Is it true what was said back there—when Jacob took the medicine, were the Icori already sick?"

Jago spoke before the magistrate could. "Yes. There was an outbreak of black fever here."

"Why didn't I ever hear about that?" asked Gideon, aghast. "The council never mentioned it. All we heard was that he broke the pact for more money."

"Because it was irrelevant." Roger leaned against the wall, tapping his fingers impatiently. "The bitterroot was promised to us, for our use. It doesn't matter who he sold it to or why."

"I'd think it matters if human lives were on the line! Do you know how many people live here?"

"No. What I do know is that if a similar affliction strikes Constancy, we'll suffer. Human lives will be on the line too—and likely lost now. That will happen whether he sold it to them in sickness or in health."

Gideon got to his feet and approached Roger with neither nervousness nor gentle words. "But surely there should have been some consideration, given the circumstances! Some compromise or solution. Did you really just outright refuse the request and consign those people to death?"

Roger shook his head. "They deny Uros and the angels and have probably killed more of our people in Adoria than that fever would have taken of theirs. It wasn't worth pursuing 'some compromise or solution' with people like that, even if such a thing had existed."

"One did," I interjected. "Jago offered to restock the town's supply but missed his chance because of the council's censure."

"Is that true?" Gideon exclaimed. His cheeks were flushed—with anger, not shyness. It was the first time I'd ever seen him so worked up. Even when we'd been threatened by the Lorandians, he'd remained calm. "You wasted that time with him—when it all could have been settled so simply?"

Roger's condescension shifted to something harder and colder. "Gideon, you have my respect as a minister—but you are a *junior* minister. You are still, in many ways, an outsider with much to learn."

Jago pulled my arm and stood up. "Tamsin, let's give them some privacy."

Before I could protest and demand some answers, Shirsha appeared in the doorway and loudly cleared her throat. "Pardon me," she said uncertainly, "but the dannas are asking for you again."

Animosity crackled between Gideon and Roger, but the two put their dispute on hold to go back to the hearth room with us. The group in there looked ready to disperse, but Orla beckoned us to where she stood with Lieutenant Harper. "I'm going to get the word out, here in the north, to hold off on any aggressive action until things are sorted out," he said, "but the south has seen a few of these weird raids too, and I want to make sure nobody jumps the gun there."

Orla nodded along. "To help him get there faster, we've agreed to let him send a small group of soldiers down the East Sister River to spread the word. They'll accompany us on the trip next week, and we'll bump some of our people from it to make room. They'll go on a second expedition leaving about two weeks later—an expedition that will have enough room to accommodate your friends and the others from the ship, Tamsin."

I gasped. "Do you mean that?"

"They'll still have to pay passage, of course," Orla added.

"Certainly. Thank you, Orla. You have no idea what that means to me, and what it will mean to them." Three weeks! I was so excited, I could barely stand still. Adding in travel time down the river and across Denham, the others girls would be in Cape Triumph in just under two months—well ahead of the three if they went with the Heirs. Jago ran a hand through his hair, and I could see thoughts spinning behind his eyes. "Can I have those spots on the later trip, Orla? And then let the *Gray Gull* passengers take mine on the upcoming one?"

Orla's wry smile vanished. "You want to give up your early passage?"

"It isn't that much of a delay," he replied with a shrug. "I'll still be ahead of most of the other northern traders, and it'll be easier on Tamsin and the others to all stay together."

"I see." Orla glanced to me, then back to him. "It makes no difference to me. As long as the space is divided out correctly, and everyone's ready to go on time, it's fine."

I turned to Jago, scarcely able to breathe. I'd struggled so hard to get my companions to Cape Triumph the moment we set foot in Adoria, and suddenly, just like that, it was going to happen. "Jago . . . I can't believe you'd do this. I don't know what to say! Thank you, thank you so much! And if there is a loss in profit—"

He dismissed my worries with a wave of his hand, his eyes shining as he regarded me. I wanted to leap forward and throw my arms around him. "Don't worry about it. Two weeks won't matter. And besides, the numbers should work out so that I can come along on the first run and get things in place. I'll have Arnaud accompany the rest of the goods."

"Don't get carried away," warned Roger gruffly. "You may be free and on your own, Tamsin, but those other girls are still under our protection and aren't leaving without a proper escort. I don't know if that can happen in a week."

I looked to Lieutenant Harper for help. "There's an argument that the older girls could come or go as they wanted," he said, "but you've got some young ones there too, right? Sixteen? Seventeen? As much as I think they should be allowed to go, they should still be answering to their guardians. I'll personally assist in accompanying them to Cape Triumph, if that helps, Mister Sackett."

"And I'll go too," said Gideon. "I'm sure if we can just get a couple more from Constancy to chaperone, that should be adequate."

"I'll also go back with you two to help get everyone here—we can go right away," Jago suggested. Roger still looked dubious, but he knew when to concede. The four of them fell into planning the logistics, and I was happy enough to dance. After obstacle upon obstacle, things were finally getting back on track. I was going to Cape Triumph, and my friends were too. We'd be free of the Heirs at last. I'd be there in plenty of time for Merry!

Almost. The feel of Jago's kiss lingered on my lips, and his words echoed in my head: *I'm crazy about you—I have been since you walked through my door.* Watching him as he talked numbers with Roger, I felt a tightness in my chest. Jago was not falling into place with any of this, because he had no place. He never had. We both understood that, and yet he'd still just made a considerable concession to help my friends—except I knew it was really for me. Maybe missing two weeks of the trading season wasn't a lot, but for someone scraping against debt the way he was, it still could've been an edge. And he'd given it up.

I wanted a chance to talk to him, but he got swept up with preparations that I couldn't help with. My turn for leadership would come
when my friends arrived, but for now, I had to bide my time.

Though he'd been busy too, I did get an unexpected opportunity to
speak with Gideon later in the day when I spied him eating alone in
the dining hall. I walked in and sat down across from him, eliciting a
glad smile.

"I thought you'd be holed up with the others," I said.

"We've finished what we can do before we go to Constancy. Jacob
is off discussing weights and measures with the Icori now, and Roger's
praying no heretics will come for him in his sleep."

"Are you doing okay?" I asked, noting his plate of food was mostly
untouched.

His smile turned rueful. "As okay as I can be having what I thought
I understood ripped apart before my eyes."

"You mean about Jago and the medicine?"

"Yes. To be deceived like that, it's like everything I thought was
beautiful and good in Constancy has fallen away into . . . a black void.
That sounds melodramatic, I suppose. But I still can't believe it—that
the council would refuse aid and cover it all up."

"There is *some* good in Constancy." My words came out a little
haltingly, given my personal experiences.

"I know. But it doesn't change what's happened. I gave the council
my loyalty, my friendship, and my trust. And they were knowingly lying to me, using me to further what they wanted. And what they did to
you . . . they didn't order it, exactly, but they allowed Dinah to initiate
it. I swear, I didn't know, Tamsin. If I had—"

"It's okay. I'm fine, and things have worked out."

"I can't go back," he blurted out. "I mean, I can physically go back
to Constancy, temporarily, for any loose ends. But I can't back to that
world—to the Heirs."

"Gideon . . ." I studied his face and saw how earnest it was. This wasn't a rash decision born from the earlier spat with Roger. "You gave up everything in Osfrid to sail here and be with the Heirs. What happened to Uros calling you? To you wanting a purer, principled life?"

"I'm still called, and I still want that. But it's not going to be with the Heirs. It's not going to be with the orthodox either. Maybe no one's way is my way. Maybe I have to create my own."

There was such strength and conviction in his words that I truly believed he would find his way. I was reminded of some of our earlier conversations, when he'd described his faith so passionately that I could understand why he was so driven.

"You'll figure it out, Gideon. I believe in you."

He lifted his gaze from the bread he'd been poking at. "You've always believed in me, Tamsin, even when I didn't believe in myself. You—" His blue-gray eyes scrutinized me a few more moments, and then he glanced away again. "Well. Anyway. I can't quite bring myself to ride back two days with Roger. I'll see if Jacob will let me ride with him."

It wasn't until later that evening that I finally caught up with Jago. He came to see me in my room, and we threw ourselves at each other the instant the door shut. Without a pause in kissing, we staggered back into the room and onto the rug before the fire. My yearning for him was driven both by the happy affection surging in my heart and the desire crackling through my body. I hadn't had a glimmer of interest in anything physical with anyone since Harry, and I'd almost thought I was incapable of it—like maybe he'd ruined it for me. But I came alive now, suddenly feeling as though I could never touch or kiss Jago enough.

"You're just being nice to me because of the river passage," he teased at one point, lying on his side, half propped up with his elbow. With his other hand, he traced the neckline of my dress and walked his fingers up to my cheek, where he brushed stray strands of hair away.

"I'm nice to lots of people," I shot back. "And believe me, I'm not rolling about and kissing them."

"Well, that's a relief. I'd hate to think you were doing it out of pity or obligatory gratitude."

I sat up and gave him a long, lingering kiss on his lips. "I am terribly grateful, though. It's a relief to know the others are taken care of. Now I can focus on Merry. I feel so much closer to her now—like she's within reach."

"She is." He shifted up too and straightened his shirt. No one's clothing had come off, but it was certainly less tidy than it had been before. "I like that name. Why did you name her that?"

I gazed across the room, but it was the past I saw. "Her full name's Meredith, but I always planned on calling her Merry. There was so much heartache and strife in the time leading up to her birth. I picked the name as a sort of reminder to myself that things were going to change—that I was going to make them change."

"Was . . . was her father ever involved?"

"Aside from the obvious? No. We had no contact until right before I signed with Jasper. My family was about to collapse under the bills, so I finally went to him and asked for money. Do you know what he said to me? 'I'm very sorry for you and your child, but you got yourself into this. You'll have to get yourself out of it.' Who says something like that? It made me realize I was right to have stayed away. Merry's better off with no father in her life than one like that."

"From what you've said, she's got plenty of other people to love her."

My heart lightened a little. "Yes. And she might as well have two fathers, with the way my pa and brother spoil her."

I leaned into him, and we sat quietly for several minutes, watching the fire. He stroked my hair, and I traced circles on his palm. When Jago stifled a yawn, I lifted my head and laughed. "Sorry, is this boring?"

"No." He tipped my face upward and pressed his lips to my forehead. "But it's been a long day. I should get to bed soon."

We kissed again and then some more before I was able to break away and ask, "Do you want to go to bed here?"

There was a slight intake of breath as he searched my face. Firelight cast golden glimmers in his eyes, which were filled with open longing. "You know I do. But . . . I can't, not when I don't have anything to offer you."

"You didn't have anything earlier either." I rested my palms on his chest. "But you were willing to go to my bed then."

"I know, I know. And I get that there's this unspoken agreement that there is no agreement, but . . ." He put his hands over mine. "You deserve more."

"Like a payment? This isn't some 'amazing deal' we're striking. The only thing I want right now is you."

"I know—I didn't mean to make it sound conditional. I just need to think some things over."

"Jago—"

"Tamsin. This isn't an easy thing for me to turn down, believe me." He kissed my forehead again. "We can talk more later—it's a long trip. But let me go now while I've still got the willpower."

Disappointment filled me, and his show of principles only made the yearning that much worse. I had a feeling that willpower might crumble with a little more pushing, but I couldn't do that to him. He talked about me deserving more, but what about him? Who was I to ask for a night together after having made it blatantly clear I'd soon be on my way to spend my life with someone else?

"Okay. Get your rest, then. But I'm going to hold you to that bit about it being a long trip."

The tension in his face melted into a cheerful grin. "I'd expect nothing less. I'll see you in the morning."

After a very lengthy kiss goodbye, he finally dragged himself away. I sat on my bed and sighed, filled with an array of emotions. I'd been there about five minutes when Shirsha knocked at the door and told me Orla wanted to see me. Puzzled by the late hour, I followed with trepidation and was taken to a small sitting room adjacent to Orla's own bedroom.

She sat in a chair near the fire, clad in a dressing robe, combing out her long hair. Seeing me, she said, "Ah, Tamsin. Thank you for coming. I was curious: Did you know Jago Robinson is about to give up everything in his world for you?"

CHAPTER 26

WHEN I ANSWERED WITH ONLY A BLANK STARE, ORLA motioned me to sit across from her with a graceful wave of her hand.

"What do you mean?" I asked, once I'd recovered myself.

She set the comb down and leaned back, a small smile playing at her lips despite her grave eyes. "If we ever get a moment, I'll have to show you my horses. Lovely little things—black, with ivory manes. A couple of years back, I saw some like them, traveling among Lorandian traders. They weren't for sale, and their owner told me they were hard to obtain. He said—with some skepticism—that to buy my own, I'd need a genius tradesman. So, I located one, and he got me the horses."

"Jago told me that's how you met," I said. "But what does that have to do with what's happening now?"

"My horses were hard to get in Adoria. Jago's silvers were *very* hard to get. And the one he's boarding in the south? Nearly impossible."

"Felicia. I thought she was his sweetheart when we first met."

That broadened Orla's smile, though her somber demeanor remained. "I'm sure it seems that way. Between her and the silvers, my understanding is that he's setting himself up very nicely to make a fortune in raising specialty horses. He's got a good head for what's going to be in demand and a good heart for taking care of animals. He just needs to pay down the debt for them and his land a little bit more." The wry smile dimmed. "So, you can imagine my surprise when he came to me earlier and asked if I was interested in buying the silvers."

I leaned forward. "Pebble and Dove? He wouldn't! He loves those horses."

"Apparently not as much as he loves you."

"But no . . ." That was as far as I got with any sort of coherent response in my shocked state.

"But yes. When I declined, he offered to sell me Felicia instead."

"What? I . . . don't understand. Why would he do that?"

"He said he wants to marry you."

I opened my mouth but couldn't manage a single word this time.

Orla shrugged. "I gather he needs a large sum of money quickly? Or rather, you do?"

I slumped back and clutched the couch's fabric, as though that might stop the world from spinning. "I can't believe this."

"So you do need money. Or . . . you want the money?" Her eyes scrutinized me in that cunning way of hers. "I understand you've come here to marry well, but maybe you could make yourself stick it out and live humbly a while? Assuming you love him back."

"You bloody well know I do!" The words came out before I could stop them, and I straightened up again. "And it's not about forcing myself to make a sacrifice to humble living! All I've ever done is live humbly!"

She took my outburst calmly, knowing my outrage wasn't directly targeted at her. "Well. I figured there must be more to it. Jago doesn't strike me as the type to upend all of his plans to impress a woman— though he's certainly no stranger to extreme actions when he thinks it's truly called for."

"Like the medicine," I murmured, still stunned.

"Like the medicine. He didn't waver about risking the stocks then, and he didn't waver when I questioned him now."

I blinked and focused back on her. "Stocks?"

"Didn't he tell you that? It was his punishment for selling us Constancy's bitterroot."

"I thought he paid a fine."

"I think he did both. I'm sure he can tell you more about it later."

"I don't know. Apparently he doesn't tell me much of anything! Are you sure this horse sale was for me?" I didn't really need her nod to confirm it. I felt sick to my stomach, upset that he'd make this sacrifice . . . and yet, hopeful that it could actually work. "He can't sell them. You said you told him no, so that's that."

"Oh, there are others he can go to. Perhaps not in Kerniall, but if he's determined to find a buyer, he will. I confess, if we didn't have the possibility of war looming on the horizon, I might have been tempted. But I can't spend that much money on my own indulgence."

"What happens if he does sell them?"

"Well, he loses the breeding stock to establish a specialty ranch. He has other horses, I know—more common ones—so maybe he could do something less lucrative with them. I'm not sure how it would play into his land in Denham."

"*His* land? He talked like he was only leasing something there."

"He is—but he's also in a complex arrangement to eventually own it. He makes payments on it, and that's where the rest of his debt is coming from. It's a huge amount of land, with a huge price. The loan is backed by the understanding that his racing enterprise has enormous potential."

"Not if he doesn't have any horses!"

"Maybe he can race some of his common ones? I guess it depends on if you're bringing in any debt."

I caught the unspoken question. "Yes. I don't know how it'd match up to a horse sale, but it'd cost a lot if he—that is, if we . . ." I looked down at my hands, unable to continue. What costs was he taking into consideration? My marriage fee, certainly. Merry's medicine and extra expenses.

"I don't know then," Orla said, her voice unusually gentle. "If he has to forfeit the horses, and then the land by default, he'll still have the traveling trade business. It's not as glamorous, but you'd be to-gether. Maybe that's worth the sacrifice."

Sparks flew up from the fire as logs shifted. I watched them a few moments and then slumped onto the couch. "A long time ago, there was a young man that—things didn't work out with. I know now he never had any intention of making them work. But at the time, when it first fell apart, I'd been certain that we could be together if he was willing to sacrifice certain parts of his life. Yes, it would shock his peers. Yes, it would anger his father. But that's what love is, right? Doing anything for the other person? It devastated me that he couldn't. I hated him for not loving me enough to keep us together, no matter what. Then I just hated him because he was an ass." I lingered on that memory a moment and then lifted my gaze from the fire to Orla. "Now, here's someone who is willing to make a sacrifice for me— an even bigger one—and I'm devastated again. Jago's built his dream from the ground up, holding on to something most would have lost as a childhood fancy."

"And it's his choice to let it go—or to postpone it," she said.

"But my participation in this isn't his choice." I turned to the fire again, but didn't really see it. My mind's eye was back with Jago, back when we'd been kissing, and I'd invited him to spend the night.

I can't stay, not when I don't have anything to offer you.

"I can't let him give up his future," I said, recalling the way his eyes glowed when he spoke about raising horses. "*We* can't."

Orla arched an eyebrow. "We?"

"He's your friend. You can't want to see him throw away everything he's worked for."

"No . . . but I also don't want to see him throw you away! I want him to be happy. And I think . . . I think you could make him happy." She ran a hand through her hair, messing up what she'd so neatly combed. "And I think he could make you happy too. You know, I recommended him to you when we met, not just because he could help but because I thought you two would connect—not like this, of course. But you both have an innate drive to help people, often going to extremes you don't fully realize the consequences of."

"And that's exactly why I'm going to save Jago from himself."

We lapsed into silence, and Orla walked over to a table at the room's side. She poured herself a glass of wine and held another glass up in question. I shook my head. "You might need it if this is going forward," she said when she returned to her spot. "I know I will."

"Then you'll help me?"

She answered by way of a long drink of the wine. "Are you sure this is the path you want, Tamsin?"

"I want him, but not like this. I don't want him spending his life with me and always wondering what would've happened if he'd stuck with his first plan."

There it was, the familiar mocking smile. "Tamsin, no one sticks with their first plan."

Wasn't that the truth. Some days, I didn't even know what plan I was on anymore.

"Orla," I said, "you act like I should go off with him, but if you believe that so easily, why did you call me here tonight? You wanted me to stop the horses from getting sold."

The smile slipped. "Yes . . . but I guess I was just hoping you'd have some other plan to take its place to get this money you need so badly."

I looked down at my hands, worried tears might come to my eyes. "I do have a plan—the same one I've had since coming to Adoria. I'm sticking with it. Now, are you going to help me help Jago stick with his?"

The next day was filled with preparations. The decision to make a second trip a couple of weeks after the first was big news. Its main purpose, of course, was to help settle the conflict brewing around us. But an extra trip meant a handful of spots were available, and many wanted to take advantage of it.

Merchants and other interested parties poured into the keep to petition Orla and her sisters. Meanwhile, Harper and Jago were trying to rustle up resources to help transport everyone from Constancy to Kerniall. They had Icori at their disposal, but Harper was hoping to stop by an outpost on the way back to pick up other soldiers, seeing as the Heirs might not react well to a group of Icori coming to town, even sanctioned ones.

I worked with them since I had especial knowledge of what it'd take to accommodate my friends. They'd need rations for the trip itself, and I bartered more of Jasper's belongings away. The distraction kept me from agonizing over my decision with Jago all day. Instead, I just agonized over it for most of the day.

When Jago excused himself to take a meeting with the merchant who'd greeted us upon entering the city, I knew what it was about. And when Jago returned, mood dimmed, I knew what had happened. Although it wasn't Orla's nature to command her subjects' decisions, she had sent word to the man this morning that she would look very, very favorably on him if he declined any opportunities to buy Jago's horses.

And I knew too why Orla called Harper for a private talk and why he looked so perplexed afterward. It all left me with a storm of conflicted feelings. I was pleased that our plan was all falling into place, but knowing what was to come tore at my heart.

Jago and I didn't have a chance to talk alone until after dinner. We sat together by the fireplace in my room, his hand over mine as we both rested from the long day.

"I'm going to miss you," he said. Panic shot through me until he added: "After seeing you every day now, I don't know how I'll go a week without you."

I relaxed slightly. "Well, maybe you'll like the peace and quiet instead of having me badger you all the time."

"Usually it's deserved, so I don't mind. I'm more worried *you'll* like the peace and quiet of not having my chatter around."

"Peace and quiet's overrated," I teased, eliciting a lopsided grin. "I've gotten so used to your chatter, I'll hardly know what to do without it."

He took hold of my other hand and pulled me toward him. Our break here had given him the chance to clean up and shave, and no matter what he said about not being "dashing," he looked pretty fine to me. But it was the earnestness in his green-and-gold eyes glittering in the firelight that mesmerized me the most.

"Do you mean that?" he asked.

I swallowed and looked away. If I could've just lied and spurned him then and there, it would've saved me the trouble of all the contingencies Orla and I were working out. But I couldn't do it. He would see the truth in me.

"About peace and quiet?" I asked in a lame attempt at evasion.

"Well. Sort of. But I think you know what I'm really talking about." He leaned closer, and I melted. "Tamsin, I know I'm not what you came here for. I honestly don't know how you put up with me. But ever since I met you, I've just felt like my world can be so much bigger than I ever dreamed. And I've always dreamed pretty big things for myself, you know. It's not like I've ever doubted my abilities or anything. Other people might have. But with my natural—"

"Jago."

"Anyway, like I was saying, I thought I had a handle on everything I needed to worry about in the future. And then you walked through my door. Literally. And suddenly, all my big dreams just weren't big enough for—"

"Jago," I interrupted again. "Be quiet."

I wrapped my arms around him and kissed him deeply. After a brief jolt of surprise he answered with the same intensity, wrapping one of his arms around my waist while his other entangled itself in my hair.

Everything about him flooded my senses—the way he felt, tasted, smelled. It intoxicated me, leaving me heady and greedy for more. I'd wanted him last night, but now, I felt like I *needed* him, like I couldn't go on if I didn't get more of him. Part of that was driven by the knowledge that very soon, I wouldn't have him at all. Everything felt amplified. Last night, I'd known he liked me. Tonight, I knew he loved me, and that knowledge sent my own love and desire to endless heights.

"Tamsin," he said breathlessly, when I began unbuttoning his shirt. "I—we—it's still like I told you. Not until I can provide more—"

"Jago," I interrupted, looking down at him. We were lying together on the rug, with me pressed on top of him, and my skirts pushed up to my knees. "You don't have to provide anything, do you understand? You're perfect like you are. Now, if you've got some other real reason to back off, that's okay. I'm absolutely not going to force myself on you. But if you're stuck on some idea of needing to show what you can offer, then stop it! I love you, and that's all that's needed. This isn't some kind of deal you have to strike."

His face grew radiant when I said I loved him. If he could've seen himself, he would've taken back his joke about not being mistaken for an angel. He cupped my face in his hands and said, "Maybe you're right. I could never strike a deal this amazing."

I shook my head and started to stand up. "If you're going to talk shop, then you can go back to your own room after all."

"Whoa, hey." He stood too, encircling my waist before I could get far. "I'm crazy about you, but I'm not crazy."

He jerked me to him, and we kissed again. Then we were kissing on the bed. And then everything melted into a delirious blur, the joy in my heart mingling with the passion in my body until I lost track of where one ended and one began. All I knew was that afterward, as he stroked my hair while I lay exhausted against his bare chest, I couldn't remember the last time I'd felt so completely and selfishly happy.

And also so sad.

I curled my fingers into his chest, still drinking him in with all my senses. I tried to choke back a sob, but he noticed and shifted so that his face was near mine. The fire had died down by now, leaving scant lighting. He brushed his fingers against my cheek.

"What's wrong? Did I do something—"

"No, no." I pressed a light kiss to his lips. "You were perfect.

Everything was perfect. I'm just—I'm just happy, that's all. It's all—tonight—it's just a lot."

Even though I couldn't see his face, I could sense him trying to puzzle that out. He eased himself back down again, keeping me close. After a long time, he said, "You know, after the way things ended at our first meeting, I never expected this is where I'd end up."

I couldn't help a laugh, despite my quaking heart. "And yet, here you are."

He laughed too and kissed my forehead. "Here I am."

Jago fell asleep soon thereafter, but I stayed awake most of the night, tormented by my own thoughts, as well as the need to cling to this as long as I could. Had I been wrong to do this, knowing what was to come? Would this moment make being away from him easier—or just more agonizing?

And *did* I have to be away from him? It wasn't too late to change things . . .

I've always dreamed pretty big things for myself, you know. It's not like I've ever doubted my abilities or anything.

No. I wasn't going to change things. We'd have this memory, and those of our other times together, and that would be it. We each had our own agendas to follow, and those agendas couldn't work together. Maybe if we'd had more time, we could've figured something out. But it wasn't to be.

I had a few remaining hours, though, so I fought sleep, savoring them as long as I could. I drifted off a little before dawn, only to wake soon thereafter as Jago was creeping from the bed.

"I didn't mean to wake you," he whispered.

"I'm glad you did."

He got dressed in the dark and then returned to me. We sat together for a few minutes more, saying little, kissing a lot. At last, he stood up with a sigh.

"You're hard to stay away from, Tamsin Wright."

"Be careful out there," I told him. "Avoid any blizzards."

"I'll see what I can do." He leaned down and kissed me one more time, setting a small bundle of cloth into my arms. "I love you. Stay warm, and I'll see you soon."

Jago left my room, leaving me sitting up in bed with my heart breaking. Even in the dark, I knew what he'd given me. I could tell by its softness and the way it smelled like him. The red scarf. I clutched it to me and lay back down, too heartsick for tears.

In the week that followed, I tried not to think about Jago, but it was impossible. Everything reminded me of him, and it didn't help that everyone in the keep brought up his name for various reasons, always under the assumption he'd be back soon. I nodded along with them and tried to keep to myself, not that my thoughts were very good company during those days. I wrote letters and practiced riding with Orla's horses. I watched the horizon a lot, anxiously scanning for any signs of storms.

None came, but seven days after Jago and Gideon departed for Constancy, I was sitting on a small balcony on the keep's tallest floor when I saw a large dark group of riders far down the road. As they approached, they materialized into wagons, sleds, and horses. Springing up from my perch, I ran downstairs, even though I knew it'd be a while before anyone made their way up the hill to us.

At last, there was a commotion at the gates, and all of a sudden people were spilling into the keep's courtyards. I spied the sailors from the *Gray Gull* and Lieutenant Harper. Icori who'd aided him returned as well, but they weren't whose arrival made me come running forward.

All nineteen of the other Glittering Court girls, as well as Miss Quincy, entered the courtyard, slowing to a halt as they gazed around their Icori surroundings with a mix of apprehension and excitement. They wore the drab fashions of Constancy but otherwise seemed well. For a moment, I did nothing. I just watched them, relieved and happy to see they were okay.

"Tamsin!"

I'd been spotted. And in moments, I was swarmed with hugs and greetings. "You did it," said Winnifred, nearly squeezing the air out of me. "You really do get things done."

The sight of their smiling faces lifted my flagging spirits, and after they'd hugged me, I found myself hugging all of them. "You're okay?" I asked. "Everyone's okay?"

"We are now," said Damaris. She looked around, enthralled. "This is amazing! I wouldn't mind staying and exploring."

Vanessa shook her head. "Not me. I'm ready for Cape Triumph." Her eyes tracked a young Icori woman passing by. "But I wouldn't mind delaying for a clothing exchange. Look at that red tartan cloak! It's gorgeous. Maybe we could set up some trade?"

"You will do no such thing. Hello, Tamsin." The sea of my friends parted, and Dinah Cole stepped forward. Her eyes narrowed at me and made the wind on top of the fortress seem warm. "I see that someone is still watching out for you. I pray it's the six glorious angels and not the six wayward ones."

"It's nice to see you too," I muttered as she walked away. Beyond her, I saw Samuel and Constancy's general store owner, Bernard Glover, speaking together. Dinah joined them, and all three looked over at me, expressions cool.

"Samuel and Mister Glover have business in Cape Triumph, so it was useful for them to come along," Polly explained.

"Does Dinah have business there too?" I asked wryly.

"We're her business," said Winnifred. "It's unclear if we still need guardians, but they insist we have a respectable female chaperone."

"Respectable, huh?" I eyed Dinah a moment longer, then put her out of my mind as I turned to my friends. "Well, no need for her right now. Come on, let me show you around. I've got everything ready for you. If there's something you need, let me know, and I'll make sure it gets taken care of."

As we turned to go inside, I heard a familiar voice calling my name.

We waited as Gideon ran up to us, his handsome face drawn with worry. "Gideon, I'm glad you're back," I told him. "Are you okay?"

"I tried to get to you right away," Gideon said. "I'm so sorry—I know you must be wondering what happened to Jacob."

I froze up a moment. Then: "Oh. Yes. I'd meant to ask. Where is he? Down in the city?"

Gideon shook his head, and a few of the other girls looked dismayed too. "It's not fair, really," said Vanessa. "Mister Robinson was so nice to us! Helped us get packed and ready to come here."

"And he helped get us passage too, right?" asked Damaris.

I nodded, forcing myself to keep a blank expression. "What's happened? Is he okay?"

"He's fine," said Gideon, frowning. "I think so. It's a long story—but there was an unexpected delay at the fort that held Jacob up. I can explain more later, but he's not with us yet."

"Oh." I clutched my hands to keep them from shaking. "That's unfortunate. I hope it's cleared up soon."

The others nodded in agreement, and Damaris said, "That lovely Lieutenant Harper said it will be. He was pretty angry about the mishap."

"Jacob's probably on his way here right now," added Gideon as we resumed walking inside. "I know he doesn't want to miss the trip. He'll be back here soon."

"I'm sure you're right," I said. "Now, we should have a tour before you settle in, so you know where everything is."

The girls twittered in agreement, but Winnifred suddenly interjected, "Oh! I almost forgot, Tamsin. Mister Robinson wanted to make sure this got to you."

She reached into her cloak and produced a folded sheet of paper. I didn't have to open it when I took it with shaking hands. I knew what it was: Olivia's drawing of our family.

"Th-thank you," I said.

Winnifred beamed. "Oh, I only carried it. He's the one that made sure it got rescued from the attic, so you can thank him when he gets here."

I gave her a shaky nod and then began a cheerful tour of the keep, barely even aware of what I said as I walked around and smiled with my friends. On the inside, though, I wanted to curl up in a ball and block the world out, because I knew what the others didn't. Jago would not be back to Kerniall anytime soon. In fact, we'd likely never see him again.

Chapter 27

"It's just like waiting on the docks in Culver to sail to Adoria, isn't it?"

Several girls chuckled at Polly's observation. A bitter wind whipped around us, tugging at hair and cloaks. On the East Sister, barges and boats rocked near the bank as Icori loaded crates and shouted orders. An overseer paced around with her list, directing each item and person to its place. The weight and size of all the objects and passengers had been taken into consideration and arranged into a precise plan.

"I don't know. This wind puts me more in mind of the tempest," noted Maria.

No one laughed at that. Today wasn't a stormy day. Gusty, yes, but nothing out of the ordinary for late winter. Nonetheless, there was enough wind to make the boats sway more than they would have from current alone, and it was hard not to fixate on that. But the wind only made ripples on the East Sister, not massive, ship-swallowing waves. And even if a boat did capsize here, the bank was in sight, just like when we rode the Quistimac.

The perils of the journey had been on my mind, and in the last couple of days, I'd made a point of speaking to every girl individually to ensure there'd be no repeats of the panic some had experienced before sailing with the Balanquans. Most were comfortable with another water journey—or at least they claimed to be. I'd appointed Damaris and a few others to counsel anyone who might get cold feet. They all wanted to get to Cape Triumph, but the storm still haunted us.

"Good morning, ladies," came Lieutenant Harper's cheery voice. He tipped his hat at us as he and a few of his men passed by. The gloom of Maria's remark dissipated into smiles and greetings among my friends.

"I wouldn't mind being a soldier's wife," said Damaris speculatively.

Vanessa frowned. "He *is* rather striking, but I don't think they make much money."

"The officers do, don't they?" Damaris insisted.

"The very high-ranking ones, I'm sure," said Winnifred. "But he's still young."

A dreamy look fell over Damaris. "Young and gorgeous. As long as he can afford the contract fee, I could stand living humbly for a while if it meant waking up to that each morning."

Gasps and giggles met her remark, both because of its brazenness and because it was coming from normally levelheaded Damaris. But *living humbly* struck my heart like a dart, made worse by the sight of Lieutenant Harper.

The "unexpected delay" of Jago's that Gideon had spoken about upon arriving in Kerniall had been Harper's doing. Actually, Orla and I had conceived of it, and he'd implemented it—with some misgivings. Shortly after arriving in Constancy, Harper had made arrangements for one of his colleagues to bring Jago to the fort for questioning on the grounds that they needed to go through the formalities of answering the Heirs' accusations of him kidnapping me. Harper had kept his involvement secret and had supposedly made quite a scene, insisting it was a waste of time to detain Jago when he'd already been cleared.

But they'd taken Jago anyway. Harper had assured Orla that Jago wouldn't face any harm or punishment. He would just be delayed for days, put off, and seriously inconvenienced. By the time Harper's colleagues got around to conducting the brief interview, it'd be too late for Jago to join us. It was an elegant solution, and Harper—who didn't even know the plot's purpose—had agreed to it only after some coaxing and dealing with Orla.

Orla had declared it all "nice and neat," but my heart was in ruins.

I was sick with the thought of what we'd done to Jago. He'd be devastated when he learned the delay had cost him the first trip south. And when he found out *I* was the reason for that delay . . . well, I had to keep stopping my mind from going there. I kept thinking of when Harry had rejected me and I'd gone through the heart-searing pain of being betrayed by someone you love. And now, I had just inflicted that same pain on another.

The overseer yelled something in Icori and looked around in annoyance to see why no one was acting. Her eyes fell on my group, and she beckoned us over. Using a mix of Icori and Osfridian, she ordered us to three different boats. We split up accordingly and made our way on board.

The Icori barges, I'd been told, were smaller versions of the great beasts that the Balanquans used on the Heart's Blood. They were rectangular in shape, with their front ends tapering to a point and slightly raised off the water. The rest of each barge was flat and had a long canopy stretching over it that was held up by narrow poles coming up from the craft's sides. Sturdy, three-foot-high railings lined the sides to keep everything in, but ropes were also lashed across the cargo as extra precaution. Ten rowers sat together in the back, and what looked like a giant set of oars was set into the very front. I learned that those basically functioned as the rudder and were used to steer.

My barge's captain directed me and six other girls to a spot under the canopy and told us not to leave our places while sailing. More of the Glittering Court rode in a barge tied next to ours, and the remainder in one a little farther down the bank. The Heirs rode together in the same boat, without any of us, which suited everyone fine—except, perhaps, Dinah. Samuel had begun to read from one of the scriptures once they were seated, and though the other Heirs listened with bowed heads, Dinah kept peeking up. I suspected she was searching for Gideon, and her grimace proved I was right when he came scrambling onto our barge, just before departure. Her gaze then slid to me. Its chill made the frosty morning air feel balmy in comparison.

Seeing Gideon, the other girls sitting around me straightened up and went back into coquette mode—except for Damaris, who still watched Harper wistfully. He was in the Heirs' boat, also at Orla's request, to make sure our "chaperones" didn't cross any lines, particularly with me. Grashond's laws had left me clear of any wrongdoing, but the Heirs' narrowed eyes and stiff words showed they felt otherwise.

Gideon greeted us all warmly and settled down beside me. Taking in my solemn air, he asked, "Thinking about Jacob?"

I flinched. "Ah, well . . ."

"Don't worry—they'll clear that up. It's a shame after all he did for us, but he'll get in on the next trip and be in Denham faster than you'd imagine."

But not fast enough, I thought. Uros willing, I'd be married before ever crossing Jago Robinson's path again. He'd forget about me and move on to dizzying success. I kept telling myself that over and over, but it didn't lessen the pain I'd felt every day since parting from him. Merry's absence was a constant ache too, but it was tempered with the knowledge that I'd have her back soon. That hole in my heart would heal up. But the one Jago had left wouldn't.

Small, two-person scouting boats launched ahead of the barges. This part of the East Sister was wide and slow and prone to chunks of ice in the winter. Farther south, into the foothills, the river narrowed and became faster. Ice rarely formed there, but the rapids presented other problems. I'd decided it was best my friends remain ignorant of that, though.

The barges untied next, the captains carefully maneuvering to keep our party within sight of one another but also spaced apart enough to avoid collisions. Icori on the bank cheered and called farewells, and I decided it really was a little like our departure from Osfrid. But once we were steady and moving on the tranquil river, there was little of the drama we had often felt in a giant ship with no land in sight.

I didn't miss that drama.

Several of the girls, saying nothing, endured our launch with gritted teeth and white knuckles. They watched every bit of ice in the river and winced if the barge moved too suddenly. But by midafternoon, most everyone began to relax.

"I know it's always warmer in the south, but one of the sailors was telling me that spring will be in full force when we reach Denham," Gideon remarked. "No snow. Everything green. One of the Icori overheard and said it was true."

Vanessa exhaled with happiness. "I'm ready for that. I'm ready for a lot of things."

In the days before our departure, I'd asked Damaris about Vanessa's atonement. "She took it like a warrior" had been the response. "Barely blinked an eye out there in the cold."

"But what about inside?" I had insisted. "Confessing to the town?"

Damaris's smile had faded. "She got through it without crying. And I got through it without choking someone. So. It's over and done."

Of course, it hadn't exactly been over and done, because Winnifred had later told me that when my disappearance had been discovered, Damaris had joked that Dinah should have to wear a CARELESSNESS sign for poor planning. Dinah had overheard, and Damaris had spent another sleepless night blackening and cleaning out the stove.

All that's behind us now, I thought, leaning against a tarp-covered crate. *The Heirs might be our escorts, but they have no more power over us. Damaris and Vanessa will be the pampered wives of powerful men and forget any of this ever happened.*

Just before midday, one of the scouts returned upriver to tell us the way ahead was blocked with ice. The captains slowed all the barges, save one. It glided ahead of the rest of us, and the Icori on board scurried about on some unseen task. By the time the rest of the barges crept ahead, that lone one had attached a large, square device made of wood and metal to its bow. We'd seen lots of ice chunks in the river today, but this particular bend was clogged with them, and in some places, those chunks had frozen together in thick barriers.

My barge pulled toward the bank a good distance behind the ice and waited, as did the other barge. The one with the plowing device pushed forward into a spot of the ice barrier that looked the least stable. As it did, some of the smaller boats joined it, and their riders began hacking at the ice with picks. Slowly, enough of the ice wall broke away for our whole party to make it through, and we continued on cautiously.

Three more times that day we had to wait for the ice to clear. One of the Icori told me we could expect the same for a few more days. As a passenger, I had the "luxury" of just sitting around, but as the hours went by, I wished I could do something more productive. I even offered to row, but the Icori captain chuckled and told me I was too short. My friends and I made up games and shared stories, and sometimes, we found ourselves lulled into the passing river's hypnotic effect.

We stopped when twilight came, for fear of missing obstacles in the dark. The spot was one well-known to the Icori, and the fact that we'd reached it today, as hoped, indicated we were on schedule. The bank was wide and clear, with room to build fires and set up tents. It felt good to walk on steady ground—to simply be able to walk for any length of time after being restricted to our small space. We reunited with the other Glittering Court girls around a fire, and everyone's spirits were high as we ate dinner.

Restless, I wandered around afterward, investigating the rest of the camp. I passed Captain Milford sitting with some of his sailors, and he held a canteen up to me in a dramatic toast. "Well done, girl."

The barges were secured and guarded for the night, but a handful of Icori were working on something at the river's edge. I made my way over, stepping carefully where the bank sloped. "Don't mind me," I said when one spotted me. "Just curious."

He waved me over and demonstrated how they were setting up fish traps for the night. Some were little more than netting; others were cages of woven sticks. The Icori seemed to like my interest and showed me the clever doors on the traps that allowed fish to come in but made it difficult for them to get out. One was in the middle of explaining how the traps were baited when his eyes lifted to something behind me. He stopped talking, and I turned around.

Orla stood at the top of the slope, watching with a smile. In a leather coat and pants, she looked very much as she had at our first meeting, only cleaner. "Tamsin," she called. "Come join me."

One didn't turn down that kind of request around here, so I climbed back up the bank. We walked through the camp, and Icori paused in their work to greet her, some nodding or bowing. I was known by many too and received my own share of well wishes. The scope of our party was incredible. There had to be at least a hundred people.

"How are you doing?" she asked.

I shrugged. "Surviving. Like always."

"Lieutenant Harper insists Jago will be fine. No one will mistreat him. He should be released later today."

"Oh, I know they won't hurt him. Harper's a good man. That, and Jago will probably walk out of that fort with a dozen deals in place from soldiers wanting to buy cornmeal and ribbons."

"Maybe he'll thank you," she said, though her rueful expression told me she knew better.

I sighed. "It won't take him long to figure out the detainment wasn't an accident. And it won't take him long to figure out I was part of it. And that . . . ugh. It kills me, thinking of how he'll feel the moment he realizes I betrayed him. I've been there. It's awful. It's like someone has your heart in their fist and is squeezing every last bit of blood from it. And yet, I almost feel just as bad about the other part."

Orla's brows knit in puzzlement. "Which other part? Because this sounds plenty bad."

I stared off ahead of me, the people and their movement blurring into the background. "The part before he finds out. When he's still detained. He's in there now, knowing what day it is, knowing he's not with me. It must be devastating. And I bet he's fool enough to be worried about me! Worried that I think he's the one who cut out and ran.

It kills me to think of that. It's almost easier thinking of him hating me once he realizes the truth."

Orla came to a halt, not far from her tent. She rested a hand on my shoulder and said, "Tamsin, I can't say for sure how it'll all fall out, but one thing I feel for certain: Jago Robinson will never, ever hate you."

In the days that followed, I tried not to think about how I was getting farther from Jago. Instead, I focused on how I was getting closer to Merry.

Always, always, she had been my driving force behind all my planning. And one morning, waking up to brilliant sunshine and melting snow, I decided I wasn't going to let heartache for a man overshadow those plans. I'd come to Adoria for a reason, and it was time I remembered that.

My friends noticed my increase in energy. I hadn't been cold to them, but I had been distant since leaving Kerniall, mostly because I'd retreated into myself. But I needed to learn to be social and outgoing again. I looked for pleasure in the world and in others, and my friends' personas likewise bloomed as we planned for Cape Triumph.

Gideon noticed the difference as well. A week into our trip down the river, I began opening up again, talking with him much as I used to.

He surprised me with his curiosity about the Icori and would explore the evening camps as much as I did. He *really* surprised me in his desire to understand the Icori's religious beliefs. "Oh, I'm not converting anytime soon," he said with a laugh when I asked about it. "But if I'm going to really try to understand divine forces in the world, it seems to me I should learn how other people understand them."

I found him one evening huddled together with two Icori trappers and the children. The boy and girl—Eroc and Briga—often tailed Gideon, which wasn't unexpected. Children seemed to sense his affinity. Kneeling beside them, I watched as Gideon concentrated hard on rubbing a stick back and forth across a larger one held on the ground with his knee. A pile of kindling sat nearby. Sweat beaded on his forehead, and I couldn't help a small laugh. He stopped when he heard me.

"Are you laughing at me, Tamsin?"

"No," I said, covering another laugh. "Not exactly. I'm just perplexed, that's all."

Shaking his head good-naturedly, he returned to his task, saying: "I've never made a fire without flint. When they heard that, they said I had to learn. Apparently even these little ones can do it."

"I could have had this lit already," Eroc told me very seriously. He turned back to Gideon. "You're wasting time."

Gideon went back to his task and finally got a spark, though his hands paid the cost in blisters. He sat back and exhaled, watching with weary satisfaction as Briga quickly blew on the small flame and the trappers added sticks.

"How'd I do?" he asked the children.

"Not terrible. But you'll have to do better next time." Briga scrambled to her feet and gave me a grin that was missing a front tooth. "I'll get some more kindling!"

Gideon wiped his brow and pointed at me. "Make her learn. I need a break."

"I already know how," I told him.

"They didn't have flint when you lived in the market district?"

"Sure. But when money was tight, you had to get creative. It's been years, though," I admitted.

"Aha," said Gideon. "Time to refresh your skills."

One of the trappers nodded and handed me a stick. The Icori method was slightly different than what I had been taught, but it was similar enough that I quickly understood. I was less quick in making the spark, though. I really was out of practice. So I couldn't help a whoop of triumph when I managed it at last—much sooner than Gideon had.

"You could use more practice too," one of the trappers told me.

"But that's not bad. What about other outdoor skills? Are you as bad as he is?"

I glanced between them all, puzzled. "What types of outdoor skills?"

"It's part of a deal I made with Eroc and Briga," Gideon said. "They asked me to teach them some conversions between Icori script and our letters. They wanted to teach me something in return, so I agreed when they offered to show me some outdoor skills. I didn't realize I'd be handed over to some harder masters. No offense." The two trappers both grinned at that.

"What else are you supposed to learn?"

"Just this so far. The others are a little . . . impractical."

Briga put her hands on her hips. "No they aren't. We could go out in the river right now and teach you to swim."

"You can't swim either?" I asked Gideon.

"You say 'either' like these are things I would have done all the time in Osfrid." Gideon looked at me suspiciously. "And I can't believe *you* were doing much swimming there. Unless you were watching from the Os River while they built that bridge?"

"No, no. But Pa sometimes got hired on for jobs out of town, and once he had one building a wall near a lake. We kids came with him for the summer, and that's when I learned to swim."

"See? You have to learn," said Eroc. "It's not that cold."

Gideon eyed the river, which was rapidly getting lost in darkness. "We passed ice this morning."

"Leave him alone for the night," said one of the trappers, his eyes crinkling with laughter. "He's worked hard and enjoys some nice company."

"Thank you," said Gideon.

"But," the man added, "come back tomorrow, and we'll show you how to carve a spear." Gideon groaned.

Later, as he and I took a meandering route back to the Osfridian tents, I said, "I bet you never thought you'd have Icori children teaching you to swim."

"I am *not* swimming in that river, at least not on this trip. Check with me again in the middle of summer."

"Still. You've made some Icori friends. They seem to like you."

"Eroc and Briga do. I think the others are just pleasantly tolerant. You, on the other hand . . ." I could sense Gideon's big smile, even if I couldn't make it out in the shadows. "They all adore you."

"Me? Why?"

"Well, even if they don't know all the details, they know you played a part in helping Orla smooth things out with Grashond. And you were, what, blessed by their priestess or something?"

"Or something."

"Then, of course, there's Jacob. You're his friend, and they *really* adore him."

"Sounds like all my adoration just comes by association," I teased. I gazed around at the dancing fires and silhouettes moving about on nighttime business. "But most of them are good people, and it's been eye-opening."

"Agreed. That's why I've enjoyed getting to know them—even if it apparently requires manual labor. I may not have a congregation yet, but I've been making notes on what I've seen to write a sermon on . . . eh, let's see. Tolerance? Understanding? I'm trying to explain how we can find peace by learning about our so-called enemies because . . . how do I put it . . ."

". . . because we'll find we probably have more in common with our enemies than we have differences?"

Laughing, he came to a halt not far from our friends' campfire. "See? You're doing it again. Just like I said. You take all these things jumping around in my head and hone them down into one efficient line."

"You would have come up with it if you weren't so tired from making that fire."

"That was my third one tonight, actually." When we both stopped laughing at that, he continued, much more seriously, "It's nice to be able to talk to you again, Tamsin. Really talk to you. I've missed our talks."

I looked up into his kind eyes and smiled back. "Me too. I'm glad we get to spend this time together before you go off and start your great spiritual revolution."

He hesitated, uncertainty spreading over his features. "Yes . . . about that . . ."

"Tamsin? Is that you? And Gideon?" Dinah rose up like an apparition from those gathered around the fire. "Finally! It's almost time to go to sleep. You shouldn't be wandering around with . . . *them*. Gideon, will you lead us in a prayer before bedtime?"

"Certainly," he called back. None of them knew yet about his decision to leave the Heirs, and so long as nothing went against his conscience, he didn't mind going through the motions with them. Likewise, my friends and I were also going through the motions of adhering to Dinah's directives. She could do little to enforce them, and it was easier just to keep the peace sometimes.

As he turned, I lightly touched his arm. "What else was it you were going to say?"

"N-nothing," he said, gesturing me forward. "Come on, let's go."

CHAPTER 28

DURING THE LAST FEW DAYS OF OUR JOURNEY SOUTH, I began to believe Adoria could be warm. That didn't mean *I* was warm yet. A chill still clung to the air in the evenings and early morning, but by noon, the clouds would burn off, letting the spring sun come out in full force. Green buds swelled on the trees, and I spied crocuses blooming on the banks. There was no trace of snow, though its memory lingered in the river. Its water level was running high from snow having melted here, and the Icori often spoke about how the lands upriver tended to flood.

"Look how warm it is," said Briga. She tossed her coat onto the barge's deck. "We could swim in this for sure."

"It's a trick, and you know it," Gideon responded. "The sun may be out, but that water's still freezing."

Eroc stood at the barge's side, peering over the wall, which was almost as tall as he was. When he tried to touch the water, Damaris and I sprang forward as one and jerked him back.

"Have a care, child," she scolded. "Tumble over, and you'll make poor Gideon have to go in after all."

Gideon shot us affronted looks. "What? Why me? You two are always bragging about what expert swimmers you are."

Damaris winked at me. "Well, it's not easy swimming in dresses, and we figured you'd want to step forward and do the manly thing."

Gideon, feigning indignation, returned to the book he and Briga were looking at. She and her brother had started spending time on our barge this week, both because our group was novel and because Gideon was helping her understand Osfridian letters. The children were light enough that the barge captains didn't mind their moving from ship to ship. The older Icori also approved of the lessons. They believed surviving the political turmoil of these times required understanding the language of those they were struggling with. Most Icori children were taught to speak Osfridian—but rarely how to read or write it.

My friends and I helped teach them sometimes, and it seemed impossible that only a year ago, I'd been a student as well, learning place settings and political parties in a luxurious parlor that didn't feel like it could possibly be in the same world. Getting closer to Adelaide and Mira made me think of Blue Spring a lot, and all the good times I'd had there. I'd been composing a thousand apologies for Adelaide. None felt adequate, but I'd deliver all of them if it might give me a shot at forgiveness. Even if it didn't work, I just wanted to see my two best friends again, to drink in the sight of them and be happy that they were alive and well.

Something told me Mira wouldn't be married yet. I could picture men being enchanted with her, but she viewed marriage even more pragmatically than I did and wouldn't be in any rush. But Adelaide? She was the diamond. If she wasn't married, the odds were very good that she'd be engaged. She'd have no shortage of options. The question would be if she could find someone who echoed her romantic nature. I hoped she could. Truly.

And . . . I also hoped that her "someone" wasn't one of the top candidates I'd culled from Esme's lists. While thinking of Adelaide and Mira filled me with warm affection, pondering my own prospects dragged me back to cool calculation. I so, so needed one of those ideal men to be available. Just one. I'd been going over their biographies in my head lately, reminding myself of every detail and how I could play to each man's personality. Between that and my other Glittering Court skills, I adamantly believed I could win someone. And if those men had been taken? Well. That was an unsettling thought, but I'd deal with it like I always did. I'd get things done. I'd find someone else who'd take on a widow and stepdaughter, and then I'd transform into exactly what he was looking for.

Honestly, that task wasn't nearly so daunting as the other one weighing me at all times: forgetting Jago. No matter how rationally I plotted my strategy for Cape Triumph, Jago always lingered on the edge of my thoughts. Well, I'd deal with that too. In the long run, it didn't matter if I ached forever because of him. I didn't need to convince myself I was over him. Just my husband.

"Didn't you hear me?" exclaimed Damaris. "Get back over here."

Briga was a diligent student, but Eroc, being younger, often grew distracted. He had wandered back to the edge and was leaning over it again, ignoring Damaris. Pointing up, he exclaimed, "Look at the smoke!"

Beyond the swathe of evergreens and maples, columns of black smoke rose into the sky. "It must be another village," said Winnifred, though she sounded uncertain. We'd passed a number on the trip, sometimes stopping for brief trading. But this didn't seem like the kind of smoke that came from stoves or fireplaces.

The Icori didn't think so either. Instructions were shouted among the vessels, and with a bit of coordination, the fleet made an unplanned landing at the bank. Orla leapt out before her barge was secured, uncaring of splashing in ankle-deep water. She issued a few commands in her language, and within moments, she had two dozen Icori assembled. Weapons drawn, they plunged into the woodlands.

The rest of us waited apprehensively, and the remaining Icori drew their weapons. The sailors and soldiers stood braced in tense, watchful poses as well. Gideon and Briga forgot their lessons. I watched at the side with Eroc, my hands clenching the wooden rail.

Everyone flinched when half of Orla's group burst back through the trees about fifteen minutes later. They shouted something to one of the captains, and he quickly lifted the tarp covering his ship's boxes.

One of the scouts called out to Lieutenant Harper's barge, spurring his men to action as they disembarked and ran upriver. The scout then hurried to my barge and looked right at me.

"Tamsin Wright—Danna Orla says you know how to care for injuries?"

"Eh, a little." Racking my brain, I recalled a dinner in Kerniall when I'd fallen into conversation with one of Orla's advisors about childhood ailments, most of my knowledge coming from caring for Merry.

The man beckoned. "Then come."

Gideon was on his feet beside me. "I'll go too."

We followed the Icori back into the woods and immediately found a well-worn trail. The smell of smoke grew stronger as we traveled, and after a few twists and turns, the trail ended in a small collection of houses—or what was left of them. Those that weren't already reduced to ashes were wrapped in flames. The smoke was so thick here that it was hard to see, and bits of ash floating on the air only made matters worse.

Icori were in motion everywhere. Some searched the remains of houses. Others had formed a bucket brigade at a well and welcomed the addition of new containers that the scouts had retrieved from one of the barges. I recognized almost everyone here. The village was deserted—mostly.

Over in a clearing, upwind of the smoke, one of the trappers I knew was tending to five people. One sat upright; the others lay on their backs. I hurried over with two Icori who'd also been recruited for first aid. One of the patients was a boy—maybe eleven or twelve—and the others were adults, three men and one woman. The scouts had brought medical supplies from the barges, and I set to work on the boy.

He had a few scrapes and lacerations that I cleaned, but as he coughed and tried to sit, it became clear that smoke inhalation was what had taken him down. "Easy, you're okay," I said, supporting his back. He didn't seem to understand Osfridian but guessed my

meaning. I handed him a canteen, and he nodded his thanks. Satisfied with him, I moved on to another—the woman. She suffered from
similar issues but had also burned her arm. With a small knife from
the supplies, I cut away her blackened sleeve to assess the damage.
The skin underneath was scaly and red, with a few blisters closer to
her wrist. I wrapped it loosely with clean, wet cloth as a short-term
fix. Depending on what the blisters did, she could need some kind of
ointment, but I didn't know the extent of our medicines.

I was treating a similar burn on one of the men when it struck me
as odd that I was already on my third patient. Where were my companions? Looking up, I saw them both huddled over another man. As
soon as I finished my work, I went over to join them. When I saw the
pool of blood on their patient, I clamped a hand over my mouth to
stop from screaming. The two healers spoke rapidly in their own language and were trying to stop the bleeding that came from a wound
on his thigh. Though they worked together without pause, they also
seemed to be having an argument. One kept pointing back toward the
river, and the other shook her head adamantly.

"What happened?" I asked, but neither heard me.

"Shot," said a voice.

The fifth patient, who appeared to be the least injured, watched
the others work, his face filled with worry. He clutched his hand to
his chest, and I gently pried it away. A long gash across his palm had
stopped bleeding, and if he could avoid infection, it would be fine.
He grimaced as I cleaned and wrapped the hand. That cut had come
from a blade, and I was about to ask more when a sixth patient was
brought over. He too had a bleeding wound, in his upper arm. One of
the other healers examined it and told me, "The bullets went through.
Just stop the bleeding and wrap it."

I hastened to obey while she called for two Icori to help carry the
other wounded man back to the river. The debate had apparently been
whether to remove the bullet here or back there. Back there had won.

"Who did this?" I asked as I bandaged the arm.

The man looked me over, taking in my clothing and language. "Osfridians attacked us. No provocation."

I paused a moment before continuing my work. "They wouldn't do that."

"I didn't shoot myself!"

"No, no, of course not. I'm sorry. Just that—they respect the treaties. If it was them, they had a reason."

"Maybe just being caught," he said with a snort. "They didn't expect anyone to be here yet." Seeing I didn't understand, he grudgingly added, "This is a summer hunting camp."

An out-of-the-way target—just like the farm encampment I'd heard about in Kerniall. Its damage had been monetary since the farm was seasonal, and no one had been there to fight back. No one to examine the attackers more closely and perhaps realize that they weren't, in fact, Osfridian. Peering around at the smoky, chaotic scene, I suddenly wondered if I'd stumbled into the aftermath of another Lorandian ploy.

Before I could give it much more thought, the trapper and another of Orla's people dragged a new patient our way but set him several feet from the others we tended. When I stood up to go to him, the trapper shook his head and spread a tartan over the man's face and body.

I backed away, stunned by the horror of it. The world blurred around me briefly, and when things settled back, I noticed that Gideon was gone. He'd been near me when I first set to work. Scanning the small settlement, I saw that most of the fires had been extinguished. All that remained burning were a roundhouse and a larger, barnlike structure with two floors. Icori were actively trying to put out both; a handful also stood around arguing. After a quick check of my patients, I went to investigate and found Gideon.

"What's happening?" I asked.

He pointed. "There's someone up there, in the loft—but Orla won't let anyone risk going in. He's Osfridian."

"One of the attackers?" I exclaimed. I joined those looking up at the barn's highest window. I had to wait for a gap in the smoke before

I could make out a pale man with sandy hair sitting in the window frame. He had a hand to his chest and a glassy look in his eyes as he struggled to keep them open. Once, he tried to rise, but the effort proved too great, and he slumped back down. His clothing suggested he was Osfridian—but he could just as easily be Lorandian.

Orla's sharp voice rose up beside me as she faced off with one of her warriors. He gestured at the window, his expression frustrated as he spoke to her. Orla shook her head and issued an obvious rejection, cutting him off when he tried to argue again. The man gritted his teeth as he peered up at the window and then at the progress of those putting out the fire.

I touched Gideon's sleeve. "He's trapped by his injuries, not the fire. If he had the strength, he could jump out and probably survive from that height. Look—that half of the barn isn't burning yet."

"It doesn't matter," said Gideon. "This side's almost done for. When it goes, it's going to take the rest of the building with it. Orla's right to keep them out."

The warrior who'd argued with Orla stared up at the window with narrowed eyes, then studied the barn's large entrance, and then glanced toward Orla. He reminded me of Eroc, assessing whether he could climb up the side of the boat without getting caught. I understood the warrior's urgency. Capturing the assailant could provide valuable information about the attacks. That, and having a Lorandian captive would solidify the case Jago and I had made.

But the warrior proved too loyal to Orla and, though obviously upset about it, held his position. Above us, the wounded attacker attempted to stand again and failed. I caught a flash of terror on his face, and then his head lolled to the side as he collapsed back down. A swathe of smoke briefly enveloped him, sending him into a coughing fit that gave me an unexpected flashback to sleepless nights with Merry. The Icori around me wore impassive expressions, and I couldn't blame them. But pity welled up in me, despite the man's crimes. He was still a human being, and it was a hard thing to watch.

Turning from the window, I spied a gap in the smoke below that gave me a glimpse inside the barn's doorway. The building appeared to be empty, and while flames raged in one side, the other was still intact, and I could see a ladder reaching up from the ground floor. The way was perfectly clear, only a little smoky. If someone just moved fast enough—

"Wha— Tamsin? Tamsin!"

Gideon's voice rang out after me as I raced through the barn's doorway. I heard people yelling behind me, and then my whole world became flames and smoke. The flames were still concentrated on the other side, but the smoke was more debilitating than I'd expected. Each breath made me nauseous, and the haze and my tears blocked my vision. But I made it to the ladder, relieved to see it too was untouched.

I climbed up into the loft, which stretched over only a third of the barn's length. The fact that the hay on its floor hadn't caught fire was nothing short of an angelic miracle. A piece of ash blew into my eye, and I tried to rub it out, only driving it in further. I stumbled over to the window and knelt by the man, taking his hand. He groaned and rolled his head toward me.

"It's okay," I told him. "I'm going to get you out of here."

From the blank look in his eyes, I wasn't even sure he'd heard me. Either the smoke or his injury had driven him into shock. Then, licking his lips, he stammered, "Molly?"

"No, my name's Tamsin. I'm going to help you. Can you stand?"

I didn't need his answer to know he couldn't. The front of his shirt was soaked in blood, so dark and wet that I couldn't pinpoint where the exact injury was. The ladder would be safe for another few minutes, I was certain, but he wouldn't be climbing down it. I wasn't even sure if he'd be breathing in a few minutes.

"Y'look just like her," he muttered. "She always said whiskey'd be the end of me."

"I'm guessing a bullet was," I said, leaning over him to peer out.

Orla and some Icori were gathered below, and upon seeing me, they began shouting, but I couldn't hear what they were saying. The man's head knocked against my arm, his eyes closed, and I gently shook him as I slid my arm under his arm. "Stay with me—what's your name?"

When he didn't respond, I thought he might already be dead. Then, after more coughing: "Robert."

"Okay, Robert. I'm going to need you to stand. We've still got a clear shot for that ladder and the front door. I know it'll hurt, but—"

As I tried to get him to rise, a figure appeared in the barn's doorway downstairs, and suddenly, Gideon was racing toward us. Covering his mouth, he climbed up and was soon beside us. "Tamsin! Are you okay?"

"Gideon! You shouldn't have come—never mind. Help me get him out."

Tears leaking from his eyes, Gideon put his arm under the man too. The attacker cried out in pain as we forced him to stand, and I murmured apologies over and over. A crash from below jerked my attention away, and I watched in horror as part of the burning side of the barn collapsed inward. Not only did it block our way out, it sent sparks and ash everywhere, igniting places that had been untouched.

"Back, back!" I exclaimed. Half-dragging the man, we retreated toward the window and crouched down as flames raced over the barn's lower floor.

"Tamsin, look!" Gideon cried.

Outside, on the ground, our friend the trapper came hurrying up with a large, bundled hide. Quickly, he and some other Icori began unfolding it.

Rubbing my eyes, I said, "Looks like you don't need to take the stairs after all—Robert? No, don't go to sleep! Hang on." The men had the hide unfolded now, and other Icori were grabbing hold of its sides. "Just a bit longer. Tell me more about Molly. Or the whiskey. How it's your end."

"Would'n'a gotten shot if I was sober." His eyes fluttered open and then closed. "But they were s'posed to be gone and—" He coughed again and didn't finish.

"Robert?" I asked. "Robert?" I put my hand to his throat to check for a pulse but already knew there'd be none.

Gideon gently closed the man's eyes and eased him to the floor, murmuring, "Ariniel, light the way."

"Ariniel, light the way," I echoed, surprised at the grief I felt for someone I didn't know.

A shout from below drew us back, and we saw that the Icori had the large hide open and ready. Six men stood around it and positioned themselves in a spot below the window that would be easy to aim for. I started to tell Gideon that we should still push Robert's body out, but a brilliant flash suddenly lit up my periphery. Sparks had finally landed on the hay, and fire instantly flared across the loft. It was at my feet in the blink of an eye. Leaving Robert, Gideon and I both climbed up into the window frame.

"Jump!" I ordered Gideon.

"You first."

"Damn it, Gideon, this is no time for— Ahh!"

So help me, Gideon pushed me out the window. I screamed the whole way down but landed safely, if not gracefully, biting my tongue and bouncing a bit when I struck the hide. One of the Icori pulled me off, and then they shouted for Gideon. He jumped, just as the whole building began to crumple.

The sudden spread of the fire to the loft was too much for the barn. The flames had already consumed most of one long side, and with the deterioration of this end, the structural integrity gave out. The Icori saw the barn's collapse coming and didn't even bother getting Gideon out of the hide when he landed. They just wrapped him up and carried him along as they ran away. We managed to flee the worst of it as the barn fell in upon itself. Wood and ash and cinders spread out in a great cloud. I dropped to my knees and covered my face, not getting up until someone touched my shoulder.

"Tamsin, are you all right?"

Gideon put an arm around me and led me to where the other Icori were assembling. Everyone seemed to be talking at once, all in Icori, and I couldn't really tell what was going on. "I'm okay," I told Gideon, covering a cough. "I just— Gideon! Look at you!"

Soot darkened his face, and nearly all of his coat's left sleeve had been burned away. The once white shirt underneath was browned and tattered, but the flames must have been smothered before getting much farther.

Gideon looked down in surprise, apparently noticing his state for the first time. "Blessed be Uros. That could have been a lot worse."

Seeing he was otherwise okay, I felt no remorse at lightly punching his other arm. "Not by much! Six! What were you thinking?"

"What were *you* thinking?"

"I saw a clear way to get him in and out."

"And I saw a clear way to come save you," Gideon retorted.

"I didn't need saving! Well . . . yes, but not when you first decided to come. You should've stayed out here where it was bloody safe!"

His eyes widened. "How could I do that and leave you in danger, Tamsin? I love you."

I stared, unable to answer both because of shock and renewed coughing. When I recovered myself, I could only stare. Gideon, at a loss as well, stared back.

We were saved—sort of—when Orla strode up with her hands on her hips. "Tamsin Wright, if you were one of my people—"

"I'm not," I interrupted, slowly turning from Gideon. "And I'm okay, so don't scold me. I had to try and get that man out, but his wound was too serious. He died before I jumped."

Orla shook her head, angry but also relieved. "I'm just glad you didn't die. Either of you. Getting us a Lorandian hostage wasn't worth the risk."

"I did it because he was human, not because he was Lorandian . . ."

Amidst all the panic, I'd almost overlooked what I had noticed in my foolhardy stunt. "I talked to him . . ."

"Yes?" said Orla. Beyond her, I heard shouts as Lieutenant Harper's men joined us, returning from scouting for any attackers.

I blinked away more smoke as I replayed that last scrap of conversation I'd had with the man in the loft. His name, his accent. None of it was made up. He'd been on death's doorway, barely able to speak, let alone craft a conspiracy. "And he actually wasn't Lorandian. He was Osfridian." My heart sank as I looked into the faces of those who'd supported my theory that Lorandians were staging attacks in disguise. "This attack actually *was* carried out by Osfridians."

CHAPTER 29

IT WAS RAINING WHEN WE REACHED KERDAUN, THE END of our journey on the East Sister. Kerdaun was a small village that made its living as a crossroads for travelers. Not far to the west was Kershid, home of Orla's betrothed. Sail farther south, and the river split, with one branch eventually going to the sea and the other to the Heart's Blood. And, of course, less than a day to the east was what I had come here for: the border of Denham Colony.

Most of Orla's people were traveling on to Kershid. Our river party had included a handful of non-Icori, and they were all going different ways. Some were taking the road to Cape Triumph with my friends and the *Gray Gull*'s crew, and we pooled our resources together to hire wagons and horses in Kerdaun to transport our collective goods. The Kerdaun Icori had arrangements with colonists in a town farther into Denham to tag-team these sorts of escorts.

As our belongings were transferred from the barges to wagons, I pulled the hood of my cloak over my head to shield some of the rain. It was a coarse, black wool cloak given to me by Bernard Glover when my old one had been damaged in the fire. The flowered dress Jago had given me had likewise been burned past repair, and I wore a bluish-gray one in the Heirs' style. Dinah, with triumphant condescension, had given it to me, saying we'd settle the cost in Cape Triumph. "No," I'd told her. "You can have it back as soon as we arrive." Orla had offered me replacement clothing too, but as much as I loathed

Grashond fashion, it was still easier for me to wear in Denham than something obviously Icori.

A couple of crates were set down next to me, and I moved out of the way. These were labeled in both Icori runes and Osfridian, and I did a double take when I saw them.

Jacob Robinson
Orchard End
Rushwick
Denham Colony

The Icori workers who had deposited them were already headed off for their next load. "Wait," I called. "What are these? Why are they going to Jago?"

"Because they're his." A hunter who'd traveled with us walked up to me. He lived on the outskirts of west Grashond and had been introduced to me simply as Mister Elkhart. "I'm making sure they get dropped off at his place since he couldn't come."

I ran my hands over the wet letters. Just touching Jago's name sent chills through me. "His place . . ."

"Well, almost his place. Over in Rushwick. He kind of owns it, kind of leases it. He should have most of it paid after this season's trade, assuming this delay doesn't slow anything down."

"I'm happy for him." I dropped my hand. "He's worked hard for it. He'll be able to start his horse business soon."

"Yup. Genius idea, that. Most wouldn't have the patience to see it through. Easier to raise and sell ordinary workhorses. But as this country gets more settled, the rich start looking for something to do. Fancy racehorses will be all the rage, and he'll be on the cutting edge of it." Mister Elkhart winked at me. "You're off to marry some rich fellow, aren't you? Maybe Robinson'll cut you a deal on a horse or two."

I looked away. "I don't know."

"Well, he must have a soft spot for the lot of you—or just likes your pretty faces. It's because of you girls he didn't come, right? He gave you his spots?"

His words brought up the memory of Jago going to a hunter he knew, and I dragged my gaze from the address. "You're . . . Louis, right? Jago's friend?"

"Louis Elkhart, at your service." He gave me a mock bow. "And if you're his friend, you're my friend. I'm not taking the road all the way to Cape Triumph, but if you need anything before I turn north, let me know."

He left, but I lingered near the boxes until they were finally loaded up. By then, the Kerniall Icori were ready to go on their way, and Orla summoned me.

"Farewell again, Tamsin." Her smile was as wry as ever. "It doesn't seem like many things have gone your way in the time I've known you. I hope that changes."

I summoned a mental image of Merry's face and smiled. "Only one thing has to go my way. I'll deal with the rest. Thank you for everything you've done for me. I wouldn't be standing this close to Denham if not for you. I'll always be grateful for that . . . but I've never understood *why* you did it."

"Impulse? Instinct? I don't know what to call it. I was amused watching all you pretty little birds flutter and fret on the way to Constancy, but when I started watching the way they flocked around you, I was intrigued. It's like I told you before—you're good with people. That's going to become increasingly important in the near future, I think." Her blue eyes lifted to the bustling mix of Icori and Osfridians going about their business. "I remember what you said: 'My conscience isn't contingent on someone else's.' It brings to mind an old proverb of ours."

"'If you're on the path of right, and someone crosses it with wrong, you don't need to turn. Build a bridge over their path and continue on your way.'"

She turned back to me in amazement and then burst out laughing. "Jago told you that one?"

"Yes."

"It's what we're going to need—all of us—if we're ever going to get a lasting peace. Listening to each other will be key, but overcoming grudges and a history of wrongs has to be in there too. That's why I thought you'd be a useful person to help. And that was a hunch that paid off."

"Did it?" I asked pointedly.

Her smile faded a little. "No one blames you for what happened at that settlement, Tamsin. And just because Osfridians attacked there doesn't mean Lorandians didn't attack the others in the north."

I couldn't muster an immediate response. The fire at the fishing camp had cast a pall over the rest of our trip south. She was right that no one had blamed me—or even the other Osfridians traveling with us—but I could see some of the Icori looking at us a little differently. Those who had been open and sociable earlier in the trip now became guarded.

"None of it matters if it can't be proved, and the only thing we have proof of is that the Lorandians robbed me in Grashond. That won't stop your people from going to war if pushed far enough."

"Then *I'll* have to stop them . . . unless it's warranted. But something still feels off to me. This mystery isn't settled yet. I'll miss having you looking into it, but I'm also happy for your success." She smoothed back hair that had escaped her sloppy bun, but that just made a few more pop out. "If I can ever do anything for you, let me know. You have a lot of friends and admirers here."

I shrugged. "Oh, people just like me because I ran into a burning building."

Orla laughed and startled me with a giant hug. "Goodbye, Tamsin. I hope you find happiness. Ah—sorry. I got ash on your cheek. No, the other one."

I rubbed at where my face had brushed her jacket in the hug. She'd worn the same clothes since the fire, and everything was covered in dirt and ash. "Are you going to change before Kershid?" I asked delicately.

"You mean before I meet my betrothed?" She glanced at her sooty attire and ran a hand over her hair again, messing it up further. "No. If he can't take me like this, then he shouldn't bother taking me at all. Safe journeys."

Traveling by road was jarring after the river ride. True, there were no rapids to deal with or captains scolding us for moving around too much, but our progress was so slow by comparison. Our caravan lumbered along—people, animals, and wagons creeping toward Cape Triumph. A few days after Kerdaun, Louis Elkhart bid me farewell when we reached a highway branching north.

"Going to drop Robinson's stuff off in Rushwick on my way to Cotesville. I'll eventually swing through Cape Triumph later in the spring, so maybe we'll cross paths. If a fine lady like you will even acknowledge the likes of me."

"Of course I will." I stood on my tiptoes and gave him a kiss on the cheek, which thoroughly delighted him and horrified the Heirs. He separated his wagon from the rest and turned his horses onto the lonely looking road. Watching them disappear made me feel like I was getting even farther from Jago.

A few miles later, we reached the small town that served as Kernaud's counterpart. Here, the Icori who'd been hired on at the East Sister turned everything over to colonial guides and went back home. The Heirs and a few of the others in our caravan were thrilled to be free of Icori. Also joining us was a handful of travelers who'd been staying at the local inn and were on their way east.

Among that group was a young man named Frank Brennan, who came from a wealthy planting family based in Cape Triumph. And suddenly, it was like someone had thrown cold water over those of us in the Glittering Court. We'd never forgotten why we'd come to Adoria. We'd talked about it often on the ship, in Constancy, in Kerniall. It was always with us, a fixed star leading the way to our future. But even if you could say with absolute certainty you were going to be the wife of one of Cape Triumph's wealthy and elite men, that sentiment could feel a little empty if you were scrubbing floors in Dinah Cole's kitchen.

My friends had always fawned over Gideon, flirting in a subdued way and trying to earn his admiration. It was understandable, given his kindness and how he looked. But, as had been discussed that very first day in Constancy, he was never viewed as a real marriage candidate. Frank Brennan was.

He had money. He had a powerful name. He had cultivated tastes. He had beautiful riding clothes. *And* he knew who we were.

"You're . . . the lost Glittering Court girls? No! I thought you drowned at sea."

"Mister Thorn didn't get my letter?" I asked. My heart sank.

"Not that I've heard of, though maybe that's changed while I was out of town. Last I knew, everyone thought you were gone . . . for good."

That grim thought gave us pause, me especially. After all, I was the only one with a lot of friends back in Cape Triumph. This group had never met Adelaide, Mira, or anyone else from Blue Spring. Knowing people believe you were dead, gone from this world . . . it was chilling. And heartbreaking.

"Did they give us a funeral, at least?" Polly asked. I couldn't tell if she was trying to be funny. "Or a nice memorial?"

"If they did, it was nothing public," Frank said. He was wearing a green brocade riding coat and led a lively black stallion. "Maybe they did among themselves. Nothing really seemed to change the way they went on, though. I was traveling when they had their opening ball, but my friends said it was quite the affair."

We got as many details out of him as he had about the Glittering Court's current status. He'd heard of a couple of engagements— one was a Blue Spring girl—and he knew who Adelaide was, which didn't surprise me. When I asked about Mira, he said he didn't know her. When I added that she was Sirminican, he said, "Oh, yes. I heard about her." And that was it.

Frank was never alone for the rest of the trip. When he didn't have a small flock of admirers fluttering around him, he'd take the time to walk alone with some girl or another. He realized quickly the lucky position he was in. He was in the market for a wife, and he had us all to himself before we went on display for the rest of the city's bachelors. It was almost comical. He showed off to my friends; they showed off to him. They—demurely—investigated him and his prospects, and he tried to find out about each of us.

I was no different. Frank wasn't anyone I'd heard of beforehand, nor did I know if he was dead set on marrying a blushing virgin, but as a respectable prospect, he had to be treated appropriately. That, and I had to start getting back in the habit of charming others, no matter how much I still pined for Jago. After observing Frank for a few days, however, I realized fawning all over him like the others did actually wasn't the best method to interest him.

"Tamsin," he called one afternoon, as our party took its lunch break. "I've hardly had a chance to talk to you. Come eat with me. You can share this lovely olive spread Archibald set out with my brioche." Archibald was his manservant, the one who painstakingly set up Frank's luxurious tent each night and pressed each day's new riding coat. Today's was indigo, almost a perfect match for Frank's eyes.

"I certainly will not." I didn't look up from our ration box, where I was sorting out my friends' allotted portions of rye bread and some sort of hard white cheese. "If I sit down with you for any length of time, Mister Brennan, it will not be while I'm in a worsted working dress, with my hair barely brushed. And I certainly hope you will be able to do better than the side of a road and olive spread from a jar that took your man all of ten seconds to open. I won't waste my time or yours with a display that is anything less than our best. But thank you just the same for the lovely invitation."

Frank stared openmouthed. He wasn't used to being dismissed by women around here or back home, I was certain. And it enthralled him. For the rest of the day he kept sneaking glances at me that were equal parts disbelief and fascination.

"How did you do that?" demanded Maria later in the evening. "We've all been tossing our hair back, putting out our wittiest lines, and praising everything he does. Then you come along with one sharp-tongued rejection, and now he can't stop mooning over you!"

I was settling down to write a letter and gave her a quick grin before putting pen to paper. "It's like you girls always say: I get things done."

Gideon overheard and waited patiently until I finished writing. I'd been so distraught about discovering the Osfridian attacker that Gideon's declaration at the fishing camp had almost slipped my mind. He never mentioned it again, and I didn't know if it had simply been an impulsive sentiment, born from the moment's heightened emotion, or if it was sincere and he was simply embarrassed about admitting it after I'd told him in Constancy that there couldn't be anything between us. My gloomy mood had caused me to withdraw into myself for the end of the trip, so I'd had little chance to speak to him or anyone else much.

"Do you actually like him?" Gideon asked.

I looked over at where several of my friends sat around a campfire. Frank sat with them, of course. He was animatedly telling a story about how his brother nearly proposed to the wrong girl at a masquerade ball after indulging in too much champagne. Frank knew how to play to an audience, hitting all the punch lines at exactly the right time, and I found myself smiling at the outlandish tale too. As compelling as the story was, the background details were just as noteworthy—like how the masquerade had taken place at his family's estate, hosting a hundred people. The plentiful champagne had been a rare Lorandian type. Frank Brennan had money, no question. He had looks too, which weren't a necessity but weren't something I minded.

"I don't dislike him," I mused. "He's pretty much a perfect example of what the Glittering Court goes for, though this really wasn't the setting I'd planned to be meeting suitors in. I'm not at my best."

"I don't know. I mean, I've never seen you wearing a silk gown in a ballroom, but after everything that's happened?" In the lantern's soft glow, Gideon's smile held its usual radiance. "I feel like I've seen you at your best. You should have a husband who appreciates that."

"Hopefully I can find one."

Gideon eyed the group by the campfire. "And you think you'll find him among Cape Triumph's elite, critiquing champagne in some tacky drawing room?"

The image, coming from Gideon especially, made me laugh. "Well, we'll see. I *do* think I'll find someone in one of those tacky drawing rooms who can help my . . . family with our bills."

"And you'll give up love and connection for that?"

"In an instant. They matter more than everything else, and I'll do whatever it takes, be whatever it takes, for their security."

"It's a shame," he said after long moments. "You shouldn't have to sacrifice one thing for another. You should have it all—being able to take care of your family, someone you can love, the freedom to be yourself . . ."

I nearly had that with Jago, I thought wistfully. *All but the one that matters.* To Gideon, I said, "Believe me, I want all those things if possible. I'll let you know if I find him."

"Well . . . what about me?"

I'd started to pack up my paper and now stopped in surprise. "You . . . what?"

Gideon was angled away from me, so I couldn't make out his expression. He took a deep breath. "Me. As your husband. Will you . . ." Slowly, he turned around. "Tamsin, will you marry me?"

CHAPTER 30

"GIDEON . . ." FOR THE BRIEFEST OF MOMENTS, I WONDERED if he was teasing me, but the earnestness on his pale face left no question. Apparently, his declaration at the camp hadn't been a spur-of-the-moment impulse. "Oh, Gideon. We talked about this. You're wonderful—truly. Worth a million Frank Brennans, to be honest. But I have to marry someone who can pay my contract fee and my other expenses."

"I-I can," he stammered. "I have it. The money."

Again, it should have been a joke, and again, his expression insisted it wasn't. "How? An orthodox priest wouldn't have that kind of money . . . let alone . . ."

"One from the Heirs of Uros?" he supplied, with a rueful smile. "You're right. But remember, I wasn't always one. Before that, I was a spoiled boy living a shallow and decadent life. What I didn't tell you is that I was also a spoiled boy whose father is one of the landed gentry."

I shot to my feet. "Stop it, Gideon! I didn't believe it before, but now I know you *are* joking."

He held up a hand. "It's the truth. May the angels strike me down if it's not. I grew up in the Oakmont district. Have you been there?"

"Sure," I scoffed. "Delivering laundry. One of Ma's regulars went to a debut there, and we had to deliver her satin ball gown."

"When was it? I could have been at that party. I told you—I went to lots and burned through my parents' money. They had every right to cut me off, but they kept hoping I'd straighten up one day. Sailing to Adoria to join the Heirs wasn't exactly what they had in mind, but they were so thrilled to see me focused on anything that they continued sending the stipend my brothers and I get from our grandfather's estate. It's not as much as if I'd stayed in Osfro and played an active part in running the land, but it's covered my expenses in Grashond for my education and board—and it would cover your contract fee. There's a bank in Watchful that's got some of it invested for me. It'd take a bit of time to send for it and get through the paperwork, but once it was freed, I'm certain I could help your family and give you a comfortable life. I can't promise champagne and tacky drawing rooms, but I swear you'd never want for love, respect, and acceptance."

Frozen, I could only stare and try to process his words. Realizing I was gaping, I finally clamped my jaw shut and turned around. "Gideon—no. I can't do— No." I stalked off into the darkness, too overcome to continue.

"Tamsin!" He caught up easily and clasped my hand to stop me. "Wait, please. I'm serious. I want to marry you. I love you."

I shook my head, though we'd gone far enough from the lantern that I wasn't sure he saw that. "Gideon . . . I meant it when I said you're wonderful, and I care about you a lot. But . . ."

"But what? If you care about me, and I have the money that'll help you, what's the problem? Are you . . . are you hoping to find someone with more money? Or someone you like better than me?"

The tremulous note in his voice at that last bit struck me deeply. "No, it's not that. It's just at this point . . . well, I came here treating marriage as a sort of business, and I feel like I need to stick to my original plan. Love and romance are wonderful things, but I can't risk getting distracted by them."

"Like with Jacob Robinson?"

I went very still. "What are you talking about?"

"It's okay." Gideon's voice held its familiar gentleness. "I saw the way you looked at him. And I heard the way he talked about you when we went back to Constancy. But I'm guessing if he hadn't been detained at the fort, you would still have cut him off."

"Gideon, it's complicated—"

"I don't have any hard feelings toward him. He's a good man. And I don't blame you for having to end things because of his money—or lack thereof. Like you said, you came to Adoria for a specific reason. But I'm guessing it still hurts—and that it's probably easier considering your marriage prospects impartially now, keeping your heart out of it altogether."

Gideon didn't know the exact details of how things had ended with Jago and me, but he had, I realized, figured out what even I hadn't. I was slipping back into my old role of focused, goal-oriented Tamsin because choosing a husband from an emotionally detached place meant I couldn't get hurt again.

When I stayed silent, Gideon continued, "But I'm telling you, you don't have to make that sacrifice. Marry me, and you can have it all. It's okay if you're not madly in love with me right now, but the fact that you care at all and we have such a good friendship is more than you'll have with some stranger you meet in a drawing room. This is the kind of basis we can use to build something beautiful. Don't resign yourself to unhappiness."

I rubbed my eyes and slowly turned back toward the wagon, Gideon falling into step beside me. "I don't want you making a rash decision," I told him. "A lot's happened in your world recently. You gave up a life of luxury in Osfro to come to the Heirs, and now you're leaving them. You don't need me right now—you need time to figure things out."

"But that's exactly it," he said, voice suddenly growing sure and eager. "You're the reason I figured things out. Long before I found out the council had lied to me about Jacob, you were making me question what I was being told." As we neared the light again, he stopped in front of me so that I'd have to look up into his face. He took my hands. "Tamsin, you are the bravest, cleverest person I've ever met. Your compassion is boundless, and you aren't afraid to stand up for your beliefs. I came to Adoria hoping I'd find people who could cut through the superficiality and excess that taints the world. And it turns out, one of them found me. Do you *really* want to marry someone like that?"

He gestured across the camp, and, almost on cue, we heard Frank call, "Archibald! Did you lay out my jacket with the red pinstripes? I wanted the one with larger red stripes. Don't go to bed until it's pressed and ready."

I winced. "That's kind of an extreme example . . ."

Gideon leaned closer. "Tamsin, I think we could do wonderful things together. You've got such a gift for helping me bring my ideas to life. We could create sermons—no, larger messages and ideals—to share and guide others along the path Uros intended."

"I have no calling, Gideon. I'm not going to pretend for a second I do."

He smiled, and it reached his eyes, making them shine. "You say that, but I think you have been called. And that's what I'm realizing. Being righteous and good isn't about how many passages you read or how modestly you dress. That's as empty as the gold robes and repetitive services I hated in Osfro. The real test of who we are is in how we live, how we embody those principles in the world each day. That's what you do. And that's why I want you by my side, to find a home and a community." He hesitated. "To create a better understanding of the divine—to create a new sort of church that gets to the heart of what matters, without the strictness of the Heirs."

"Your own church . . . Gideon, that's . . . wow. That's amazing," I said sincerely. "I think you could do some really good things."

"And with you, I could do some really great things. Please, Tamsin." We could hear the others disbanding. He released my hands, but his voice grew more urgent. "Let me prove to you that you can have it all. That opening your heart doesn't lead to pain. Be my partner in a new venture—not just someone's pretty trinket. You're a woman without equal. You deserve the world."

My heart racing, I glanced over my shoulder and then back to him.

His words were thrilling and beautiful. Not enough to make me instantly get over Jago, of course. But they did give me hope. A minister's wife wasn't what I'd envisioned, but nothing was, anymore. Was it so crazy to marry him? It might not be an opulent lifestyle, but it would surpass what I'd had in Osfro and ensure my marriage plans were settled when Merry arrived. And he was right that I was unlikely to find anyone who'd want me to help build his dream with him in such an equal way. Maybe I really wouldn't find anyone who loved me like this.

Jago did, an inner voice said. *He was willing to give up his dream for you.*

"Gideon, there's something you need to know before you ask this. I'm not who you think."

"There's nothing you can say that'll change what I think of you," he said.

The others had almost reached us. In a rush, I suddenly blurted out the impossible: "I have a daughter. No one knows. She's nearly four, and she means everything to me. Her father—we weren't married— never acknowledged her, and she's been sick a lot. She's why I'm here, to get her a better life. I'd planned on telling whoever I married that I was a widow. I respect you too much to lie, though, because I know you value the truth. So." I finally took a moment to breathe, just as Winnifred and Joan walked by, calling greetings. "You should know that before you really ask me to marry you. Good night."

I hurried away after the other girls, wondering what I'd just done, and leaving Gideon staring into the distance.

"We could reach Cape Triumph today."

The proclamation came two days later, from one of our guides, and it made every conversation stop. Eyes widened, mouths dropped.

Startled by the reaction, he added, "But . . . there's no guarantee. The Flower Festival's tonight, and if it looks like we won't reach the city until evening, we should just camp until morning."

"Why?" demanded one of the sailors. "After this nightmare, I think we're due for a celebration." A few echoed his sentiment.

"The city's chaotic. Try to bring in a caravan like this after dark, in the midst of all that? It'd be a mess. If you're trying to visit someone, they'll probably be out. If you're planning to stay at an inn, there won't be room. And it'd take forever to drive some of these wagons through the streets, as crowded as they get."

But he assured us we'd do our best, and we moved with a renewed vigor. Cape Triumph. Finally. I was well ahead of Merry and eager to get things prepared for her . . . whatever those things were.

Since telling Gideon my secret, we'd had no extensive conversation together. He behaved the same as always to me when others were around, but we never had a moment alone, and I often spied him watching me thoughtfully. I'd questioned myself constantly over whether telling him had been the right thing to do. But I'd meant what I'd said about honoring how he valued the truth. I couldn't go into marriage with someone like that under a lie.

Of course, if I'd just outright rejected him, there would have been no need to tell him. But I hadn't. His words had made me realize I did want to have it all—or, well, some of it. I wanted someone I could care about—maybe even truly love. I'd written that off, but Gideon had given me hope in his declaration and then in the fact that he didn't immediately rescind the offer.

But he also hadn't returned to me with open arms, issuing assurances of his continued love for me and acceptance of Merry. As time passed and his silence grew, I began to doubt myself. *Could* I have it all in a marriage? Or had I once again slammed into another obstacle in Adoria?

Evening brought us to a small town called Helm, and here our guides called a halt, eliciting groans. We were only about three hours from Cape Triumph, but that would put our arrival right in the middle of the city's revelries. Captain Milford agreed with the guides and had to do a great deal of threatening to keep some of his men from sneaking off. It helped that Helm was holding its own Flower Festival, and while the scale was probably nothing next to Cape Triumph's, it was a happy diversion for us. The town's bachelors were equally happy to have twenty young women show up.

I was tempted to sneak off to Cape Triumph too. But, as anxious as I was to get settled there and reunite with Mira and Adelaide, I would see my "pretty little birds" through to their nest.

I pushed aside my worries and let myself actually have fun. A fiddler and piper played music in Helm's square, and those of us in the Glittering Court fell into the delightful task of teaching the locals some of the complicated ballroom dances we'd had to master. I even showed Captain Milford how to do a waltz, and we were both surprised at how good he was.

After two hours of dancing, breathless and laughing, I took a break and went searching for a vendor who'd been selling lemonade and mead. As I was about to hand her a copper for my lemonade, a voice behind me said, "I'll cover that and have one myself."

I looked up at Gideon and smiled. He smiled back and paid the vendor for our drinks. "I wondered where you were," I said as we strolled away. "I didn't see you here and thought maybe you didn't approve of dancing."

"I approve, though *others* don't." He nodded across the square to where the Heirs sat to the side, watching in disapproval. "Seeing as they don't know about my leaving yet, I figured I should keep the peace. Can we go back to the wagons and talk?"

My heart accelerated. "Of course."

We wound our way through the festivities, back to the quiet of the caravan. I had to stop myself from shaking. Was this it? The moment I officially accepted a marriage proposal in Adoria? That had been the whole point of everything I'd endured, and the possibility of it becoming a certainty was both exciting—and frightening. Was I fool to consider Gideon over some shipping baron or plantation owner?

Leaning against a large wagon, underneath a hanging lantern, Gideon sipped his drink and seemed to be preparing himself. After long moments, he smiled at me and said, "Tamsin, what you told me . . . that was incredibly brave."

"W-what?"

"Not that I'm surprised. I've been saying forever that you're brave, and that just proved it. I just wish you'd told me sooner. I can't imagine what it must be like carrying that kind of secret. It must be so hard being away from her. I wish I could have been helping you long before now."

My hands began to shake. "You . . . you mean that?"

"Absolutely." He finished the rest of his lemonade and set the cup down. "What's her name?"

"M-Merry. It's short for Meredith."

"Merry," he repeated, and I again experienced the joy of hearing someone else say my daughter's name. "It's beautiful. I bet she is too. Does she have red hair like you?"

"She does."

His grin broadened. "I can't wait to meet her."

I had to stop myself from gaping again. "Gideon . . ."

"Yes, Tamsin. This doesn't change how I feel about you. I still want to marry you. I'm sorry I didn't tell you sooner. I never could catch you alone, and I admit . . . it was a surprise. But I understand why you'd keep that secret close to you—I imagine you don't always get the best responses from others."

"That's putting it mildly," I said, still in shock.

He shook his head. "Like I said—I can't imagine. It must be hard on both of you, dealing with that judgment from others who certainly aren't perfect. I know I'm not. I made my own share of mistakes when I was younger."

I came out of my daze enough to note, "She's not a mistake. Some of my actions were—but not her."

"I'm sorry," he said with a grimace. "I didn't mean to— Ugh. There

I go again, messing up what I want to say. See? This is why I need you. If you'll still have me."

I put a hand on the wagon to steady myself. Was this it? Should I do it? Though I still hurt, I would have to move on from Jago one way or another, so why not with someone who loved me and could support my child too?

I had to wet my lips a few times before I could speak. "Yes. I will. But—just to be clear—you're sure you have the money? My contract could be close to two hundred gold. And some months, Merry's medicine has cost three gold. It won't be this way forever—she'll outgrow this ailment. But it adds up now. I want her to get a good education too. And I promised to send for my parents and siblings—"

Gideon stopped me by putting a finger to my lips. "Yes. I can afford it all, once I get the rest of my money from the bank. I can't promise you a hundred silk gowns or real silver cutlery, but we'll live well enough. And we'll live with love."

"Thank you," I said softly. "And I'm sorry to keep coming back to money. It's nothing personal against you. It's just—"

"Merry's a priority," he finished. "You have to accommodate that. *We* have to."

I wasn't in love with him, but I did love him a little for that. "I can't wait to see her again. I'd like to have everything in order right away. Do you think we can get married immediately?"

He laughed. "Wasn't I just begging you the other night? Of course we can. I'd marry you now if I could. When does she get here?"

"Six weeks."

His smile remained as his eyes grew thoughtful. "That's enough time to get everything settled. We can start putting out word about her, so it doesn't come as a surprise to others. I really want this to be easy for both of you—no more judgment or censure."

"I want that too."

"And that's why I was thinking . . . your story about being a widow might not go far enough."

I frowned. "How so?"

"What if someone asks for details about her father?"

"Don't worry—I've thought about that. I've got a whole biography ready."

"But some might think it's suspicious that you never mentioned her before. And some might just start overanalyzing the fact that you have a daughter at all."

A sense of unease began to run over me. "Where are you going with this, Gideon?"

"I think you need a new story. I think we should say that she's your little sister who's come to live with us. It'll chase away any doubts about her heritage, and when we bring the rest of your family over, it'll seem more plausible still."

The whole world came to a screeching halt around me. "You want me to lie about her?"

"You were already going to."

"About whether I'd been married or not! Not about if she's my daughter! And it's not really going to work when she calls me 'Mama.'"

"She's young enough to adapt. We'll keep correcting her, and eventually, she'll forget." He tilted his head to peer more closely at me. "Tamsin, what's that look for?"

"What do you bloody think?" I exclaimed. "I'm not going to stop being her mother!"

"You won't be," he said, startled. "Nothing can change that. This'll just be in how the world sees it. You want to be free of judgment, of people looking down on you—and her? This is it. We remove any doubt or suspicion. Make sure it's never an issue. It's especially important going forward with our new venture. If I'm trying to teach people to lead a principled life, I shouldn't have any questions coming up about my own household."

My mouth opened, but nothing came out right away. "Is that what this is about? Not saving us from judgment—but saving face for you?"

"It's for all of us."

"You said you understood! That you made your own 'mistakes' when you were young."

"I do, and I did. I don't judge you, but others will."

I stared at him for a long time, trying to figure out if he was telling the truth. Astonishingly, for the most part, I believed he was. He thought he was doing the right thing.

"Gideon, I'm not going to say she's my sister. We've done that in the past on certain occasions, but going forward? No more. I am her mother. She will know that. The whole world will know that. Do you know why I write those letters every damned night? To make sure she remembers I'm her mother! I'm not going to undo all that."

"Then you could risk undoing all that I'll have done!" He put a hand to his forehead, face anguished. "You know how carefully we'll have to tread. Any deviation of belief from the orthodox faith gets scrutinized for heresy! We don't want others thinking badly of my new church. We have to be beyond reproach. If I'm going to encourage people to lead meaningful lives free of corruption and façades, then we have to be a shining example of it."

"By creating a façade?" I snapped.

A spark of anger glinted in his eyes, the only time I'd ever seen it, aside from his quarrel with Roger. "You want to create one too. Remember how you said the money wasn't personal, but that it was essential with Merry as your priority? Well, following my dream—this vision of mine—is my priority. Changing the story isn't personal either. It just makes it less likely that someone'll figure everything out. That's good for me—and for you too."

I couldn't believe what I was hearing. I was so used to condemnation and humiliation for my past that this new twist caught me off guard. Gideon accepted me . . . but not all of me. And it was maddening to have someone so ostensibly understanding be so completely clueless. The fragile hope of a loving marriage I thought I had in my hands began to crumble.

"It's not good for me," I said, trying to be calm. "It's unacceptable for me. I've compromised on so much, sacrificed on so much—but being her mother is not negotiable. I'd rather have everyone in the world know the truth—that I got pregnant when I wasn't married—than believe a sanitized story about her being my sister."

Gideon threw his hands up. "Well, you might get your wish if something goes wrong!"

"I'll take the chance!"

"I won't!"

The words fell down like thunder. We could only stare at each other, both too worked up to speak, while the revelry continued in the background.

"Well," I said after an eternity, "that's that."

Gideon put a hand to his forehead and seemed to wilt where he stood. "Tamsin, please be reasonable. I love you. And as her mother, you should do what's best for her."

A cool, razor-sharp sense of purpose settled over me, and I shoved away any last sentimental thoughts. "You don't love me enough, Gideon. And yes, I *am* her mother, and I'm going to do what's best for her. Happy Flower Fest, Gideon."

"Wait," he called as I began to walk away, "what are you doing?"

I paused and gestured toward the square. "I'm going to have another dance or two, and then I'm going to get a good night's sleep so that I can get to work in Cape Triumph tomorrow."

"Tamsin . . ."

"I came to Adoria for a reason." I turned my back on him and didn't stop again. "Thank you for reminding me, Gideon."

CHAPTER 31

WE MADE GOOD TIME TO CAPE TRIUMPH, BETTER THAN
the guide expected, considering how late most of us had stayed up.
We left at dawn and reached the old fort that stood just outside Cape
Triumph's main entrance about two and a half hours later. A wooden
wall, left over from more-vulnerable days, surrounded the city, though
there were a number of gaps throughout. Relative peace in recent
years had lessened the need for constant fortifications.

I stared up at it with a chill running down my back. I'd been in
Adoria for weeks now, but until then, every place I'd traveled had been
an obstacle to this. Now, the full weight of where I was hit me. Cape
Triumph. The oldest Osfridian city in the New World, one that had
survived against the odds. Constancy was still trying to establish itself.
Cape Triumph had already succeeded. It wasn't a transient settlement.
It was a true city. *The* city. Here, lives could be changed.

Most of the main roads in the area terminated at the large gate on
Cape Triumph's west side. Its doors were left permanently open, and
two soldiers keeping watch from on high gave our caravan a wave as
we passed through. I returned their waves with a grin and then fixed
my attention back on the sights before me as we entered. There was so
much to see; I didn't know where to look.

Winnifred squeezed my hand. "Can you believe it?" she whispered.
"We made it."

"We did. Everything's going to be okay now. Better than okay."
I swallowed as an unexpected surge of emotion threatened to bring

tears to my eyes. "Everything'll be perfect now."

Nothing about Cape Triumph was predictable. Some buildings were old and finely crafted; others looked like they might have just been thrown together yesterday. One neighborhood looked meticulously planned, its streets in a perfect grid. Other sections showed the signs of decades of gradual settlement, built upon and expanded as needs required. There were no subdued colors or attempts at austerity here. Homeowners and shopkeepers painted buildings however the mood struck them. The city made no pretenses to conformity. It seemed to be saying, "I'm here, take me as I am." When I could lift my eyes from the array of sights, I became aware of the massive trees just outside the city's perimeter. They too seemed to have a message, reminding everyone that Cape Triumph still survived in the shadow of the wilderness.

As wondrous as the city itself was, a new excitement began to stir within me. "Where's the Glittering Court?" I called to our guides when our party came to a halt in one of the city's more commercial districts. The streets were fairly empty, either because of the hour or recovery from last night's Flower Festival. Those few residents I did see were as diverse and fascinating as the city.

They didn't hear me because Captain Milford was loudly going on about needing to get to the docks and check in with the sailors' guild to report on the loss of his ship. The Heirs wanted to find a respectable inn, admitting at the same time that they thought no such thing existed. The guides hired to see our belongings delivered glanced about uncertainly. I tried in vain to get someone's attention, much to the amusement of an elderly man in a raccoon fur cap whittling outside a fine jewelry store that wouldn't have looked out of place in Osfro.

"Excuse me!" I finally yelled. The others stopped talking. "You can do whatever you want, but the rest of us are going to the Glittering Court. Mister Brennan, do you know where Charles Thorn's home is?"

Among the travelers not affiliated with my friends, Frank was the only one from the caravan who'd stuck around. And Archibald, of course.

"Wisteria Hollow—it's a house not far outside the city proper. I can give you directions or take you there myself."

"I'm sure you mean well, sir," said Samuel, "but they are our responsibility. We can't let them go off alone with a stranger."

"You're not going off without us either," insisted Captain Milford. "Thorn needs to know there's a debt to settle."

In the end, Captain Milford sent his first mate and some of the sailors with us to help with the cargo and discuss payment with Jasper. Frank went on his way, telling us in a hopeful tone that he looked forward to seeing us again. He and one of the merchants who'd been with us took enough of their belongings to free up a cart, and those of us on foot piled in, happy to rest before reaching our new home.

Gideon rode in the cart as well, sitting on the opposite side from me. He'd said little all morning, and his eyes were bloodshot, as though he hadn't slept. I glanced at him once and then spent the rest of the ride talking to the other girls. Our fight still stung. He'd been my friend, after all. But I couldn't spare any more energy on him, not when I was on the verge of getting my life back on track—and reuniting with my very best friends.

If they were still my friends? Mira would welcome me, but what about Adelaide? I ached to see her but suddenly feared for my reception. Polly glanced over at me and did a double take.

"What's wrong?" she asked, misinterpreting my expression. "Do you think . . . do you think it's too late for us? That they're done arranging marriages?"

Joan blanched. "They can't be . . . can they? Will they turn us out?"

Everyone was suddenly looking at me, and I shook my head. "Don't be silly. There's always a need for women around here. At the very least, some destitute bond servant will be looking for a wife. I'm kidding," I added, seeing shocked looks. "Plenty of well-off men still need us, and besides, Mister Thorn should've gotten our letter by now and will have things prepared."

We took a well-traveled road out of the city and quickly found ourselves passing through forest and land cleared for farming. Our excited chatter eventually faded away, and we simply watched and waited for any sign of our destination.

"There!" Vanessa shot to her feet and pointed. "Look—look at that house. It's what Mister Brennan described. And it even has wisteria on the porch!"

Said wisteria was only just showing signs of spring renewal. It hung on a stately three-story white house with black shutters and large glass windows. A burly man in overalls and a straw hat sat on the porch, yawning, though he jumped to his feet when he saw us approach the house.

An almost comical moment of indecision followed when we'd all assembled on the house's lawn. "We have been their caretakers," Samuel announced. "We should be the ones to officially present them. Gideon, since this trip with the Icori was done at your insistence, you can take the lead."

Gideon jumped, startled at the recognition. He'd been staring off into space and clearly didn't want to take the lead on anything. But after a few moments to compose himself, he managed to put on the pleasant, practiced face of someone who dealt with the public. He stepped up on the porch, flanked by the other Heirs. The rest of us followed closely.

He knocked.

It took seconds, maybe, for the door to open, but it felt like one of the longest waits of my life. The young woman who appeared was about five years older than us, and I recognized her after a few moments: Miss Bradley, the Dunford Manor mistress who'd chaperoned the *Good Hope*. Her jaw dropped when she found what was waiting on the porch.

Gideon took off his hat. "Good morning, mistress. My name is

Gideon Stewart. Can you tell me if this is the household of Mister Charles Th—"

His words were cut off by the shouting of a delighted voice. "Winnifred! Joan!"

A girl I didn't know hurried out of the foyer, bumping Miss Bradley along the way. Winnifred gave a squeal when she saw the girl, and the two met in a hug. And suddenly, the rest of us were rushing forward, spilling into the house as all attempts at orderliness vanished. Oddly, most of the resident Glittering Court girls appeared to be right there in the foyer. If not for their stunned expressions upon realizing who we were, I might have thought they'd been expecting us. Most of them didn't know us, divided as we'd been between manors. The girl who'd greeted Winnifred and Joan was the one who'd switched with me on the ship.

But soon, a few Blue Spring girls recognized me. I heard gasps of "Tamsin! It's Tamsin!" Some hugged me, and I returned the embraces gladly, but my eyes were elsewhere, searching and searching.

The next time I heard my name shouted, it was by a voice I knew and loved. Everyone else in the room seemed to fade as Adelaide appeared, her eyes enormous and disbelieving as she stared at me. Maybe she thought I was a ghost. The next thing I knew, she was hugging me, clinging so tightly that she must have thought I'd disappear again if she wasn't careful.

"Oh, Adelaide . . ." I felt myself crumple, unable to find any words that could convey what was in my heart. Adelaide held on to me, and suddenly, Mira was there too, hugging us both. All three of us cried.

Adelaide recovered the powers of speech first. "Where have you been, Tamsin?" Her lovely face, always so filled with mirth and wit, held a pain I'd never seen in her, and it tore at my own heart. "Where have you been? We thought . . . we thought . . ."

I wiped tears from my eyes, but more promptly took their place. "I know. I know. I'm sorry. I wish our letter had gotten through, and I'm sorry for everything back in Osfrid—"

"No, no," she interrupted. "You have nothing to apologize for."

By that point, Jasper had apparently joined the throng and tracked down answers. He stomped on the floor to get everyone's attention, his face glowing. He hopped onto a chair and exclaimed, "Friends! Friends! You're witnessing a miracle right before our eyes. Something none of us thought possible. I've just learned that—as you can no doubt tell—the *Gray Gull* wasn't lost at sea! It sustained great damage in the storm and was blown off course—far, far north to the colony of Grashond. Who do I have to thank for this? Who do I have to thank for saving my girls?"

After some shuffling, Gideon came forward and introduced himself, explaining very briefly how their community had taken us in. Jasper fawned over him like he would his own son. Actually, I was pretty sure I'd never seen him show so much affection to Cedric. Gideon tried to deflect the excessive thanks, saying, "It was simply our duty under Uros." His eyes looked past Jasper just then, meeting mine. I turned away.

Jasper wasted no time. He offered accommodations to the Heirs, promised to meet with the sailors, and set the house's caretaker, Mistress Culpepper, to seeing that we received rest and refreshment. "And now that their journey is over, I'm sure they'd like to change out of traveling clothes and into their finer wares."

That was when we had to deliver the news that most of our fancy evening dresses were gone. After some initial surprise, he took it more in stride than I'd expected. "Well, then, I'm sure we can put together a wardrobe from the other girls—especially the ones who are engaged." I wondered how well he'd take it when he saw how much else was gone.

Mistress Culpepper assigned us bedrooms, and I was of course put in with Adelaide and Mira. The three of us closed ourselves away, still breaking into spontaneous hugs and ever on the verge of tears.

We'd barely sat down on the beds when a visitor knocked. A girl I didn't know entered with an armful of green dresses. "You were the emerald, right? I inherited your spot, but I don't need these anymore. Not now that I'm engaged."

I thanked her and looked over the pile of organdy and silk after she left. She had been named the peridot back in Osfrid and then rebranded an emerald here, since the gems had similar colors. The peridot wardrobe was a shade lighter than my emerald one had been, but it was still stunning. *Green is my best color.* I'd longed for these clothes so much, but now, it was nothing compared to seeing my friends. I shook my head, remarking, "To tell you the truth, I don't care what color I wear anymore, so long as it's not this blasted cheap wool."

Adelaide and Mira had all sorts of questions, and I couldn't blame them. If my friend had come back from the dead, I'd want to know everything too. But the rush of energy that had spurred me here this morning had drained away, and all the exhaustion of coping with Constancy, the Icori, Jago, and Gideon came crashing down upon me. I didn't even know where to begin. I answered in vagaries, and Mira, at least, picked up on my mood. She suggested I change and clean up, and when I came back, I could tell she'd had a talk with Adelaide. They pulled back on their interrogation, but the suggestion that they were ready to hear my story any time always lingered.

As for me, I was ready for *their* story. And after food and rest, I found my energy restored. I felt like a new person, but maybe that was the green silk poplin. The spark I'd felt last night when I'd walked away from Gideon flared up in me again. I was ready to claim my fortune and fight for Merry.

"It's late in the season, but I plan on making up for lost time," I told Mira and Adelaide. "I hope you've left some men for the rest of us. You must have both gotten slews of offers by now."

Mira's lips twisted in a half smile. "Not that many in the way of, ah, official ones. But I feel optimistic about my future."

That was a typical Mira answer. It was nice that some things didn't change. I looked to Adelaide, expecting more because of her chatty nature and diamond rank. "What about you? There's no way you haven't had all sorts of offers. Have you settled on some promising young man?"

The silence that met me was unexpected but not nearly as unexpected as the story that eventually poured out of the two of them. Adelaide had found a young man, it seemed. In fact, she'd found him long before setting foot in Adoria: Cedric Thorn. With a dreamy expression, she explained how they'd unintentionally fallen in love and finally decided to stop fighting their feelings. The scene I'd arrived to this morning had, in fact, been part of the fallout of Jasper discovering the relationship the night before. He, Charles, Cedric, and Adelaide had been having a meeting about the scandal and had been unexpectedly joined by Adelaide's leading suitor.

"His name's Warren Doyle," Mira explained. "He's the governor's son."

I sat up straighter. I knew that name. He was one of the handful of men Esme Hartford had claimed wasn't opposed to a wife who'd been previously married. In her letter, she'd mentioned his parents had tried to arrange a marriage with a young widow from a minor noble house but that the woman had ended up accepting another offer. Esme had also mentioned his father was governor, but the rest of Mira's remarks were unexpected.

"And he's about to become governor of his own colony. He seemed pretty infatuated by you, Adelaide. He couldn't have taken it well. I'm sure Jasper didn't take losing the money well either."

"He actually offered to help us," Adelaide said.

Mira leaned forward. "Jasper?"

"Sorry, no, Warren."

"Warren's going to help you and Cedric? After finding out that you were already in love with someone else the whole time he was courting you?" Mira's face said she didn't believe that for an instant. "What happened?"

Adelaide took a deep breath. "Cedric and I can get married, with conditions. His father and uncle won't advance us money to cover my contract—but Warren will. He says he doesn't want someone who doesn't love him in return and would rather cut his losses by recruiting upstanding citizens for his new colony. So we're going with him to Hadisen next week. I'll find a family to board me in exchange for housework and teaching their children. Cedric's going to work a gold claim. He'll get to keep some of the profit, and Warren gets the rest. When the contract's paid off, we can get married and go somewhere else."

It was something of a relief to see that Mira looked as flabbergasted as I felt. Of course, she was probably shocked at the new arrangement. Me? I was still stuck on something else.

"What were you thinking? You turned down a future governor for... what, an impoverished student?"

Adelaide made a face. "Well, he dropped out of the university. And he's not impoverished. He's just . . . um, without assets. But I'm sure that will change."

"This would have never happened if I'd been around to look after you," I announced. "Mira, how could you have stood for this?"

Mira looked embarrassed. "I had no idea," she said.

"You're her roommate! How could you not?"

Neither had a good answer. My friends hadn't faced the threats I had over the last several weeks, but they'd fallen into trouble nonetheless. Would things have been different if I'd been here? Maybe. My protective instinct wanted to believe they would have been, but after a while, I wasn't sure. Adelaide was Adelaide, always dreamy and following her heart. Mira was Mira, caught up in her own quests.

And later, when Cedric came to welcome me back and discuss plans with Adelaide, I grew more certain there was nothing I could have done. They were head over heels for each other, and in hindsight, I realized they had been back at Blue Spring too. I was glad Adelaide had found love, and wanted her to be happy, but it was unsettling to think of her going off to the fringes of Osfrid's colonies. Hadisen was even less settled than Grashond. It was mostly rural, lacking some of the most basic amenities. An isolated gold claim would be taxing and dangerous.

But Hadisen's governor . . .

I needed more details, but I was certain Warren Doyle wouldn't be living in a claim shanty. He had his family's money in addition to a governor's income and, according to Adelaide, already had a house built in Hadisen's one city. Eventually, those gold claims would pay off, and the colony would prosper. A governor's wife could live very well. A governor's wife could have a lot of sway in how things ran. And a man accommodating enough to help when the woman he wanted was in love with another might have exactly the nature needed to accept a widow and her daughter.

As Adelaide, Cedric, and Mira continued their conversation, my thoughts raced. I'd gotten off track in a lot of ways in Adoria—far more than just geographically. I'd joined the Glittering Court with an agenda: Find the most advantageous situation to protect Merry and elevate my family. I'd been single-minded in that pursuit. I'd been ruthless. And then, I'd let love entangle me with a man who couldn't offer any of those things. After that, I'd chosen a man who offered the promise of idealism and self-respect. That had also gone horribly awry.

Attempts at love and affection hadn't worked for me, so it was time to stick with my original plan, the one guaranteed to best help Merry. A husband—and the life he could offer me—had to be a matter for my head, not heart.

"So. This Warren. He's available then, right?"

Everyone stopped talking and looked at me. "I suppose so," Adelaide said uncertainly. It had to be weird talking about the man she'd been trying to keep her distance from. "And he's motivated to find a wife . . . but he's only got a week left before he leaves."

I couldn't help but smile at everyone's bewilderment. I'd apparently been gone so long they'd forgotten I was the Tamsin who got things done. One week.

"That's all I need," I told them.

CHAPTER 32

"WOULD YOU DO ME THE HONOR OF A DANCE?"

"Excuse me, *I* was just about to ask Miss Wright to dance."

"Well, I beat you to it."

It could have been Shibail's dream all over again—except this time it wasn't just in my head. This was real. Tangible. And it would not end in disaster.

"I'll have plenty of time for a dance with each of you," I said, holding out my hand to the first man. "But no more than that. I've already had other offers."

Four days after my arrival in Cape Triumph, I felt as though I'd been here for ages. The austerity of Grashond and harshness of roadside travel seemed like something that had happened in another life, not this one filled with comfort and entertainment. I'd had two, sometimes three, social engagements each day. A nighttime event was a given. There was always some party, dance, or formal dinner. Daytime activities varied. Teas, luncheons, simple social calls. All of them required meticulous care in appearance and charm. I couldn't slack in anything.

Damaris joked that this new life was more exhausting than the hard labor of Grashond. It *was* work in the sense that I pushed myself relentlessly. I flipped back into the mode I'd had at Blue Spring—ever vigilant, always looking for an opportunity to advance. I thrived in the momentum of it, both because I had Merry's security within my grasp and because if my mind was focused on advancing into high society, it had little room left to ruminate on Jago, Gideon, and the Icori unrest.

"There's something I've been wanting to tell you," my partner, Mister Page, said. He shifted his grip a little; his palms were sweaty. "And I hope it won't seem too forward."

I looked up with what I hoped was coquettish surprise. "Why, whatever could you mean by that?"

He swallowed. "Well, after we were seated by each other at yesterday's luncheon, I haven't been able to stop thinking about you. And I realized last night that we have a profound, soul-reaching connection—I'm sure you noticed—and I want to spend the rest of my life with you. Will you marry me, Miss Wright? I can speak to Mister Thorn right now, if you'd like."

"Mister Page, I had no idea you'd even noticed someone like me." I'd known perfectly well and suspected his intent when he approached me tonight. "Naturally, I was captivated by your many charms, and I'm overwhelmed that you'd show me such regard."

"Then you accept?" he exclaimed, face lighting up.

"Being your wife would be a dream come true, I'm sure . . . but I can't accept. Not yet."

He stumbled, but I effortlessly kept us in time with the music. "W-what?"

"Well, I've already had some offers, and I have it on good authority that there will be others. I promised Mister Thorn I'd hear all of them out—it's only fair, isn't it?"

"How many more do you think there'll be?"

"It's hard to keep track, and some of them are from truly lovely gentlemen who've offered more than my contract price."

Mister Page didn't comment on that, which I'd expected. Anything I couldn't find out about a man's background and finances from talking to him could be learned from Jasper. I studied up on everyone in my free time. Mister Page was doing well, but there were others doing better, and that came through in what they were willing to offer. He wasn't off the table yet, but he wasn't an immediate yes either. If I was going to play this game, I'd play it to win. I'd learned my lesson in the dangers of sentimentality and would be all calculation and strategy from here on out.

"I'll of course keep you at the top of my list—I'm very fond of you, as you know. But I simply must wait. I hope you understand."

"Of course," he said, trying to hide his disappointment with a weak smile.

"I knew you would! You have such a kind and open nature—I saw it right away."

When the dance ended, my next partner didn't immediately materialize. Rather than feel affronted, I welcomed the lull as a chance to breathe deeply and let my face rest—a little—from smiling. I strolled toward one of the many elegant refreshment tables, coming up alongside a man in a dark coat whose back was to me as he stared into a wineglass, lost in his own thoughts. Recognizing him a few seconds before he noticed me, I decided to try a bold approach to get his attention.

"Excuse me, you seem to have run out of the rosé champagne that was here earlier. Could you go back to the cellar and bring some more?"

Warren Doyle turned toward me, eyebrows raised in astonishment.

I gasped. "Mister—Governor Doyle! How embarrassing! I hope you'll forgive me. I thought you were one of the servants."

His expression turned wry. "Nothing to forgive, Miss Wright. That's what I get for skulking over here, I suppose."

My heart raced, not from true embarrassment but from nerves. Of Esme's eligible gentlemen, only two were actually eligible anymore. Warren was one. The other was out of town with an unknown return date. While there were likely other suitors I wasn't aware of who'd be amenable to a widow, I no longer had the time or luxury to investigate new possibilities. And of those I found, it seemed unlikely any would beat out the prospects a future governor held—unfortunately, he was leaving soon to lead his expedition to Hadisen.

He and I had been formally introduced at a recent party, and although we'd had a lively discussion, I hadn't walked away with the sense I'd piqued his interest. It wasn't through any fault of mine, I was certain. I got the impression he was too distracted by his upcoming responsibilities to pursue a wife—particularly after the disaster with Adelaide.

"Well, don't let me interrupt your skulking," I said, reaching for a glass of red wine. "I'll take this and be on my way."

Warren caught hold of my hand and moved it away. "I can't really do that now, knowing you'll be pining for champagne all night. Besides, it's excellent. I toured Evaria a few years ago and had my fair share in Lorandy. You there—excuse me." He waved down a passing servant and requested the champagne with the self-assurance of someone who was used to getting what he wanted, quickly. As he spoke, I covertly studied his features. Chiseled face, sleek black hair, a head taller than me. Yes, he was the way to win this game, if I could only pull it off in time.

After he'd sent the servant scurrying away, Warren turned back to me. "If you can bear the agony a little longer, he says he'll track some down. And if he doesn't, then I really will become a servant and handle matters myself."

I averted my eyes, wishing I could force a blush, though that wasn't a skill I'd ever managed. "I'm still mortified about that. Thank goodness no one overheard."

Taking my hand again, he led me toward the other dancers. My spirits soared as he said, "You can make it up to me with a dance."

Just then, inconveniently, my missing partner ran breathlessly up to us. Mister Wells nodded a greeting at Warren and quickly turned to me. "I'm so sorry—I hadn't noticed the song had ended. Shall we?"

Warren pointedly put a hand on my waist. "I had just asked her to dance—didn't realize you'd staked a claim, Howard. There's always the next dance. Let that be a lesson on attentiveness."

Mister Wells was left behind, and I couldn't help a laugh. "Are you mocking that poor man?" Warren asked.

"No, no. I'm just thinking he got off easy—as far as lessons on attentiveness go. Up where we were staying in Grashond, that sort of lesson would have involved copying pages of scripture, not missing out on a dance. Well, actually—they don't dance."

Warren's eyes grew thoughtful. "I still think it's incredible you spent so much time with those people. I'll be honest—it sounds terrible."

"Not all of it. And we're certainly grateful for their kindness."

"There's a way you say 'kindness' that makes me think there's a story there."

"There are several. If you want to hear them, you'll have to schedule time for another day."

"Do you even have any?" he asked with a laugh. "From what I hear, you're pretty in demand. A friend of mine was saying he regrets settling for one of the girls in the first group."

I glanced away, feigning interest in the other dancers. "Well, it's lucky you didn't make that same mistake, now, isn't it?"

I held my breath, wondering if I was being too bold, but he chuckled again. "So it seems. And I suppose I was lucky to be mistaken for the help just now too."

"Hush. You said this dance settled that. But I *am* surprised you would be skulking, as you put it. If it's not too forward of me to say, you're about to march off in triumph to your own colony. It seems like you should be the center of attention tonight."

He sighed, the amusement slipping away. "Oh, I could be, but I don't have the time. I don't really have the time to be here, period, not with all that I have to do. But my father wants to show me off, so I'm going through the motions."

"What all do you have to do? I'm good at getting things done and will help you if I can. Not that I have a lot of time myself, of course."

That brought a return of the smile. "Of course. It'd only bore you, I'm afraid. Just the endless logistics of leading people who are constantly demanding one thing or another from you and then have the audacity to be offended when you have no time to lead."

I didn't have to fake my scoff. "Mister Doyle, you've clearly forgotten how I spent my first six weeks in Adoria. Now. Tell me one of your problems."

"Okay," he said, after scrutinizing my face. "I'm having trouble keeping regular supplies coming into Hadisen for the settlers there. Most came with their own goods, but those don't last forever. You can't imagine how hard it is getting respectable shopkeepers to settle out in the wilderness when they can stay comfortably, say, in Archerwood and earn a steady income."

"Easy. Money motivates people. So offer them a better-than-steady income."

"By letting them price gouge? Certainly not. And I don't have extra funds to offer incentives."

"No need to give what you have. Give what you don't. Tax breaks, favorable trade regulations. It costs you nothing and keeps your settlers around—and hopefully attracts more."

Warren stared off for a few moments, face speculative, before turning back to me. "That's an elegant solution. An absurdly simple one— and that's a jab at me, not you, because I should have thought of it."

"Well, remember, I was actually spending time with traders in the wilderness not so long ago . . ." A sudden longing for Jago stopped me. My host's home, filled with velvet upholstery and rose-scented candles and burnished fixtures, became suffocating and superficial. It was a world away from sitting outside in Jago's sleigh, surrounded by endless land and fresh, crisp air. A knot formed in my chest.

"Miss Wright? Tamsin?" Warren prompted politely. "What were you saying? You ran into traders during your trip?"

I pushed aside the mental image of hazel-and-green eyes and fixed my attention on Warren's dark ones, slipping back into form. "Oh, yes. Traders and just about every other kind of people in Adoria. I don't suppose your next problem is recruiting Balanquans, Icori, or the Heirs of Uros to Hadisen, is it? I have *a bit* of expertise there."

"I'm sure you do," he said with a grin. "I still can't believe you traveled with the Icori. I still can't believe they let you, given the stories I've heard about them attacking our people." His brow wrinkled as he considered it further. "Weren't you and the others afraid of them?"

"Not of the group we traveled with. Besides, we had our own soldiers along for protection—although they probably needed protection from *us*. Their leader—Lieutenant Harper—had a few admirers, to put it mildly. A good friend of mine was especially devoted. It made for an interesting trip."

I laughed prettily and expected him to pick up the cue and ask for juicy details, but he wasn't quite there yet. "Harper came here with the Icori? No one told me that! When I heard he was in town, I assumed he'd come to ask for backup on the border *against* the Icori. Typical. My father loves bragging about how I've become a governor, but he still insists on treating me like an underling."

The scowl on Warren's face took me aback, though I could tell I wasn't the target. Keeping my tone light, I said, "No one who meets you would ever think of you that way. And there's no need for Lieutenant Harper to ask for backup. The way I, ah, hear it, there was some misunderstanding about the Icori attacks. He's been working toward peace with Kerniall, so that's good news, isn't it?"

Warren, apparently still irked at the perceived slight, didn't process my question right away. When he did, he sighed, and the dark expression smoothed. "I'm sorry for that outburst—it just caught me off guard to hear about this. I need to know these things to do my job. When I'm out of the loop on something—"

"—then others get an edge you don't have," I supplied.

He looked me over again, but this time, I felt he was really, truly seeing me. "Yes. You understand that—how important it is to get an edge sometimes."

I shook my head. "Mister Doyle, I believe it's important *all* of the time."

Something sparked in his eyes, but before he could comment, a man in gray approached deferentially, a pink bottle in his hand. "Sir? I have the champagne you requested."

The song ended just then, and Warren glanced around. "How's that for timing? Open it over there and bring a glass for the young lady. Thank you." To me, Warren said, "Can I join you and share another dance?"

It took all of my self-resolve to say, "As lovely as that sounds, it'd be unfair to Mister Cambridge over there. He made his arrangement hours ago."

"Unfair? It'd be downright cruel from the looks of it," Warren remarked, following my gaze to where the aforementioned gentleman shifted from foot to foot, eyes wide and hopeful—though he was too timid to intrude on Warren. "Perhaps it's for the best. I can leave now to get some work done without my father's censure. He's not even here tonight, but word always gets back to him." At the mention of the elder governor, Warren's tone grew bitter. "No doubt he's off collecting more information to keep from me. If I'd known about Harper sooner, I would've pushed harder for a meeting and set him straight about the Icori. It's difficult scheduling time with the officers these days—and now it's too late."

A chill ran over me at those words, and ignoring Mister Cambridge and the champagne-bearing servant, I caught Warren's sleeve and asked, "Set him straight how?"

Warren hesitated. "I know you're friendly with the Kerniall Icori—and I'm glad of that. I'm glad they treated you decently. But I hear a lot of things—you know about the patrols I run?"

I nodded, not trusting myself to comment. There'd been growing unease about heretics in the colonies, and Warren had personally organized patrols to investigate reports of illegal religious activity. A year ago, I would have endorsed it—if I'd even given it much consideration at all. The dissident Alanzan group had strange practices—such as worshipping outdoors—and keeping them away from ordinary followers of Uros seemed right. Now, after my time with the Heirs and

Gideon, I was starting to appreciate how those with different beliefs might have valid reasons for their choices, even if I didn't share them.

"Most of those patrols stay in Denham, but we get around the neighboring colonies too. And I've heard rumors of Icori in the north and the south spying and planning a joint attack. The clans in South Joyce have already stirred up trouble. And in the north . . . there's another clan, the Kernady? Over the border, farther up by the Balanquans. There are all sorts of reports of their raids. Maybe the Kerniall aren't involved with them—I hope not—but Harper and the rest of the armies are fools not to watch that area. Who knows what could happen if all those clans united? My friend Dale Eubanks was up in Bakerston and talked to actual victims."

"You hear *a lot* of things," I said, surprised. From what I'd observed in Cape Triumph, most of Denham was oblivious to the outer colonies' affairs.

"I have to stay informed. I'm not insulated like these colonies. *My* citizens are out there on the borders—they're the ones at risk. My father can brush these rumors and reports aside, but I can't. I don't want to wake up one morning and find Icori razing White Rock. But you shouldn't be burdened with this." Almost chagrined, he took my hand and kissed it. "Thank you for the dance. I hope we can talk again before my trip."

I stared after him as he walked away and Mister Cambridge scurried over. Unlike our last meeting, I believed that this time, Warren really did want to see me again.

"I saw that kiss," Mira said later, as we rode home to Wisteria Hollow. "Things must be going well."

She sat beside me in the coach wearing crimson silk. I'd seen her dancing a couple of times tonight, but I'd been too preoccupied with my own conquests to think much about hers. I didn't get how she wasn't being flooded with offers. She was smart, beautiful, and kind. Being

Sirminican shouldn't matter, especially with such a shortage of women. One would almost have to purposely dissuade suitors in her situation.

"We'll see. I definitely made headway." I settled back into the seat, suddenly aware of my sore back and feet. "But what about you? Why don't you have more than that elderly man pursuing you? Suitors should be lining up for you."

"They're all in your line," she teased. "But seriously—don't worry about me. I'm fine."

I put an arm around her, still overjoyed just to be near her again. "It's hard not to. I never know what you're going to do. Just please don't go tramping off to some gold claim on the fringes of society like Adelaide."

"You're telling me that?" Mira dissolved into laughter. "Isn't that your whole goal with Warren?"

"He manages the gold claims," I corrected. "There's a difference. And he lives in a real house, not a tent or shed or whatever it is Cedric has."

"Yes, but—never mind." Mira rested her head on my shoulder. "I'm just so glad you're back and safe."

Our party had run late; most everyone else was going to bed when we reached the house. I was eager to sleep as well but had to stop by Mistress Culpepper's office first to direct her attention to a tear in my cloak that had happened when an inebriated gentleman stepped on it. As I was returning through the foyer, I spotted a man in a familiar uniform preparing to leave.

"Lieutenant Harper? I didn't expect to see you here. Is everything okay?"

He glanced back from the door and smiled at me. "Oh, Miss Wright. It's nice to see you again. And all's well. I was just, ah . . ." His eyes lingered on the staircase a moment. "Just in the area and thought I'd stop by."

I tilted my head to better study him. He almost looked like he was blushing. "Were you . . . you weren't here to see Damaris, were you?"

Yes, he was definitely blushing. "I like to check in on everyone. You, for example. How are things? You've been out tonight?"

I wavered a moment and then let him get away with his change in subject, largely because of where it might lead. "Yes—every night. It's nonstop. And you know, I just heard the most puzzling things. Is there another group of Icori north of Kerniall? The Kernady?"

Lieutenant Harper's expression instantly sharpened. "Kernighy. Why?"

"Someone was telling me about them tonight, that they're conspiring with Icori in South Joyce for a joint attack."

"There've been a lot of raids in South Joyce, yes, though I'm suspicious they might be fabricated by the Lorandians too." His earlier fluster was completely gone now as he turned over my words. "I hadn't heard anything about a plan with the Kernighy. Who told you this?"

"Warren Doyle. He's anxious about Hadisen being caught up on the outskirts. He said his friend Mister Eubanks knows more."

Harper's eyes knit in thought. "Eubanks . . . I don't know the name, but I don't know a lot of people here. If he's in Doyle's circle, he's probably easy to find. I could talk to him . . . but the Micnimara sisters seemed sincere in wanting peace."

"They're one group," I pointed out. "And we know . . . well, the group that raided the fishing camp wasn't Lorandian. Maybe some of the stories are true."

I could see my dismay reflected in him. "I don't want to believe it either, but I'll look into it. Thank you for telling me, Miss Wright. It's kind of amazing you can still keep track of political tensions while having your head in all of this." He gestured around us.

"I can't help it," I said. "I keep track of everything."

Not long after my encounter with the lieutenant, I encountered Warren at a party on another day—one he couldn't avoid, since it was a going-away celebration. He was surrounded in well-wishers and all sorts of important colonial citizens who'd turned out, and as I made small talk with other suitors, I mulled over how to politely interject myself amidst his admirers. But when he noticed me, he promptly separated himself from the throng and headed in my direction.

"I was hoping you'd be here," he said, eyes eager.

I hadn't expected such a promising reception, but I ran with it. "I figured as much, Mister Doyle. That endless flattery must get so boring. Do you want me to send you off on an errand or two?"

The grin he gave me was filled with genuine delight, and it lit up his perfect features. It was easy to admire his striking appearance, but it didn't stir the same warmth within me that Jago's multicolored eyes and crooked smile did.

"You can send me off on more than that," Warren said. "Is it true you talked to Lieutenant Harper for me?"

I took a moment to respond, uncertain of where this was headed. "Well, I ran into him this week, and the Icori came up while we were talking, that's all."

Warren shot me a knowing look. "That's all, huh? You can play coy as much as you like, but your 'casual' conversation with him got the message through that I was hoping for. Harper convinced the garrison here to dispatch troops south to investigate the stirrings there, and he's going to send some of his own men up near the northern Icori to keep watch there."

The unabashed admiration reassured me I'd done nothing wrong, but the news still startled me. Those were big actions, and I wasn't sure enough about the Icori's involvement to feel comfortable with the military moving in. Hiding my shock, I said, "I'm used to making men jump when I talk, but I never expected to send armies on the move."

"All in a day's work for you, I imagine," he said with a laugh.

"Certainly. It might actually be the one thing I've done that the Heirs approve of. Maybe it'll buy the lieutenant some goodwill with them too."

"Didn't he have it before? Most people say he's pretty charismatic."

"He is, but charisma doesn't always get you far with the Heirs. And they weren't happy he didn't take action against the Icori sooner. He also made a few thinly veiled threats about calling their practices into question with the Crown."

Now Warren wore the shock. "Did he? That's pretty serious. The whole point of the colonial charters is to let each one set up its own laws and ways, without Osfrid's interference. Have you heard about that new Westhaven Colony? Where people can practice any twisted religion? If that's free of oversight, surely Grashond should be."

"I'm a little biased," I admitted, "seeing as the Heirs tried to starve me and wanted to cut my hair."

"Your . . . what? Really? Maybe *some* oversight is warranted. Your hair is divine, you know. But is that something they run into a lot? Friction with the Crown?"

"Sometimes," I said. The delight of having my hair called divine was a little unsettled by the intense tone of the question. "I mean, they're not openly antagonistic. Osfrid is there to take care of us, after all."

"Yes, of course," he said, relaxing a little. "But sometimes it's in a heavy-handed way. Remember my infrastructure problems? Much of that is because the Crown's taxes sweep away half of our gold income! And then I'm left to figure out how to build roads and schools with their leavings."

"That does seem unfair." I started to frown but then caught myself. I didn't want wrinkles—or to sound like I was talking treason. "Well, whatever comes of it, I'm sure you're clever enough to find a solution."

"I hope so. But if I'm not, I'm sure *you* are."

The note in his voice was unmistakable. I went very still and tried to keep a serene expression. "That's sweet of you. Of course, I'm not the one who's a governor."

"No, but I think you could be invaluable to someone who is." He took my hand, and I lowered my gaze to look at it, lest he notice me hyperventilating. "You weren't kidding about getting things done. You have a mind for the logistics of managing others. You persuaded an officer. You understand the situation in northern Adoria better than most people who've lived their lives here."

I had myself under control now and looked back up at him. "Mister Doyle, you know I'd listen to your flattery all day if I had the time, but I've already seen half a dozen young men trying to catch my eye. I'd hate to think you were wasting my time when you know very well how in demand it is."

"Oh, I'm aware," he said with a laugh. "And I'll get to the point, because I know you like that. And that's something I like about you. I also like that you are unattached, and it would mean a lot to me if you stayed that way for the next two weeks. Once I've seen my charges settled in Hadisen, I'll be coming back here by the water route—it can be done in a day, you know."

I nodded. Hadisen's position on the western side of Denham Bay made it an easy trip across the water—if you were just trying to get a boat or small ship over. The shore on that side was rocky and unpredictable, so large parties of people, animals, and supplies—like the one leaving tomorrow—had to go across land, cutting through Denham on a ten-day route not far from the one I'd taken coming from the East Sister.

"If we weren't leaving tomorrow . . ." Warren's face grew momentarily wistful. "Well. Nothing to be done about that now. I'll be back before you know it, and then we'll have plenty of time to discuss things. And by 'we,' I mean you, me, and Jasper. Do you think you can do that—hold off on any decisions with someone else? Can you take it on faith that I'll make the wait worthwhile?"

It was getting hard to breathe again. My free hand was clenched in a fist, and I chastised myself for being so silly. *Get a hold of yourself, Tamsin!* I mentally scolded. *This is what you've been waiting for. You're on the verge of making it all worthwhile, all the sacrifices with Merry and Jago.*

It was Merry who steeled me to proceed, but it was the wistful thought of Jago that made me unexpectedly say, "Can I take it on faith you'll think of me once in a while during that time? You don't have to be madly in love with me—not that I could blame you if you were—but I'd hate to think you were pining for my friend Adelaide those whole two weeks."

Surprise flickered in Warren's eyes, replaced quickly by amusement. "Nothing to pine over. I wasn't in love with Adelaide. I see that now. She's a lovely, accomplished girl—which is what I was infatuated with. Her standing. But I've come to realize she isn't what I need to govern Hadisen. I need someone who stays fixed on a goal, someone always looking for an edge. Someone who understands that respect and shared vision get you farther than rampant emotion."

I did understand that, though a nagging part of me wondered just how far you could get with love. But I ignored that part and unclenched my fist. Meeting Warren's gaze unblinkingly, I responded airily, "Well, since you're being so charming about it all, I suppose I can hold off on any decisions until you return. But just so you know, I'm not going to stop taking callers or invitations."

Warren brought my hand to his lips, the kiss lingering longer than before. "I'd expect nothing less."

CHAPTER 33

As I excited as I was for the Hadisen expedition to depart so that Warren could return and finalize matters, I dreaded it too, because it meant losing Adelaide. My dismay went beyond a selfish desire to keep her close; I worried for her safety as well. The evening before she left, I attempted one more earnest talk.

"Adelaide, I know it all seems like some grand adventure right now, but I've spent the last month and a half on the edges of the colonies. Living like that was hard for me—and I grew up in tougher conditions than you did."

She looked up from a bag she was packing and gave me a wry grin. "Are you saying I can't handle it?"

I studied the belongings spread out on her bed before answering. Heavy leather boots. Plain but durable blouses. Wide-legged suede pants. Earlier that week, Mira and I had gone with her to buy attire for the trip at a store specializing in wilderness gear. It was owned by a man they'd met on their voyage, one Grant Elliott, who hadn't much impressed me with his gruff and blunt manner. But he did seem like the kind of man who'd seen his fair share of rough situations, and the fact that even he thought her impending adventure was a harsh one hadn't been lost on me.

"I'm saying I remember you trying to do things like wash dishes and build a fire when you got to Blue Spring. This'll be worse than that. And have you ever slept on the ground before?"

"No . . . but I'll only be doing that during our trip to Hadisen. Once we're there, I'm boarding with a family who already has a cabin ready to go. I'll have a bed."

"It won't be like this bed. And you'll be surprised at how many ordinary household things you take for granted once you don't have them."

Adelaide closed the bag and stood up, stretching. "Are you trying to talk me out of this? You think I should just tell Cedric it's over and stay here?"

"Well, not when you put it like that! But I'm just worried about you. It'll be hard—not just the labor. There are all sorts of dangers on the frontier. And it's not like there are a dozen stores around the corner to buy what you need," I added, recalling Warren's supply issues. "If something runs out, you may be waiting a very long time."

"I'll have to go without, I guess. Or maybe if I hope hard enough, some peddler will stop by. Aren't they out there?" The joke made her smile, and she didn't notice I winced. "But whatever waiting there is, no matter how hard, I have to do it. I know it sounds crazy. I wish I could help you understand. I love Cedric, and I'd rather have him than a house full of luxuries."

Again, I didn't answer right away. I'd first been jealous of Adelaide for her refined background, then for her diamond status . . . and now, I realized, I was jealous that she got to be with a man she loved. It wasn't the type of envy that wished her ill. I wanted her to be happy—truly. But I couldn't help but compare myself and think how I had lost a man I had loved. Taking a deep breath, I reminded myself that I still had the one I loved most: Merry. And maybe, one day, respect and a shared vision could lead to more with Warren.

"I just want you to be happy," I said at last. "If this is what you want, then I want it too. And if there's anything I can do to help you secure that happiness, just tell me."

"Oh, Tamsin!" She nearly knocked me over with a massive hug. "And if I can help you find your happiness, I will. Not that you'll need it. You've always got everything under control. You really will get the best position for yourself, just like you've always said you would."

I swallowed back my own tears. "Was there ever any question? Now—ease up there, because you're wrinkling that silk, and I've got to be at an important party in an hour."

I saw her, Warren, and Cedric off the next day. Their caravan departed from the gates of Cape Triumph amidst a sea of fanfare and well-wishers, and I cheered them on. The prospective settlers headed out with hope in their faces, some well-off already and hoping to expand their success in this new territory. Most of the others looked as though they'd had little success of any kind in their lives and were now staking all they had left on this enterprise.

After Mira and I returned home, the long wait began. Two weeks. Two weeks of hoping Adelaide and Cedric would make the journey safely and continue to stay safe once in Hadisen. Two weeks of hoping Warren didn't change his mind about me.

I held true to my word about not accepting any other man but did still ensure I had plenty of backup choices. My delay in Grashond hadn't ruined my prospects, and I had a short list of half a dozen suitors who could support me and my family *and* whom I also liked reasonably well. I even managed to tease out of some that they would have no qualms about marrying a widow, so that was a relief. One way or another, Merry's future would be secured.

At last, I heard during an afternoon tea that Warren had returned to Cape Triumph via the bay and that the rest of his party was safely settled in Hadisen. I breathed a sigh of relief for Adelaide and Cedric, and then I spent the rest of the day anxiously awaiting any news from Warren. It came the following afternoon when he showed up at Wisteria Hollow and asked to speak to Jasper.

I hovered at the top of the stairs as Warren entered the house, and as soon as he and Jasper were locked away, I ran back to Mira in our bedroom, hardly able to contain myself. "Do you know what that means? He's going to make an offer! This could be it! What I've been waiting for."

Minutes later, I was called too. After a quick check in the mirror, I put on a calm countenance and walked serenely into Jasper's office. "Hello, Mister Thorn. It's nice to— Mister Doyle! What a pleasant surprise. I hadn't realized you were here. How was your trip?"

Warren waited until I was seated before taking a chair himself. "Excellent. Everything was on schedule, everyone is doing well. Including Adelaide," he added, guessing my thoughts.

I beamed. "I'm so glad to hear that. It was nice of you to come give us an update."

An amused glint in his eyes told me he knew that I knew there was more to his visit to that. "Mister Thorn tells me you aren't engaged or married, which is a considerable relief, because I have an offer for you."

I clenched my hands and swallowed. "Oh?"

"I'll be returning to Hadisen in two days—by water—and would like you to come with me and tour the area."

"Oh."

"White Rock is coming along nicely, and my own home is quite comfortable, but Hadisen is still a rather wild colony. I wouldn't want my wife to be shocked or feel like she'd been misled by the time it's too late. So, come as my guest, see what Hadisen is all about, and then if you approve . . . we can have a further discussion."

I relaxed a little. It wasn't as good as an outright engagement, but it was promising.

"One of Mister Doyle's associates lives in White Rock with his wife, and she'll come stay with you at the governor's house," Jasper continued. "So you'd have a proper chaperone."

I nodded along. "Of course. I wouldn't have presumed otherwise."

"Then you'll do it?" asked Warren. "I was afraid after the rest of your adventures, it might be too soon for you to plunge off into the unknown."

"Mister Doyle, I am ready to go right this moment if needed," I told him, head held high. "Especially if I don't have to sleep in a tent or wear unfinished wool."

After a few more details, Warren left, and Jasper held me back. "Tamsin, I expected great things from you, but you've surpassed my expectations. You've secured more prospects in three weeks than girls who've been here from the beginning have. And not just any prospects—one of the very best. Warren's hinted that he'd be offering more than your base contract post. There'll be enough to cover your debt."

"Then you think there *will* be an offer, sir?"

"I'm positive of it. I think he's taking this extra step for propriety's sake. I've seen men propose after one meeting, but an engagement looks more serious if the couple's actually had real time together."

"I understand. Thank you for all of your help."

Jasper stood up and opened the door for me. "Honestly, this was all you. You're the one who won him over so quickly, but that was probably nothing after all you did to get the other *Gray Gull* girls here—even if it did cost me some goods."

It was hard to keep a straight face at his dry tone. "I am sorry about that, sir. But believe me when I tell you: It could've been a lot worse."

"I do believe that. Loss is part of business—one has to expect the unexpected. Say, like, when your diamond throws away amazing opportunities." His face settled briefly into a scowl, then smoothed. "Well, what's done is done. I'm just thankful you aren't like her."

"Thank you, sir." But as I walked back to my room, I found myself wondering if I should really see that as the compliment he'd meant.

The day I was scheduled to leave for Hadisen banished any concerns about Adoria always being cold. The weather had already been steadily warming in my time in Denham, but I awoke that morning half believing it was summer already. By noon, everyone was sweating, and the humidity made me feel like I was wrapped in blankets.

Mistress Culpepper and Miss Bradley were beside themselves trying to keep everyone powdered and sweat free, but it was clear early on that the battle might be hopeless.

More than half of the girls were engaged now. A few had already married and left. Most of the attached ones came from the early group, but some *Gray Gull* girls already had fiancés. Other than the very elderly gentleman, Mira had had no one show serious interest, which worried me. She seemed restless and agitated, and I wondered if her romantic situation was finally taking its toll. When I hinted at that, she looked totally surprised.

"What? That? Oh, no. That's all fine."

"Then why are you pacing like a trapped cat?"

She abruptly stopped said pacing, not seeming to have realized what she was doing. "Other things," she said evasively. "And I'm worried about you, about Adelaide."

I crossed my arms and walked to the window. "Well, the only thing you need to be worried about for me is if Warren's actually taking me to Hadisen."

It was well past the time he was supposed to have arrived, and anxiety was eating me alive. I wandered the house, saying hello to those preparing for evening engagements. All the while, I was constantly peeking out the windows. It was one such moment, with my back turned, that Gideon seized a chance to sneak up on me.

"Hello, Tamsin."

I closed my eyes a moment and then turned around with a cool smile. I'd been doing an excellent job of avoiding him. He and the Heirs were still around, and no one knew when they were leaving. The girls who hadn't lived with them in Grashond were complaining about how odd they were, little knowing how much worse it could be.

"Hello, Mister Stewart."

His eyes made a quick assessment of me. I probably bore little resemblance to the Tamsin back in Constancy. Even my traveling clothes were luxurious: a green velvet riding habit consisting of a full skirt and a form-fitting jacket with a scoop neckline edged in gold. A plumed hat decorated with the same golden lace was tied with a silk ribbon over my hair, which I'd worn loose today. The other Heirs had made no secret of their disapproval of the outfits paraded through Wisteria Hollow, but something told me Gideon didn't mind them.

"I wish you'd call me Gideon again," he said. When I didn't respond, he shuffled his feet and glanced away. "You look . . . very nice. You're sailing to Hadisen today?"

"Yes."

"With the governor's son."

"With the governor of Hadisen. Though, yes, he's also the governor of Denham's son."

"Right, right. That's what I meant." Gideon dragged his gaze back to me. "Are you . . . happy?"

"Of course. He's a cultured, industrious man who's going to be in charge of an entire colony. He's financially secure and will have the respect of everyone in Hadisen—and outside of it."

"And what about his wife?"

"His wife will have the best of everything."

"Do you love him? Does he love you?"

"We respect each other. And from what I've seen, that'll get me further than love."

Gideon winced, catching the barb. "And what about . . . her . . ."

I might have called him out for avoiding saying Merry's name, but given the open setting, vagueness was probably better. "I'll deal with that after we're married, and bring it up in a way that he'll be accommodating to. You've helped me realize waiting is the best strategy, and I'm grateful to have learned that before I ruined a legitimately good prospect."

There was no sunshine in Gideon's face today. "I deserve that," he said unexpectedly. "And . . . Tamsin . . . I've been thinking a lot about what I said . . ."

"No." The prim, cool demeanor I'd been holding up was tossed away.

"Do not go down that road, Gideon. Don't start confessing your regrets."

He glanced around anxiously. "But I have them! Tamsin, I've done a lot of thinking and praying, and you were right—you're always right. I was being a hypocrite. I advocate for people embodying their ideals, yet I was embodying what I despise. The empty customs and rules that I complain about . . . well, I was applying them to you to cover my own insecurity."

"Your apology is accepted."

"Tamsin, I want to do more than apologize. I was wrong. I was shocked and said things I shouldn't have. I still want to marry you—it's not too late!" His gray eyes were wide and frantic. "There's a colony being chartered—it's called Westhaven—"

"I've heard of it."

"Then you know they allow freedom of religion. Early settlers have to buy into it, but after we're married and rebuild my money, we can move there and work on my new enterprise. You can be part of that—an invaluable assistant to a wondrous creation."

The passion and anguish on his face did move me. No matter what had happened, I didn't want him to suffer. But the thought of me going back to him was ludicrous.

"Gideon, I already get to assist in a wondrous creation—the forming of a colony. If you want my advice, don't wait to join Westhaven. Spend your savings on buying into it now, not on paying off a bridal contract. Go. Be happy. That's what I plan to do."

He wilted. "Isn't there any way I can change your mind? I'll do practically anything!"

I wondered if he realized the impact of his word choice. *Practically anything.* Jago had been willing to do everything.

"I'm fixed on my path," I said. "And now you need to find yours."

"Tamsin . . ." Gideon reached toward me, and I stepped back. "I really do love you."

I examined his face, the raw emotion burning in his eyes. "But not enough," I said. "Goodbye, Gideon."

Warren was full of apologies when he finally showed up that evening, explaining how business and bureaucracy had tied him up longer than expected. Two of his associates were with him and quickly loaded my trunk into a waiting carriage. "We'll have to make part of our trip in the dark," Warren added, "but we'll still arrive tonight. I hope it's not too exhausting."

Jasper answered for me: "No need to worry. Our Tamsin can handle anything."

Mira stood near him, trying to hide her sadness, but her dark eyes gave her away. I wished I could have offered a longer goodbye, but there was little to be said that we hadn't already shared earlier. I gave her a hug, told her I'd see her soon, and then followed Warren and his men.

I'd grown well acquainted with Cape Triumph in my time here and had often seen the busy part of the port—the section of the bay where ships going to and from Osfrid or coastal colonies docked. Farther west along the bay, a smaller cluster of buildings along the water managed ships sailing inland, not to the ocean. Here, we boarded the boat bound for Hadisen.

When I'd heard how only small vessels could dock on the far side of the bay, I'd worried we'd be traveling in a dinghy. But Warren's boat was about forty feet long and even had a small enclosed bit of cabin on its deck. The cabin had a partition dividing it into two sections. A few chairs sat inside one half, and Warren urged me to make myself comfortable. Gazing at the red and purple sky of sunset, I told him I'd stay out on the deck for a little while. It was wide and flat, with plenty of space to sit, and being near the water was already cooling me off.

The boat had a crew of two, and the captain had a hushed conversation with Warren before we set off. He pointed at the sky, then gestured at the bay. After a little more back and forth, the captain shrugged and ordered his crewmate to start untying.

Warren and his two men, Lawrence and Earl, sat near me and watched the shoreline depart. Shrugging out of his jacket, Warren said, "Forgive the informality, but this heat is cooking me alive. The captain says it's going to cool off soon, though. He expects it to rain—but that cabin is snug and dry. And once we arrive on the other side, we'll have a covered carriage too."

"I'm surprised you can get in a boat at all, Miss Wright," Lawrence told me. "After what you went through at sea."

"Well, I still arrived safely, didn't I? And I did a lot of water travel in Grashond, so I've gotten used to it again." The shore had become nothing but a black edge around the water now, dotted with the lights of buildings and streetlamps. "It helps being able to see land. At sea, there's nothing but water and more water."

Earl shuddered. "I've never left Adoria. Can't say I want to."

"Of course you do." Warren gave him an easy smile. "You've got to see the old country. And Evaria too. I spent almost two years over there touring the continent. You see the old cathedrals of Lorandy and statues of Ruva, and it'll make Adoria seem like an upstart."

"All the more reason not to go," said Earl. "I'll keep my happy delusions."

We laughed at that and discussed various light subjects as the voyage continued. Warren had a picnic dinner of sorts for us, and there was an almost party-like atmosphere to it all. I felt like I had wings, like I could have launched off and flown to Adoria. Everything I wanted was within my grasp.

The weather soon cooled, and the promised rain began, just a sprinkle at first. I traded my plumed hat for a hooded velvet cloak. It was around that same time that the boat began angling toward the shore, and I looked over at Warren in concern. "Is something wrong?" I asked. We were heading south, when Hadisen was due west across the bay.

"No, no. I should have mentioned it earlier—we're picking up two additional passengers. Associates of mine. I'm sorry for the added delay when we're already late. You must be exhausted."

"I'm just fine. You take care of what you need to." The wind had picked up by then, and a low rumble of thunder made me clench at the railing. Warren patted my shoulder.

"We're not in the middle of the ocean, and this is no tempest. Everything's going to be okay, Tamsin. May I call you that?"

"Of course," I answered, smiling. He strolled over to the captain and had a murmured conversation. Because of the late hour, they had to navigate in the darkness and were questioning the small port where Warren's associates waited. They found it, though, bringing us up to a long wharf in front of a small fishing village. Lights shone in the windows of scattered houses, and two men in cloaks waited at the wharf's end. One held a lantern and waved a hand in greeting as the other caught a line tossed by the captain's assistant.

The two new passengers stepped aboard, hunched over and holding their cloaks. As the captain shoved off, Warren shouted brief introductions over the increasing rain. "Tamsin, this is Mister Smith and Mister Carpenter. Gentlemen, Miss Wright."

We all stammered out appropriate greetings, though I barely heard theirs, and mine likely sounded mumbled too. A gust of wind threatened to rip off my hood, and I pulled it low, huddling in upon myself.

Warren leaned his hand down to mine as he steered me toward the cabin. "No need for you to get drenched. There's a tiny cabin with a bed you can rest on. We'll be in shortly and hopefully won't bother you while we go over business in the dining area. Earl, take her in, and see that she's settled."

I started to follow, pausing a moment to watch the captain and the other crew member as they fought with the lines of the sail in the lashing rain. Inside the main cabin, Earl told me, "I heard Mister Doyle talking to them. The captain says it'll be bumpy but that we'll be okay if we just keep riding the swell of the waves. This boat's low and solid enough that it's not likely to tip."

"Not likely to?" I asked uneasily.

Earl grinned. "It's fine. He says the biggest problem is just staying on course. Coming down here meant getting closer to some of the southern buoys than he'd like, so now's he got a job ahead of him to fight the wind and pull us back out."

"What are the buoys for?" I asked, rubbing my hands together. This small cabin contained only a simple table with benches and a lantern, but it was warm and dry and wonderful.

"They mark the shoals and shallow rocks on this half of the bay. They're dangerous for bigger ships—not us. But we need to be well north of them to stay on the course to Hadisen. Here you are." Earl opened a small door that slipped from his hand when the ship suddenly pitched sharply to the starboard side. Thunder boomed outside, and the door swung out and clattered against the wall. He winced and grabbed the door again. "Sorry. Let's try again."

I peered inside the second cabin. There wasn't much to it, just a pallet big enough for one person, which took up most of the room. I thanked Earl, and he told me to let them know if I needed anything. I pulled the door shut and couldn't quite make it catch. Leaning closer, I saw part of the latch had broken, probably when it slammed against the wall just now. I got the door to stay shut as best it could, though it left about an inch gap. No matter. Warren might think I'd be more comfortable here, but I wasn't sure I could actually stand being in a room without windows for very long.

I stretched out on the thin mattress, which was more comfortable than it looked. The rest of the men stomped inside the other room, and the wind's volume rose momentarily until they closed the outer door. I stared up at the wooden ceiling and listened to the combined sounds of rain, wind, thunder, and the others' patchy conversation. I tried not to think about how similar this was to the *Gray Gull*, but it was impossible not to. Lying in here, waiting, felt just like when I'd sat with Winnifred in our cabin and prayed to Ariniel. Maybe I should do that now. Would she listen, or was she tired of helping me?

The memory of a different storm flitted through my memory—the blizzard in Grashond. I found myself smiling as I recalled Dinah in-sinuating that my friends and I had endured so many trials because we were being punished. And then Jago had responded: *Doesn't seem like a punishment if they keep coming through it just fine. Maybe it's more like a sign of favor, the way the angels look out for them. Maybe they're carrying some divine message for the rest of us and don't even realize it.*

"Oh, Jago," I murmured. The pain I kept pushed down in my heart reared up without warning. I missed Jago. I missed his wit and how easy it was to talk to him, without any need of the caution and for-mality that had governed my social interactions these last few weeks. I missed his kindness and open nature. I missed the way he'd held me against his chest in bed, how his fingers had stroked my hair while I'd listened to his heartbeat.

I covered my eyes, trying to banish tears and memories. I couldn't let longing for the impossible keep me from a future so full of promise. I couldn't.

". . . can sail across a blasted bay, then they can raid one ship!"

I jerked upright as Warren's voice cut through the din of the storm. He'd raised it in anger but dropped it promptly, returning conversa-tion to its previous volume. I scooted over to the door and leaned near the gap, forgetting all my mother's lessons against eavesdropping.

". . . boats are small," Lawrence was saying.

"He knows what to do," a new voice said. "That's too big a prize to pass up. He knows we won't get a chance at that much ammunition again, and he always sees a job through."

The unfamiliar speaker must have been either Mister Carpenter or Mister Smith. I frowned, listening to the deep voice's quality. Those surnames were solidly common Osfridian ones, but this man spoke with a distinctly Lorandian accent.

"Which is more than can be said for some people," Warren snapped. "If you'd done yours, the northern army would have been on the move a long time ago."

"We did do ours!" exclaimed the Lorandian voice. "Both sides, just as discussed. One of my men nearly got killed attacking that farmstead, and we even got some ridiculous Icori clothes when we hit Grashond. I don't know why the army didn't go. No one suspected."

"Someone obviously did. The regiment up there met with Icori leaders to investigate the 'misunderstanding' and held off taking any action."

"What? Well, when we go back—"

"No need," Warren interrupted. "My bride-to-be did what you couldn't. The north will be going soon, and Campbell's going to take most of the fort's number south. She helped do that too, though it also sounds like the attacks our agents did there and in the central colonies were a little more effective."

The Lorandian speaker's voice came out as a growl. "I told you, we did what we were supposed to—"

Another huge wave tossed us around, and with it, the door's faulty latch gave way. It swung open again, smacking the wall loudly, and I gripped the doorway so that I didn't tumble out. That left me in the awkward and embarrassing position of crouching right there by the door.

I stared stupidly at Warren and felt the others watching me. After what felt like an agonizing time, Warren said, "Hello, Tamsin. Are you okay? I'm sorry if your rest was disturbed."

An uneasy tone in his voice made me realize he was more concerned about the notion of being overheard than that I might have been purposely trying to listen. Swallowing, I got to my feet and attempted a cheery laugh. "No, don't worry, it's hard to really rest with that racket out there! But the room was getting stuffy, and I . . ."

The words died from my lips. Until that moment, I'd been focusing on Warren. Now, my eyes lifted from him to the others. Earl, Lawrence. A lanky, unfamiliar man in a brown cloak over worker's clothes must have been one of the associates. I hadn't really been able to see their faces outside. Beside him sat another man, much bigger in build, with a bushy blond beard. And he, as it turned out, was familiar.

He was the same Lorandian who'd challenged me and Alan and then had later appeared at Lo Canne. The man clearly hadn't gotten a good look at me on the deck, and his eyes widened as recognition shot through him. I shrank back instinctively, though of course, I had nowhere to go.

Warren noted our reactions. "Do you know each other?"

My tongue felt thick, and even if I could've spoken, I had no idea what to say. What I knew with certainty was that there was no good answer I could give. After a few more moments of shock, he lumbered to his feet and pointed. "She—she was there! In Grashond!"

Perplexed, Warren glanced between us. "I know. She came to Cape Triumph by way of the north."

Flushing, the man shook his head. "She was in Constancy! We held up some of those Heirs, and she was with them. I know her face."

"I do too," said the other man slowly, also speaking with a Lorandian accent. He stood beside his partner, forehead wrinkled in thought. "Lo Canne. She was there with that trader . . . Robinson. Jacob Robinson, right? But she was Icori . . . wasn't she?"

From the larger man's startled expression, he hadn't noticed me at the trading camp. I had tried to stay out of his sight then, never expecting that someone else would get a good look at me and later cross my path.

"She was with the Heirs," Warren said. "But Lo Canne? That trading post? She wasn't there . . . were you, Tamsin?"

"Lo—what? A trading post? I ran into traders up north, I told you that. But I don't know that place. Is that the name of a company?"

My words were a perfect mix of confusion and guilelessness, but I hesitated too long in responding. I could see it in Warren's eyes. He knew I was lying, and a rush of emotions flashed over his face at that realization. Panic. Uncertainty. And sadness.

"I think you and I should go outside." He stood up and gave a small shake of his head when Earl and Lawrence did too. "Perhaps some air will help."

"All right then," I said, forcing a smile. "I won't mind seeing how everything's shaping up out there."

"Mister Doyle," said the bearded Lorandian, his eyes narrowed.

"I know," said Warren with a sigh. "I know."

He opened the door for me, and as I stepped out, I saw the others inside sit down and exchange grim looks. On deck, the captain and sailor barely noticed us as they hurried about. Most of their work was in the stern, controlling the rudder and sails, with occasional trips to the starboard side of the bow to check our trajectory. Warren led me to the port side of the bow, where the cabin mostly blocked us from view but not from the rain.

"Tamsin," Warren called over the wind, "I'm sure you heard some pretty strange-sounding things in there. A lot of odd things happen in stressful situations."

"Yes, of course."

Lightning flashed, the brief illumination showing a tight set to his features. "What exactly did you hear us talking about?"

"Not much of anything, to be honest. Too much noise from the storm."

Warren did nothing for several moments, and as the rain continued pouring down, I was about to ask if we could go back in when he said, "Tamsin, I can almost believe that, looking at your face now. There's no fear, mostly irritation at the rain. And the answer was good. Insisting you'd heard absolutely nothing wouldn't ring true. Maybe you really didn't hear anything. But those men—do you know them?"

I shook my head indignantly. "No! And it makes me terribly uneasy to have them looking at me like that—especially that big one. I don't understand what this is about."

Another brief flash showed him studying me intently. "You sound so sincere about that too. You're good, Tamsin. And clever. You can be whatever you need to be—adapt to any situation. I could've used that. Truly."

I shifted from foot to foot, again acutely aware that I had nowhere to go. "I'm not following, Mister Doyle. Can you explain it more, back inside?"

He didn't budge. "Given more time and trust, I think I could have made you understand our plans. I think you would have kept my secrets. But we didn't reach that point. And you *do* know those men. Or you recognize them, at least. You know what they were doing—and that's too big a secret for even you."

"I told you, I don't know them! I don't understand any of this."

"I'm sorry, Tamsin." Lightning forked, and his face really did look remorseful. "I can't risk that cleverness being used against me."

"Warren, I—"

He was so fast, I hardly saw him move. One moment, we were standing there, and the next, he was barreling into me. I fell back against the railing, and he was right there with me. He caught hold of my arms and shoved me up over the edge—and then I was falling down, down, down. Thunder trampled part of my scream, and the rest was lost in a mouthful of icy water as I plunged into Denham Bay.

CHAPTER 34

THIS IS DEATH.

It had to be. Nothing else could be so black, so cold, so smothering. As I flailed in a panicked attempt to gain any sort of bearing, some distant part of my mind was waiting for Ozhiel to take my hands and drag me down to his underworld.

Calm down, Tamsin. You're going to drag yourself *under.* I slowed my frantic struggles, which had no real result. I started to sink and then moved my arms in a gentler, more controlled way, rolling to my stomach and straightening my body. I floated up, just enough for my head to break the surface. I spit out the water in my mouth, took a gulp of air, and was promptly knocked back under when a wave hit me in the face. I emerged again, coughing, and managed to tread water, despite the heavy layers of skirts tangling my legs.

Blinking, I tried to get some sense of where I was. There was water everywhere. *Everywhere.* Coming from the sky, surrounding my body, still in my nose and throat. Sometimes I floated right along with the waves, bobbing up and down. Other times, they crashed into me, splashing my eyes and mouth. As I turned in place, I finally found what I sought: the boat. It was only a splotch of blackness, set with a few yellow lights, but there was no mistaking what it was. Or that it was moving away from me.

"Wait!" I yelled, instinct driving me to seek help from the only human source I had—even though that very source was the reason I needed help. The storm was too loud for anyone to hear me, though, and in the time it had taken me to recover, the boat had put a good deal of distance between us. I started to swim after it, using the long, sure strokes I'd learned as a child, never guessing back then that they could save my life after someone attempted to kill me.

But I soon stopped. There was no way I could catch up with it. I watched it get farther and farther away, soon melding into the rest of the black bay. Was Warren there, staring at the boat's wake? Watching where he'd sent me to drown? Probably not. He'd have to go to the stern for that, where the captain was. Warren had hurled me far enough, and I'd been under long enough, that the crew probably hadn't even noticed a thing. Surely the boat would be doubling back if the crew realized someone had gone over . . . right? Or was Warren's sway too strong?

I pushed those musings away. What went on in that boat made no difference to me now. My biggest priority—my *only* priority—was staying alive. Already, I was tiring from treading water. I was out of practice, and my clothes were heavy. Constantly having to readjust after waves struck my nose and eyes didn't help. And it was cold. Everything was so, so cold. A flare of lightning gave me a brief glimpse of the coast before darkness swallowed it up again. Yes, I could still see land, just like when I'd started out tonight. But did it matter, if I couldn't swim to it?

I had no choice. If I was going to drown, it might as well be trying to reach shore and not staying in one spot in the middle of the bay. In the lightning's unreliable illumination, the nearest land seemed to be in a more leftward direction than the boat had gone. Another wave broke against me, and after a moment of coughing, I set off for the coast. Decision made, I experienced a rush of energy as the adrenaline of determination went through me. I moved well, stayed strong, and didn't even swallow that much water.

And then . . . the fatigue came again. I had to stop a couple of times and rest from the more aggressive swimming just to catch my breath. But when I'd start up again, my muscles were still tired. I couldn't move as forcefully or cover the distance I had earlier. And when, on another break, I reassessed the shore, it seemed I'd hardly made progress at all. Panic started to make me falter. I was weakening. I didn't have the stamina to reach the shore. My strokes grew smaller, hardly moving me at all. I became less adept at keeping water out of my nose and mouth. And Six, it was cold.

Another bolt of lightning. They were becoming infrequent, and the wind and rain had lessened too. But in that flash, I saw something up ahead on the water—something red. It was there, and then gone. Was there another boat? If so, why didn't it have any lights? Hope gave me a second wind, and I swam in the direction I'd seen the blur of red, praying for more lightning. When it came, I saw I'd made progress toward that phantom object but that it was too small to be a boat. It had a roundish shape, and something stuck out from its top.

A buoy, I realized. The ones the captain had seen that marked the shoals. It wasn't a boat, but it did float. My second wind had faded by then, and I mustered what I could of a third one, pushing my body until my muscles burned and then pushing them some more. More than once, I thought I'd sink in exhaustion. But I kept thinking of Merry, Adelaide, Mira, Jago, and all the other people counting on me.

I reached it at last, my lungs bursting. The buoy was about three feet in diameter, with a flat top that gave it the appearance of a squashed barrel. A wooden pole with a wildly whipping flag jutted up from its center, and I used the pole as a handle to pull myself on top of the buoy. Gasping, aching, I collapsed against the flagpole and offered a silent prayer of thanks. I was alive.

I lay there for a long time, staring without seeing, just regaining my strength. The waves tossed the buoy around a bit, but I was never in danger of getting dunked. The wind grew still, and the rain diminished, spurring me to utter another prayer of thanks. But when I squinted, I could see lightning dancing among the clouds on the horizon, steadily coming closer. This was the eye, as deceptively calm as the ocean storm's had been. The onslaught would be back. I sat up a

little, using the pole for support again, and then realized the last place
I wanted to be in a thunderstorm was next to a tall, pointed object.

Actually, that was the next-to-last place I wanted to be. The *last*
one was the open water, and there was no way I was leaving the buoy.
As the storm's wrath rolled back in, I felt up and down the pole. It
was old and soaked, and I found one section I was certain was weaker
than the rest. I got on my knees, pushing and pulling with all of my
tepid strength, and incredibly, I broke the pole. Not gracefully. It was
splintery and jagged, but I'd taken a few feet off it. I was still the highest thing around, but there was nothing else to be done. Grasping the
broken pole, I curled up on the buoy, making myself as low as I could
while staying out of the water. And then I waited.

And waited. I not only had to wait out the storm as it returned with
its former intensity, I also had to wait out the night. I passed it in a
sort of exhausted daze but never truly slept. When morning arrived,
the sky was clear, and the rising sun finally gave me some sense of
direction. Following the curve of the coast, I could see that I appeared
to be in the southwestern part of the bay, which fit with what the
captain had said about seeing southern buoys. But again, just like last
night, even the closest section of shoreline was too far for me to swim
without a break. I put a hand to my eyes, trying to discern any other
buoys I could use as waypoints to land. There likely were some, but I
couldn't count on finding one.

So why not take this one with me? Knowing it'd have to happen
sooner or later, I jumped back into the water, crying out as I went
from just cold to freezing. I swam around the buoy, diving under a few
times to determine its setup. A rope extended from its bottom surface,
presumably down to an anchor somewhere. There was no way I could
untie it. The rope didn't feel like it was on the verge of disintegration,
but it was worn and waterlogged.

I climbed back up on top of the buoy and examined the flagpole
I'd broken. The little pennant was held on with two metal clasps. I
slid one off, and after hammering it against the buoy enough times,

managed to flatten it somewhat. One of the metal strip's corners was quite sharp, and I used it as a knife, beginning the long and painstaking process of going underneath the buoy, sawing away at the rope with my makeshift blade, and then coming back up for air. It was well into the morning when I finally broke the last strands of rope. The buoy popped free of its anchor and listed to one side.

I was worn out enough by then that I would've liked to rest again, but with nothing to hold it, the buoy was already drifting at the whims of the waves and light wind. Holding on to the buoy with my arms, I turned toward the shore and used my legs to propel me forward. I moved faster than I had swimming on my own, and although I was still worn out, I at least had the comfort of something to hold on to when I stopped—instead of simply sinking.

The sun was at its zenith when I finally staggered onto a shore of jagged gray rocks. I pulled the buoy with me and then sank onto the flattest spot I could find. I buried my face in my hands and started crying, softly at first, and then giving myself over to great sobs that shook my body and snatched at my breath. If my throat wasn't so raw, I would have screamed my frustration to the world.

When I finally calmed down, I took stock of what I knew. If I'd come from the southern section of Denham Bay, then I was in the northern part of Denham Colony. Northwest, I supposed, scrutinizing the shape of the coast. I was days from Cape Triumph, but in theory, all I had to do to reach it was follow the shore east. Or, if I headed due south I might hit a road like the one I'd taken in from Icori territory.

What else did I know? I was freezing. Even though the day had warmed up into another almost summery one, the icy water had chilled me to the bone. I kept moving my toes and poking my numbed limbs. They all still seemed to work.

I was hungry, thirsty, and exhausted. I had nothing but the drenched clothes I wore and whatever tools I could scrape together from the buoy. No one knew I was here, so no one would come looking for me.

Oh, and Warren Doyle wanted me dead.

Actually, he probably assumed I already was. I would too, in his position. Images from last night tumbled back through my mind, hardly seeming real. How had I gone from boarding a boat with dreams of being a governor's wife to being left for dead by said governor?

You do *know those men. Or you recognize them, at least. You know what they were doing—and that's too big a secret for even you.*

I didn't know what they were doing! And I'd never even seen the smaller one. I rubbed my forehead, trying to piece together the scraps of conversation I'd heard and what it could mean that a Lorandian who raided under the guise of an Icori was spending time with Warren. But it was all too much in my current state. The memories and bits of information slipped through my hands when I tried to hold on to them. The only thing I could be sure of was that I'd stumbled onto something powerful enough for Warren to try to kill me and face whatever fallout came of it in Cape Triumph.

It was that chilling thought that finally drove me to my feet. Someone paranoid enough to kill another person for overhearing a conversation might very well be paranoid enough to double-check his work. I salvaged everything I could from the buoy that might be useful later: the metal clasps, the pole, rope fragments, and even the flag itself. The rest of the buoy I hid in the forest behind the gravelly beach.

Then I slipped off into the trees, trying to use the sun as a guide to keep me headed south. If I could find a road, then maybe I could find help. I would have even settled for a trail to save me from picking my way through all the roots, undergrowth, and fallen branches. The weather might be pleasant now, but signs of the storm's passing were everywhere. Surveying all that it had knocked down in this forest made me wonder how Cape Triumph had fared. Had the storm taken out trees there? Buildings? Were my friends okay?

They were probably better off than me, I thought bitterly. No one had tried to kill them last night.

As I walked and gleaned some warmth from the sun, I tried again to pick through the jumble of last night's events. Five minutes before pushing me overboard, Warren had been planning to marry me. From his comments, he might have even been planning to make me a coconspirator in . . . what? That was the life-or-death question.

He had Lorandian associates, that I knew for a fact. Lorandians who'd been trying to make Osfridians and Icori think each was under attack by the other. Jago and I had been right about that—at least in the north.

My bride-to-be did what you couldn't. The north will be going soon, and Campbell's going to take most of the fort's number south. She helped do that too, though it also sounds like the attacks our agents did there and in the central colonies were a little more effective.

My steps slowed, and I leaned against a tree, partially to pull my thoughts together and partially because I was getting dizzy. *The attacks our agents did there and in the central colonies.* What agents did he mean? Not Lorandian ones, judging by the big man's indignation. *Our agents.* Osfridian agents? Was that the implication, that the Lorandians had staged skirmishes in the north and conspiring Osfridians had done them in other places—like the hunting camp along the East River?

I closed my eyes. If that was true, then Jago and I had been right about the reports of all the Icori raids being fabricated. They were just being done by different factions.

A drop of water splashed onto my forehead, and I blinked back to my surroundings. Another drop followed. Stepping aside, I squinted upward and saw the culprit: Water had pooled on a large leaf above me and finally lost its balance. I didn't know the tree type, but the other leaves that were open were also broad and curved down in a way that let water collect. I backtracked to a log I'd passed earlier and dragged it to the tree. Using it as a stool, I climbed up. I carefully plucked water-filled leaves off and slurped their contents. A few times, I found it easier to let the leaves stay as they were and just bring my mouth up to them.

When I didn't feel so parched anymore, I continued on but took a few of the cup-shaped leaves with me. My traveling outfit was actually in no way designed to be helpful for traveling, aside from two gold-embroidered pockets on the front of the skirt. I kept the leaves in there with some of my salvaged buoy bits. The water went a long way toward restoring me, but I wanted food too. Denham was in true spring now, but the pickings were slim. The most plentiful things I found were dandelion greens, and though they were edible, I knew too many would hurt the stomach, especially when dehydrated. I'd have to keep looking.

Just as twilight was approaching, I finally came to a road. It wasn't as wide or packed down as the one our caravan had taken to Cape Triumph, but it had seen enough wear to suggest it was used a lot. I turned onto it, putting the sunset behind me. I encountered no other travelers, but the road did cross a small, bubbling stream via a bare-bones wooden bridge. My thirst had returned, and I hopped down the bank. When I reached a particularly rapid part of the stream, I used my leaves to gather more water.

I'd have to camp for the night, I realized. I had no tent or cloak for protection, though. In their attempts to teach Gideon to live in the wild, Briga and Eroc had talked about shelters, but I'd only half listened. Could I build one? I had no construction knowledge, save watching Pa on some of his jobs. The storm had made the woods a feast of building materials, so surely something could be managed.

Earlier in the day, I'd hoped to find other people who might offer direction. Once evening's shadows grew longer, though, I decided it might be wiser to pass the night without encountering any strangers. I walked upstream until I felt I was far enough from the road to avoid detection. After a lot of trial and error with various tree and plant materials, I ended up with a lean-to type of structure composed of fallen limbs set against a sloping section of land above the streambed. I "thatched" the outside of the limbs with pine boughs and dried leaves, weaving some in and just piling up others. It made a snug little enclosure that would keep me out of sight and reasonably warm.

I decided to pass on a fire, as much as I longed for the extra heat. It was another way to attract attention, and I had nothing to cook over it. I'd have to put it out before sleeping anyway. My clothes, though stiff, had dried, and the weather was far milder than what I'd camped in farther north. That left me with deepening shadows as the sun set and no way to banish them. It was probably just as well; I needed the sleep. I trekked down to get one last drink of water, and as I knelt at the rushing stream, the fleeting light caught a flash of silver that quickly vanished.

Fish. The clawing sensation in my empty stomach intensified, just thinking about fish cooked over a campfire. That, at least, was something I'd paid attention to with the Icori. I'd learned all about how they set their clever fish traps and cages out in the river each night. The problem was, I had nothing even remotely close to that on hand and no way to build one. Maybe by weaving dried vines? I had no time to find them. I stared at the stream, my insides aching. Some of the Icori traps had clever flaps that let fish come in but not exit. A couple of baskets had simply relied on the current funneling fish in who then had trouble finding the way out.

Conscious of the rapidly growing darkness, I scouted the closest parts of the stream and found one where the bed bulged out a little. I gathered every rock and stick I could obtain quickly, not screening for size or uniformity, using them to construct a barrier that was a hybrid of wall and fence, stacking rocks and shoving in sticks until I'd sectioned off the bulbous part. I made my barrier like the Icori baskets, open and wide on the upstream side, narrowing to a point on the downstream side. The Icori used bait, which I didn't have time for, so I'd just have to hope for fish straying in on their own and being too stupid to find the way out.

And with that, I crawled into my lean-to, pulling a few more branches against it to close off the opening. I rolled to my side and was wondering how I'd ever fall asleep in such strange conditions when, pushed past exhaustion, I dropped into a deep slumber.

∽

I woke to birds singing and bright sunshine pouring in through the cracks of my roof. I wiggled my way out and stretched muscles that had stiffened from both the cramped quarters and hours of swimming. Walking to the stream, I brushed off leaves and dirt that had stuck to me overnight, as well as a few bugs I tried not to think too much about. Yawning, I crouched at the river for a morning drink and tried to gauge the time. Well past sunrise. I'd slept in, which was understandable. Now I had to—

I sprang to my feet. I'd forgotten all about my hasty fish trap. But there, about ten feet downstream, one fish not quite as long as my hand butted obstinately against the rocks. I whooped with joy before I could stop myself, feeling as victorious as I would have taking down a wolf with my bare hands. I quickly snatched the fish out before it could escape, and built a fire that Briga wouldn't have criticized too much. I gutted the fish as best I could with sharp sticks and the blade I'd made from the buoy latch and then set it to cooking on a skewer. The minutes dragged by as I stared at it, and I had to stay my hand from pulling it off too early.

When I finally deemed it edible, I nearly burned myself in my haste to get it off. I ate with little grace and no silverware, and it was delicious.

I found the road again and resumed my journey east—or east-ish, seeing as the road didn't stay perfectly straight. Food and sleep had done wonders, and I moved at a brisk pace. About midday, I finally encountered other travelers on the road. The sound of hooves alerted me to them before they came into view, and I quickly ducked behind some roadside bushes, hoping for a safe and friendly family. Three men on horseback trotted by instead, their clothes rough and practical, and after a moment's deliberation, I stayed concealed. I couldn't say from a glance if they were trustworthy or not, and yesterday's events had left me wary. What I did note was that they carried no supplies. Even considering the ground a horse could cover, they must have come from a settled place.

That gave me hope. I felt a lot better about finding help in a small town than from strangers on an isolated road. I set off again, and about two hours later, I came to a small crossroads marked with a hand-carved wooden sign that named my current road as the Bay Highway. The small intersecting road had no name, but beside an arrow pointing south, letters read: 30 MILES TO GOVERNOR'S HIGHWAY, 100 MILES TO CAPE TRIUMPH.

I knew the Governor's Highway. We'd taken it from the East River. It was the most direct route across Denham to Cape Triumph. But 130 miles! That'd take almost six days on foot. I was farther west than I'd realized, but I had little choice if I wanted to get back to the Glittering Court and Merry.

An arrow pointing east, where I was headed on the Bay Highway, was labeled: COTESVILLE ROAD, TO NEWVILLE—10 MILES.

Cotesville? Where had I heard that name? In a flash, the memory came rushing back: Mister Elkhart, parting ways from our caravan, shortly after we'd crossed the border into Denham. *Going to drop Robinson's stuff off in Rushwick on my way to Cotesville.*

Rushwick was where Jago's land was! Was I near it? I peered around as though the forest with its rustling leaves and singing birds might offer some direction. Mister Elkhart had gone north from the Governor's Highway, and his comment had suggested Rushwick came before Cotesville from that direction. If I was putting everything together correctly now on my mental map, I was on the opposite side. I'd reach Cotesville first, with Rushwick somewhere after.

Except Cotesville itself was not marked on the sign—only Cotesville Road. But generally, roads named after towns led to those towns. If I could find Cotesville, could I find Jago's home? Could I find Jago?

All the feelings I'd been trying to bury these long weeks, all the longing for him . . . it came bursting forth in a great rush. I nearly ran off then and there. But what would I accomplish? What would finding Jago mean?

Safety. There was no question I had to eventually return to Cape Triumph for Merry, but I didn't know what would be waiting for me. Did anyone even know something amiss had happened? Had Warren told them anything? Or had he continued on to Hadisen, leaving others in blissful ignorance about me? I knew I'd find safety at Wisteria Hollow, but I had no idea how long it would last if someone was intent on killing me.

There were very few people I could trust right now, I realized. But Jago was one of them. And he had the resources and wits to help me make sense of this disaster I'd fallen into. The urgency to go to him burned within my chest, and while, yes, my overall well-being was on the line, I also selfishly, desperately wanted to see him again.

But would he want to see me?

Yes, I decided. Or, well, he would see me, even if he didn't want to. And he would help me, despite what I'd done to him. Because that's how he was. That realization should have relieved me as I began to walk, but mostly, it made me sad.

Two hours later, a small and unmarked road crossed mine. It had to be the Cotesville Road, based on the timing. But where was Cotesville? North or south? Where was Newville, the town referenced on the sign? Unease filled the pit of my stomach as I glanced back and forth and weighed my options. At last, I turned south. The road's northern section looked less traveled. If there were three towns that way, I'd expect more traffic. And due north led to the bay. I hadn't traveled that far from it; it seemed unlikely there'd be three towns in so small a distance. The odds leaned south, and if it turned out I'd misjudged, I'd most certainly hit the Governor's Highway eventually and could continue on to Cape Triumph.

There were a lot of *ifs* and leaps in my deduction, but that was pretty much all I was going on lately. I traveled the rest of the day without finding any sign of human habitation, which made me worry I wasn't even on the Cotesville Road. As it grew a little wider and more worn, though, I took comfort in knowing I was at least on some main thoroughfare. But would it lead me to Jago?

I camped another night and set out at first light. Not long after that, I scored a victory when I came upon the town of Newville. "Town" was something of a stretch, though. It mostly consisted of a few bare buildings set back from the road. Beyond them, where the forest grew deeper, I heard the sound of wood being chopped. Newville was some sort of lumber camp, it seemed. I saw no residents and wouldn't have given those buildings a second glance if not for another road sign identifying the settlement. And on it, underneath NEWVILLE, were words that made my heart sing: COTESVILLE—10 MILES.

I was on the right course! Half a day's travel, and I'd hopefully find some answers. I might even find Jago, depending on how far Rushwick was. Even though that had been my plan in turning south yesterday, the idea of actually seeing him was startling. Part of me had doubted it could ever happen again, and I spent those next ten miles in a nonstop whirl of emotions. Exhilaration. Regret. Nervousness. Fear.

I would understand if he didn't love me anymore. I almost expected it, after what I'd done to him. But what if he didn't . . . like me anymore? What if he didn't respect me? Imagining those warm, friendly green-and-gold eyes turning cold made a pit open up in my stomach.

That dreary thought sapped some of my vigor, and my steps began to flag, until I caught the faint sound of wagons and voices ahead. As I regained my speed, the noises grew louder and louder, and before I knew it, I was strolling into Cotesville. There was no missing it. It was a real town, a little bigger than Constancy, bustling with people going about their daily tasks and businesses selling their services.

I found a general store and sold my broach, which was about the only thing of value I had on me. Most of the money went toward food, but I also got a few other handy things: flint, a tiny knife, twine, and a water skin. It all just fit in an old sack the storekeeper gave me for free after eyeing my bedraggled state. I was almost tempted by a fresh set of clothes but instead settled for a plain cotton apron to cover the dirty and matted velvet. Food mattered more.

The storekeeper told me Rushwick was another twenty miles south, and I wanted to be prepared. I didn't know what I'd find there, if I'd even find Jago at all. I might very well be right back out in the woods or on the Governor's Highway. And though I had gotten pretty adept at building fish traps on the creek running alongside the Cotesville road, I couldn't count on that option either.

I left Cotesville in late afternoon, making camp around sunset. When I set out again in the morning, the land began to change. After the endless forest of western Denham, I was surprised to see the trees thin out, giving way to rolling hills and meadows of some of the greenest grass I'd ever encountered. Once, I spied a large, affluent country house a ways off the road. Several horses pranced happily on the emerald-green pasture, and I felt tears well in my eyes, thinking how Jago must love this place.

When I reached Rushwick proper, I found it was more developed than Newville but a long ways from being anything like Constancy or Cotesville. Rushwick was a fledgling town emerging as a result of the increased development of those swathes of green. They were apparently especially well-suited for grapes, hemp, and—horses.

"Most residents live outside of town on farms and plantations," a harried storekeeper named Branson Myers told me. He specialized in seed and was also a member of the town's governing council. Someone on the street had referred me to him when I'd come asking about Jago. "I don't know half of the townspeople," he said. "Excuse me a moment."

I waited until Mister Myers finished up with a customer before asking more about Jago. "Isn't there some . . . I don't know, directory?"

He guffawed. "That would be great, wouldn't it? The area built up too quickly. Last year, the governor opened up land here, and *bam*!" Mister Myers clapped his hands for emphasis. "There was a mad rush. Which is great, ultimately—I mean, most of them buy their seed from me—but we didn't have the manpower to keep up with the details, if you know what I mean. When there were a dozen landowners, me and the other four councilmen took turns playing clerk. Never even bothered with a town manager or assessor. Now, there's more than fifty. Hang on."

"But I have an address," I said, once he'd tended to his next task. "Orchard End."

"Still doesn't help. Not me, at least. I'm sure it's in one of the ownership deeds. We've got those—but they're not very well organized."

"I think he only just bought it. Or he might be about to—he was leasing it."

"Oh, one of those? They aren't organized at all. Hey, Bill? Hold on a minute, I'll be right back."

Mister Myers led me two doors down to a building labeled TOWN OFFICE. He unlocked the door and waved grandly at a small room with a dilapidated desk and dusty stacks of paper.

"If you want to try and find it, you're welcome to it," he said. "You can't really make things worse."

Gaping, I stared in disbelief at the chaotic scene. I walked around and perused some of the stacks, which had no system that I could identify. Official stamped and sealed documents from Cape Triumph were mixed with handwritten notes. There were land deeds, tax records, birth certificates, business licenses, budgets, and requisitions for basic town needs. Alphabetical and numerical ordering didn't exist. The closest thing I saw to organization was a stack marked FOR CLERK TO DO. The top page in that stack was a job advertisement for a clerk.

"Are you serious?" I finally asked.

Mister Myers leaned against the door. "Yeah. It is kind of a mess, isn't it? On second thought, how about this: Stick around town a week or so, and I'll see if I can get the banker's boy to come work on it for you." He paused to take in my appearance, which had improved since yesterday. It might have been silly given the circumstances, but conscious of seeing Jago again, I'd taken the time to clean myself up as best I could, even going so far as to plait my hair. "Someone like you shouldn't have to fix our problems."

I might have agreed with him, but his word choice made me do a double take. "Someone like me?"

"Sure." He waved a hand in my general direction. "You've got a little travel wear and tear, but you're obviously a young lady of some refinement who doesn't deal with disasters like this."

I looked around again, assessing the quiet, messy office. Then I mentally contrasted it with being tossed about in an ocean tempest, accosted by Balanquans, punished by followers of a fringe religion, descending into a giant chasm, running into a burning barn, and being shoved off a boat to drown. Mister Myers gave me a puzzled look, and I realized I was smiling—not so much because this was funny but because it was ridiculous. After all I'd endured, this next stage in my survival came down to organizing papers.

"Mister Myers," I said, trying not to laugh like a lunatic. "Lately, all 'someone like me' deals with is disasters. And this? This is not a disaster. Give me a meal and a bed that's not a pile of leaves, and I'll fix this up in no time."

Without waiting for his response, I dove right into the first stack I saw. He stood around for a few minutes, watching me like I might be a crazy person, and then he quietly slipped out. When he shut down his store and returned that evening, I had about three-quarters of the office organized. But I still hadn't located Jago.

Mister Myers' face filled with awe, either because of my accomplishment or because I was still around. "Why don't you call it a night," he said. "My house is down the street. Ellen—my wife—will fix you up a bed and some supper. No leaves."

The offer beat building another fish trap. I accepted, and then came right back the next morning. It was noon when I finally located any mention of Jago, and I almost missed it. He was a footnote—as Jacob Robinson—at the bottom of a deed for land owned by someone else. The note said that a deal was in place for Jago to take ownership upon paying a prearranged sale price, at which point the estate's name would change from Grassy Hill to Orchard End. In the meantime, Jago had rental rights, and details of the payment schedule's current status were on file in Rushwick's bank.

I was so excited, I wanted to hurl the paper aside and run out the door, but there was no way I was messing up all my hard work. Before returning it neatly to its place, I reread all of the financial terms. It was a lot of land and had a steep price. I clenched the paper and bowed my head as a wave of anguish washed over me. Jago had nearly sacrificed all of this.

Branson knew of Grassy Hill and hadn't realized a sale was pending. He gave me directions, and I set out with trepidation. When I reached the location, I could see instantly how it had gotten both names. The farm's house sat on a hill that was, in fact, grassy. The rest of the property swept out, smooth and flat, and most of it was covered in apple trees. Some were green and full, likely to sprout blossoms any day. Others were dead, twisted, and gray. The buildings on the property were just as mixed. The home on the hill was in disrepair, and part of its roof was sinking in. A storage shed and barns were in equally bad shape.

On one end of the property, though, a large stable was flanked by two small shanties. All three stood straight and sturdy, gleaming with new yellow timber. No apple trees were near them, and a couple of stumps suggested recent clearing. Beyond the stable, a fence of that same new wood enclosed a broad pasture. My old friends Pebble and Dove were within, along with four other horses.

There was so much peace and beauty here; I was almost afraid to intrude on it. But Jago was somewhere in this dreamland, and I had to find him. Even if he wouldn't help me, I needed to see his face again and hear his voice. If I could just have those things, I felt certain I'd be able to handle whatever madness came next in my journey.

I crossed the property and walked up to the fence to get a better look. One of the horses was a silvery gray, remarkably similar to Dove and Pebble. A solid black mare grazed by a colt almost identical in color, except for a white star on its forehead. And on the farthest side of the pasture, the fourth horse lifted her head and looked at me. She had a tawny coat, almost brandy colored, speckled with ivory. Her hair, however, was the extraordinary part. She had a mane that was pale gold in color, with a length and volume I'd expect more in a lion. I'd never seen a horse with a mane that long or with that kind of thickness. Her tail had the same kind of drama, and more of that golden hair grew on her feet, ringing her hooves like little clouds.

I leaned against the rail and smiled. "So you're Felicia, eh?" I murmured. "You *are* a pretty thing, I'll give you that."

Movement in my periphery made me jump up. A tall, hulking figure approached me, his bearded face puzzled. I gasped when I realized who he was. "Arnaud! I can't believe it." When he just stared, I took my kerchief off, in case that was confusing anything. "It's me, Tamsin Wright. From Grashond. Don't you remember? Arnaud?"

No flicker of recognition showed in the big man's face. A voice off to my other side said, "That's not Arnaud. It's his brother—Alexi. I told you you can't tell them apart."

Slowly, disbelievingly, I turned around and found Jago smiling at me.

CHAPTER 35

HE WAS THERE.

He was there, and he was real, and he was wonderful. After all the ups and downs—mostly downs—I'd experienced, one good thing had finally come my way. I was afraid to take my eyes off him, lest one blink make him disappear. I had to rest my hands on the fence to stop myself from trembling.

Jago wore that smile of his—that easy, open smile that somehow seemed to know all your secrets. It undid me. That, and those eyes. Those wondrous, bewitching eyes. Feeling flustered as the silence stretched—and also conscious of Alexi's puzzled gaze—I attempted an air of control and said: "Well, are you just going to stand there and stare, Jago, or are you going to invite me in like a civilized person?"

His grin grew so wide, it was a wonder his cheeks didn't hurt. "Oh, Tamsin," he said. "I've missed you." He spoke to Alexi in halting Belsian, and the big man nodded and trotted off. Jago watched him a moment and then waved me forward. "Okay, Tamsin. Come see my palace."

I expected him to lead me to the big house, but we instead went to one of the newly constructed shanties. The one we entered was even smaller than his cabin in Grashond. It was more like a tent that happened to have wooden walls. "'Palace' might have been overselling it," he told me, taking a kettle from the hearth.

I laughed and sat on a braided rug, seeing as there were no chairs or table. "If you knew what I'd been sleeping in, you'd know this is pure luxury. Sleeping in your sleigh was pure luxury, actually, compared to a riverbank."

He poured two cups of lukewarm tea and then joined me on the rug, taking off his hat. His sun-streaked hair was damp with sweat, his cheeks ruddier than the last time I'd seen him. He wore an old button-up shirt that might have been white once, its sleeves rolled up to the elbows. He couldn't stop smiling, and I realized I wasn't the only one doing a lot of staring.

"A riverbank? What do you . . ." His eyes flicked down, and the smile faltered just a little as he took in my clothes. "Good grief, Tamsin. What happened to you? Green is still your color, but . . ."

I ran my hands over my skirt. I'd cleaned most of the dirt off, but the velvet was matted and dull. I untied the apron, revealing the rest. "I figured you would've noticed right away and tried to sell me something new."

"Why would I be looking at a dress when I had your beautiful face in front of me? But I probably can rustle something up for you. Now. Where have you been? Did you . . . you did get to Cape Triumph, didn't you?"

"Yes. And then I went some other places. The middle of Denham Bay, for one."

I launched into my story, stumbling briefly when I described how I was nearly engaged to Warren Doyle. That was a necessary part, though, and as I delved into everything else, the awkwardness faded. I grew more impassioned as I spoke, my emotions bubbling over. For the last few days, I'd lived through incredible circumstances, forcing myself to focus on survival. Now, removed from them, actually describing them, I felt the full onslaught of just how dire my situation had been. It slammed into me, and all the fear I'd had to repress to get through each day now came out. I didn't realize how much I was shaking, how frantic my words became, or that I even had tears in my eyes until Jago drew me to him, resting my head against his chest.

"Okay, okay. It's okay now," he said gently. "You're safe. We'll figure this out."

I squeezed my eyes shut. "I was afraid you'd turn me away. I was afraid you'd never want to see me again."

"All I've wanted for weeks is to see you again." His fingers curled into my hair, winding the strands around his hand.

"But after what I did to you . . . it was terrible . . ."

He leaned his head down, resting his cheek against my forehead as he thought over his response. "I know why you did it. You *shouldn't* have done it. But I know why you did."

"Of course I should have. I wasn't going to let you give up everything you've worked for!" Even in my bleak state, I couldn't help a spark of indignation.

"It was mine to give up," he insisted.

"And mine to refuse!" Realizing the argument was quickly going to spin around futilely, I sighed and let it go. "I'm sorry, Jago. I don't regret saving you from yourself, but I am sorry it had to happen like it did. You must have been so angry when you realized the fort was a trick."

"Angry? No. Shocked, maybe." He paused. "Heartbroken."

I felt my own heart break at those words. "Oh, Jago. I'm so sorry for hurting you."

His tone turned rueful. "Well, it was a little comfort to think you'd at least be safe and well-provided for with some other lucky lovestruck man."

Silence.

"I want to laugh at that," I said finally. "But I think I'd start crying pretty fast."

"Well, we can't have that." He helped me stand. "Come take a look at what you saved. We'll get you fed and cleaned up. Then, we'll figure out what to do next."

"But I—"

"Food and bath first."

Outside, the sun beat down, daring me to claim it had ever been cold in Adoria. Jago formally introduced me to Alexi, as well as the horses. The silver mare was Breeze—Pebble and Dove's mother. The black mare was Winsome, and her colt was Desmond. Jago's face shone as he described their personalities and petted the ones who came to see us at the fence. Felicia stayed away, though.

"She's jealous of you," Jago teased.

"Well, I'm jealous of her hair. I've never seen such a thing on a horse. Is that why everyone gushes over her?"

"Partly. But she's agile too, lots of endurance." His eyes lit up. "And when you let her run, she's faster than lightning."

We climbed the grassy slope up toward the house, pausing at the door to survey the vista around us. Green, green everywhere. Smooth and rolling like the sea on an easy day. A gnarled lilac bush by the house perfumed the air, and the horses grazed contentedly in the pasture. Near the barn, Alexi knelt near a leafless tree, digging at its base.

Jago pointed. "The old owners never thought about using this land for horses. It was all apple trees when they came over from Osfrid, and they maintained them for almost thirty years. When the husband died, his wife went to live with their son out east. They hired workers for a while but soon stopped and just let things go."

"And that's when you came along?" I asked.

"Not right away. I came along about ten years later. The mistress's son had been wanting to sell, but she wouldn't allow it. When I saw it, I knew it was perfect, but I didn't have nearly enough money." He crossed his arms over his chest, gazing about fondly. "I tracked them down, got a feel for her, and made a deal that won her over. I can be pretty persuasive, you know."

"Yeah, I think I heard that somewhere," I remarked straight-faced.

"I agreed to keep some of the orchard and restore the house. In exchange, we worked out a longtime payment plan, during which I could keep the horses here and start some of the labor. Her son would've preferred to sell it all in one go, but by then, he was ready for any sale."

"And so, here you are."

Jago answered with a lopsided smile and slipped his arm around me. "Here I am."

"If you're supposed to keep the orchard, why is Alexi digging that tree out?" I asked.

"Because it's dead. Half of them are. We're trying to clear those out, but it's a long, hard process. Makes fixing up this house seem easy, and that's quite a feat too. Take a look."

He used an ancient key to unlock the front door, opening it with a creak. Entering the house reminded me of stories I'd heard of great tombs in faraway lands, where emperors were buried with all their goods. The rooms were all furnished and decorated, just as if they were in use. The layers of dust suggested otherwise, as did the disrepair. It wasn't just the house's structure that had worn with time. Some of the furniture and rugs were also falling apart.

"This is why you guys sleep in the sheds," I said, peering up at a warped section of ceiling.

"Yup. I'd rather welcome you here, but I also don't want the attic collapsing on you." We continued through the kitchen to the house's still room. The scent of herbs lingered in the air from where they'd been hung from the vaulted rafters.

"This'll be incredible when it's restored," I said. "It's a rival to any of the fine houses I saw in Cape Triumph."

"You visited a few of those, I imagine?" Jago moved to one wall where an old bathtub was lying upside down. He flipped it over and knocked away some spiders.

"Did you doubt me?"

"Never," he said good-naturedly, hoisting the tub up. "Grab the door there, please."

We trekked back across the property to his shanty. He set the tub down with a thump and wiped sweat from his forehead with a wrinkled handkerchief. "If you don't mind the heat, you can have a bath now. Otherwise, it should start cooling down in a few hours."

It took me a moment to realize what he was getting at. "Oh, I don't need a hot one. Cold water's fine."

"After swimming in Denham Bay? No. You get a hot one."

I ran a hand over my hair, which was limp and oily from days without a proper washing. "Then I don't mind the heat."

"I figured. Be right back."

When he returned, he carried a basin of steaming water and had Alexi in tow. Alexi greeted me in Belsian and handed over a basket of bread, cheese, and dried apples. Jago dumped the water into the bathtub and covered it with a tarp. Then, after urging me to eat, he and Alexi departed once more. When they came back, each with a hot basin this time, I tried again to deter them.

"What are you doing? That's enough," I exclaimed. "You don't need to be traipsing about with tubs of hot water on a day like this!"

"It's no bother," Jago said in his cheery way. "We've already got more heating up on a fire out there."

Guiltily, I ate the food while they labored. When the bath was finally ready, Jago left me with soap and a large trunk. "I offloaded a lot of my goods when I got to Denham, but lucky for you, I've still got some women's clothes. Take what you want. We've got a few things that need to be taken care of this afternoon, but I'll check on you later."

I looked around at the steaming tub, clothes, and remnants of my meal. A lump formed in my throat. "Jago . . ."

He opened the door and winked. "I know."

I didn't get around to the clothes before he returned because I never left the tub. Once I'd given myself a thorough scrubbing, I went through and scrubbed again, even though it left some of my skin pink and raw. I just kept feeling like I had layers of grime to remove and had to hold back from a third washing. Instead, I contented myself by lounging back in the sudsy water, luxuriating in this brief respite.

Jago didn't look entirely surprised to see me still there when he came back. "Isn't it cold now?"

"Lukewarm."

He poured himself a cup of water and then knelt down in a corner, putting a polite distance between us. "Then we should heat more water and refill it."

"No! I'll be out soon." I leaned my head back against the tub's edge and stared upward. "And then it really is time to figure out what to do. I know I have to get back to Cape Triumph, but from there . . ."

"Wait a few days," Jago advised. "He might be able to put off dealing with your disappearance in the short term, but if enough time goes by, he's going to have to commit to some story. Your return will contradict that. Otherwise, he'll be able to improvise."

"I'm in no rush to get back there," I admitted. "Not until Merry comes, of course. But I hate the thought of Mira and the others thinking something's happened to me. I can't put her through that again."

"Better others think something happened to you than something actually happening." He mulled that over and then focused back on me, meeting my eyes over the side of the tub. "Something very nearly did! I think you really do have an angel looking after you to keep getting out of these scrapes."

"That, or I'm just too stubborn to die."

"I'm glad of it either way, but it's time to make sure these close calls end. You can't go back to Cape Triumph just so Warren can try to kill you again, and the way to prevent that is by figuring out why he wanted to kill you in the first place."

"Because the Lorandian man recognized me—and I recognized him. I knew that he wasn't really Icori."

"You knew that before. Harper believed you."

"Yes, but when we realized an actual Osfridian had attacked that fishing settlement, Harper didn't believe all the reported skirmishes were staged. I'm sure that's why the other reports he heard—thanks to me—helped spur him to shuffle soldiers around."

"But you think that Osfridian wasn't so much a disgruntled settler breaking the treaties as someone ordered by Warren to stir up trouble?"

So much of that night on the bay felt surreal and fragmented, but there was something in the way Warren had referred to his agents conducting attacks—and the way the Lorandian had bristled at the comparison to his own acts—that made me certain of the theory.

"Yes," I finally said. "I don't think Warren singlehandedly is arranging all these attacks along the borders, but he's part of whatever group is. The Icori and colonists each think the others are attacking, and that's going to lead to real retaliation—if it hasn't already. Now, the central armies are off to intervene, which could make things worse. Why would Warren want a war with the Icori?"

"Someone usually profits in war. You said he was talking about ammunition. Maybe he wants to sell it?" I could tell Jago didn't really believe that, though.

"Surely there are better ways to make money. Especially for someone whose colony's biggest export is gold." I started to sit upright, then stopped, too uncertain of my situation with Jago to parade around naked. "But maybe it's not for us to figure out. Warren obviously doesn't want others to know this information, so there must be someone it makes sense to."

"Agreed. And we'll make sure it gets shouted in the streets. We'll head out to Cape Triumph later this week."

"We?"

"We," he replied, giving me a pointed look. "I mean, we all know you're a master fisherwoman, but there are parts of the Governor's Highway that aren't near water. I've got to go with you, if only so you won't starve. Besides, I've got some things I wouldn't mind selling in the city."

"Oh, well, if it's that, then I don't mind," I teased. "I was worried you thought I couldn't take care of myself."

"Don't suggest ridiculous things, Tamsin. Now, if you want to stay in there, you're going to have to let me get more water."

"Just something to dry off with."

He handed me a worn but clean flannel blanket and then moved away, keeping his back to me. I stepped out, dripping, and dried myself off before wrapping the blanket around me as a makeshift dress. Jago glanced over when I knelt by the trunk.

"If nothing fits, feel free to just wear that."

"Jago Robinson, *you're* the one who needs to stop suggesting ridiculous things."

"Right. Sorry. I'll try harder to be a gentleman."

"Oh, it's not that," I said, lifting out a simple dress of sky-blue lawn. "It's just that you'd never be able to get a lick of work done around here, and I could hardly live with myself." Getting to my feet, I held the dress up to me. "I don't suppose you've got a sewing kit in your treasure trove?"

"I do—right over there, actually. I was trying to mend one of my shirts."

I peered at the pile of cloth he indicated. "'Try' implies you actually did something."

He shrugged. "I was getting to it. There's just a lot to do. In fact, I've got to get back to work—can't let Alexi dig those trees out on his own. And there'll be no living with Felicia if she's not groomed soon."

"What am I supposed to do while we wait to go to Cape Triumph?"

"Whatever you want. There are books in the house to read. I've got things to write with. Or just relax. You've earned it." He walked over to me, rested his hands on my shoulders, and kissed my forehead. "I don't have heaps of jewels, but you can still practice being a lady of leisure."

I placed my palms flat on his chest. "Thank you, Jago," I said softly. "I don't know why you're so nice to me."

"You know why. I'm crazy about you. That hasn't changed."

"After everything I've done to you? More like just crazy."

"Same difference."

I inched forward and kissed him, my lips just barely grazing his at first and then moving in with more certainty. His fingers slid slowly from my shoulders, down along my bare arms, and finally settled around my waist. I reached up and hooked one of my hands behind his neck to bring us closer, my lips parting further. A rush of heat radiated through me, and taking one of his hands, I moved it up to the edge of where the blanket folded around me. His fingers immediately started to loosen it, and then he abruptly sprang back.

"What?" I asked, startled. A bit of panic—and embarrassment—started to flicker in me, that I might have misread him. "I'm not judging you on gentlemanly behavior right now."

"Yeah, I gathered that." His gaze pointedly flicked to where my hands had caught the blanket as it started to slip. "But you should be judging me on how sweaty I am. I'm the one who needs a bath now."

"Really? I didn't notice. I was too busy looking at your beautiful face."

"You didn't seem to be looking at it that much, but I get the sentiment." He gave me another quick kiss on the forehead and then retreated toward the door, his eyes running over me one last time. "I'll see you at suppertime."

I followed him to the door and leaned in its frame to watch him walk away. Or was he sauntering? It was hard to say, but I liked the way he moved. I liked the way he felt too, and my flesh still tingled from our brief encounter. After a few more moments, I sighed and shut the door. Wrapping my arms around myself, I looked around the tiny room and wondered two things. First, how exactly one went about being a lady of leisure. And second, how I ever thought I could be serious about anyone besides Jago.

As it turned out, I could not, in fact, do the leisure thing so well. After hemming the blue dress, I continued on to mending Jago's shirt. Then I found a few of his other clothes that needed cleaning, so I filled one of the smaller basins with water and soap to wash his laundry and mine. I didn't know if the velvet could be salvaged, but I used every trick Ma had taught me.

When that was drying, I poked around the shanty looking for other things that needed cleaning or fixing. Jago was a neat housekeeper, all things considered, though he also didn't have much in his house that actually needed keeping. I found the writing implements and penned a letter to Merry. Just as I was taking down the laundry, the door swung open, and Jago rushed in with a small covered kettle. Behind him, the sky blazed orange.

He set the kettle down and brushed a kiss across my lips. "Sorry I can't stay for supper. Desmond chipped a hoof."

And like that, he was gone. I found what tasted like venison stew in the kettle and wondered if it was Alexi's handiwork. I washed the dishes when I was done eating and then noted that the tub of my bath-water had been forgotten. I couldn't lift it by myself, so I emptied it in batches, one basin at a time. By then, it was almost fully dark outside. A light shone from the barn window, and I heard the sound of clanging.

When the tub was emptied, I started heating new batches of water. I couldn't do it as efficiently as the men had, but by the time Jago returned, the tub was filled again and had retained enough heat to still give off a little steam. He didn't notice it right away. He took off his hat and boots and started telling me about Desmond. When Jago did see the tub, he came to a halt.

"Did you do that?"

"You said you needed a bath."

He studied it a bit longer and then took in the rest of my small chores. "Tamsin, you might be stunningly smart, but you don't understand what 'leisure' means."

"Quiet," I snapped. "It's going to cool off if you keep wasting time."

And so, we switched roles, with him immersing himself into suds and me waiting discreetly to the side. He told me more about the farm, and I listened, my heart happy to see him happy. It was a rare, comfortable moment of peace.

"You haven't said anything in a while," he observed, when he'd finished describing some mishap with a stump. "You okay?"

"Just thinking, that's all."

"About what?"

"That I don't want to leave." I gestured to the neatly folded laundry.

"I think I was happier working here today than I was at any of those fancy parties I've been at this month."

His bright expression sobered a little. "Ah. Well. I don't really want you to leave either. But of course, you have to."

"Yeah," I said, wilting a bit. His answer wasn't a surprise; we both knew the nature of the life I'd signed on for.

And then he said, "But once you've reported on Warren and picked up Merry, you can come back."

I lifted my head. "What? Jago—"

"Don't. I know what you're going to say. And no, I won't give up the horses and the land. And no, I don't know how we'll make it work yet." A spark of his earlier amusement returned. "Besides, you've been here for one day. Let's see what you'll say in a few more. You might be running back to Cape Triumph without me."

"Jago," I said quietly, "I don't want to go anywhere without you."

He was left at one of his rare losses of words. Finally: "Don't look at me like that, not when I'm soaking wet and can't come hug you."

I stood up with a blanket and strolled over, tilting my head to peer at the water. "Hmm."

"That's not a very ladylike way to look at a man in a bathtub," he noted, reaching for the blanket. I kept it away.

"No. I was just noticing that the water's not really dirty. Is it still warm?"

"Mostly."

I dropped the blanket and began to unbutton my dress. "I bet it'd be warmer with two."

"I bet half the water'll end up on the floor with two," he said wryly, though he didn't take his eyes off the buttons.

I paused. "Do you want me to stop?"

He sat up and shifted over. "Stop suggesting ridiculous things and get in here."

CHAPTER 36

I WORKED AS HARD IN THE NEXT COUPLE OF DAYS AS I had among the Heirs, as hard as I had in Osfro. And I loved every moment of it.

I saw little of Jago during daylight. He always had something to do. The horses needed exercising and grooming. The orchard needed clearing. The buildings needed constructing. He and Alexi worked doggedly along in the hot weather, both ready with a quick smile when our paths crossed.

Jago refused to give me any directives, but the more I explored, the more I found to do too. Along with all the little domestic tasks I couldn't help but tend to, I discovered plenty of jobs inside the house. Part of preserving it and getting it ready for Jago's eventual residence involved cleaning it out. He and Alexi had done little of that so far, since their priority was in structural repairs to keep the place standing. So, I ended up spending long hours sorting through the jumble of items, deciding what could be saved, sold, disposed of, or sent to the estate's elderly mistress. It was dusty work, but it really did feel like exploring an ancient treasure-filled tomb at times. I'd get absorbed reading or looking through collectibles and then be surprised to find I'd hardly made a dent.

I'd found a stash of old newspapers one day and was trying to decide what to do with them when I heard a knock and a man's voice. Jago had few guests, and those who knew him well knew he didn't live in the big house. Then the visitor called, "Miss Wright? Are you here?"

I carefully set down the flaking newspapers and made my way to the foyer. "Mister Myers? Is that you?"

Rushwick's councilman beamed when I stepped outside. His face was flushed from the heat, and nearby, an old mare was tethered. "You are still here! I'm so glad."

"Is everything okay?" I asked, wiping my dusty hands on the apron.

"Oh, yes, yes." Looking beyond me, he held up a hand and waved. "Hello there."

I turned to see Jago and Alexi swiftly approaching over the green slope. Both men wore wary, tense expressions, and Alexi held a large pine plank over his shoulder. "Tamsin?" Jago queried.

"It's all right," I said. "I know him. This is Mister Branson Myers—the one who helped me in Rushwick."

After a moment's scrutiny, Jago relaxed and murmured something to Alexi. The big man nodded and eased his grip on the plank. Slipping into his salesman mode, Jago strode to my side and shook Mister Myers's hand heartily.

"Well, how do you do, Mister Myers? Jago Robinson. I sure am grateful for the help you gave our girl here."

"My pleasure! But really, she's the one who helped me." He paused to push his spectacles up. "Some of the other councilmen and I were surveying your work, and they were completely awestruck! As well they should have been. And so, I've come with a proposition for you. Would you be willing to continue to help us out until we hire a full-time clerk? We're getting around to it . . . honest. Along with the other positions. We could give you a stipend for your troubles—a silver a week—and perhaps, if the budget allows, we could keep you on as an assistant to the clerk if you are interested and still around." The words came out in a rush, and he had to catch his breath before continuing. "*Are* you staying around?"

I glanced over at Jago, who looked supremely delighted by this afternoon diversion. To Mister Myers, I said, "That's so incredibly kind of you, sir. I can't say how flattered I am that you'd think of me. But we're actually going on a trip in two days, and even if—when—I get back, I'm just not sure what my exact situation will be."

Mister Myers's face fell, but he nodded in acceptance. "I see, I see. Well, if you change your mind when you come back, I'm sure we'll still be in need of the help."

I tried to keep my face straight. "I'm sure of that too."

The councilman, though scattered, glanced between Jago and me and noted the familiar way we stood near each other. "Are you leaving to get married? You know Esau Rivers on the east side of town used to be a judge. No need to go far if that's what you're after."

"N-no," I stammered. I could feel my cheeks heating. "That's not what our trip is for. We don't have any plans to get married."

"Oh. Well. I'm sure . . . well, yes." Mister Myers looked equally embarrassed and hooked his thumbs through his belt loops as he turned away. "Nice piece of land you have here, Mister Robinson." His eyes widened. "Those are some horses."

"Would you like a better look?" Jago waved him forward. "Come this way. And while you're here, Tamsin had mentioned that some of the new town buildings don't have proper window coverings. Now, I don't have any glass on me, but I know a guy, and I bet we could work out a fair price . . ."

I watched with a smile as Jago led the councilman away, sucking him into a web of amazing deals. Forgotten, I returned to the house and my work. I still wasn't sure what to do with the newspapers, though they barely earned the name. They were nearly thirty years old, one page each, printed with very simple presses. Most of the "articles" were just a few lines of news from Cape Triumph and Bakerston, followed by a handful of classified advertisements. Considering how undeveloped things had been in Denham back then, these had probably been long out of date before reaching Grassy Hill.

The front door opened, followed by creaking footsteps. Jago soon entered the parlor, his mood high. "Did you fleece Mister Myers of everything he owned?" I asked.

"Since when have I fleeced anyone?" Jago knelt beside me. "I made him some incredible deals, and now I don't have to haul all that wax and dried beans to Cape Triumph."

"Did you see his face when I said we didn't have plans to get married? He thinks I'm some sort of wicked seductress."

"Oh, Tamsin. You aren't wicked."

I jabbed him with my elbow. "I thought I'd be getting away from gossip when I came to Adoria, and now I'm openly walking right back into it. I mean, what must Alexi think?"

"He thinks you're too good for me. And he's probably right."

"He knows we're sleeping together."

"Well, unless someone in Rushwick knows Belsian, you don't have to worry about him gossiping."

"Jago." I leaned against him. "You know what I'm referring to."

"I do. And it's the least of our problems. I mean, I'd go find that judge right now if you wanted, but I know you won't until things are settled in Cape Triumph. So, we'll go settle them, and that'll be that."

I shook my head. "You make it sound so easy."

"Well, being on the road again won't be easy. We'll have to sleep in a wagon. It's not nearly as comfortable as that luxurious straw-filled mat we're using right now. But exposing Warren's crimes, freeing you from the Glittering Court . . . I'm sure that'll be no problem. In the meantime, don't let Myers make you feel bad. If anything, he should be ashamed of that offer. One silver. I'm sure that's not what they're offering the regular clerk."

I couldn't help but laugh at Jago's indignation on my behalf. "The irony is I don't think they'll ever get around to hiring one. They don't have the time or organization for it. That's what a town manager's for—but that job advertisement's sitting in a stack with the clerk's." I pointed at the newspapers. "Of course, a silver a week's a fortune compared to what things used to pay years ago! You should read some of these. They're fascinating. I just wish I knew how to transport them safely. Half of them fall apart when you touch them."

"There's probably someone in Cape Triumph who knows about preserving this stuff," he said, leaning in. "We can ask. Are they worth saving?"

"A historian would think so. Back in Osfro, one of our clients was a professor who'd travel all over, bidding on things like this." I pointed to a few of my favorite headlines. "There are all sorts of fascinating stories about Adoria's early settlement. It was a lot more disorganized than my textbooks taught! There was one . . ."

A strange, improbable thought occurred to me. I rose on my knees, looking around the various sheets I'd laid out. When I spied the one I wanted, I gestured for Jago to join me.

"Look there, at this one from Bakerston. 'His Majesty's Loyal Army Squashes Rebellious Troublemakers.'" I pointed at the words as I read them, carefully avoiding contact with the paper. "'Soldiers from Fort Shorebank were called in on Vaiel's Day to address rumors of insurrection in Bakerston. Treasonous ruffians, led by a Mister Harold Vance, were advocating the rebellion of Archerwood Colony from the Crown, due to recent tax changes imposed upon the charter. The rebels were quickly rounded up and imprisoned, with Mister Vance scheduled for death by hanging next week.'"

Jago grimaced. "Bad day, huh? Let that be a lesson to people who complain about taxes."

"That's just it. Warren was complaining about taxes—he was really upset about the cut the king gets of Hadisen's gold. And he kept wanting to know just how upset the Heirs were with Grashond's charter being questioned."

Neither of us said anything for a long time. I knew Jago had grasped my conclusion immediately. But it was a hard thing to know how to process.

"I don't know Warren Doyle personally," he finally said. "Do you think he's the type who would try to get the colonies to rebel?"

"Not on his own. But I could see him being part of a larger group. He has a lot of powerful connections."

"You'd have to. One lone colony couldn't successfully rebel. You'd end up like poor Mister Vance there. It'd take a coalition of colonies, and even then, even with manpower and weapons, you'd be hard-pressed to take on the royal army. And they can move fast. One speedy rider could relay news of a rebellion in Bakerston to Cape Triumph in less than a night. Denham's army could be there in the morning."

"Not if they were up in the outer reaches of Grashond or down on the far southern edge," I said grimly. "Not if they'd been summoned out there to handle trouble with the Icori."

"Yeah. And you and I both know how long it takes messages to get here from those distant borders." Jago groaned and rubbed his eyes. "Well, then. I guess that settles it. How attached are you to that luxurious straw-filled mat?"

I raised an eyebrow. "Not very."

"Good. Because we're going to have to get on the road earlier than planned."

It was hard to sleep that night. I tossed and turned, consumed with the revelation that Warren was orchestrating conflict with the Icori in order to clear the way for his own rebellion in the central colonies. I'd actually been sympathetic to him when he'd explained how Osfrid's steep taxes were hurting Hadisen, but using that tax frustration as a way to justify the slaughter of innocent Icori and border settlers was unforgivable. And if he was helping acquire weapons and had enough support to make him and his coconspirators believe rebellion was possible . . . well, the outer colonies weren't the only places innocent people would die.

"Would it help if I told you a story?" Jago's sleepy voice murmured beside me. "I could explain the mechanics of racing bridles. That'd put you to sleep pretty fast."

I rolled toward him, propping myself up on my side. The shanty had one small window, its moonlight faintly illuminating the gold of his hair. "I'm sorry," I said, touching his face, "I don't mean to keep you up. There's just a lot on my mind about tomorrow."

He kissed my bare shoulder and brushed my hair back. "It's okay. It'd be weird if you didn't have a lot on your mind."

With a sigh, I sat up and drew my knees to me. I had no clothes on, and even in the middle of the night, it was still hot and muggy. "I just hope we can pull this off. Even knowing what we know . . . will anyone believe us?"

"We've got enough scraps to get people's attention, especially if Harper hasn't gotten too far away yet. And you know me. I can talk them into anything. Then we'll get Merry and get married and live out the rest of our days in peace and bliss."

I looked down, trying to see his face. "Did you say we'll get Merry or that we'll get married?"

"I said both." He covered a yawn. "Assuming you want to. And that she likes me. You know, on second thought, let's change the order. Let's get married before she gets here."

A rush of pleasure went through me, despite knowing things wouldn't be quite as easy as he breezily made them out to be. "Well, Merry's probably not going to be a problem so much as Jas—"

"Shh." Jago sat up beside me, tilting his head. "Did you hear that?"

A chill ran down my spine. "Hear what?"

"One of the horses."

"Oh." I exhaled. "You scared me."

He felt around for his pants on the floor and then stood up to get dressed. "I've got to go check on them. They should be fast asleep."

"Maybe they have a lot on their minds too."

He planted a kiss on the top of my head. "Try to get some rest. I'll be back soon, right after I tell them a story."

I lay back down after he left, draping my arms over my head. The frustration of knowing I needed to sleep was now keeping me from sleeping, and I couldn't afford to be tired when we got on the road in the morning. We needed to get to Cape Triumph fast.

We'll get Merry and get married. I smiled to myself as I turned his words over and over in my mind. If I was going to keep myself awake, at least it should be for something positive. But was it really? Just because we were sleeping together and uncovering treason, our logistical and financial problems weren't vanishing. We had no solution for that yet, and no matter what else happened, Merry still had to come before my own romantic longings.

I sat up again, feeling glum. So much for positive thoughts. And where was Jago? A sudden fear that something had happened to one of the horses, particularly Pebble or Dove, seized me. He certainly had no shortage of horses, but they were his best driving team, and one of them getting sick would alter tomorrow's plans.

Getting up, I pulled on one of Jago's work shirts and headed for the door. Then, in case I ran into Alexi, I sought the clothes I had laid out for the morning. Between Jago's motley assortment of supplies and my own sewing skills, I'd made a split riding skirt out of linen. It hung near the hearth now, and I tugged it on with the shirt.

The door suddenly squeaked open, and I started to ask Jago what had happened . . . and then I saw the shadow that fell in the spilled moonlight on the floor. It was too big and too wide. I held my breath, shrinking back as a large man crept into the shed. I knew I had only a handful of seconds to play my advantage. There was enough lighting outside that his eyes would have to adjust in here, and even in darkness, I knew every single part of this shack. Never taking my eyes off the hulking figure as he stalked toward the window, right by the straw mat I'd just been on, I reached back toward the hearth and wrapped my hand around the iron poker.

The intruder's feet bumped the pallet, and he leaned down to examine it. I advanced slowly from my hiding spot, weighing my chances of slipping past him. He'd left the door open in such a way that to get out, I'd have to pass right behind him and—

He straightened up and turned around, and in that brief moment our eyes met, I recognized the dreaded, blond-bearded face of Warren's

Lorandian associate. And then I swung the poker as hard as I could.

He roared in pain, and I tore out the door, not waiting to see how much damage I'd done. My heart thundered as I peered frantically around. Where to go? The barn. That's where Jago was initially headed. I ran for it, and halfway across the yard, I heard shouting in Lorandian. I rounded the barn's corner and saw the door was open. Once inside, I skidded to a halt as I was plunged into blackness. Unlike Jago, I didn't know every inch of this place.

I heard the whicker of a horse and moved toward it. Suddenly, a hand clamped over my mouth. Poker still in hand, I flailed against my captor and then heard Jago's quiet voice: "Easy, Tamsin. It's me."

"Jago!" I whispered, once he released me. "What's going on—"

A gunshot rang in the distance, and I heard uneasy shuffling and snorting from the stalls. "That could be Alexi," came the grim response. "I hope it's him. Come on."

Taking my hand, Jago led me to one of the stalls and unlatched it. He guided one of the horses toward the exit, and as we neared the light of the doorway, I saw he had Felicia.

"I hope you haven't forgotten how to ride without a saddle. I'm not sure how many of them there are out there, but last I saw, most of the men were near the house. So, take her out around the far side of the pasture, out where the good apple trees are. Ride straight between them, and you'll get to a road that branches off the main one to the east. Then you'll—"

"Wait, wait. Jago, what are you saying? Where are you going to be?"

"Dealing with whichever ones stay. They're here for you, so most are going to follow you once they notice you leaving. They won't be able to catch you, though. Not on her." He patted Felicia's flank and began putting a bridle on her. "Especially with how light you are. The hardest part'll be when you first get out of here, if you're still in shooting range. I'm hoping not. Most of them are still searching the buildings. By the time they react, you'll be out of reach."

He sounded so impossibly calm, considering the hysteria bubbling up within me. "Jago, I can't leave you! Let me fight. Or come with me—"

"I'd slow you down. None of the other horses can keep up with her. You'll be safe once you're out of here with that head start, and most of them will follow you. That'll make it easier for me and Alexi to handle the rest." A gun fired again, and I jumped. Jago pressed a quick kiss to my lips. "That's by the house. Now listen. I need you to get to an Icori outpost."

He rattled off directions, and I tried to absorb them, though it was difficult, given my terrified state. When he finished, he took the poker and helped me onto Felicia's back. She danced in place a bit but otherwise remained docile. Satisfied I was steady, Jago reached up and squeezed my hand.

"You can do this," he said. "This is easy for someone like you. Just ride, and she'll get you away."

He released my hand and then ran his hands over Felicia's luxurious mane. Letting out a small, wistful sigh, he reached for his belt and unsheathed a long knife. Its blade flashed in the light, and then, disbelieving, I watched as he hacked away at her long hair, cutting about six inches off it.

"You don't want that blowing in your face," he explained. Moving in front of Felicia, he peered out the barn door. Satisfied, he looked back up at me, tension and concern taking the place of his usual merriment. "Okay. Time to go."

Swallowing back my fear, I gave him a jerky nod. "You'll come to me?"

"Always."

At Jago's command, Felicia shot out the door and ran. No, more than that. When I'd let Dove run free outside Kerniall, I'd likened it to flying. But now, racing by the pasture, I expected to look down and see wings on Felicia, launching us through the air.

The silence that had preceded our exit vanished, and a flurry of noise and movement took place. I saw little of it, not with my speed and sights fixed ahead, but things unfolded much as Jago had said. Men—I got the sense there might be half a dozen—shouted and scrambled for horses. Shots were fired, one bullet striking part of the fence right as we passed it. Felicia didn't waver, though. She stretched her neck out, her long legs tearing over the ground at an incredible rate.

Soon, I heard hooves behind me, but I didn't look back. I kept faith in Felicia, believing that she would stay ahead of them all. And as we continued on, following the maze of small roads Jago had described, the sounds of pursuit grew fainter. Eventually, they faded entirely. I didn't think I'd lost the Lorandians for good, but I was sure they weren't a threat for the time being.

But what about Jago and Alexi? Fear for them gnawed at me as we thundered down the roads. I felt sick, thinking I'd abandoned them. Maybe most of the intruders had followed me, but what would they do when they accepted I was out of reach? If someone had been afraid enough to send this group after me even though it seemed more likely I'd drowned, then they were probably paranoid enough to go back and deal with loose ends. They'd have to know that I would have told others what had happened, sharing more secrets Warren couldn't let go.

When Jago had first gone outside to investigate the horses, he hadn't taken a gun with him, which was why he'd been forced to rely on the knife and then the poker when he discovered the attack. If most of the assailants cleared out after me, he'd have a chance to better arm himself and regroup with Alexi. The advantage would shift to them. The Lorandians wouldn't stand a chance if they came back and found their roles reversed, with them being the ones hunted in the dark.

That thought eventually settled me a little, though the calm was short-lived when Felicia's hooves thumped across the wooden planks of a bridge. I drew up the reins and brought us to a stop. She hadn't shown signs of tiring in our run, though she was breathing heavily. I patted her neck and contemplated my location. In his directions, Jago had specifically called out this bridge, saying if I reached it, I'd missed a turn.

Steering her back in the direction we'd come from, I squinted at the edges of the road as we moved at a much slower pace. We'd left the grasslands of Rushwick for more-forested land. This was not a well-traveled road, barely big enough for two riders traveling abreast. Around it, the brush and trees were overgrown, some spreading on the road. When I reached an earlier intersection, I knew I'd missed it again.

On my next pass, I finally spied the break in the vegetation that indicated our next course. It was about the same size as the previous road, but as it curved through the woods, our way grew narrower and bumpier, forcing us to a less aggressive speed. This was expected, though. The Icori weren't supposed to have any sort of permanent presence in the colonies, but they still maintained eyes and ears. My destination, according to Jago, was an extremely out-of-the-way camp the Icori manned to watch Denham and serve as a waypoint for messages going to various clans on the other side of the borders.

"It's hard to find, but if it is discovered, the Icori'll help you," Jago had told me in the barn. "Someone there might recognize you. And they'll definitely recognize Felicia."

Of course, that had been before her haircut. "Poor girl," I murmured, stroking her stubbly mane. "I'm sure it'll grow back in no time."

I'd learned all about how this breed of horse was prized for beauty and speed. As noted, however, the beauty of that mane became problematic if it was whipping around at the rider. For races, the manes were usually braided into more-aerodynamic but still-whimsical styles. Obviously, we hadn't had time for a hairstyling session tonight.

We stopped again as the path forked before us. I was growing weary, and this had been near the end of a string of directions. A lightening of the eastern sky allowed me to see my surroundings more clearly, but that didn't aid my decision. Both ways were narrow trails.

Left, I decided. I was certain that was what he'd said. We moved ahead at little more than a brisk walk. Felicia's energy seemed good, but she had to be feeling the effects of our mad dash. Her type was bred for fast and furious races, not overland treks at those same speeds.

When the path grew wider, I began to question my direction. We were supposed to be hiding. Had I gone the wrong way and was now headed toward one of Denham's main thoroughfares? Slowing, I gauged my directions from the sunrise. Should I turn back? I could have sworn Jago had said the left fork was north, and that matched with what I could see. I urged Felicia on, and that was when the other horse emerged from the trail behind me.

It was a black gelding with white markings on its head. And sitting on top of it was my Lorandian adversary. His bearded face split into a grin, and I cursed myself for the time I'd lost missing my turn. Now, I had no room to take advantage of Felicia's speed—or dodge the gun he held.

"Lucky hunch for me, turning off the main road," he said in his accented Osfridian. "Just like my hunch was right to track you down after the storm. Doyle said you couldn't have survived it, but my instincts wouldn't let it go."

"I don't know why you're doing this." My eyes darted around, trying to watch his gun and find any possible escape. "I don't understand what's going on. Let me go. Please. I don't have anything to do with this."

His lips twisted into a smirk. "I'm sorry, little one, but we both know that's not true. You saw me in that joke of an Icori raid, and then you and Jacob Robinson were apparently pulling some scheme at Lo Canne." He raised the gun. "You may not know everything, but you know enough."

Zing.

An arrow shot out from the brush, right into the hand holding his gun. He cried out and dropped it, just as a gun was fired. The shot struck his leg, knocking him off balance and out of the saddle. Both horses reared, and out of nowhere, people holding guns and other weapons swarmed around us. Two men tackled the Lorandian, and in dawn's light, I caught a glimpse of green tartan.

"Well, well, well," said a familiar voice. "It *is* you. I wasn't sure when I ordered them to attack, but I figured we couldn't risk it."

Orla Micnimara stepped out in front of me, dressed for the wilds, and I nearly toppled over in relief. "Thank you," I breathed. "Thank you so much."

She crooked me a wry smile. "Well, I was actually talking to Felicia, but I'm happy to see you too, Tamsin."

CHAPTER 37

"When Jago said there was an Icori watch here, I didn't expect you to be part of it," I told Orla later, once the commotion on the trail had settled down. "Or so far east of the river."

Orla and the others led me and the now-restrained Lorandian man back to their bare-bones shelter deeper in the forest. I sat down near a cold fire pit, drinking some sort of green herbal tea she handed me. Some of the Icori I knew from Kerniall joined us and greeted me warmly. A dozen or so Icori from other clans worked around the camp, glancing at me curiously.

She made a face. "It's not a normal activity for me. There's a . . . situation that requires me to be here. I'm waiting for some news. I'd say you were a pleasant diversion, but based on your arrival, I'm guessing the truth is a bit darker."

We both looked toward the far side of the shelter, where the Lorandian man sat tied up and gagged while an Icori woman knelt near his bloody leg. Orla called something to her in their language and received a curt reply.

"He'll live," Orla translated. "The bullet didn't hit anything vital. He probably hurt himself more when he fell out of the saddle. What should we do with him for you?"

I played with the edge of my cup, weary from the long ride but eaten up with anxiety over what had happened back at the farm. "I don't know. He just tried to kill Jago and me. And he's one of the Lorandians who was disguised as an Icori up in Constancy."

Orla's body went still, all traces of warmth disappearing from her face. "Where is Jago?"

"Hopefully on his way here. When we were attacked, he sent me away on Felicia." I tried to recap everything as succinctly as possible, which wasn't easy, since the story actually began back in Cape Triumph, when I'd first met Warren.

"I have faith in Jago." Orla's eyes narrowed as she studied the Lorandian. "But this man and his companions have caused damage that's rippling through Adoria." One of the servants made a suggestion in Icori. The woman who'd bandaged the wound overheard and chimed in, nodding along. Orla, however, grimaced and shook her head, giving a sharp rebuke.

"What?" I asked.

"They're suggesting we execute him as an example," Orla told me. "And I'd like to. Very much. But something tells me you'll want him brought back to your people."

"I-I suppose so." I was still in shock and hadn't thought that far ahead. But she was right. If we were going to prove this conspiracy, he was an essential piece of evidence.

Shouts from the forest interrupted my rumination, and moments later, a scout emerged from the trees. Behind him came Jago, leading Pebble. All the control I'd barely been keeping collapsed, and I sprang to my feet. He met me partway, wrapping his arms around me as I buried my face against his chest and swallowed back sobs.

"Six, Jago. I was afraid you were dead."

"No one left to do the deed," he said gently. "Alexi knocked one of them out, and the rest came after you. I assume they scattered when they lost you."

I pulled back slightly and pointed. "Not all of them."

Jago's eyebrows rose as he noticed the Lorandian. "I see. Oh—hello there, Orla."

"Hello, Jago." She rose gracefully. "I hope there are no hard feelings over what happened in Kerniall."

"Oh, there were a few when I found out just what roles everyone had played in my 'detainment.' Luckily, I'm the forgiving type."

Her face shifted back to a smile as she glanced between us, noting his arm around me. "Things seemed to have worked out for you."

"They're getting there," he said, pulling me back to him. His eyes lifted when he heard a soft neigh from the clearing's edge. "There she is. Still going strong, from the looks of it—but it's a shame about the hair." After surveying her a moment further, he turned back to the rest of us. "Okay, Orla. What's happening? It can't be good if you're here with such an entourage."

"No," she said, face hardening once more. "Not good at all, especially knowing what I know now. Kershimin was attacked recently—severely attacked, not one of the nuisance raids we've been tracking. Several people died."

"Kershimin is south of here," Jago told me. "Near the border of North Joyce and South Joyce."

"The attackers were Osfridians." Orla's gaze flicked to the Lorandian. "Or maybe not Osfridians. Or maybe Osfridians hired for a purpose. Whatever they were, they succeeded in enraging both Kershimin and its neighbor, Kermoyria—*and* Kershid. That's Padrig's home. My betrothed. One of the people killed was an Olaron."

"The ruling clan in Kershid," explained Jago.

I rubbed a spot between my eyebrows, where a headache was forming. It was hard keeping track of all the unfamiliar clan and city names. "So what's happened?"

"Kershimin and Kermoyria want to strike back," Orla continued. "They've been trying to get the Olarons to join them. It's triggered a pretty heated debate in Kershid, and I've just barely been able to convince Padrig not to. He's wavering, though. Your accounts of the Lorandians in the north have lost some of their impact after this recent attack and Tamsin's confirmation of Osfridian involvement at the hunting camp. It looks more and more like deliberate action by the colonies to violate the treaties and move into our lands."

"But it's not!" I exclaimed. "Some are Osfridian, but they're not acting with any official directive."

Orla rested a hand on my shoulder. "I believe you, Tamsin. But others don't know what I do. They haven't seen what I've seen. If Padrig throws his support in for joining the other clans, all of Kershid will stand with him."

"So what's he doing now?" asked Jago.

"Well, that's the big question," she said with a bitter laugh. "Two days ago, we received word that there was a delegation from the southern clans here in Denham, wanting to talk to the Olarons."

I turned to Jago and saw he looked as confused as I felt. "Why Denham?" I asked her. "Why not call a meeting in the southern colonies? Or why the colonies at all? If they wanted to talk to him, it seems like they'd send their delegation to Kershid."

She spread her hands out in a gesture of confusion and began to pace near the fire pit. "That's the other big question. I came here with my company, and he's out there at the meeting with two dozen of his own riders. We expect him any time now."

Jago began his own pacing. "That's *a lot* of Icori on this side of Denham's border. If that gets discovered by anyone in charge, Warren's people won't need to fake further conflict."

Jago and I accepted Orla's invitation to share a meal after that. We weren't in any rush to ride back to Grassy Hill just yet, and we were hoping to catch Padrig and learn about the mysterious meeting. When we finished eating, Orla gave me a change of clothes. I'd made the ride here with Jago's oversized shirt and no shoes. My homemade riding skirt had torn at some point I couldn't even recall, possibly when I'd run from the shanty. The only extra outfit Orla had brought was a long green dress, edged in plaid, which seemed excessive. But the voluminous skirts were at least split for riding, and I supposed it beat my other option.

She sat with me while I braided my hair and Jago tended to Felicia. Watching him eased her tension a little, and she told me with a smile, "If I had any doubts about his feelings for you, they're long gone. I never thought I'd see the day he let someone run off with that horse. I never thought I'd see the day he chopped off her mane. Does this mean you've solved your problems?"

"No. Not by a long shot. Everything's out in the open now, which feels better. I didn't like running out on him like that. But we still don't have an answer for the money I need. And I don't think I can bring myself to marry someone else to get it. But what else can I do without Jago losing his livelihood?"

"Forget the money," she said bluntly. "Isn't the man you love more important than that?"

I was tired of dancing around Merry, especially with someone I respected as much as Orla. "It's for my daughter. And she matters more than a husband."

"As well she should," Orla replied, no trace of judgment. "So, the money matters. Do you have to get it from a husband?"

"I would if I could. There aren't many other ways for someone like me to do it, unfortunately."

Orla stared off in puzzled contemplation. "From what I've observed, 'someone like you' can do all sorts of things. You beat back nature and arbitrate between different groups of people. You lead and manage the needs of others. It seems like there's got to be money there somewhere. If you could get paid for overcoming impossible situations, you'd be a rich woman."

I laughed at that. Hearing me from across the clearing, Jago glanced over his shoulder. His bright, generous smile tore at my heart and filled it up at the same time. "The problem," I said to Orla, watching him fondly, "is that I'm a woman. You should've heard the ridiculous pay I was offered for—"

My tirade was cut off by the arrival of a troop of Icori in red tartan. In moments, the small camp area was packed and confused. Jago slipped through the crowd and clasped my hand, pulling me along as we tried to locate Orla again. We found her near the trailhead, speaking with a man who made me gape.

My heart wasn't fixed on anyone but Jago, of course. Still, it was hard not to be taken aback by the sight of Padrig Olaron. That might have been because he was bare chested, just like in the classic Icori stories. That and his chest and arms were hard with muscles, and platinum hair flowed down his back. Icy blue eyes glittered underneath a golden circlet.

"I can't believe I ever likened Gideon to Kyriel," Jago muttered to me.

"I can't believe I thought Felicia had the best hair I'd ever seen," I whispered back.

He and Orla were engaged in a rapid and heated discussion in Icori. Well, it was heated on her part. I had the sense he was worked up too, but his cool and aloof manner made it difficult to tell. We, and a number of Icori, waited in silence as the two continued their exchange. Neither seemed satisfied when it concluded. Noticing Jago and me, Orla beckoned us forward and made introductions.

Padrig studied us with a stoic expression, and his lack of surprise made me think Orla had told him everything about us. Ever one to get to the point, she stated flatly: "The delegations from Kershimin and Kermoyria are here in advance of their armies—which will have already crossed into Denham."

She glanced at Padrig for confirmation at the last bit, and he nodded. "They should reach Cape Triumph in less than a week."

"Wait, wait," said Jago. "*Cape Triumph?*"

"Why in the world are they going there?" I asked, sharing his disbelief. "Not that I want them marching on any place, but aren't their problems with the southern colonies?"

"They were," Padrig replied, his voice as impassive as the rest of him. "Until Cape Triumph's army was sent out to attack them."

I turned to Orla in a panic. "Tell him—"

"I did, I did," she interjected.

"I'm sure your intentions are good," Padrig began, his tone suggesting he didn't believe that at all, "but it doesn't matter what misunderstandings or conspiracies have brought us to this point. The bulk of Denham's army is coming—their movements are being tracked. And if Osfrid insists on such a hostile action, Kershimin and Kermoyria are going to answer in kind by striking at the colonies' greatest cities."

"It's madness," Orla hissed, a sentiment she had clearly already expressed to him repeatedly.

"Not if there's no one to defend it," Padrig countered.

"The militia is there," said Jago. "It's not like the city's completely open for the taking."

"Near enough—especially for their combined armies. I've been to Cape Triumph. I've seen the state of its militia. If we join up with the others and show up at the gates, the city will likely surrender without a fight."

Orla turned on him, eyes flashing. "We are not marching up to their gates!"

He met her anger unflinchingly. "You can lead your people as you like. And I will lead mine."

"And *are* you leading them to Cape Triumph?" prompted Jago. The radiant, friendly face I'd admired just a short time ago had gone pale and tense. "Maybe you can take the city without a fight, but you can't hold it without one. You know that. It might take a little longer, but they'll get the armies back. Probably get the navy involved too."

For the first time, Padrig appeared hesitant. "I didn't agree to it yet—much to the other clans' disapproval. I came back here to discuss it with my bride-to-be, only to be met with more censure."

"You shouldn't have left them with any question." Orla crossed her arms and angled herself away. "You should have refused!"

"They're going with or without us and left it to me to join them along the way. I made the best decision I could at the time, Orla." He was still formidable, but there was a glimmer of something in his eyes that made me think, despite the sparring, he did actually want her approval. "And it's reaching a point where this can't be allowed to go on."

"It wasn't going to go on with you much longer." I flinched when that steely gaze turned on me, but I didn't back down from my argument. "It was about to erupt in the central colonies! But if we can get to the people in charge—the ones really in charge—we can stop all of the fighting, both on the border and in the interior."

"The other Icori are already on their way. It's too late," he said.

"Can we beat them?"

Everyone fell silent at that. It was almost more disconcerting than the earlier arguing. At last Padrig said, "From what I gathered, they were at the Yost River ford. That's about four days out, just like us. Maybe five, but I imagine they're moving at a good pace. They wanted to get by before the army realized they'd been passed."

"You could jump ahead of them." Jago ran a hand through his hair and gazed upward as his thoughts spun. "You'd want to keep off the colony roads, of course, but you could use them if you travel at night too. And then you'd save time both because of the longer hours and more-direct routes. Then cut anything else that'll slow you down. No one on foot. Fewer breaks. As fast a pace as the horses can safely handle."

"I won't go there with my forces diminished." Padrig nodded toward his gathered soldiers. "If only the militia opposes us, we could take the city with a group this size—with a fight, but so be it. I'm not going in alone and giving them the advantage."

"It won't matter if you don't have backup if you stop it from being a fight in the first place!" I pointed out. I was trying to keep calm, but it was hard when images of Cape Triumph, burning and besieged, kept playing through my head.

"And you really think I can? Just by getting my army there ahead of the others?"

"Yes. Well, I can. We can." Seeing Padrig's skepticism, I said, "Get there quickly. As fast as we humanly can. Believe me, you'll get their attention and secure a meeting with the government. Let Jago and me help you talk to them. We'll tell them what we know—show them our prisoner. And we'll just be bloody convincing. We're good at that. Then once things are negotiated, it'll be up to you to convince the others to back down when they arrive. Can you do that?"

The challenge took him aback for a moment, but he recovered quickly. "If the leaders there acknowledge the wrongs that have been done to us and make appropriate compensation? Of course. That's easy compared to what you're claiming you can do. Your people don't have a history of treating us fairly."

"They've never dealt with Jago and me," I retorted.

I was confident I could do what I said—mostly because I couldn't accept not being able to do it. If I failed, Adoria could be plunged into war. My friends would be in danger. Merry would be in danger.

What I was less confident of was that Padrig would let Jago and me try to negotiate. And so, it was more than a shock when he agreed to the plan. With time suddenly an issue, everything became a whirlwind, giving me little chance to agonize about what I'd just gotten myself into. As the camp buzzed around me, packing and preparing to head out as efficiently as possible, Jago pulled me aside and kissed me. It was no passing kiss either. It was a long kiss. A deep kiss. The kind of kiss that would have scandalized my mother. The fact that everyone was in too much of a hurry to even notice proved what a state we were in.

"What was that for?" I gasped when Jago finally pulled back.

He cupped my face in his hands, eyes brimming with an odd sort of wistful happiness. "Because I love you."

The words and the expression both thrilled me and flustered me. "Well, yes, and I love you too. But that's never made you put on a spectacle in public before."

He grinned. "I love you for all sorts of reasons, one of which is the amazing bravery and persuasiveness you showed with that Padrig guy.

And I know you're going to do the same in Cape Triumph. The governor won't stand a chance."

Something in Jago's voice raised an alarm in me. "*We're* going to do the same."

"Afraid not." He pressed another kiss to my lips. "You're going to have to do it alone. Because I'm not coming with you."

CHAPTER 38

THE SMALL CAMP WAS A SEA OF NOISE—BARKED ORDERS, clanging weapons, restless horses. But for me, it all faded to a deafening quiet, and the echo of Jago's words was the only sound in the world.

I'm not coming with you.

Wild thoughts began flying through my mind so quickly, I could barely grasp any of them. *This is it. This is where he leaves me. This is the settling of debts for what I did to him.*

"Tamsin. Tamsin!" Jago's raised voice broke the spell, and the lively camp came rushing back in on me. Hands still resting on my cheeks, he leaned over so that our foreheads touched. Seeing he had me back, he dropped his volume. "I'll see you again, I swear. I'm not leaving you—I'm just not going with you to Cape Triumph."

I took a deep breath, still shaking with the aftereffects of that brief scare. "Why not?" I finally managed. "You have to. Look what's on the line! If negotiations break down—"

"That's why I'm not going. As soon as this group departs, I'm heading north, as fast and furious as I can. Based on when you said Harper's regiment was leaving, I think I can catch up with him. He'll stop at Fort Shorebank to relay news and resupply. I'll find him there or nearby and tell him what's happened. We need him to bring his men back, just in case . . ." Jago's gold-and-green eyes looked past me, and he cleared his throat. "Well. I think Cape Triumph should have more than the militia on hand for defense."

"But there won't be a 'just in case' if you're there! You'll make the peace. You can talk anyone into anything."

"It probably seems that way, seeing as I managed to win you over, but this isn't going to come together on charm alone. Yeah, it's going to require a good negotiator for sure, but there's nothing special I can do that you can't with Padrig and Governor Doyle. The strength of the evidence, plus each side's real desire for peace, will be critical, and if those fail, it won't matter which of us is there. I don't want to send you on your own, believe me, but we can't risk the city. Besides, getting those soldiers back will snarl up Warren's own war plans."

I'd been physically drained all morning, and now, I felt as though all my mental energy was going too. I couldn't argue against him, because I knew he was right. I hated that he was, but he was right.

Staying close to Jago let us keep our conversation private under the guise of a lovers' sweet moment. "I don't think Padrig's going to let you go," I murmured. "Even if he really doesn't want war, he'll be suspicious if you're going off to bring soldiers back to the 'wide-open' city."

"Agreed. That's why I didn't ask him. I told Orla I want to take Felicia back home and that I'd eventually meet up with you all on Dove. She knows how much I fawn over Felicia, and one fast horse won't speed up a party of this size."

"But she'll make a difference if you're trying to catch up to an army. It's okay," I said, seeing his glum face. "I know you don't like lying to her, but it's for the best. Don't pit her against her fiancé."

"I know, but it's still hard. I keep trying to tell myself it just evens things out after she cheerfully sent me from Kerniall without mentioning she knew I was going to be detained for questioning."

There were shouts to mount up, and I pressed closer to Jago, my fingers curling into his shirt as I clung to him. "This is it," I said.

He sighed. "This is it. And you can do it. Think of all the different people you've had to arbitrate with since coming to Adoria. There aren't many who can claim that kind of experience. If they're all sincere, you'll get them to where they need to go."

"I just want you to get to where you need to go safely." Orla called my name, but I held on to Jago a moment more.

"I'll be safe. Felicia's forgiven me for the hair." Jago kissed me and then released my hands as he backed away. "See you soon."

The throng of Icori swept us both away, and by the time Orla and Padrig had their companies lined up, Jago had already taken off on Felicia. As I began my own journey, sitting on Pebble, I found myself replaying some of his parting words: *Think of all the different people you've had to arbitrate with since coming to Adoria. There aren't many who can claim that kind of experience.*

He was right about that. But in reflecting over all my interactions, I couldn't help but recall how the *Gray Gull*'s crew had nearly left us on the beach, the Heirs had imprisoned me, and a suitor had tried to drown me. Maybe I did have experience in dealing with all sorts of people . . . but was I any good at it?

Considering how fast we moved, the journey felt agonizingly long. I was worried about Jago, worried about the great task before me. And behind all of that, driving everything as usual, I was worried about Merry. Her ship was due in about two weeks, and I'd heard that in lucky conditions, ships could arrive a week or more early. What if hers had? What did I have to show for myself? I had no husband, nor a desire for any available ones that could improve our prospects. More than one person wanted to kill me. A negotiation to prevent bloodshed and despair rested on my shoulders.

Some of the Kerniall Icori I knew talked to me along the way, but mostly, I kept to myself. We were riding long days—and part of the night—and no one felt much like conversation. Orla had her own concerns to deal with, and when she noted my dreary mood, she said kindly, "Don't worry, he'll probably reach us soon. He won't have lost much time going back on Felicia, and the other silver's fast too."

I smiled my gratitude, even though her concern made me feel worse. Ironically, the one traveling companion who spoke to me the most was Padrig. He was suspicious of the Osfridians and the circumstantial evidence surrounding the conspiracy, but once he'd committed to this path of trying for a truce, he threw his weight behind it and interrogated me on what to expect and what I thought Governor Doyle and the other leaders in Cape Triumph would do.

"They'll be uneasy about a group of Icori knocking on their door, to put it lightly," I told him once. By day, we'd traveled on stealthy ways, meaning our arrival should come as a surprise. "It'll be important for everyone to stay calm. That's when I should also take on my biggest role—they need one of their own people to reassure them. From there, I'll work to get you a meeting with the governor. Everyone involved is proud and looking out for their people. Everyone has their own procedures and formalities. If we all remember that and act accordingly, this will work."

"I was uneasy when Orla advocated for you to speak for us," Padrig said, once he'd taken in my advice. "I still am. You're very young. But I think you might be a little wise. If we all get killed, it probably isn't going to be because of you."

Orla, overhearing as she passed, remarked, "Wow, Tamsin. He really thinks well of you."

We reached Cape Triumph in just under four days, thanks in no small part to riding almost nonstop the night before our arrival. We were all tired and sore, but that fatigue evaporated as we rode up to the city's gates during late morning. Tension electrified us all, and those who'd been slumping or yawning now sat up straight, weapons held tightly and eyes fixed ahead.

We came in through the city's second biggest entrance. The other was guarded by the fort, and even if most of the army was gone, caution seemed best. We met no armed resistance. In fact, we didn't meet much of anything. The gate was surprisingly deserted, and that gave us pause, more than a fighting force might have.

"We did beat the other clans . . . didn't we?" I asked. A horrific image of all the city's citizens imprisoned and subdued by Icori invaders flashed before me.

Padrig scrutinized the entrance with wary eyes. "Yes. If the city was occupied, we'd know."

Just then, a man pulling a cart passed by the gate. When he noticed our retinue, his eyes bugged out. He dropped the cart and ran off screaming.

"That's more what I was expecting," I muttered.

Similar reactions greeted us from the handful of people we encountered as we marched farther into the city, and I tried to put myself in their shoes, imagining what it would be like to see almost fifty Icori entering unceremoniously. I'd probably be running and screaming too. A few of our number had stayed outside the gates, including our bound Lorandian prisoner. He was going to be vital in our dealings with Governor Doyle, who might very well have an easier time accepting a truce with the Icori than an accusation of his son's treason.

There were still fewer people out than I expected, and I couldn't shake the feeling something was wrong. Even without a full military on hand, shouldn't someone have challenged us?

A scout who'd gone ahead when we entered the city came racing back to Padrig. "There's a huge assembly of people up ahead, over to the east."

Padrig tensed, and the other warriors pulled out their weapons. "Militia?"

The scout shook her head, dumbfounded. "No, they're not there for us . . . I'm not really sure what's going on. But I gathered the governor is there."

Padrig glanced back at me, and I shrugged. "I have no idea what's happening. Be cautious. Be smart."

We continued our stately pace in, and I tried to control my

breathing. My sweaty hands slipped on the reins. I was afraid I'd get so overanxious I'd faint, fall off, and wake up to a war.

It didn't take long to reach the assembly, which I promptly recognized, even if the Icori didn't. A hanging. A gallows was set up in front of the courthouse, and a huge crowd had gathered around it—a crowd that started to panic and break up as we trotted forward. I searched for the governor and found him standing on the gallows, watching our approach with shock. But he couldn't have been more shocked than I was to see who else was on the platform: Adelaide, Cedric, and Warren. Cedric's hands were bound behind his back, and a noose hung nearby. A man I didn't know climbed up beside them, and the governor began shouting for the militia, but it was hard to say if anyone heard over the frantic onlookers.

"Cedric, no," I murmured, going cold all over. What was happening? How was this possible? One of the Kerniall Icori gave me a quizzical look, and I pointed at the gallows. "My friends are up there. They're going to kill one of them!"

Her confusion only seemed to grow, and I couldn't blame her. The talk here had all focused on behaving carefully around the Osfridians, in order to prevent violence, and here we were walking right in on them trying to commit violence among themselves. The only bright spot was that our arrival had distracted everyone from the hanging. Cedric was still alive. Adelaide seemed unharmed. How were they even back in Denham? And where was Mira?

Focus, Tamsin. I couldn't worry about them yet. We'd come here to speak to the town's leaders face to face, and now, bizarrely, we'd managed it. I had to make sure things proceeded the way we'd planned. This was the part where I needed to put myself forward as our spokesperson.

The Icori riders stopped in front of the gallows, taking the place of the dissipated crowd. As I started to edge Pebble ahead in our group, Padrig, his voice booming over the din, suddenly said: "Where is the governor?"

I turned to him with a start, hoping to catch his eye. That bold demand wasn't in the delicate pleasantries we'd gone over! Some of the crowd's anxious chatter quieted. Beyond the courthouse, I spied a few men who weren't fleeing. They were coming this way, steps cautious, and carried guns.

"Where is the governor?" Padrig asked again. I urged Pebble toward him, weaving through the other riders.

Governor Doyle stepped to the center of the platform, visibly unnerved. "I am the governor. You have no business here. Get out before my army beats yours to the ground."

Padrig had the courtesy to let the bluff slide. "We do have business. We've come seeking justice—your help in righting a wrong done to us."

"You've had no wrongs done to you," the governor shot back, mustering a bit of steel. "We've all agreed to the treaties. We've all obeyed them. You have your land, we have ours."

"Soldiers are moving into our land and attacking our villages— soldiers from the place you call Lorandy. And your own people are aiding them and letting them cross your territories."

"Impossible!" spat Governor Doyle. "Lorandians moving into your lands means they would flank ours. No man among us would allow such a thing."

Now it was my turn. I finally reached Padrig's side.

"Your own son would," I called, surprised at how clearly my voice rang out.

Almost all the colonists who hadn't fled mistook me for Icori. But I saw Adelaide's eyes widen when she spotted me, and recognition flashed over the governor's face too. I focused back on him and continued, "Your son and other traitors are working with the Lorandians to stir up discord and draw Osfrid's army out of the central colonies—so that Hadisen and others can rebel against the Crown."

"It's a lie, Father!"

Warren had recognized me too. He stepped forward, a gun in his hand and face snarled with anger. Swallowing, I forced myself to meet his outrage with coolness.

Warren looked over at his father. "There's no telling what these savages have brainwashed this girl into believing." The scorn in his voice, the derision . . . it reminded me startlingly of how so many people had put me down throughout my life. "What proof does she have for this absurdity?"

"The proof of being thrown off a boat in the middle of a storm when I discovered your plans," I called back.

"Lies," Warren insisted, though he looked more panicked than skeptical. "This girl is delusional!"

The Icori near me shifted the hold on their weapons. The set of Padrig's jaw was tight. He didn't think this was going to end well.

"She's telling the truth."

I jerked my gaze back as the next player in this unfolding drama took the stage. Grant Elliott, the brusque shopkeeper, had climbed onto the gallows between Warren and Governor Doyle.

"Who is that?" Orla hissed from behind me.

"He sells survival gear," I whispered back.

"There are stacks of correspondence," Grant added. "Witnesses who'll testify."

"Elliott? What the hell are you talking about?" Warren demanded.

I wondered that too, but if Grant could support my claims, I'd take it.

"I think you know," said Grant. There was a dangerous glint in his eyes. "About Courtemanche. About the heretic couriers."

That part lost me—but it made Warren lose control. Panic and desperation seized hold of him. He raised his gun, and Adelaide sprang forward into Grant, knocking him aside just as Warren fired. The bullet missed Grant, but Warren had another shot lined up—this time with Adelaide in front of the barrel. A scream lodged in my throat, but rather than a gunshot, I heard a noise that sounded like *thwack*. A heartbeat later, Warren fell backward, with what I thought might be an arrow sticking out of his leg. Grant dove in quickly, restraining Warren through screams of pain.

"Six," I muttered, watching the spectacle unfold. But Adelaide and Cedric were okay now, so something was going right. Both looked bewildered and were scanning the crowd, finally fixing their sights on something behind me and the other riders. I turned in my saddle, trying to figure it out.

Moments later, I saw her. She stood on top of a wagon, holding a crossbow, her expression as fierce as an eagle coming in for its prey.

"Who is that, Tamsin?" Orla asked, noticing where I looked.

I smiled and hoped I didn't start crying. "That's Mira. One of my best friends."

"This isn't going how I expected," said Padrig. The understatement was even funnier because he wasn't trying to be funny. Jago would have loved it.

Gazing around at the chaos and outright weirdness, I took a deep breath and was surprised I didn't feel more anxiety about the unexpected turn of events. Maybe it was because everything that happened to me in Adoria was unexpected, and I'd learned to adapt to it. Maybe that was my strength, more than arbitrating with people.

"Well," I told Padrig, "we were hoping to get a face-to-face meeting with the governor. Looks like we got it."

CHAPTER 39

"WHY SHOULD WE HAVE TO DO ALL THE WORK TO CLEAR your land?"

"Because it's your fault this happened!"

"As if we'd sanction attacking our own people! Don't blame us for the crimes of traitors acting for their own reprehensible reasons."

"Like your son?"

I jumped to my feet, resting my hands on the table and leaning forward. "Gentlemen, gentlemen. Let's not get sidetracked from our topic. What's important is making sure there are no more Lorandians or rebels lurking on the border."

"How are we getting sidetracked?" demanded Padrig. "His son *is* one of those lurking rebels."

In navigating my way through the rougher places of Adoria, as well as in the formal ballrooms of Cape Triumph, I'd become something of an expert at maintaining a smiling face when conversation took a turn into boring or appalling territory. In the last two weeks, however, even my skills had been pushed to their limits.

That's how long I'd been helping colonial and Icori leaders work out a truce. Technically, the truce part was done, in the sense that neither side was going to war. But matters in Adoria had escalated to such an extent in the wake of the conspirators' meddling that more now needed to be settled than simply not killing each other.

To my left, Governor Doyle's face was reddening, growing dangerously close to purple. I turned to my right, meeting Padrig square in the eye. "Governor Doyle's son is in custody, about to sail back to Osfrid and be punished for his crimes—crimes that the governor had no knowledge of and which have gone against all of his principles. And it's a sign of just how strong those principles are that he's with us right now to reach an accord." Angling back to look at everyone gathered at the table, I said, "We've all suffered. Dwelling on the past won't improve that."

Padrig took the hint and nodded gravely toward Governor Doyle. "I apologize," he said stiffly. "Your son's actions are not yours." Then, even more haltingly: "This . . . must . . . be very difficult for you."

Governor Doyle cleared his throat and looked away. "Yes, well. No need for hand-holding. I'll manage. This has been difficult for all of us."

In most other contexts, that exchange would have been described as awkward at best. In this context, however, it was one of the more personable ones I'd witnessed.

"Which is why we all have to work together," I concluded smoothly. Giving each man a smile, I settled back into my chair at the head of the table. "Now, I think in going forward with rooting out rebels, we shouldn't be thinking about whose responsibility it is, but rather who can accomplish the most. From what we've heard, the holdouts are hiding on the Icori side of the border. Dann Padrig, Danna Orla . . . your people know that land best. But, Governor, the Lorandians have impersonated Osfridians before, so someone should also be there who can determine friend from foe . . ."

On it went. Another day, another set of meetings. Honestly, though, they were tame compared to the drama of my arrival with the Icori. The stories that came out after the courthouse spectacle were equally astonishing, all seeming to want to outdo each other in outrageousness.

Warren had apparently told everybody I'd run off when we were about to board the boat to Hadisen. He'd claimed the storm had spooked me with its memories of the *Gray Gull* and that, despite the valiant efforts of him and his men, I'd been lost in the chaos of the tempest, though it hadn't even begun when we departed. Cape Triumph organized a search party the next day, but it turned up nothing—because they were looking where Warren had told them I'd disappeared, not at the other end of the bay. Warren had paid my contract fee as a sign of his "sorrow," and my friends had had to experience my death all over again.

I wasn't the only one Warren had attempted to murder. It turned out he hadn't been so forgiving about Adelaide's spurning, and he'd subsequently tried to kill Cedric in Hadisen. Cedric had survived, only to have Warren's machinations get him arrested and sentenced to execution. Even now, I shuddered thinking about how close Cedric had come to death that day. If the Icori hadn't moved as fast as they had . . . if they hadn't thrown Cape Triumph into disarray . . .

"That was some nice work you did in there. You've got the patience of an angel."

I smiled at Lieutenant Harper as we walked out of the meeting hall later in the afternoon, freed of another day of negotiations. "I think that's where the resemblance ends," I told him. "And if this goes on much longer, you might find yourself reconsidering your words."

We stepped into the late afternoon sunshine, and I waved a farewell as Padrig, Orla, and the other Icori went their own way, heading to their camps outside the city limits. They'd be back again in the morning, and I knew they were restless to end this too.

"It won't go on much longer," Harper said, putting a hand up to shield his eyes from the light. "We've made good progress. And everyone's so tired, they'll agree with anything now."

"That's not really a testament to my skills." I stepped to the side of a bustling street and crossed my arms. "You haven't heard anything from Jago, have you?"

"No. I swear, the instant I do, I'll tell you. But I think he'll be here first. He said it wouldn't take long, and I know he wants to get back to you."

"Well, he's sure taking his bloody time," I muttered.

Lieutenant Harper and his men had arrived in the city a few days after I had. The southern Icori clans had shown up around the same time, and there'd been a bit of scrambling to reassure everyone that the other side hadn't called for backup as part of some ulterior motive. I'd been thrilled—once animosities were smoothed away—because I'd assumed Jago had come with the army. But instead, I'd been told he'd lingered in Archerwood on "business" that no one knew anything about.

The lieutenant grinned. "I'm sure his reasons are good. Jago Robinson doesn't miss an opportunity. You're proof of that."

I rolled my eyes. "Oh, stop trying to cover for him with your flattery. Go put on a dress uniform so Damaris can show you off."

The mention of his new fiancée sobered Harper right up. Tonight would be their first outing since becoming engaged this week. "You're right," he said, backing away. "And I've still got to file a report at the fort. I'll be in a lot of trouble if I miss this."

"You and me both," I said with a smile.

Adelaide made a beautiful bride. She was always beautiful, of course, but that night, it wasn't the glittering white-and-silver gown she wore, or even those perfect curls, that entranced us all as she exchanged vows with Cedric. She glowed from within, made radiant by the love she'd held fast to and was now finally able to celebrate.

When the ceremony ended, the two of them mingled with their well-wishers, shaking hands and kissing cheeks. Watching from where I'd stood as a bridesmaid, I gave a wistful sigh before I could stop myself. Mira, beside me, glanced over in amusement.

"Now, now, don't be sad. I know you wanted her to do better than a student, but I'm sure they'll make it work."

I nudged her with my petite bouquet. "Stop. You know that's not what I'm thinking. I'm happy for them, truly. It's about time some-thing good happened to us."

Mira slipped her arm around me and steered us forward to join the others. "You've come back from the dead twice. That's pretty good as far as I'm concerned." Her jovial voice grew more serious. "And who-ever you're waiting for, I'm sure he'll be here soon."

"What makes you think I'm waiting for someone?" I asked quickly.

"Because no matter what you're doing lately, you're always look-ing around for something—someone—else," she laughed. "*And* you're blushing now."

"I certainly am not, Mira Viana. I've just been out in the sun a lot. That's what comes of having a delicate porcelain complexion like mine."

But that only made her laugh more. "Nothing about you is delicate, Tamsin. And that's what's so great."

We all went back to Wisteria Hollow to celebrate the wedding. Hosting it there had been a great concession on Jasper's part, seeing as he still harbored a lot of resentment over what he saw as Adelaide and Cedric betraying the Glittering Court's rules—even though her contract had been paid off as part of the settlement for Cedric's labor following Warren's arrest.

Mine, though paid as well, had a few loose ends.

"Excuse me, Mister Thorn?"

A couple of hours into the revelries, I caught Jasper alone by the rum punch. A party was still a party, and he'd been making use of the time by chatting up any prominent bachelors crossing his path.

He'd been about to walk away and halted in surprise. "Yes, Tamsin?"

"I wanted to talk to you about my fee, sir. I know Mister Doyle 'settled' it when I was away."

Jasper scowled. "I'd say it was kind of him, except we all know there was a bit more to it than his sympathy."

"Yes, sir. And I also hear there was a bit more to it than the base fee. He paid over it."

"Yes—another happy outcome. It more than cleared your loan from Osfrid."

"That's the thing, sir. The 'more' thing, that is. Anything over and beyond the fee and outstanding debts should get split into a commission for you and surety money for me." I paused, just to make sure he didn't miss the next part. "And I haven't received any surety money."

"W-well . . ." he began, taken aback. "You also didn't get married."

"The contract just says anything over fees and debts gets split with me."

"These weren't normal conditions."

"Then perhaps you shouldn't have collected the fee, Mister Thorn." I glanced across the decorated yard where guests laughed and danced. "Adelaide and Cedric have an attorney friend here I could ask to help us solve things."

After a long, thoughtful silence, Jasper finally shook his head and made a sound that could have been a grunt or a laugh. "Blizzards and shipwrecks haven't changed you, Tamsin. You're as assertive as ever. More so, I think."

"Why, thank you, Mister Thorn. That's kind of you to say. Although assertiveness isn't why the money's owed. It *is* in the contract." Orla's words suddenly played through my mind: *If you could get paid for overcoming impossible situations, you'd be a rich woman.*

"What?" asked Jasper, seeing me hold back a laugh.

"Nothing," I told him. "Just thinking that maybe those blizzards and shipwrecks really did pay off."

I was in high spirits as I left Jasper, delighted to finally have a sum of money to call my own. It wasn't enough to fix everything, but it would let me get a decent stock of Merry's medicine to have on hand when she arrived. Distracted by my victory, I didn't notice Gideon until I practically walked into him.

Unsurprisingly, the other Heirs hadn't attended the festivities. By now, it was well known that he was breaking with them and going off to settle in Westhaven Colony tomorrow—as were Cedric and Adelaide.

"Tamsin," Gideon said, catching my arm. "I've been trying to find you. I wanted to say goodbye now in case I miss you in the morning."

My anger at Gideon had faded, and I gave him a swift hug. "Well, you could see me sooner than you think. I'll be getting out there at some point to check on Cedric and Adelaide—and now you too, I suppose. I'm excited to see the amazing things you'll be doing with your new church."

"You and me both." He smiled in his beatific way, and even after all this time, I saw it still affect some of my friends when they walked by us. "And I expect you'll be doing some amazing things too."

"I don't know about that. I'm just trying to get by—not found religions or new colonies."

"You would've been good at those things, you know," he said, growing a little more serious. "You're good at anything that's ever handed to you—but it always seems to be assisting or adapting to someone else's vision. But I wonder . . ."

"Wonder what?" I prompted, puzzled by this odd, philosophical tangent.

"I wonder what greatness you'll be capable of when *you're* the one in charge and giving the directions?" His smile returned. "There's a saying, 'The angels have a plan, and we assist.' I think the opposite's true for you."

"Gideon, it's a good thing you're going off to an experimental religious colony, because that was complete blasphemy."

"Goodbye, Tamsin," he said fondly. His gaze focused on something behind me, and he gave a slight nod. "Tell him goodbye for me."

"Tell who—"

Gideon was already walking away, and I looked toward the far side of the lawn. There, leaning against a tree in the evening shadows, was Jago, watching me with one of his half smiles. Ignoring the scandalized looks of Cape Triumph's well-to-do, I lifted my skirt and tore off across the grass. I wanted to throw Jago against the tree and kiss him passionately, but in a show of great restraint, I simply clasped his hands tightly.

"When did you get to town?" I exclaimed. "You should have come to me right away!"

"You think I didn't?" he laughed. "I stopped by the fort on my way into the city to ask for Harper. They told me he was at a wedding and then launched into this whole tale about how the groom was almost executed but saved at the last minute by the bride's dazzling, divinely beautiful best friend as she led an Icori entourage."

"Entourage indeed! And no one really said 'dazzling, divinely beautiful.'"

"Well, they were thinking it," Jago retorted with mock solemnity. "Just like I am now. You are . . . a vision."

I flushed under his appreciative gaze, secretly thrilled that he finally got to see me in Glittering Court glory. The dress I wore was made of celadon silk, its off-the-shoulder bodice decorated with deeper green crystals. "You're just saying that because you've mostly seen me in drab Heirs dresses or Icori traveling clothes."

"Hey, I happen to like those leather traveling pants. A lot."

I tugged at his arm. "Come meet my friends, and tell me where you've been."

He shook his head and stayed put. "I'm underdressed—and don't tell me no one cares. We aren't married. We can't flout society quite yet."

"We'll be able to soon enough," I said. I went on to explain to him how I now had a paid contract and a little money on the side.

His eyes lit up, both with delight and speculation. "Huh. That makes a lot of things easier, doesn't it? And you know what else'll make things easier? The fifty gold I secured for us. That's why I was late."

"Fifty gold? Did you rob someone?" I clamped a hand to my mouth in horror. "Jago! You didn't sell the horses, did you?"

"Look at the outrage! Why, Tamsin, is it possible you've grown to actually care about those horses?"

"I've grown to care about you fulfilling your childhood hopes and dreams! Now how'd you get the damned gold?"

"Well, I don't have it in hand, but I will once we preserve and transport those newspapers you found at the house. I made some inquiries in Bakerston, and you were right about their value. They're starting a college up there, and one of the professors offered a pretty hefty sum if I could deliver them. Of course, they aren't mine. My deal with the old mistress is a small cut of anything I sell on her behalf in the house. She lives between here and Bakerston, so we had a chat, and I coaxed her into more than a 'small' cut for the sale since we'll have to do some work to preserve them *and* because no one would have known they were worth something, if not for you."

"Fifty gold . . ." I breathed.

"Not for a while, but, yes. I thought I'd be scrambling for the rest of your fee, but it looks like we can get married right away and get all the things you'll need for Merry. We'll have to buy most of it here, I imagine, seeing as Rushwick's pretty limited. You didn't hear if they're getting a school, did you?"

"No, and I'm not optimistic about it happening soon, what with how small they are. But with that much gold, we'll make do. We'll buy books."

His smile seemed to be as much because of my happiness over the news as the news itself. "Don't write that council off yet. You know who I saw on my way in? Myers, of all people. He made the trek out here. He's going to drop off all the job advertisements at the newspaper office."

"Really?" I was impressed enough to turn my thoughts from the windfall. "Maybe they're getting their act together."

"Maybe. He was chattering about how he didn't have the time to go through applicants, asked again if you'd reconsider being assistant clerk and do the interviews for him." Jago gently touched my cheek and then quickly withdrew his hand, remembering we were in public. "Can't blame the guy for trying, though. We all depend on you."

Some of the other girls began calling for me from the other side of the grounds. "Oh! They're going to decorate the coach. I need to go—are you sure you won't come with me, Jago? You should get something to eat."

He shook his head. "No, not this time. I'm bone tired anyway. I'll find you tomorrow, and we'll start talking wedding plans. Wait'll you see the deals I can get on decorations! Do you want to do it before or after Merry is here?"

"Oh. I . . . I honestly wish I could do it after all of my family's here. Part of the plan was to bring them over when I . . ." The cheery mood humming through me all evening took its first dip. "Well, we'll figure things out, I suppose. We always do."

"Tamsin!" came Mira's voice. "Where are you?"

"Go," Jago said. "They need you."

I squeezed his hand again and started to turn. "Hey, you don't know where Mister Myers is staying, do you?"

"Myers? Branson Myers?" Jago asked, like he hadn't just been telling me about him five minutes ago. "He mentioned some inn with . . . Arms in the name, I think. You aren't going to take him up on that pitiful offer, are you?"

"That offer? No." I lifted Jago's hand and sneaked a kiss onto it. "See you tomorrow."

After all the celebrating, most everyone at Wisteria Hollow wanted to sleep in the next morning, but the caravan to Westhaven departed just after sunrise. It left with as much fanfare as the one to Hadisen had, but this time, watching Cedric and Adelaide lead their horses, I no longer felt filled with dread. The world was bursting with optimism and beauty, and anything seemed possible.

"Stay out of trouble," I teased Adelaide, hugging her for what felt like the fiftieth time.

"Me? Your record's much worse than mine." Her bright laughter faded as she blinked back tears. "Tamsin, I can't say again how sorry I am for my role in it, for everything that happened back in Osfrid—"

"Oh, hush," I scolded. "What happened to me is on me."

"Still. I should've told you about Cedric, and my past . . ."

"I should've told you about *my* past."

It was an awfully big secret to tell in such a hasty manner, but I'd kept it from her for too long. So, out it came, as quickly and coherently as I could manage, all about Merry and the medicine, and even a little about Jago. She listened with wide eyes, and I don't think she blinked.

"Tamsin, I wish I'd known!" she exclaimed when I finished. "I wish I could've helped you . . ."

"That's the past. But I could use your help now. You said you had a sum of money in Osfro, didn't you?"

"Yes . . . I inherited it by getting married. But I'd have to send a letter to Osfro and then wait for it to come back here. But if you need money—"

"I need a loan," I corrected. "And what I need it for is actually back in Osfro . . ."

The sendoff took longer than I expected, and I had no time to find Mister Myers before meeting with the governor and the Icori. Restless energy ate me up as the arbitration continued, but I kept up my smile and my calm. When we had a small lunch recess, I skipped eating and instead hurried off to an inn I'd inquired about earlier: the Duke's Arms.

Through a bit of luck, I found Mister Myers as he was sitting down to eat in the inn's common room. He jumped up when he saw me, nearly knocking his plate off the table.

"Miss Wright! You're here! Will you do it? Are you accepting the job offer? That's such a relief!" He nodded to a stack of papers. "I was actually on my way to the newspaper office, and it'd be so helpful if you could—"

"I'm not here to accept your offer," I said, sitting in the chair opposite his. "I'm here to make you one. And I don't have a lot of time, so I'll just come right out with it: I could've practically run your office that first day. I *was* running it! I did more in that time than anyone else has done since . . . I don't know. How long ago was Rushwick incorporated?"

He shifted uncomfortably. "I don't know the exact date. It's in some of the paperwork somewhere . . ."

"It doesn't matter. What does is that you were offering me an assistant clerk's job when I was neither assistant nor, in fact, clerking."

"I don't understand," he said, his thin eyebrows tugging together into an almost straight line. "Do you want . . . the *clerk's* job?"

"I want the town manager's job." I leaned in and tapped the papers on the table. "I know you need one, because I saw the advertisement. I'm the one who filed it with the other ads."

"The manager? That's not an easy job . . . I'd figured we'd give it to someone more . . ."

"Male?"

He winced. "It's very complicated. There are a lot of things to keep track of. Town projects. Staff. Council meetings. Not many people can keep up with all of it."

"I've noticed that," I said dryly. "But by all means, you can go turn these ads in and hope a good candidate will apply, even though it's unlikely you'll have the time to interview them. Meanwhile, you've got me right here, ready to go as soon as I tie up loose ends in the city— loose ends that involve negotiating a bloody truce between two nations in Adoria! That alone should qualify me to manage your town's government, even if you hadn't already seen what I can do."

"It's unusual to have a woman . . . especially of your age . . . in that role, but . . ." He took a deep breath as he wrestled with the decision. "But . . . these are unusual times. Very well, Miss Wright. I will take responsibility for hiring you—and you'll deal with all the rest of this?" He slid the stack of papers toward me with a hopeful look.

"Yes, but not for one silver a week." I flipped through the pages until I found the manager posting. With his pen, I scrawled a new number on it and showed him. "Don't look like that," I warned, seeing his shock. "We both know that's the going rate. And honestly, with my background, it's a bargain." I pushed my chair back and stood up. "It's also my final offer. I have to get back to bringing about peace and prosperity now, but when you decide to accept, come find me at the town's hall or Wisteria Hollow. Good day, Mister Myers."

I'd only taken a few steps away from the inn when he came running out. "Miss Wright? Miss Wright? I accept!"

A job. A real job, one that would earn me respect and a hefty wage.

The thought of it left me walking on clouds as I returned to the negotiations. The money Jago and I had secured would take care of us in the short term. And the loan Adelaide was giving me would buy passage here for the rest of my family. As great as those windfalls were, the need for a reliable, consistent income had been eating at me.

Well, I had one now. Most incredibly of all, the money was coming from me and my talents—not the indulgence of a wealthy husband. I controlled my future.

We'd barely sat down for negotiations when the doors to our meeting room were flung open. Half the people at the table jumped, probably thinking an attack was coming, but it was Jago who burst in.

Orla brightened upon seeing him. "I'd heard you were back."

Governor Doyle exchanged puzzled looks with his colleagues. "Who in the world are you, and how did you get in?"

"Jago, what's going on?" I asked uneasily. As happy as I was to see him, the timing wasn't exactly optimal.

Jago, as usual, didn't look particularly unfazed at intruding. He'd cleaned up since last night but still wore his usual casual attire. Jerking a thumb behind him, he said, "Oh, old Lawson let me in. We go way back—cotton deal, you see. But that's not why I'm here. Tamsin, the *Sterling* just came into port."

Slowly, I stood up, my hands clenching the edge of the table. After a few steadying breaths, I said very quietly, "Gentleman, ladies . . . I'm going to have to step out for a moment. Lieutenant Harper, I'm sure you can fill in."

Without waiting for approval, I followed Jago out the door, ignoring Orla and Harper's concerned calls. As soon as I emerged outside, I broke into a run toward the docks. Jago fell right into step with me.

When we arrived, customs inspectors were just leaving the *Sterling*. Other ships were loading and unloading too, and we kept getting pushed back in the bustling crowd as we stood on our tiptoes to see what would happen next on the ship. Why were there so many tall people here today? Suddenly, a woman behind me squealed and surged forward, hugging an elderly man carrying a suitcase.

"It's happening," I gasped. "The passengers!"

And then—a flash of red hair. She saw me as I saw her, her rosy-cheeked face splitting into a grin. "Mama!"

Merry pulled away from the woman who held her hand and dove into my arms. I swept her up and felt everything inside of me burst. My heart had to keep so much held in over the last year, and now, this was the key that finally released it. All the heartache, ambition, exhilaration, and so much more. Everything that had driven me on this quest. I could scarcely draw breath as I showered her with kisses and held her against me.

"Stop all that crying, Mama. People will stare."

"Why, Tamsin, look at you!"

Ester Wilson and the rest of my old neighbors made their way over, hugging me as I kept hugging Merry. When the whole family was off and had their belongings, we set out through the congested shipyard for easier parts of Cape Triumph. Jago scooped up Merry's trunk and ambled alongside us.

"I've missed you so much," I told her, still hardly believing I was touching her. "You're so tall now."

She nodded gravely. "Well, I'm four. I was afraid you wouldn't recognize me."

I kissed her again. "Don't be silly. I'd know you anywhere. I was afraid you wouldn't remember *me*."

"Of course I would! Aunt Livvy's always drawing pictures of you. And we read those letters you left every day. I brought some of my favorites along, but I like having the real you even more." She leaned against me and stared wide-eyed at the city. Noticing Jago, she lifted her head and said, "Who are you?"

"Jago Robinson, miss. At your service."

Merry scrutinized him with the tactlessness children excel at. "Did you know your eyes don't match?"

"I've heard that once or twice," he replied solemnly.

"I like them."

She started to put her head on my shoulder again but perked back up when I said, "Mister Jago is a good friend of mine. Once I've taken care of a few things here, we'll be going out west to live with him."

Glancing between us, she asked suspiciously, "Is this who Granny was talking about? The rich man who's going to carry us off to a castle?"

"Oh, I'm rich in character," he told her, "and it's not so much a castle as a, uh, farm."

"That's not the same at all," said Merry, though she sounded more curious than disapproving. "Are there animals on it? Cows and chickens?"

"Not that kind of farm. I have horses."

She made a face. "Oh. Horses are everywhere."

"Not like mine. I'm serious," he added, noting her skepticism. "Mine are faster and smarter than other horses. They're for racing. Just ask your mother there—she's ridden them."

"Have you, Mama?" And then, not waiting for an answer: "Can I?"

"When you're older," I answered, at the same time Jago said, "Yes."

"Jago," I warned.

Merry jumped to his defense. "They're his horses, and he says I can. We should go right now."

Jago grinned behind her, and I shook my head at both of them. "It's five days away, love. And you just got here. There's lots of the city to see."

"I've seen cities. I used to live in one. Did you know that, Mister Jago?" In one glance, she dismissed all of Cape Triumph's wonder. "I don't need to see another city. I want to go live on a farm."

"And I'm anxious for you to," Jago said. "But I'm also anxious about getting our affairs settled."

Merry looked at him like he was crazy. "Why are you anxious? Mama's here. If things need to be done, she'll get them done. Didn't you know that?"

I shifted her to my other arm and brushed curls out of her face. "Don't be rude, Merry."

"I'm not! I'm just telling him things. I like telling people things they need to know. Someone's got to."

Jago winked at her. "I absolutely agree. Feel free to let me know anything else you think of."

"I'm starting to think I know what it'd be like to have two children," I said deadpan.

That made him smile even bigger, but Merry was deep in thought. "Apples," she said suddenly, her voice a challenge. "You need apples for your horses. Did you know that? They love apples."

"I do know that," he replied. "And I have apple trees at the farm."

Merry was rendered speechless. But not for long. She and Jago *did* have that in common.

She looked at me with sparkling eyes filled with such hope and joy, I worried I'd start crying again. "Did you ever think, Mama, that we'd be on the other side of the world, going to live on a farm with horses and apple trees?"

"No, I didn't." I glanced over her and met Jago's eyes. "And yet, here we are."

Merry rested her head back against me and sighed. "Here we are."

DON'T MISS A SINGLE HEART-POUNDING MOMENT!

THE COMPLETE *Bloodlines* SERIES!

GO BACK TO WHERE IT ALL BEGAN...

JOIN THE CONVERSATION   /BLOODLINESBOOKS

Razorbill • An Imprint of Penguin Random House   BloodlinesSeries.com • VampireAcademyBooks.com

IN A VILLAGE WITHOUT SOUND,
ONE GIRL HEARS A CALL TO ACTION

SOUNDLESS

AUTHOR OF THE INTERNATIONAL #1 BESTSELLING
VAMPIRE ACADEMY AND BLOODLINES SERIES

RICHELLE
MEAD

"Fans of Rose Hathaway and Sydney Sage will flock to
this impressive stand-alone novel."
— *Booklist*